BILL FOX was born in Clapham, London. One of six children, he was educated in an 'all age' Roman Catholic school attached to the monastery and church of St Mary's. Further education was received in the 'Day Continuation' schools. He did military service in the Royal Signals in the latter years of the war and served in Italy during the collapse of the German forces. Subsequently he served in Palestine during the Jewish terrorists' campaign for independence.

Bill entered the Civil Service then undertook three years of teacher training before taking various teaching posts in London and the southern counties. He was a headmaster for six years.

Bill is interested in art and reproducing copies of 'Old Masters'.

The Curtain Falls

The Curtain Falls

A trilogy by

W J Fox

ATHENA PRESS
LONDON

ISBN 1 84401 719 2

First Published 2006 by
ATHENA PRESS
Queen's House, 2 Holly Road
Twickenham TW1 4EG
United Kingdom

Printed for Athena Press

To Penny Fox-Colbourne for her involvement in some of the writing, much of the characterisation and the hours of fun we had discussing the 'plot'.

A trilogy...

The curtain rises. The scenes are set. The tale unfolds. Players strut and posture. Expectancy is sharpened.

Let the words speak...

Contents

ACT ONE:
ICE HOUSE

Chapter One

Simon West strolled up the steps to the garden, absent-mindedly taking stock of the earth scattered over the paved patio and of the hole, some fifteen inches across, in the centre of the flowerbed.

This day was no different from other days this month. Since they had acquired their new dog – a large raggedy affair with a penchant for digging – each morning there had been heaps of soil needing to be replaced in the cavities she had kindly and rigorously dug for them during the evening before.

He idly pushed at the earth with his foot and it was several seconds before he realised the hole was not filling up at all and the earth was quickly disappearing down a larger hole that was developing under his feet. He stepped back hurriedly and the sides of the hole collapsed, revealing a pit now about three feet across and still growing.

'You've really been busy this time, Judy,' he said affectionately to the dog, whose muzzle was now well down in the soft soil. 'Looks like you've uncovered a mine shaft.'

He strode up the garden to the garage, a tall man, now in his sixties, but fit and with a hint of athleticism in his movements. He soon covered the fifty yards to the garage and returned with a large spade.

'Let's see what you've got here, Jude,' he muttered, more to himself than to the dog, and began to dig down in the bottom of the hole, throwing the earth into a heap in front of him. It was a matter of moments before the spade struck something hard. Stone or concrete he thought and scraped away further. A large flagstone was gradually exposed and he banged his spade down onto it to judge if it was firm. It was only half covering a black hole and Simon could see where his soil had been disappearing down a triangular opening. The flagstone must have been recently dislodged, he mused. He remembered the storm that had brought down the fir tree only a couple of weeks back. The stump was still lying a few feet from the hole, as the tree surgeon had been unable to remove it from the small garden.

Simon cleared away the last remnants of loose soil from the stone's surface and bent down for a closer view. He felt around the top of the stone, discovering an iron ring set into it, rusted and completely unmovable. As Simon eased himself upright again, he considered what manner of a construction would be hidden under a couple of feet of earth and rubble in his garden. Many questions came tumbling into his mind as he turned and hurried indoors to put the news of his exciting find before his companion, Lydia. The dog followed closely on his heels.

'Lyd! Lyd! Where are you, Lyd?' he shouted as he entered the kitchen. He had difficulty keeping his voice under control so eager was he to share his discovery. 'Lyd, Lyd – hear what I've found!'

'For heaven's sake, what on earth's all the noise?' Lydia replied. She was a tall, dark woman with black hair, belying her fifty-four years, cut into a straight bob. She wore large glasses, and with her olive skin and the highly coloured clothes she invariably wore, Simon thought she cut a striking figure. An intelligent woman with a slightly cynical outlook on life, she could be extremely perceptive and quickly sum people up. She did not suffer fools gladly but she had a ready smile and a sharp sense of humour, and Simon blessed the day they'd met and their decision to set up home together. It had been taken about three years ago and was one he had never regretted.

'Come outside!' he said, taking hold of her hand and half dragging her towards the door. 'There's something under our garden, something in stone... I don't know how big it is or what it is, but it's something unusual.'

'What d'you mean, it's "something"?' she asked, beginning to laugh, just because Simon was laughing and excited.

'A stone – and it's under our flower bed. I don't know how big it is but I'm going to find out.'

Now outside, he let go of her, reached for the spade, pushing it down so that she could hear the contact of steel on stone.

'There!' he said triumphantly. 'I'm going to clear it away so that we can see better.' He jumped into the hole and began throwing out more soil.

'What on earth is it? How did you find it? How long has it been there?' Lydia fired the questions at him.

'I don't know. All I do know is that the soil disappeared as I tried to fill in one of Judy's holes so I thought I'd better investigate. Then I felt the stone under the spade. Look, here's a ring in the middle, so it must be a lid or some sort of trapdoor. I'll just make a bit more room. Then I'll pull it up and we can look down it.'

Simon fetched a crowbar from the garage and, fixing it under the edge of the ring, he forced it until the ring gradually eased up from the stone. He slid in the crowbar so that he could use it like a jemmy and put all his weight on it.

At first nothing happened but then came a grinding sound and a very slight movement. He bent over and cleared more soil from the edges and tried again with the bar. Gradually, it lifted about two inches on one side, but it was so heavy he had to let it slip down again.

'How about putting a rope through the ring?' Lydia suggested. 'We could use the tow-rope – it's very thick – then I could push the crowbar under the edge of the stone as you pull it up.'

'Good idea,' puffed Simon. 'Gosh it's heavy! It must be a solid flagstone. I wonder what's in there... shouldn't be long now. I say, I hope it's not full of water – or even something worse.'

Lydia appeared with the rope and Simon pushed one end through the ring and then put both ends over the stone wall nearby. He leant over the wall and pulled with all his weight on the rope against the wall. He felt the stone lift.

'Quick, Lyd, push it under now!' he called.

She moved quickly and placed the crowbar in the gap and then, for good measure, also put the spade halfway in as well. As Simon lowered the stone it rested on the bar and the spade some four inches above the level of the opening.

'Good, now if we pull the rope across we should be able to slide it off.'

They both pulled on the rope, slowly dragging the stone across the heap of soil, and then let it rest.

Lydia leant back against the wall, her breath coming in little gasps. 'Golly, that was difficult! Let's have a look,' she said, and stepped forward.

'Careful,' shouted Simon, 'the edge might not be firm. Here, I'll lie on my stomach and peer in... wish we had a good torch.'

'I know!' said Lydia. 'There's one in the spare room cupboard – if the batteries are all right – it hasn't been used for months. You stay still while I get it. No heroics, now!'

Simon grinned as she hurried indoors. The air coming up felt cold and damp on his face and there was a smell of dankness but it was quite fresh, nothing bad. Maybe the flagstone, being set crooked, had let the air in over the past weeks; any old odours would have cleared away since the storm.

Lydia was coming back. 'It still works,' she announced, with excitement in her voice. 'I've brought a mirror in case you can't get down far enough.'

'Good thinking,' replied Simon, and he edged himself forward and lowered his head into the opening, the torch in his left hand and mirror in his right.

'Don't tip in, we don't know if there's a floor,' said Lydia.

'Don't worry; I don't think I'd fit, anyway. I'm not sure I could get my shoulders through this entrance. Ah! There we are. Looks like bricks all around. It's like a room! There's a lot of earth and bits of rubble on the floor but it looks solid. Nothing down here... Oh, I can see a bit of the ceiling – it's slightly arched – I suppose that's to keep it up. I can't think what it would be for. It's quite large, a proper room.'

'About how big?' asked Lydia. She was hopping about beside his horizontal body, keen for a look herself.

'Oh, about seven foot high and six foot wide. I can't see how long it is. Just a minute, I'll see if I can get a bit lower and shine the torch right down, and I'll put the mirror behind the torch. I say, you'd better hold my legs, just in case.'

He edged forward. His shoulders were scraping the sides of the opening as he tried to manoeuvre the torch and the mirror with his arms outstretched. He was worried about dropping the torch but gradually he got himself in a position where he could see the end wall of the 'room'. It was just a brick wall, like the sides, quite disappointing really.

'Hey! What's that white bit?' He tilted his mirror downwards, as a heap of lighter coloured bits and pieces were reflected in his mirror. 'Something down in the corner, could be bits of chalky stone. No, it's whiter than that, and there are different shapes… looks like bones.' He thought to himself, surely it wasn't used for putting dead pets in? A fox, perhaps, got in before the flagstone was in place. But there seemed to be rather a lot of pieces for a fox… perhaps there's more than one, he mused. He eased himself out of the hole and up into a sitting position.

'Well?' said Lydia questioningly. 'What can you see?'

'It seems like a proper room, I should think about nine feet long, and it looks as if it's all brick. There's nothing down there but some earth and bits of stone – the earth's covering the floor, so I can't really see if it's firm but in the corners it looks like more bricks, as if it's all made completely of bricks, as in the coal house and the outside loo. There's something strange, though, in one corner. It looks like some bones, quite large and spread across the end where the wall meets the floor. I thought, at first, they might be from a pet dog that someone had buried here.'

'*Bones!*' exclaimed Lydia, 'Oh, how grisly! But you wouldn't build a room that size and use all those bricks if you just wanted to bury a pet dog. You'd just dig a hole, surely, however much you loved it. Let me have a look.' She was getting down on her hands and knees on the other side of the opening. As she stretched out her head was practically touching his, crown to crown. He looked up and planted a kiss right on top of her hair, which smelt clean and of shampoo.

'Hey, you!' she giggled. 'Give me the torch, please.'

He got up onto his hands and knees and passed her the torch. She wasn't taking any chances. She didn't lean down into the hole as he had done. She just peered through the opening straight down, so her view was very limited.

'It's a bit creepy. Are you sure there are bones here? I can't see anything except mud.'

'You're not down far enough,' he replied. 'Anyway, we can't do anything about it at the moment but I'm pretty sure that's what I saw. What we want is to get some steps down there and see if someone younger and fitter could go down and have a good look. I still haven't a clue what it could be.'

'Perhaps Greg could go down,' said Lydia, thinking of their

neighbour's nineteen-year-old son, home from university for the summer break. 'Let's ask him this evening. It's no good going around now, as he'll be helping at the nursery. He's got a holiday job there.'

'We could pop round and tell Stella, and ask her if she'll ask him to come round when he gets home. Mind you, once we tell her the whole village will know fairly soon. She can't resist passing on news.'

It was after six that evening when Greg knocked at their back door. 'Mum's told me about your find, isn't it exciting? He said. 'I'd love to go down. I've put on my old jeans and Dad's bringing round the aluminium ladder, say's it'll be lighter and easier to lower down. And Mum's coming round too.' He was grinning. 'Well you know...'

'Yes we know.' Lydia and Simon both smiled at Greg. Stella wouldn't be able to bear not being a part of their discovery.

Simon led the way. 'Come on, then, let's go up the garden. Greg, I want you to have a rope round your waist.'

'Whatever for? It's not very deep is it? Mum said about eight feet.' Greg looked puzzled.

'Yes, but we can't see the floor because of earth and rubble. We don't want you to fall down a hole or trip over anything we can't see and perhaps twist your ankle. You wouldn't be able to climb out.'

Greg considered this eventuality. 'Okay,' he said, 'I don't mind. Whatever you think best really.'

In the garden, Stella and her husband, Tom, were standing by the trapdoor, which had been dragged back in place to prevent cats or dog from venturing into this new 'annexe', as Lydia and Simon had been jokingly calling their mysterious room since its discovery.

There was only just room for Greg to squeeze down the hole when the stepladder was in place, even though he was very slim.

Simon remarked, 'It's a good job I didn't try to go down. I'd have got jammed and probably wouldn't have been able to go up or down. It's quite a small opening. Either the people who were expected to go down there were small or they just threw things down, whatever it was for, and left ropes attached to pull them up again. I can't imagine what its true purpose was. Are you down, Greg?' he called.

'Yes,' Greg shouted up. 'The ground's quite firm – at least, it is where I'm standing. Can you pass me the torch now? It's a bit eerie down here. You feel quite closed in because the entrance is so small. I'll see if I can move around a bit. Pass out a bit more rope, will you?'

He took hold of the torch that Simon handed down to him. Simon then tied the end of the rope round a tall conifer standing about twelve feet from the hole. 'Okay, you've got all the rope,' he called. 'Will you see if you can get to that heap of what looks like old bones up the far end?'

They could hear Greg shuffling around below them. Then he shouted up, 'It's a bit wet here. My feet are wet – never mind. They definitely seem to be bones… *Ow!*' There was a sudden shriek. Was it fear or surprise?

The watchers above all rushed to the hole and peered down. 'Greg, are you alright?' called Tom. 'What's happened?'

Stella was looking agitated. 'Greg!' she called nervously. 'Are you all right? For heavens sake, what's happened?' She was yelling now.

Greg's face appeared at the edge of the hole. He had gone rather pale and looked a bit sick, but there was also a flicker of amusement in his eyes as he wriggled his body to get his arm out of the hole.

Suddenly his hand emerged into the daylight and he thrust it upwards so that they could all see what he was holding. There, looking particularly incongruous in the sunny garden, was a human skull!

Chapter Two

Although Hugh Fitzhugh and his wife, Gladys, were really Simon and Lydia's next-door neighbours, their house and garden were some distance away because of a vacant plot between them which had never been developed. Simon had tried to find the owners several times but without any success. He would have liked to put in an offer for the land and increase the size of his garden, but Hugh seemed decidedly unhelpful any time the subject was broached.

Simon thought it was because they'd like it for themselves, but Lydia said they probably couldn't afford it and just didn't want anyone else to have it as they'd overlook their property. It was apparent that Lydia didn't like Hugh very much. Both the Fitzhughs kept themselves to themselves, but Hugh had actually snapped at Lydia one day when she'd made a joke about his name. Gladys had tried to pass it off, saying that he'd had so many comments made he'd no patience left with the jokes but Lydia put it down to his bad temper. A lot of people in the village complained about Hugh's abrupt manner and the way he put his wife down in public, often making out she was stupid when she obviously wasn't. Many people had wondered why she stayed with him, she'd never been known to complain about him; and because of her loyalty, which many people thought was misplaced, she had the respect of most of her neighbours.

Hugh and Gladys had lived in the village longer than most of the other inhabitants. Both in their seventies now, they had moved down from Newcastle when Hugh had finished his medical training and secured the post of junior partner to the very old and ailing Doctor Jacobson. Hugh felt he'd been lucky getting the position, as he'd had no experience and there was also the chance to live over the surgery at a very economical rent and make use of the extensive gardens, which were extremely overgrown at the time.

Hugh had a passion for trees. Coming from the centre of South Shields, with its shipbuilding and fishing industries, he had rarely seen that many, except on school trips and family holidays, but he had vowed as a young boy that one day he'd have a large garden and plant lots of trees himself. Hugh was a short man in stature as well as in manner; he often wished he'd been taller but there it was, nothing he could do about that; but he could admire the height, the slender grandeur and the seeming immortality of trees. His favourite was the silver birch, but he liked all the varieties, even conifers; and seeing the overgrown plot behind the surgery and being told he could do what he liked with it was an added attraction to the position.

'There's all we want here, Gladys,' he'd told her, his voice full of enthusiasm for once.

'Aye, we could settle here; it's grand, really grand.'

That had been 1921. They had settled in as he'd predicted, and the following year Bunty had been born.

She'd been christened Elizabeth, but Hugh liked to sing 'Bye, baby bunting' to her in the evenings after surgery, when he'd bounce her on his knee and revel in the soapy, clean, baby smell of her before taking her to her cot and setting her down. He always put her to bed. He told Gladys it was because he didn't spend as much time with her as he'd have liked because of his work, but Gladys knew he'd have spent every minute with her if it had been possible. She was the apple of his eye. He never tired of talking about her, and his patients soon knew when she cut her first tooth, started talking, walking, and all her other attributes – of which, according to Hugh, there were a great many.

Now, in 1971, there were no other residents in the road who had lived there all those years. In fact most of them had arrived during the past twenty years, and Simon and Lydia had only been in their cottage for three years since he'd retired from the office and they'd sought somewhere 'really peaceful but not too far from civilisation', as Lydia had put it.

Lydia wondered whether they should tell Hugh and Gladys about the bones straightaway or whether they should wait till they happened to meet and just drop it casually into the conversation.

'I think we ought to tell them, now,' said Simon. 'It might be weeks before we meet them. We don't often see them, even though we live so close. It wouldn't be very nice if they read something in the local paper, or heard about it from someone else when we are their neighbours after all.'

'Okay, I'll ring them first, shall I? Ask them if they'd like to come round for a drink. Mind you, I hope Hugh's in a good mood. He can be so grumpy sometimes that it's difficult to make conversation with him.'

'Yes, but you'll be telling him about the bones, won't you, so you'll have something to talk about straightaway. He's bound to be interested, having lived next to them all these years, even if he didn't know anything about them. I say, you don't think he *did*, do you?'

'What?'

'Know anything about them?'

'Of course not silly! They wouldn't still be down there if anyone knew anything about them. I don't suppose anyone even knew there was a room down there. They've probably been under the earth for years and years,' said Lydia, reasonably.

'Yes, but he's lived here for years and years you know, and didn't they use our place our place as an extra surgery at one time?'

'Oh, that's only a rumour; anyway, if he'd know the room was there he'd have looked at it. If he'd looked in it he'd have found the bones, and if he'd found the bones then they wouldn't still be here – would they?' Lydia applied logic to the situation.

'Yes, of course. Of course you're right. If anyone had known they were there then they wouldn't still be here—'

'Except the person who put them down there,' Lydia cut in.

He looked at her, there was silence between them while they both considered her revelation.

Chapter Three

This was how Berlin was in the year 1938. Hurrying furtive figures. Shoulders hunched, with looks almost apologetic for being allowed to walk the streets. Trying to hide the sign that branded them untouchables. The yellow Star of David and the word *Juden*, displayed on their jackets. Due to an accident of birth they had been classified 'subhuman'. Groups of uniformed thugs, legitimised by their brown shirted uniforms parade outside shops and businesses that had the word *Juden* scrawled obscenely over the outside walls and windows. This was National Socialism displaying the malicious anti-Semitic part of its political 'manifesto'. Behind the open facade of their hatred was the hidden and more sinister discrimination against the professional *Juden* – the bankers, doctors, dentists, lawyers and staff in educational establishments. Here, the embryo seeds for the genocide of six million Jews were being sown. Such visible and invisible evidence failed to move Karl Langstein as he travelled from the Chancellery in the sleek Mercedes. Reclining back on the leather upholstery he ruminated on the meeting of the masters of Germany that he had just left. There had been many milestones in the Nazis' rise to supreme power.

The mass meetings of the uniformed *Herrenvolk* – the Nuremberg rally. A massive demonstration of German unity. The military precision, the banners. Huge red standards showing the crooked cross of the swastika, borrowed from ancient mythology. The podium with the Nazi hierarchy in full view. A superb stroke of propaganda.

Adolf Hitler, the master of political rhetoric, had held his audience spellbound with rallying clichés and the massed ranks had risen to the emotive occasion. *Sieg heil! Sieg heil!* Hail Victory! Hail Victory! It was masterful hypnotism on a grand scale. Heady stuff that could only take the people onwards, whereby 'onwards' was held in the grasp of the future. Today he had heard where that 'onwards' was destined to be. It was the summer of 1938, and there were massive German troop movements in the guise of army manoeuvres taking place near the Polish borders. East was to be the greatest 'curtain-raiser' since 1914.

Karl sat there pensively. His eldest son, also called Karl, had telephoned. Hauptsturmführer Karl Langstein had gazed at his reflection in the large mirror at the Chancellery. Six feet four inches tall, and broad-shouldered. An athletic figure for his forty-five years; a hint of grey in his thick blonde hair. He had a pale, expressionless face and a piercing gaze; the blue eyes had a determined look of coldness that could not be compromised. The square jaw-line, the aquiline nose with a saving hint of sensuality about the mouth. He looked the epitome of the military order. One who had been brought up in the strict Prussian military traditions of self-sacrifice for the cause and complete submission to higher authority.

He was tough and almost handsome in his arrogant Prussian manner. Under his overcoat of soft black leather loosely thrown over his shoulders was the exquisitely tailored SS uniform with its RFSS cuff title of Himmler's personal staff, the Waffenfarben. The uniform cap showing SS security, with its silver death's head badge. Oak leaves on the collar patches indicated rank and were in silver thread. The buckle of the belt showed the eagle with a swastika in one claw and SS runes in the other. The gold oak leaves of the Iron-Cross, first class, hung from his breast pocket and the insignia of hauptsturmführer gleamed from his epaulets.

He had just come from the Reichsführer's office at the Reichskanzlerei, where he had attended the highly secretive and informative conference attended by Adolf Hitler, the Reichskanzler himself. Reichsleiter Martin Bormann. Doctor Josef Goebbels, Minister of Propaganda and Public Enlightenment. General von Manteuffel, Commander, 3rd Panzer Army. General Tippelskirch, 1st Panzer Army. Commander von Neurath, aide to Admiral Doenitz. Field Marshal Keitel, senior military adviser to Hitler. Herr Generatfeldmarchalt Hermann Goering, Reichsführer of the SS and Chief of both State and Secret Police. The most feared man in Germany, Heinrich Himmler, chinless and bespectacled in his pince-nez. Admiral Doenitz, the big lion, and the Reichsminister for Armament, Albert Speer.

It was a conference that had sealed the fate of Poland and possibly the whole of Europe.

Karl was very pleased with himself. His dedication to National Socialism was complete and his position secure. A scion of the Prussian officer class, he had served in the war of 1914 as an oberleutnant in the crack Prussian Uhlan cavalry, where he earned his Iron Cross 1st class. The humiliation of the Versailles Treaty had festered in him throughout the post-war years. In 1930 he had begun to interest himself in politics and he had been attracted to National Socialism and Adolf Hitler, who had given new hope to the disillusioned masses and restored the pride of the German nation in its military power.

Adolf Hitler came to power in 1933 and was appointed Chancellor. Karl had been rewarded for his dedication and had quickly risen to power as personal aide to Reichsführer Himmler.

After a heady courtship he had married Liesl shortly after the 1914–18 war. They had met at one of those political rallies that appealed to the disaffected youth of those post-war years. She was the daughter of the publisher of the right-wing newspaper *Das Volks Politika*. He had first noticed her hair, silky blonde with cascading curls framing an oval, almost oriental face. The high cheekbones. The large honest blue eyes. The generous mouth which complemented the warmth of her smile. She had been wearing a large copious coat, which was fashionable with avant-garde politicals of that time, modelled on the old military trench-coats. The calf-length boots looked almost dainty on her shapely legs. The coat hung loose, revealing her fulsome and exciting figure, accentuating the curves of her breasts and hips. The attraction had been unashamedly physical with all the longings of frustrated youth. They had married and within six months, Karl, their first son was born.

Their political views had bonded their relationship. Both were convinced that Germany needed a strong authoritarian leadership if it was to become once again a leading world power.

Karl's father-in-law had offered him a career with his right-wing publications and he had found himself increasingly attending right-wing rallies of the newly emerging National Socialist movement, reporting the speeches of its founder member Adolf Hitler. An Austrian by birth, he was a brilliant orator who mesmerised his audiences with his dazzling predictions for the future Germany which would emerge from the conservatism of the 'old guard' to be once again a dynamic and vibrant world power.

These infectious speeches had convinced Karl that his future must be part of this dream. He joined the movement and his military background made him ideal recruiting material for the paramilitary units being formed alongside the political wing of the National Socialist movement: the Brownshirts and the storm troopers who were to become the founder members of the elite and ruthless Waffen SS.

His journalistic experience, Aryan good looks and military training, together with a ruthless dedication to a greater and all-conquering order, had brought Karl to the brink of a dazzling career within the newly formed internal security forces of the SS under the direct command of Heinrich Himmler.

Today Karl was hurrying from the Reichskanzlerei to the headquarters of the Gestapo in Prinz Albrechtstrasse. The message from Karl junior, his eldest son, sounded urgent.

The marble walls of the Reichspolizei headquarters echoed to the strutting uniformed figures hurrying about their repulsive business. The secret intelligence department of the SD was housed here and was responsible only to Himmler himself.

He had arranged the meeting for that afternoon. His son had declined to discuss the matter over the telephone. The tapping of telephones was extended to everyone, irrespective of rank or position, confirming loyalty or rooting out treachery. Reasons were not necessary or given. He glanced once again along the corridor of the Reichspolizei headquarters with its marble walls and colonnades.

Karl was proud of his eldest son, who had fulfilled all his father's ambitions. An enthusiastic graduate from the Volkssturm, the Hitler Youth, his physical likeness to his father was uncanny. The same blonde hair, the same blue eyes, and the same arrogance were all there. However, there was obsessive fanaticism in those eyes that betrayed a ruthlessness that went beyond ordinary family loyalties and bordered on the workings of hell and an allegiance to the devil.

Karl junior was consumed by the Nazi ideologies: purity of race; blind obedience; contempt for and intolerance of weakness. Might was right and right was the absolute right. Dangerous obsessions, which recognised racial superiority over all other cultures to the point of obliteration.

Karl gazed approvingly as his eldest son approached him, noting the immaculately tailored black uniform. In his gleaming jackboots in black leather, he was a true Aryan officer of the Third Reich. He wore the insignia of the rank of Oberstleutnant with the SS runes on his collar and the gleaming silver death's head on his black hat. He was an officer of the SS Panzer Lehr, now held in reserve on the outskirts of Berlin. Its massive Tiger tanks had already embarked on the low-loader rail trucks, ready for any call.

Karl couldn't help comparing this eldest son with Paul, his younger boy, now on vacation from his university. Paul had also been an enthusiastic member of the Hitler Youth. Now he was a university student and a keen member of the socialist party. He, like Karl, had inherited his father's physical appearance: blonde hair, blue-eyed, tall and athletic. Paul had, however, also inherited a gentleness from his mother that had somewhat blunted his father's ruthlessness and ambition. He had a passion for flying and wanted to join the Luftwaffe at the first opportunity. Not, however, without some opposition from his father, who had foreseen a more glittering career nearer the hard core of the Party leadership.

However, partly through family influence and partly through his own ability, Paul would reach high rank in the newly formed fighter wings of the Luftwaffe.

His vacation had been extended and rumours were circulating of massive troop movements towards the East. Vast amounts of equipment and tanks had been seen on railway transports. It was the summer of 1938.

Paul was also attending the Berlin Academy for English Studies, as part of his university course. There he had met Bunty, a young English girl. At first he had been attracted by her freshness and innocence when he had been introduced to her by his

English-speaking fellow students. The Institute had a strong tradition of English scholarship.

She was on a working holiday to improve her knowledge of German. Her father was an English doctor and they lived in a sleepy English village in Somerset. He had learnt this on their first meeting. Their friendship had, however, deepened, and they had met many times. He had shown her the Berlin of the non-tourist; clubs where conversation flowed light-heartedly. They had talked about life, art, music and England.

Paul loved his country, and his knowledge of other cultures was limited. School had been strict and conformist, nurturing rigid attitudes of work and discipline. The Hitler Youth had been a source of physical expression. It was about the great out-doors, fitness and comradeship. He had never seriously questioned the racial and political propaganda. Healthy bodies and youthful minds being moulded towards excessive fanaticism for the future of Germany.

With the enthusiasm of youth, their conversations ranged over the frivolous as well as deeper issues. Bunty was obviously of another culture. In English schools, laughter was not far beneath the formal rituals of teaching. She often laughed at herself and ridiculed the fetishes of English middle classes.

At first Paul found these attitudes confusing when compared to his own controlled and disciplined background. Yet in many ways they complemented his impatience with blind obedience and disquieting questions about the indoctrinated racism of the National Socialists, who condemned non-purists to contemptuous ridicule.

Paul's liberal thoughts had become increasingly difficult to suppress. The more he saw of this girl the more intolerable he found the attitudes prevalent in German society. They both spoke openly of the inherent dangers of National Socialist aims within a democratic society.

The mental conflict was further complicated by his own family background. His father held high office within the Nazi Party. Karl, his brother, was a bigoted idealist. Purity of race, blind obedience and contempt for weakness; might was absolute right: these were dangerous obsessions, which only recognised racial superiority and the obliteration of opposition.

Paul had introduced Bunty to his family. His mother had been courteous and kind. The English came from a land of eccentricity and insularity. His father had shown a curious and unexpected tolerance. After all, he had earned his Iron Cross, first class, in the conflict with the English. Karl, his brother, was polite, cold and suspicious. Aryanism meant purity of race, and Bunty meant contamination. Who could say who the English were? Karl became increasingly hostile as the friendship developed. A casual friendship he could accept between his brother and this English Fräulein, but any hint of further commitment would be highly dangerous and completely unacceptable.

He had been aware for some time that Paul lacked total commitment to the Nazi ideology. He showed little enthusiasm for the discriminatory decrees against the Jews. He was weak, Karl realised, and needed watching.

The relationship took a new turn when Bunty spoke of returning home to England. It was then that Paul found that his feelings towards her were far from casual. He was in love.

He spoke to his mother, asking for her advice. Could he visit England to meet Bunty's parents? His father remained coldly aloof and distanced himself from any discussions or commitments. His brother, Karl, seethed inwardly at the disastrous turn in the liaison. His father was immensely powerful and was held in great esteem by his masters. This made his position more vulnerable. Power engendered envy from those less powerful. Karl could foresee only disaster in any further development in this affair between his brother and the English Fräulein.

As Karl approached his father, his face betrayed the gravity of the news that he was carrying.

'Karl! How are you? And why the urgency and secrecy?' Karl asked his eldest son.

'Not here, Father. Can we go somewhere more private and secure?

To go to one of the many offices that he could use for his private affairs would be courting danger, Karl realised. Every public room was bugged and under surveillance.

'Let us walk in the grounds... but look casual,' he suggested.

They left the main building of the Reichpolitei and entered the lawned square outside.

'Father,' said Karl, trying desperately to look unconcerned, 'there has been an accident. A terrible accident. Bunty, the English Fräulein, has been found horribly mutilated and dead alongside the railway track. It looks like an accident. Either she fell from a carriage or was hit by a train.'

Chapter Four

Tuesday morning

Joseph's leg was aching. That piece of shrapnel from the Englischen mortar at Verdun in '18 still bothered him, particular in wet weather. He had been out since early morning and the rain drizzled down like showers of fine glass. The sky was grey and overcast. He was looking forward to the hot coffee and sausage which Martha would have ready and waiting for him. She liked him back on time from his early morning inspection of the rolling stock parked in the railway siding.

Where was that dog! He could hear her barking. Too much hound and not enough dog. Always chasing off at the slightest scent.

'Here, Judi, here! *Kom! Kom!*' Perhaps she wasn't a German dog... perhaps she started life in some Frog family, or Polish or Scandinavian one maybe, abandoned by some tourist.

There she was, tail wagging, barking or howling at something in the undergrowth by the perimeter fence. A fox, maybe, too scared to leave the safety of the bushes. Odd, there was a flash of colour amongst the greenery. Peering closer, he saw the feet and sprawling legs belonging to what looked like the body of a young girl. The head was obscured by the mass of blood and matted hair. More blood had soaked her clothing.

Wednesday afternoon

Kielmann had been Chief Inspector of the Berlin Criminal Polizei for ten years or more. He had risen from the ranks, avoiding politics and agreeing with whoever held the purse strings. *Don't make waves* had been his motto, and his masters responded gratefully with further promotions. The sergeant looked down at the corpse lying on the morgue slab, and then gazed at his chief.

'About fifteen or sixteen year's old, I would say. Pretty young thing too. Someone had made sure of her dying. Multiple stab wounds to her chest and throat and the back of her head battered. Yes, someone had desperately wanted her dead.'

Monday afternoon

The responsibility of having Monica and Bunty staying in her home was resting heavily on Monica's aunt, Gretchen. She'd welcomed Monica last year when her brother, Monica's father, had first broached the idea. She was a good girl, helpful and pleasant company, but since her mother's niece had written to ask if she could stay Gretchen had begun to have misgivings. For one thing, Bunty was three years younger and a lot less mature than Monica, and she was known in the family to have an eye for the boys. She'd never actually been in any trouble and she was bright and friendly but she didn't seem to have the sense of responsibility Monica had. She'd laughed at their fears when they'd said she should be careful visiting cafés and clubs with Paul, and staying out so late nearly every evening.

Gretchen comforted herself with the fact that Bunty would be returning to England in twelve days' time. She glanced at the clock, after eleven and still she had not returned. She hadn't even been back for supper or to get changed after classes.

'Did Bunty say where she was going tonight, Monica?'

Her niece was frowning. 'She didn't tell me, in fact she didn't even say she'd see me after classes! I asked some of the others, and they said they thought she'd gone to meet Paul. One of them thought she'd had a message unexpectedly. She should be back soon. I told her it was dangerous on the streets at night, and we have classes again tomorrow. Well, you go up, Auntie. I'll wait up for her. She shouldn't be long, and then I'll lock up. Night-night.' Monica stretched out on the comfy sofa.

'Goodnight dear,' said Gretchen.

Monica let her thoughts stray. She wished Bunty hadn't got so involved with Paul. His brother was a nasty type. She thought she wouldn't be sorry to return to England herself at the end of the month. Things were very uncomfortable in Berlin; so many people seemed to be suspicious and anxious about each other. There were a lot of restrictions on Jewish people, and she heard talk that some people had just disappeared – gone out to work, or shopping and just never returned. What a worrying time it was. No she wouldn't be sorry to get back home and settle back into university life. She was pleased with what she had achieved at the Institute. She could now speak German pretty fluently and held her own in most conversations with her German friends.

Tuesday morning

Monica was surprised to see daylight when she opened her eyes. She must have dropped off to sleep. Bunty must have come in and gone straight to bed. She stretched herself and then went upstairs to get washed and changed.

But Bunty had not been home, nor did she return during that day or the next and Monica had reluctantly reported her missing to the police and a very polite detective had taken down all the relevant details and promised to do his best. 'These things do happen, you know. Perhaps she was staying with friends,' he said.

Monica was anxious. She had known that Bunty was becoming increasingly involved with Paul. There had been talk of running away or returning to England together.

For two months Bunty had stayed with Monica's aunt and uncle in the Berlin suburbs. They had attended the Institute together where Monica was researching the Germanic culture of the Habsburgs and the Holy Roman Empire, while Bunty was working on a project for her Higher Matriculation.

Bunty's parents, Hugh and Gladys, had expressed their anxiety, particularly in view of the news reports of violent demonstrations against the Jews. But they could refuse Bunty nothing, and she had persuaded them to allow her trip to Berlin. England seemed a faraway place now. The quiet village; Bunty's father going about his doctor's practice; babies, pills, death certificates. It all seemed so settled. Now there was all this talk of Germany, the Nazis, and Mr Chamberlain flying back and forth waving pieces of paper.

Wednesday morning

No evidence of sexual abuse. A puzzle, Kielmann thought. Violent death was not uncommon these days, particularly with all the political and murderous beatings of Jews and the politically disaffected. But those took place openly in the streets, witnessed by passive bystanders. The perpetrators were usually uniformed and organised thugs – members of the 'New Order'.

This was different. A young girl from, it seemed, a good middle-class background, judging by the quality of her clothes. He picked up the skirt and glanced at the label. Odd... the name was in English.

It was now two days since Bunty had last been seen at the Institute and there had not been any communication from any of her friends or colleagues. Could those rumours of running away with Paul have any truth in them? The police had not been touch, which could be taken as a good sign. Monica's mind was beginning to play tricks, conjuring up the worst possible scenarios despite her optimism.

Thursday afternoon

Chief Inspector Kielmann glanced at the list of missing persons. He noticed the name. *Girl, sixteen, English, Berlin*. He picked up the telephone.

The policeman stood at the door. Would Monica please come to the station?

Anxious and fearful, Gretchen and Monica were shown into the mortuary. The plastic sheet was drawn back. Anxiety became extreme distress. Yes, it was Bunty. They'd tidied up the body. The hair was pushed back. The fatal wounds remained covered.

Friday morning

Kielmann glanced down at the memo then up at the green-uniformed colonel from the SD headquarters. 'You understand, Chief Inspector,' said the colonel. 'Make all the necessary arrangements for the body to be returned to England. All forensic records to be destroyed. Cause of death – 'accidental', following a fall from a train and subsequent additional multiple injuries from other passing rail traffic. I'm confident that you can handle this with the utmost discretion.'

Kielmann knew the pattern and nodded in acquiescence. His career was secure. Another promotion, perhaps. He closed the file and saluted the colonel.

As they drove away, Karl looked at his father. Relief showed in his blue steely eyes. He said 'it was the only way. She refused to agree or cooperate, and there was too much at stake.'

'I understand.' replied his father. There was a detachment there that was frightening. 'Does Paul know?'

'Yes! He was devastated, of course,' replied Karl.

His father looked thoughtful 'It may be a good time to show Paul the advantages of patriotic service. There is an opening in our foreign intelligence service. I will speak to him,' added his father.

The following Thursday

Numbed and miserable, she sat rocking gently in the chair. A week had passed since that dreadful visit to the mortuary. The police had taken a full statement. They would pursue their enquiries. She had written to Bunty's parents. Their grief would be devastating. She was glad in a way that she had not gone straight back to England.

Sunday morning

The knock on the door sounded almost apologetic. The girl stood there looking anxiously over her shoulder. 'May I come in?' she asked.

'Of course,' said Monica, and showed the girl into the comfortable sitting room.

The girl perched herself nervously on the edge of the chair. 'My name is Elsa,' she said, 'and I am a student at the Institute. I knew Bunty very well and we were good friends. I often noticed her with Paul, who is also a friend of mine. We know each other from our school days. In fact I know the family quite well. Paul is quite different from his brother, Karl, who is full of the Party and Germany and thoroughly boring. The reason for my visit is that I have just heard the dreadful news about Bunty. We are all devastated. She was such a nice girl. We talked a lot. You see, I am in Paul's English language class. I have been away for a week or so visiting my aunt in Austria,' she explained.

'From the reports that I have heard the death was due to an accidental fall from a train. In view of this I must tell you of what I know. I saw Bunty just before I left Berlin. We were having coffee outside the Institute. She left to come home and we parted at the tram stop. It was while I was waiting for the tram that I saw the black Mercedes car pull alongside Bunty. The driver spoke to her and then got out of the car. It was Karl and two other men in SD uniforms. They were having what looked like an argument when they suddenly bundled Bunty into the back of the car and sped off. I thought that as it was Paul's brother it was something to do with him. That was on Monday; Bunty did not come back to the Institute.'

Monica was puzzled. Paul had called after the disappearance but had not mentioned his brother's meeting with Bunty.

Monica thanked Elsa, who declined the coffee she offered her. Monica closed the door and went to the telephone,

Kielmann picked up the telephone. 'Yes, this is Chief Inspector Kielmann. Her body was discovered alongside the railway sidings. She had obviously fallen from the train. No doubt about the cause of death.'

The following Monday afternoon

Monica gazed at the station sidings. The ticket office was open. She entered.

'Can I help you, miss?' The porter was standing by the office door.

'I wonder if you could?' She began. 'My cousin was involved in an accident near here about a week ago.'

The porter showed an interest. 'I wonder could you tell me who discovered the body?' The porter gazed at her. He began to feel important. People only approached him usually wanting their heavy cases carried without giving him a second glance.

'Yes, miss. I can remember it well. Caused quite a stir at the time. The police were all over the place.'

'Who actually found the body?' Monica put in, trying to keep the urgency out of her voice.

'Let me see… Yes, it was old Joseph. He's the nightwatchman. Keeps an eye on the sidings. Making sure no courting couples get into the carriages, if you know what I mean?'

'Where can I find him?' asked Monica, keeping calm and looking in her purse for a suitable coin.

'He lives over there on the edge of the yard. You can see his house from here – the one with the garden fence,' replied the porter, his eyes gazing at the proffered reward.

Joseph's wife, Martha, opened the door. 'Yes! What can I do for you?' she asked cautiously of the young woman standing there. Obviously one of those city types.

'I wondered if you can help me?' asked Monica as she gazed at the formidable Martha.

'Well, depends on what you have in mind?' replied Martha, still on her guard.

'Could I speak to Joseph the railway night-watchman?' persisted Monica.

'You'd better come in!' replied Martha. 'He's out in the back looking after his racing pigeons. He's always in the back with his blasted pigeons.' She added fretfully.

Joseph straightened up as his wife, followed by a smart young woman, came into the garden.

Monica gazed at the man. Must be more than fifty, nearer sixty, she thought. Obviously proud of the beautiful birds that strutted and cooed about him.

'This young lady wants to ask you some questions,' Martha said, relishing the chance to get him away from his pigeons for five minutes.

'My name is Monica, and I'm cousin of the girl who was accidentally killed alongside the railway here about a week ago.' Monica tried not to sound too anxious and came to the point as quickly as possible.

'Ah! Yes. Bad thing that,' replied Joseph. 'A cousin, you say? A pretty young thing, she was. Though she didn't look very pretty when I found her—'

'I'm sorry to trouble you,' continued Monica, 'but can you tell me, was she very badly injured? Only I have to tell her parents when I return to England, and they may be comforted if she died without too much pain or suffering,'

'Oh! She was English, was she?' asked Joseph.

The police had already hinted that they wanted the details hushed up. Still, what was the harm if this woman was returning to England. The truth might help.

'Well, I've seen many a body that's met a nasty end and your – cousin, you say?' He had wanted to tell someone the true story ever since that dreadful morning. He was in full flood. 'That was no accident! She'd been stabbed and her head all battered and bloody. I should know. I was in the last lot in 1914. Fallen from a train…? Not from what I saw!'

He looked at Martha and realised he had said more than he should have.

'But if the police say "accidental" then it had better stay accidental,' he added quickly. He was feeling more cautious. 'Keep what I have said to yourself. These days you never can tell. Too many people ready to say the worst about you.'

Monica thanked him and realised that he was regretting what he had said. 'I won't repeat what you have told me but it helps to know the truth,' she reassured him. 'Goodbye,' she said, and thanked the old soldier once again.

This was shocking news, but she would need to be careful. If Bunty had been murdered, then Paul's brother was implicated and her own life could be in danger. Somehow she must return to England and let the authorities there know all the details and make all the necessary investigations.

Chapter Five

Monica returned to her aunt's house. 'Is that you, Monica?' Gretchen called from the lounge.

'Yes, Auntie,' she replied.

'There has been a telephone call for you, and two men called to see you,' her aunt continued.

'Oh! What did they want?' Monica asked, keeping her voice as casual as she could. Her stomach muscles had tightened and she felt her hands beginning to sweat.

'They wouldn't say,' her aunt replied, 'but they seemed anxious to know where you were and when you would return,' she added.

Monica entered the large comfortable lounge with its heavy Germanic furniture. 'Auntie! I have a favour to ask,' she said. 'I must return to England as soon as possible.' She paused. 'My travel papers are still valid, but no one must know I have left. If I leave most of my luggage here and take just a travelling bag, would you tell anyone who enquires that I am still here but that I have gone out on one of my course studies?'

Her aunt looked puzzled, but she knew that they lived in dangerous times. Too many of her old friends, particularly those who were Jewish, had disappeared. Even the old doctor no longer practised.

'I have very good reasons for asking you,' Monica declared, 'but the less I tell you the safer it will be for yourself.'

'You must do what is best,' replied her aunt. 'I will do anything you ask.'

Gretchen was quite happy to accept Monica's excuses for returning to England. The tragic death of Bunty had been traumatic and no doubt her parents would need to be informed more sympathetically than through the official channels.

'There is a train leaving the bahnhof in Friedrichstrasse at 10.30 p.m. tonight travelling to Nuremberg. From there I will travel overnight to Karlsruhe and into France. Once there I should be safe; though I must not relax until I am in England.'

At eight o'clock Monica slipped out of the house. Dusk was falling. She carried only her small travelling bag slung over her shoulder. She caught the tram rather than the suburban railway, the Deutsche Reichsbahn, in order to remain hidden and mix with the casual suburban travellers. The tram would take her to the Institute, which was part of the Humboldt University complex in the Unter den Linden. From there the Friedrich-strasse Bahnhof was within walking distance.

The black Mercedes was parked in the deepening shadows but moved slowly forward as the tram gathered speed. Monica tried to appear as casual as possible. The Institute was a short walk from the tram stop in the Friedrichstrasse. A newspaper kiosk stood nearby. She hurried to the kiosk and bought a copy of the *Berliner Kurier*. While appearing to glance at the headlines, she observed that the Mercedes had parked about thirty yards from the kiosk.

'Hello, Monica! What are you doing here so late?'

Looking up, she saw one of her tutors, who was obviously going to the Institute for a late evening class. A great feeling of relief came over her.

' Oh! I'm just going to collect some papers that I left behind for tomorrow's seminar,' she replied. 'I'll walk along with you, if you don't mind?'

Grateful for the chance encounter, they entered the building. The Mercedes had not moved.

How to get out from the building unnoticed was going to be a problem. Her tutor left her at the foot of the wide staircase that led to the upper lecture rooms.

Monica slipped into a small cloakroom at the foot of the stairs. Several outdoor hats and coats hung on various pegs. Selecting a large heavy coat and cap, she quickly put it over her own light-weight raincoat. Then, pushing her hair up on top of her head, she pulled the large cap low over her eyes. Fortunately she had decided to wear her casual trousers. Gazing into the mirror that hung on the wall, she was satisfied that in the gathering dusk her disguise would fool the casual observer, and she could pass as one of the many workmen that were employed for cleaning and maintenance.

Emerging from the building and lengthening her stride to appear more masculine, she passed out of the lighted entrance and into the shadows. Stepping into a doorway, she glanced over to where the Mercedes had been parked. With some relief she saw that it had not moved. Then one of the occupants, a burly uniformed figure, got out of the car and began walking towards the entrance of the Institute.

Monica hurried away. Before entering the main line station, the bahnhof, she discarded her borrowed coat and cap in a large litterbin.

The station was alive with people hurrying to catch the many commuter trains. Groups of uniformed figures stood here and there waiting for transit to their units. The civilian polizei patrolled in pairs. Near the entrance to the platform the Feldgendarmerie, military police, with their metal gorget hanging from their necks, armed with Walther handguns and Schmeisser machine pistols, stood menacingly watchful. Their main concern, however, was the military personnel.

With her heart beating a rapid tattoo Monica approached the ticket office and purchased a return ticket to Nuremberg. A return ticket would be less suspicious to any future enquiries about single travellers that evening.

The train was waiting at the platform and she passed the ticket collector without incident. The journey took three hours, and the compartment had filled with an assortment of travellers, mostly businessmen and two officers of the Wehrmacht. However, the journey passed without incident.

At Nuremberg she had shown her passport and travel documents. Once again her luck was holding. If there was a search going on, it must still be localised in Berlin. But for how long? Her aunt would tell her story, but the Institute might notice her absence the following day. It was essential that she travel out of Germany without delay. She bought another ticket to Strasbourg in France.

The train had left Nuremberg at two in the morning. In four hours they had crossed into France via Karlsruhe. Once again her luck held and her documents aroused no suspicions.

With relief flooding over her, she took a train to the French coast. She caught the ferry to Dover and travelled down to Somerset. The whole journey had taken a day and a half, and Berlin seemed a million miles away.

'We still can't accept that she has really gone,' Gladys had kept repeating; hoping, perhaps, that the nightmare would be eased by the sheer repetition of her disbelief.

Monica had thought long and hard on her journey home on how to break the news of the circumstances of their daughter's tragic end. How could she tell them of her suspicions? Would it not be better to let them believe that it had been an accident?

Hugh sensed her troubled thoughts. 'Is there anything that we should know?' The official letter had been cruel in its brevity: *Accidental death – fallen from a train…*

'Perhaps I could speak to you alone?' said Monica.

Gladys seemed puzzled and bewildered. 'What is there to add?' she pleaded.

Sensing there was more pain to come, and wishing to spare his wife further anguish, Huge said 'Perhaps I had better hear what Monica has to say alone my dear.'

Gladys's eyes were brimming tearfully. 'I'll make a cup of tea for us and leave you two alone for a while,' she said.

'There's more to tell about this.'

The doctor turned slowly towards Monica. 'You must tell me all you know.' He pleaded.

Monica began to tell her story, beginning with the friendship Bunty had formed with Paul and filling in the background of Paul's family. She recalled the deepening friendship that had blossomed into a tragic love affair. Then, the suspicious circumstances told to her by Bunty's friend; the visit to the station and the talk with Joseph, the nightwatchman; the circumstances of her own danger and the flight from Germany.

The doctor said nothing as Monica unfolded the whole tragic story. His grief soon gave way to a terrible anger. That he had lost his own beloved daughter had been a blow which he could barely come to terms with. To discover that her death was part of some devilish plan concocted by a warped mentality filled him with unbearable rage towards the perpetrators of the crime.

His voice sounded artificially cold and calm. 'Have you told this to anyone else?' he asked. 'No,' Monica replied, 'there is no proof, and the German police have closed the case.'

He continued, 'Yet you yourself believe that she was murdered by this brother of the boy she had befriended.'

Monica replied, 'I'm sure if you were to meet Karl you would understand my suspicions. He is a dedicated follower of the Nazi movement. Ambitious both for himself and his family. Any threat to his ambitions would be intolerable.' She paused.

'Bunty, I believe, he saw as a threat. His brother Paul was prepared to sacrifice everything, and had spoken of coming to England with her. I'm sure that they had planned to run away together and such an alliance would have undermined the careers of both the father and the elder son.' She added, 'To live in Germany is to realise how awful the cult of the fanatical Nazi really is.'

'Thank you for telling me all this, Monica. Perhaps I'll not tell Bunty's mother. Her grief is so great that I don't think she could bear to hear all you have said to me. Would you be kind enough not repeat this to anyone else, but leave the whole matter with me? You have been very brave, and I am sure that you have taken a considerable risk with your own life.'

Two months later Hitler's armies invaded Poland and war was declared between England and Germany.

Chapter Six

After the death of Bunty, Paul Langstein had been devastated. It had taken his father quite some time to reconcile him to the fact that perhaps, after all, it had been an infatuation. After all, she had been quite young and he was himself not long out of his late school years. She had been English, which would have appealed to his sense of curiosity and novelty. Nevertheless, the tragedy had left him with an aching emptiness. Karl, his brother, had behaved rather strangely throughout the whole affair, remaining aloof and detached.

His father had offered him an interesting post in the Intelligence Service. 'Full of promise and opportunity' was the way he had put it. However, Paul had declined. His interests and ambitions lay in joining the Luftwaffe and to fly some of the latest designs – particularly in fighter planes. In the end his father had given in and used his influence to enrol him in the Fliegerschule to train as an 'Oberleutnant' and realise his ambition to become a fighter pilot. Thus the pain of Bunty's loss was considerably eased.

The war and time had further dulled these memories. He had made several tours in various war theatres. Russia, the new enemy, had been particularly vicious: atrocious weather conditions, vast distances, and the loss of many of his original friends and comrades. The Polish Air Force had been desperate and brave but the Polskie Lotnictwo Wojskowe had been ill equipped and no match for the new German Messerschmitts. The Russians were tenacious, not seemingly affected by their heavy losses.

A period of rest was followed by a transfer to the Mediterranean where close support was needed for the various campaigns of the Fallschirmjager regiments in their parachute invasions of the Greek islands, particularly around Crete. Off duty hours were, however, to be looked forward to and enjoyed.

The Italian allies were friendly, especially the upper classes of the Italian society.

For Paul, Italy was like the beginning of a love affair. Stationed at Udine in northern Italy, he spent most of his leaves exploring the country's ancient culture, its buildings, statues and magnificent paintings.

Rome he had found fascinating. The ancient Forum, and the Coliseum with its echoes of ancient gladiatorial combats; St Peter's and the Vatican City; the Victor Emmanuel Monument called by the Roman population 'The Wedding Cake'. And the River Tiber – what stories those waters could tell! Cleopatra, Mark Antony, the Caesars and their conquests...

Paul visited Pisa, with its spectacular Leaning Tower and Baptistery. Verona with its associations with Shakespeare and Romeo and Juliet; the balcony and 'Juliet' – a statue with its left breast brightly polished by the stroking hands of hopeful romantics seeking the lovers of their dreams. Venice with its unique waterways; the Palace of the Doge and St Mark's Square; the overwhelming architectural splendour of its buildings and bridges.

Then Florence, Paul's *Grande Amore*, captivated his imagination. It was compact and enfolded the river Arno with its bridges ancient and modern. The Ponte Vecchio with its silversmiths and historic houses. The bridge where Dante waited to catch a glimpse of Beatrice as she walked with her lady companions. Founded by Caesar Augustus in 59 BC as a Roman camp, 'Firenze' its Italian name – derived from the Latin *Florentia*, meaning 'flower' or 'flora'. Florence became the indisputable centre of cultural life expressed in a manifest of literary works by Boccaccio, Patrarch and especially Dante. Artists such as Botticelli stood out among the powerful of the city. But it was the Medici, more than anyone else, who were destined to be interlinked with the history of Florence for centuries to come. Two members of the family in the 1500s became Popes: Leo the Tenth, son of Lorenzo the Magnificent, and Clement.

'Can you tell me how to find the statue of Michelangelo's David,' Paul asked the Italian guide in the Uffizi. He used German, as his Italian was not very good.

'*Come, Signore?*' the guide replied. '*Scusi – parla Italiano?*' Paul looked puzzled.

'*Scuso, Signore, posse aiutarla?*' The speaker was slim, with her dark hair tied loosely behind her head. A simple white skirt and blouse draped her attractive girlish figure. Her legs had that teasing Mediterranean tan and her feet fitted casually into floppy sandals. Her large dark eyes were casually scrutinising him. A generous smiling mouth showed white, even teeth.

'*Il mio Italiano non bene,*' he replied. Maria, for that was her name, looked at him. A German officer of the Luftwaffe. Handsome with his Nordic features. Extremely elegant in his grey blue uniform. She liked what she saw.

'*Mi chiamo Maria,*' she said, '*Lei come si chiamo?*'

He understood. 'Paul,' he replied smiling.

'*Capisco – io sono all'universita qui a Firenze, dove studio Francese e anche Inglese. Lei conosce il Francese oppure l'Inglese?*'

'*Inglese…* English,' Paul repeated 'Yes! Of course I studied English for three years at the Berlin University.'

She was visibly relieved. 'Let us start again,' she replied.

'My name is Maria and I study modern languages here in Florence.' Paul felt instantly drawn towards this attractive Italian girl. 'This is a stroke of luck,' he said, smiling. 'I'm looking for the statue of Michelangelo's David but cannot find it here in the Uffizi,' he added.

'It isn't here,' she told him, 'it is in a smaller gallery called the Galleria dell 'Accademia. It is quite a walk north of the Duomo. Do you want me to show you?' she offered.

'I'd be most grateful,' he said, smiling.

They left the Uffizi and eventually found the gallery, where Paul gazed at the statue of David. 'Much smaller than I expected. Look… I am very grateful for your help. Can I buy you lunch?'

That was how it all started. There was a mutual attraction between them both.

Paul had to return to his unit, however, and there followed a period of separation as he was engaged in night sorties. British bombers were operating from Malta and North Africa, bombing targets in Southern Germany. The Americans had undertaken the daylight raids and the British operated at night.

Their absence from each other made Maria realise that her feelings for Paul were far from casual.

On his next leave they decided to spend two or three days in Rimini with its large open beaches.

They swam lazily in the calm blue waters. The sun shone steadily in a clear blue sky and the vast expanse of beach with its shimmering sands was like a haven. The shore was deserted as they raced back to their chosen spot with the water glistening on their youthful and athletic bodies.

They had brought with them a picnic: a bottle of Chianti, some white bread with butter, cheese and some tomatoes Paul had managed to obtain from various sources and at the right price. It was not a day, or the occasion, to be concerned with the ordinary things of this world.

They laughed and giggled and conversation flowed easily.

After they had eaten Maria slipped out of her costume. It seemed the most natural thing to do.

He gazed at her slim brown figure, his eyes lingering on her petite and beautifully moulded breasts. Her nipples were standing rigidly erect. He noticed her firm rounded buttocks and flat stomach, with thighs meeting in a fine down. He moved closer and she slowly slipped off his swimming trunks. His arousal was evident. There was a yearning that he found impossible to bear. They reached for each other, hands exploring, reaching, seeking. Each caressing, thrusting, accepting. The climax was a devastating consuming passion. Both lay in a beautiful exhaustion for some time. Neither spoke; words seemed unnecessary.

Maria was the first to move as she dashed to the sea, splashing and thrashing like some youthful gazelle. Paul followed, grasping her and holding her close. The cool water soothed their bodies. Neither of them would ever forget this day.

Paul returned to his flying duties. He had to channel his thoughts away from Maria and concentrate on his more practical actions. Up there in the moonlit skies, high above the silvery clouds, there was a stark beauty that he had been unaware of on his previous missions.

'*Achtung! mein Oberst!*' The radio crackled. As Jagdfliegerführer Paul was commander of a flight of night fighters 'A British bomber group ahead and slightly below.'

He shook himself from his reverie. '*Ja!* I see them.' They were a formation of *grosser nachtflug* – night bombers – Lancasters. Four engines, unlike the old Wellingtons with their two engines. Capable of a bomb load of over 2000 lbs. The pilot and flight engineer sat next to each other. Behind them in his compact compartment sat the navigator. The gunners were isolated in the front and rear. The navigator usually manned the central gun position when in action. This was the most versatile and formidable of the British bombers. In formation they were near impregnable. The flight engineer of the lead aircraft spotted the Mes. He tapped the pilot on the shoulder and pointed. 'Leader to squadron – Messerschmitts, probably 109s, overhead. Look lively and stay in formation.'

'Oberst to flight. Pick your target. *Geh los! Geh los!* ' But the bombers were ready.

The tail-end Lancaster was in his sights. A short burst and the bomber's rear cupola shattered. He had a glimpsing vision of the gunner slumped forward grotesquely over his gun. As he reared over the bomber he realised his underbelly was exposed; a careless manoeuvre.

Paul felt the impact of the burst in his rear fuselage. The control column went slack. He was hit and the plane was slipping into an uncontrollable dive. Fighting to bring the machine under some sort of control, he managed to level out. To return to base was vital. Could he make it? 'Calling Luftwaffe Kommand Udine. This is flight XX9!' he called desperately.

'Luftwaffe Udine here. Pass your message, XX9,' came through his receiver loud and clear. Paul quickly reported his damage and requesting emergency landing assistance. Approaching the flight path, his aircraft was swinging alarmingly. One wheel touched down and the aircraft slewed in a wide arc. The port wing touched the runway and sheered off. The fear of fire was uppermost in his mind. A quick release of the canopy and he let his body fall to the ground.

He awoke in a hospital bed. 'Güten Morgen, Herr Oberst,' said an efficient-looking nursing orderly. 'You are in the military hospital overlooking Verona. You had a nasty collision with the landing strip, but other than multiple bruising and a slight concussion you will live!'

Maria came a week later. '*Caro! Carissimo!* I have only just found out, I enquired from your unit!' There was a desperation in her voice and there was a strained look in her eyes.

'*Liebling*, there was no need for you to worry so! I could not get in touch with you as I had a slight concussion. I am well on the mend now and I should be out of here in a few weeks' time.' Maria relaxed; after all, he was doing dangerous work and such an incident could happen anytime. 'Of course, *caro mio* I do understand... but I cannot help being anxious whenever we are apart, and I am so relieved to see you are not seriously hurt.'

She came as frequently as she could and they enjoyed their precious moments together. Their happiness was short-lived. Two weeks later Paul received fresh posting orders. He was to report, with his squadron, to the military air base at Lyon in France. It was shattering news for them both. Maria was devastated and even considered moving to Lyon. They both knew that this was out of the question. She must continue her studies and he must pursue his career and obey any orders given to him. Any thought of marriage was out of the question, for life was too uncertain and the future a fragile dream.

Paul had been stationed just to the south of Lyon for three months. The 'wing' had been heavily committed to bomber escorts over the southern mainland of England. The Dorniers concentrating their bombing the RAF fighter bases at Tangmere and Biggin Hill and other bases strung out across the South Coast. He had regularly corresponded with Maria and they had made plans to meet on his next long leave.

Now the fighter 'wing' was under his command as oberstleutnant. His promotions were all substantiated, but he had refused any ground postings despite the offer of further promotion. His passion for flying was undiminished.

The fighters were to rendezvous over the coast of Brittany with the bomber groups – the *Kampfgeschwader* – comprising three wings or more, mostly Dorniers. He walked towards the Messerschmitt 109s – his favourite fighter, superior in speed to the much vaunted Spitfire of the RAF, but not as manoeuvrable. Mechanics were working on the aircraft, making their last minute adjustments to already finely tuned engines. The *Feldwebel* and

Unteroffizier were checking the cannon and gun mountings and ammunition.

The bombing of the RAF fighter bases had been switched to the southern ports, once Goering's proud boast of destroying the British Air Force and giving Germany control of the air had failed. Hitler now wanted the bomber forces to turn their attention to the civilian population and the shipping facilities of the ports of Southampton and Portsmouth and continue attacks on London. Today's raid was to concentrate on the southern ports.

The Messerschmitts were taking off one after the other, making a circuit of the field and assembling in their flight order.

Soon they were over the Brittany coast. It was an impressive sight. Flight after flight of the Dorniers seemed to fill the sky from horizon to horizon.

Levelling at 20,000 feet, Paul called up his 'wing' commanders. '*Achtung! Achtung! Leiter* calling all commanders. The flights of fighters will provide an umbrella over the Dorniers. Maintain this height. Keep a sharp look-out for enemy fighters. *Gluck mit!*'

It wasn't long. Out of the sun they came: Spitfires and the latest Hurricanes, capable of climbing to higher altitudes than the Spitfires, thus depriving the Messerschmitts of their previous advantage. They were like hungry grey gleaming wolf packs descending on their unsuspecting prey. Radios were picking up those peculiar English call signs… 'Bandits! Bandits! Just look at the bastards. Right, chaps, pick your targets and keep an eye open for the Mes – they're around somewhere. Tally ho! Tally hoooo!' Something to do with those strange public schools. *Gott!* These English were a most peculiar race…

'*Leiter to flights – angreifen! Geh los! Geh los!*'

The skies were full of weaving, whirling and twisting machines. The thud-thud of cannon mixed with the staccato rattle of machine guns. Smoke trails showed casualties, like wounded beasts staggering across the blue skies.

A *Spitfeuer* was in Paul's sights. One burst and pieces were breaking off the stricken enemy. '*Gott!*' There was a shuddering crash – he was hit! No smoke, but the hit was mortal. He was plunging and spinning. The whole tail structure must have sheered. No time for assessment... the Messerschmitt was tearing itself to pieces. Canopy back, pushing against incredible forces of gravity. His body was free and falling. Pull the rip-chord. Pull! – pull! No time to spare. His body was gathering momentum. The jerk nearly pulled his arms from their sockets – relief! The canopy billowed open...a slow descent...but to where? He landed heavily by a roadside, winded but undamaged.

A vehicle pulled up and disgorged khaki-clad figures. One of the company detached himself and ran towards him. As he drew near it was obvious he was a mere boy, maybe seventeen years old. The rifle he was holding an old .303 from the First War. He worked the bolt action and put a bullet into the breach then slowly raised the rifle to his shoulder. Would he pull the trigger? It was a tense moment.

Fortunately a much older man, perhaps a 1914–18 veteran, came running up. 'Easy, Tim. Put your safety catch on nice and slowly now, we don't want any accidents. He looked at Paul – clearly a German, the uniform told him that. He glanced at the pistol holster. '*Giben-sie mir pistote*' the old soldier ordered.

'I speak... English,' Paul said, as calmly as he could under the circumstances.

'Well that will make life easier' said the old man. 'Come with us and you can meet our officer.' They approached the van and a little rotund man with a captain's insignia on his collar came to meet them.

'Ah, Stan, it looks as though we have one of those Nazi pilots here. He doesn't seem injured. Put him in the van and we'll get him to the police station,' the officer instructed.

'He speaks English, sir,' Stan added.

'Well you speak English, Fritz?' said the captain, finding it difficult not to speak in that slow manner English people use when addressing foreigners.

'Ja – my name is Paul Langstein and I am an oberstleutnant and offizier in the German Luftwaffe' said Paul.

Taken a little aback by this fluent English, the Englishman replied, 'Well. I'm Captain Wilson of the Home Guard!'

They bundled Paul into the van and drove off.

At the police station they put him into a cell. He heard

through the cell door the pompous tones of the Home Guard captain.

'Good show, chaps. The army can take over from here!'

Mein Gott! These English have a way of speaking quite unique to themselves and he will never understand them... Paul thought to himself.

Later the police sergeant brought in a meal. There were eggs, bacon, sausage and bread and butter. 'Sorry, but we only have tea,' said the sergeant. Another peculiarity of the English, Paul mused. 'Tell me sergeant. Who were those men that brought me here?' he asked.

'They're members of the Home Guard' answered the sergeant. 'They are all volunteers. They do their civilian jobs when they aren't on duty. Most of them are old First War veterans, but there's a sprinkling of youngsters waiting to be called up to the regular service. Some get carried away. You were lucky you didn't get some trigger-happy youngster or some old soldier with a score to settle!'

Paul was pensive. These were supposed to be the decadent enemy. No resistance to be expected to our glorious Wehrmacht.

The regular army unit arrived soon afterwards. These men were quite different from the Home Guard. Many were tanned and had obviously served in North Africa. All looked extremely fit. They wore the red caps of the British Military Police.

The escort travelled at a fast speed north until they reached the Interrogation and Prisoner of War camp in the county of Somerset. It was an isolated place in the heart of the English countryside. It had a somewhat unusual name: *Dimmer.*

Chapter Seven

It was June 1942. War fever had consumed the German Nation. Political opposition had disappeared almost overnight. The dream of a greater Germany was an all-conquering clarion call.

It was as if a nation had retired in civilian clothes and emerged in a multiplicity of uniforms. There could be little doubt that discipline, military displays, the pomp and glitter of marching men were part of the German culture.

Conquest after conquest fed this ideology. Poland, the Netherlands, Belgium, Czechoslovakia, France. The invincible Master Race marched on. The concept of 'blitzkrieg' was an outstanding success and the much vaunted Maginot Line was simply bypassed.

The western democracies reeled under the onslaught. Benito Mussolini, Il Duce of fascist Italy, threw in his lot with Hitler's Germany, and Britain stood alone.

Adolf Hitler abandoned Operation Sea Lion, and the non-aggression pact Hitler had signed with Stalin became so much waste paper. This was a consequence of the failure of Hermann Goering to annihilate the Royal Air Force in the Battle of Britain. Operation 'Barbarossa' launched the German military machine against Russia.

The Afrika Korps advanced to the gates of Cairo under the brilliant leadership of Field Marshall Rommel.

The watershed had, however, been reached. General Montgomery was appointed commander of the British forces in North Africa. In the battle of El Alamein the Eighth Army engaged and overcame the two Panzer divisions of the Afrika Korps, plus more than one hundred thousand combined German and Italian ground forces. It was the first major defeat inflicted on an invincible German army. Churchill with his brilliant gift for the rallying call: 'Not the end! Not the beginning of the end! But the end of the beginning.'

By July 1943 the tide of war was turning. After the 'scorched earth' policies of the Russians, the disastrous defeat of the German 5th Army at Stalingrad led to the surrender by General Frederick Paulus. It was Germany's turn to reel.

General Montgomery's forces continued their advance to Tripoli. The Americans entered the war in Europe. The invasion of Italy was successfully launched. Sicily was quickly overcome and mainland Italy invaded. General Badoglio, Italy's new leader, surrendered to the Allied forces following Mussolini's humiliating departure.

Field Marshal Kesselring, the German commander in Italy, a brilliant tactician, constructed a series of strong defence lines across the Italian peninsula. The Gothic, Gustav and Bernhardt lines were all formidable obstacles to the American and British forces. The American 5th Army under General Mark Clark was the first to enter Rome. The British 8" Army advanced up the western Adriatic seaboard. Progress was slow and costly. The monastery at Monte Cassino proved a particularly stubborn obstacle, being doggedly defended by the Hermann Goering parachute division. The decision to destroy the monastery by mass air bombardment would always remain a contentious action.

Now it was late summer in 1943. Karl Langstein had not long returned from the Chancellery. There had been an air of despondency over the war's progress. Many of the Wehrmacht generals would support an approach to the Western Allies for a negotiated peace. Rudolf Hess, the deputy Reichsführer, had already flown to Scotland and made contact with Lord Hamilton, a Scottish landowner. Hitler, however, was adamant in his pursuit of the war. There had been suggestions of new and devastating weapons being developed. The Allies' insistence on unconditional surrender had not helped.

Karl glanced in the mirror that hung in the hall. There were definitely signs of strain. The grey hair was becoming more evident.

He entered the lounge. Liesl was sitting in her usual chair, a strained and haunted look on her face. A letter was in her hand resting on her lap. Whatever had happened to that attractive girl he had fallen in love with all those years ago? She was still a handsome woman. Her hair was pulled severely back from her forehead, enhancing her oval facial features. There were the streaks of grey here too, and anxiety lines were appearing around her mouth.

The whole of Germany was now involved in the war. The bombing of German cities was continuous and the civilian population was bearing the brunt of the conflict.

'How are you, my darling?' she enquired.

'Weary,' replied Karl. 'There are growing divisions amongst the leadership. Hitler is, however, determined to prosecute the war with all his usual fanaticism,' he added wearily 'Who is the letter from?'

'It is from the Flieger gruppen Hauptkommand. They are informing us that Paul has been reported missing from an escort mission over Southampton in England. His Oberstleutnant, however, observed him bailing out of his aircraft after being hit.' Tears were not far behind those anxious eyes.

'No news from Karl?' he asked.

'The last I heard was from Italy. But he couldn't say much about what he was doing.'

Karl senior knew exactly what he was doing and with what his eldest son was involved.

As a special mission officer of the Himmler SS Elite, his son was answerable only to the head of the security forces – Heinrich Himmler himself.

There had been several 'special missions'. Promoted to Oberst, Karl was given complete autonomy over his specialised and hand-picked force. There had been the aftermath of the assassination of Heydrich, the Gauleiter of Prague. Then the obliteration of Lidice. Every man woman and child massacred and the whole village reduced to rubble and bulldozed from the face of the earth. This was followed by the massacre of 300 Italians in the Ardeatine Caves outside Rome. The caves were subsequently sealed. It was a reprisal for the killing of thirty of the Wehrmacht in a partisan bomb attack in the narrow streets near to the Spanish Steps. Major Keppler of the Roman garrison had taken responsibility for the action. The actual perpetrators a mysterious unit that had quickly disappeared after the incident.

Then came the rescue of Mussolini from his mountain prison by Major Sikorski, a brilliantly executed mission, which had been supported by a similar group that had also disappeared after the successful operation.

Karl junior was now living in a luxury villa on the outskirts of Florence.

The sentry saluted as Karl drove through the front entrance of the villa. Dashing up the marble staircase, he called to Lucia, '*Un bagno, carissima con molte acqua calde, anche un grande brandy!*' She knew exactly what he wanted before he had asked. A brimming hot bath and a very large cognac.

Lucia had been Karl's mistress ever since they had met at the glittering reception given at Kesselring's expansive villa on Lake Como.

She was an Italian beauty in the classical style. Dark black hair fashioned in the Roman manner. Sultry dark eyes and a generous mouth. A figure that was full to the point of voluptuousness.

She had no illusions about Karl. A ruthless and ambitious officer, his attitude towards women was unsubtle bordering an coarseness. Physically attractive, he had a masculine magnetism that she found irresistible. '*Toglieti i vestiti, mia cara*' he almost demanded. She had no qualms about removing her clothes.

He laid back in the steaming water and watched as she undressed. The sight of her body always excited his crudest emotions.

She was full-breasted with large dark circles around her pronounced nipples. The curve of her slim waist blossomed into the fulsome lines of her thighs.

He was thoroughly aroused and rose from the water. His sheer animal aggression excited her. She almost purred. He ran his hands eagerly over her body. There would be little finesse in his lovemaking. Almost brutal, it was more like a rape than a gentle possession. She responded eagerly as he pulled her towards the bedroom.

The battle-stained motorcyclists with the Spandau machine gun mounted on the sidecar slewed to a halt in a cloud of dust in front of the villa behind the sprawl of Fort Belvedere overlooking

Florence. The sentry called for an escort to conduct the courier to Karl's apartments.

The message was short, direct and explicit. The Allies were approaching Florence at a faster rate than anticipated. Forward units may have already entered the suburbs. There was also increased partisan activity.

Karl was to assemble his unit and ensure that every bridge over the Arno was destroyed. He sent Lucia off to her villa in Como, providing her with a small but well-armed escort. Dressed in their airborne smocks and carrying only small arms and light machine pistols with explosives and detonators, the convoy set off from the fort.

A strange, menacing stillness hung over Florence. Furtive movements of figures were observed but quickly faded among the labyrinths of the city. Small arms fire could be heard in the distance, together the louder reports from tanks or artillery: either the much feared 78s of the German artillery or maybe the 4.5 medium artillery from a British AGRA support group.

The city itself was quiet. They rounded the Palazzo degli Uffizi after reconnoitring the areas around the Duomo and the Baptistery, avoiding the group of three Wehrmacht bodies sprawled in the road. Their boots were missing – a sure sign of a partisan execution.

The unit rendezvoused at the northern end of the Ponte Vecchio. The Arno's murky waters lapped around the ancient piers.

Dividing his men into smaller groups, Karl assigned each group to a bridge. From the Ponte Vittoria to the Ponte Giovanni de Verrazzano, there were five bridges extending over the breadth of the city. 'Place your charges,' said Karl, 'and blow them to pieces without any further orders from me. Obliterate any opposition, civilian or military.'

He glanced at the men. They were tough, ruthless and dedicated, and he had little doubt of their capabilities. They had been together for a long time. 'We rendezvous in Bologna. Make your own way if we are separated.'

With his closest commanders, he undertook the destruction of the Ponte Vecchio. He would get some personal satisfaction to see this ancient pile of Italian culture reduced to rubble. In fact, given the time he would have done a really good job on the other so-called historical treasures the Palazzo Pitti and the Palazzo degli Uffizi, with all those decadent 'works of art'. He'd teach these treacherous 'Artschlock' Italians.

The sound of grenades or mortars nearby broke into his thoughts.

'Charges laid, Herr Oberst!' called the Feldwebel. The Unteroffizier brought the detonator and placed it in front of him.

'Clear out!' he called to his Oberleutnant.

There was a sudden crash as a mortar landed near the bridge. He cranked the detonator and pushed down the plunger. Nothing! *Gott in Himmel!* His eye followed the detonation wires.

There it was – the mortar had severed the wire. Dashing forward, he had only taken a few steps when the flash and noise filled the air and he was thrown violently against the parapet.

Then blackness.

Through the painful haze, Karl had a vision of khaki. He struggled to a sitting position. They looked like a major and a captain, with a sergeant close by sitting in what looked like a jeep.

Beyond them was a group of glowering partisans, armed to the teeth and looking very menacing. They were like wolves cheated of their prey.

'He looks quite important. Maybe more useful alive than dead,' said the major.

'Come along, mein Herr, if you value your skin let's vacate – pronto! Pronto! How's your German, Tom?' asked the major, directing a request to the lieutenant.

'Not very good, sir I'm afraid. Look here, Fritz – *raus! Andiamo presto! Pericolosa! Partigaanni kaputts! Capisce?*'

Karl got the message and staggered to his feet. As they half dragged and pushed him into the jeep and sped off, he saw the Pointe Vecchio was still intact and standing there in all its ancient glory.

He was flown to England and interrogated. There was little that they could gain from him. His hatred for these decadent English was so complete. To add insult to injury, the interrogating officer had been so obviously a Jew...

The prison camp was segregated for officers. There was a mix of the Wehrmacht and the Luftwaffe but no members of the Reichsmarine.

As far as he had found out, the camp was in Southern England in the county of Somerset. The exact location bore some peculiar English name like 'Dimmer'.

Karl was given a medical check up by some bespectacled little English doctor.

The whole experience was thoroughly humiliating. There must be a way out of this place, he thought. He began circulating around the camp, hoping to pick up some information or news of the outside world.

He had befriended some fellow SS, though they had kept their units and allegiance hidden from their captors. It was during one of these sorties that a fellow SS officer mentioned that there was another Langstein in the camp whose name was Paul – an officer of the Luftwaffe. He was an Oberstleutnant who had been shot down on a mission over southern England but had bailed out and been picked up by some military group called the Home Guard.

Karl went straight to the Camp Commandant's office, made enquiries and was told the hut number of Paul Langstein.

He entered the hut and walked slowly dawn the bunks. He was treated with suspicion. The Sicherheitspolizei was still active, even in the camps.

There lying on the bunk was the unmistakable figure of Paul.

They had both experienced the harsh realities of war. The glamour and the glory were now tarnished. Guilt, however, was not on the agenda of either of them. There was a searching and questing for a scapegoat. Arrogant leadership, misleading propaganda – somewhere the spectre of a Third Reich to last another thousand years had vanished. Germany was a besieged fortress.

The practicalities of their current situation were more pressing. They needed to break free from this stultifying incarceration, to return to the conflict and rekindle the still glowing ashes. But how?

Paul had been acting as camp interpreter for the visiting English doctor. His duties afforded him considerable freedom of movement, particularly in assisting the good doctor with his equipment and transportation from home to camp.

Karl was impressed. His own knowledge of English was good, almost fluent. What were his chances of enrolment into this arrangement? His SS background had not been discovered, and as a relative of Paul's there was a certain trust placed in their cooperation.

It all worked smoothly, and Paul and himself were soon involved in the work of the doctor.

It was a week or so later, and Monica was cycling towards the surgery. The army 15 cwt was drawing away. Next to the driver sat two German officers from the camp at Dimmer.

With a shock, she recognised Paul. Admittedly he had aged considerably from those days back in Berlin, when he had befriended Bunty. His face had hardened and the harshness of war had left its mark. The boy had surrendered to the man.

The other officer resembled Paul in his facial features. Could it be...? *No!* The whole scene seemed like a macabre nightmare. Barely healed wounds were being cruelly ripped opened with a vicious suddenness like some ghoulish nightmare.

Gladys was in the kitchen as Monica entered looking as though she had seen a ghost – two ghosts!

'What is the matter, my dear?' asked Gladys ominously. 'You look as if someone's walked over your grave!' She dropped the knife with which she had been preparing the vegetables.

'Those two German officers – do you know their names?' Dreading the answer, Monica listened as if from a great distance while Gladys replied.

'Well! Yes, of course. One is called Paul, the younger one. The other is Karl... Langstein. I think they're brothers, and they are helping Hugh. Why do you ask?'

The nightmare had become a hideous reality.

Chapter Eight

Although Simon had planned to invite Hugh and Gladys round for a drink before revealing their discovery of the bones, it didn't work out as planned. Now that Greg knew what was down there, the priority was obviously to call the police before it got all round the village; but he was still anxious that Gladys and Hugh should know of their discovery before gossip got a hold.

Gladys opened the door to his knock. 'Oh, hello,' she said, 'hello, Lydia.'

'Can we come in, Gladys? Is Hugh at home?' asked Lydia breathlessly. She was already stepping over the threshold and holding Simon's hand, pulling him along with her. 'We've something to tell you,' said Simon. 'We want you both to know something straightaway...'

'We've found something so amazing!' Lydia butted in. 'It's pretty gruesome, really – you'd never believe it!'

Hugh appeared in the doorway of the kitchen where they were standing.

'Hello, you two. Do you want something to drink?' He seemed to Lydia to be already on his guard. Why did he never relax?

'We've come to tell you something, Hugh, you'll never believe. It's horrible really, but we want you to know before we call the police.'

'Call the police? If you've something to say just say it,' said Hugh.

'Okay, here goes.' Simon swallowed. 'We've found some bones in our garden – human bones – not *in* the garden exactly but *under* the garden.' He thought he was not making a very good job of his explanation. 'Let's sit down and I'll explain it properly,' he suggested, going through to the conservatory.

When they were all sitting down, Simon went through everything that had happened that day.

'Of course now that Greg knows he's bound to tell his friends, so we must call the police as soon as possible.'

'I expect they'll send a pathologist; I wonder how long they've been there – it's quite exciting isn't it?' babbled Lydia. She looked at Hugh and Gladys. Gladys's face had turned quite grey.

'Are you all right, Gladys? It is rather a shock – shall I get you something?' Lydia suggested.

Gladys seemed visibly to pull herself together. 'I'll be all right, really, it's just such an unpleasant discovery. Are you sure they're human? Well, of course you are if you've seen a skull. Ugh! Yes, let's all have a drink, Hugh. Then Simon'd better call the police – you can ring from here, if you like.'

Simon and Hugh both left the room. Lydia looked at Gladys.

'You find your mind buzzing with all sorts of questions,' she observed. 'How long have they been there? Did they die down there, or was a dead body pushed down there? Is it male or female? Oh! So many things to find out. Mind you, they can do so much these days. They'll probably be able to find out exactly who it is.'

'Yes, dear. Well I expect they'll sort it out and you'll soon get answers to all those questions. It will create a bit of excitement in the village, although they'll probably take everything away with them,' replied Gladys.

Hugh returned with a tray of glasses and sherry and brandy bottles and then Simon came in.

'They're sending someone over straightaway, but the sergeant said they probably won't be able to get the pathologist until the morning. He said that seeing as they're just bones there wasn't really any urgency; the officer will seal off the site tonight and everything will start happening in the morning.'

Hugh poured out the drinks and Lydia reflected that it was the first time she'd sat down with her neighbours to enjoy a friendly drink, and what an astonishing incident had led to this convivial meeting. Perhaps they'd be on a more friendly footing from now on.

The following morning the pathologist and a team of police officers arrived with spades and boxes and sacks and various other equipment. They prowled around the garden in their white overalls, putting soil into sacks, lowering the ladder down the hole. They'd have to remove the roof of the underground room as access was so restricted.

Several people from the village called to chat about the discovery. Lydia was keen to find out if anyone could remember the underground room and she enquired from all the visitors if they knew who might have lived there before the war or had connections with anyone who may have resided in the village for a long time.

It actually turned out that Hugh and Gladys had probably lived there as long as anyone and they had been as surprised as everyone else that there was anything down there.

'It was just a garden when we used the house for a spare surgery,' said Hugh. 'There were a few shrubs there; I only used the place if we had infectious cases. The district nurses used to use one of the rooms as an office, but I don't suppose they even went into the garden.'

The police were there for two days. They cleared the earth from the roof of the room and then removed all of the bricks from around the trapdoor. They brought up several boxes of bones, cleared all the debris from the floor, and when it was completely empty put same heavy metal plates over the whole area.

'What shall we do with it?' asked Simon.

'Well, I shouldn't fill it in or dismantle it yet, sir,' replied the inspector. 'Better leave it until this business is all wound up; we may need to go down there again. You could put some flower tubs on the top if you like – brighten up the scene, as it were. We'll let you know our findings in due course sir. We'll be off now, then. If you find anything else get in touch straightaway, but I think we've removed everything we need. Goodbye, sir.'

They all packed up, got into their vans and were gone. Apart from the hole in the garden it was as if nothing had happened.

'Bit of an anticlimax,' remarked Lydia. 'I wonder when we'll hear something. Oh! There might be something on the news, and in the local paper of course. I can't wait to find out who it is. How long do they take with these sorts of things, Simon?'

'I've no idea,' replied her husband. 'I've never been involved in anything like this before, but the inspector assured me he'd let us know all the developments. I think I might keep a sort of "diary of events". I might start it straightaway too. Shall we go out to dinner?'

With that he went upstairs to his study. It was 6 p.m., less than sixty hours since he had discovered the loose earth in the garden. You never know what's in store for you he mused to himself. Life's certainly not boring.

Chapter Nine

It soon seemed as if the whole village knew about the underground room. English Heritage sent someone along, and the editor of *Somerset* magazine came with a photographer to put an article in next month's issue. Opinions varied as to what the room had actually been built for, but Simon was not concerned. His interest was all directed towards the bones. He found it amazing that no one in the village ever knew of the room's existence and also that no one seemed to have been reported missing. At least, it was not part of the historical knowledge of the village. Things like this often formed part of the folklore of a place. He'd never heard rumours of any such thing.

He tried to contain his impatience and refrain from ringing the police station but every morning he wondered if there'd be any news.

After two weeks he could wait no longer and rang through to Inspector Goodbody.

'Any news, Inspector, about the bones? The ones found in our garden?' He couldn't believe the inspector wasn't as interested as he was, but of course the police had a lot of cases; they weren't letting their imaginations run riot as Simon was.

'Nothing yet, but pathologists are busy people,' said the inspector. 'However, he probably won't mind if you ring his office.'

Simon rang through on the number the inspector had given him. The pathologist's assistant answered.

'He's not here at the moment, but I know he's preparing a report. It's no secret, so he won't mind me telling you our findings so far. What we've established is that the bones have been down the hole for about twenty to thirty years. They're quite well preserved, for several reasons; it's dark and cool down there, and they haven't been disturbed in all that time; at least it doesn't look like it. Oh, by the way there are two complete sets, so there were two bodies down there – both young men. No evidence of any injuries though. They were tall, quite well set up young men. There were some odd pieces of metal and what looks like leather, too. We'll be passing these objects on to the police, see if they can make anything of them. That's about all I can tell you at the moment. Our report will go to the inspector any day now, so you'd best talk to him.'

'Thank you very much,' said Simon. 'I didn't realise there were *two* bodies. Of course, now I think of it there were a lot of bones for just one person. How mysterious it is, though. Did they die down the hole, or beforehand, do you think? What a horrible way to go if they were trapped down there and died slowly. But surely someone would have heard them calling out. They must have been dead or at least unconscious when they were put down there?'

'Well, we haven't exhausted all the tests to find out how they died. There are some more things we can do. Sometimes you can get evidence of illness from the bones; the tests are quite complicated but we shall exhaust all possible means before we give up. Call me again next week and I'll let you know how we're getting on. And keep in touch with the inspector, he might be glad of your help with general "enquiries" if he's very busy.'

Simon couldn't get the whole business out of his mind. As soon as he awoke each morning it was there in his head and stayed all day long. Whatever activity he was busy with, pictures of the bones kept intruding. He was going to become completely preoccupied if he didn't do something about it. If only he could help! He thought he'd ask the inspector if he could try and trace the items found alongside the bones, once the forensic scientists had finished with them. Surely he couldn't do any harm…

He rang the police station. 'Actually, as long as the scientists have finished, we wouldn't mind a bit of help,' said the inspector. 'We're really busy with routine police work at the moment as several chaps are on leave, it being school holidays, so as long as you report anything you find out back to me I can't see any harm. Drop by and pick up the bits of metal and leather next week and you can look at the pathologist's report at the same time. Thanks for ringing. Bye for now then.'

Simon was excited. To do some real sleuthing – that was something! He rushed off to tell Lydia.

'The best thing would be to try and find someone living here during the time of death,' he said. 'I think they might be able to narrow down the estimated length of time the bones have been down there. If we could get that down to one season, or even one year, then I could really make some proper enquiries. I'm going to talk to Gladys Fitzhugh; she's lived here for ages. She is much more approachable than her husband.' With that he planted a kiss on Lydia's forehead and was gone.

He knocked rather gingerly on the Fitzhughs' front door. If Hugh answered he'd have to be prepared for a terse greeting. Happily, it was Gladys. 'Hello, Simon, would you like a cup of tea? Hugh's gone to the auction this morning, he's on the lookout for a chest of drawers for the spare room. Come through. I'm in the garden.'

Simon followed Gladys through the house and into the back garden. It looked lovely – very green and cool because of the number of trees and shrubs. Hugh really loved his trees; there were many varieties of ornamentals and evergreens here, including cypresses of varying heights.

He sat on a wooden bench while Gladys bustled indoors to fetch the tea tray. He looked around and wondered to himself what it was about Hugh that made him so difficult to get on with. Gladys settled down on the bench next to Simon and poured the tea.

'Any news about your find?' she asked him. Simon brought her up to date.

'I'm just waiting to get the go-ahead to look at the things they found alongside the bones. I expect they'll be in very poor condition; it's pretty damp down there, apparently. The leather is beginning to disintegrate already.'

'That'll be from the exposure to the air,' said Gladys. 'I expect the other bits will be rusted pieces and I doubt you'll be able to see very much. Once you get the air onto things that have been shut away for a long time they deteriorate very quickly.'

'You seem to have considerable knowledge,' said Simon.

'Well I started out studying forensic science, but I met Hugh before I finished my degree. He'd just completed his training and was keen to take up general practice, so I left to become his practice nurse.'

'Goodness, that must have been quite a sacrifice! Have you ever regretted that decision?'

'Not really,' replied Gladys.' Sometimes you think of what might have been. I suppose I could have made a good career in forensic science but I wouldn't have had so much time with our daughter when she was growing up, and I'm glad for that, considering what happened.'

Her eyes were misting over, and Simon's curiosity was aroused. He didn't think it the best of times to push her, but the opportunity was too good to miss. How often would he have the chance to talk to Gladys while Hugh was away from the house?

'What happened, Gladys?' he asked gently.

She seemed to pull her thoughts back from far away. 'Oh, she – Bunty – was killed in Berlin, just before the war.

'Oh? How terrible! I'm so sorry, I didn't know. How did it happen?'

'It was difficult to be sure really what happened, they told us she'd fallen from a train. She had... multiple injuries. I never did understand exactly what she was doing on the train. The trouble was we couldn't go out there and talk to the police or anyone. There was a lot of agitation going on, not long before the war started. We shouldn't have let her go, really. We did think about it quite deeply, and we were both so concerned as she was only sixteen.'

'Oh, Gladys, that's so sad. What happened about the funeral and everything. Is she buried in Berlin, then?'

'Oh no. The body was returned to England via the embassy. One of their staff escorted it back and we met it at Dover and brought her home. It was all so unreal. Because we had so many unanswered questions we didn't seem able to come to terms with it. It changed Hugh; he loved her so much...' Her voice faded away.

Simon thought that this explained a lot of things, especially the way Hugh seemed to shun society and always appeared rather morose. But then it had been more than thirty years ago. How long could you go on mourning?

'So did you never hear any more? No one ever told you how she came to be on the train? No one saw what happened? Have you been back to Berlin and had a chance to speak to people who knew her out there? Since the war, I mean. Who was she staying with?' Simon had lots of questions, but thought he'd better slow down. It wasn't his business really.

'She was staying with my sister's daughter, my niece, Monica. She was already out there staying with her aunt and attending the Institute to learn German. She was four years older than Bunty, so we thought she'd keep an eye on her; but of course she couldn't have done anything. She was so distressed but Bunty was always headstrong. It was naive of us to think she'd have done what Monica advised.

'According to Monica, she'd got very thick with a boy at the Institute. The police seemed to think they'd arranged to meet in one of the trains at the marshalling yards. Apparently it was a popular place for courting couples – all those empty trains, warm and comfortable. They think one of them may have been shunted out and Bunty panicked and tried to jump out and then was hit by a shunting engine…

'We did try to find out about the boy. We wrote to the Institute, and then Hugh spoke to the principal on the phone; this was about 1947, when things had settled after the war. But he said the boy concerned had been killed in the war and that his parents were distraught, so we left it.'

'What a sad tale! Another tragedy of the war, really, then. I'm so sorry, Gladys. Where is she buried?'

'Oh, she's in the churchyard. We had a quiet funeral, just the family, but it's a very peaceful spot just beyond the lychgate. Hugh keeps it immaculate, with Bunty's favourite flowers growing on it. She used to like polyanthus, all those colours, we always keep some on the grave. Lots of people lost their children during the war. I try to think of them when I feel self-pity coming on, perhaps if we'd had other children… but it wasn't to be. All our hopes and energies were invested in Bunty. She was so lively, with such a generous, outgoing nature. We used to marvel that a rather serious couple like us actually produced such a merry extrovert for a daughter.'

Silence descended but Simon recalled why he'd come round.

'Gladys, you were living here through the 1930s and '40s,

weren't you? Are you sure you didn't hear any talk at the time about the chamber we found? It must have been exposed at some time for people to be down there, and I can't believe no one knew of it. Can you think back and try to remember if anything at all comes to mind – say, a lot of digging going on next door, or young men being seen round the village – anything at all?' pleaded Simon. 'The pathologist says they are the bones of two young men. It is unbelievable no one can remember anything.'

'Well, I don't know anything about it. I've never seen it before or heard anything about it before and I certainly don't know anything about young men.'

Gladys's tone had changed dramatically, and she sounded really annoyed. She went on, 'Really Simon, don't you think that I'd have told the police by now if I'd known anything?' She started noisily putting the cups and saucers back on the tray. 'You'll have to go now, as I've got to go down to the shop. Sorry I can't be of any help. Goodbye, love to Lydia.' And she picked up the tray and walked briskly back to the house.

Well, what a change of attitude! thought Simon. One minute she's all sad and gentle and friendly, and next she's sending me packing, as if I'd been annoying her or wasting her time. Very strange!

Chapter Ten

Simon went round to the police station to pick up the artefacts. He saw the pathologist's report, which said the nearest they could narrow the time of death to was between twenty-four and twenty-seven years. They had exhausted all their tests, and the most dramatic finding was traces of some foreign substance in the larger bones. There were only faint traces but as there was no other evident cause of death it had to be a probability that it may have been poison or some chemical reaction to the environment.

The inspector said, 'If they were hungry or on the run or something, they could have eaten meat which was put down for a trap, say, for rats or something. I know it sounds ridiculous, but at the moment we must keep all options open. Look, here are those bits of metal I was telling you about. Now you can just see some writing on this bit and one of our lads think it may be German. If you clean it up you might be able to see it better. The thing is, the time of death would fit in with wartime so it is possible it's from a German buckle or necklace, or even an identity band. It doesn't follow they *were* German; they could have taken it from a German whilst on active service.

'There was one interesting idea one of our old PCs put forward. Pete Samson – he's retiring soon, done his thirty years – he thought it might be to do with the prison of war camp at Dimmer… might have been a couple of runaways looking for shelter. Anyway, that gives you plenty to look at for now.' He paused and looked at Simon closely.

'You sure you're still interested in doing this? It would certainly help us out, but make sure your keep me informed and don't go off on lines of your own without letting me know, okay? I'll wait to hear from you. Goodbye.'

Simon took the bag of pieces home and related all the information he had received to Lydia.

'Isn't it amazing!' she said. 'Here we are in 1971, and yet over a few days we've heard about Hugh and Gladys' daughter dying in Germany just before the war and these two chaps possibly connected with the war and maybe Germany. You can go for ages and not hear anything about either subject. Seems like a real coincidence to me.'

'Oh, I don't know, it's just given us the opportunity to talk to Gladys, that's all. We hadn't had any reason to beforehand, and that's why we didn't know about Bunty. After all, she died before the war began. I do think it's worth following up about them being POWs, though. I wonder where the records are kept from when there was a camp at Dimmer? That old bobby at the station says it was quite a large place, so it seems a distinct possibility. It was the done thing to try and escape, wasn't it? It was encouraged as the patriotic thing to do, and if that is German writing on the pieces of metal it may confirm some connection. I wonder where I should try first. What about County Hall at Taunton?

'No, I think what I'll do first is get a list of the people who lived here from 1943 and are still living here. There's several chaps down on the allotments who profess to have lived here all their lives; I'll go down and talk to them first. What I really want is someone who used to have dealings with the camp, delivered goods there or did work there; they'd probably give me a good start. And I'll ask Greg's father about the German writing when I've cleaned it up. Being a languages teacher he'll probably be able to help me once I've got something legible.

'Right, those are my plans for the next couple of days. What are you going to be doing?'

'Well, what with cakes to make for the W.I. sale and the vegetables and flowers to get ready for the horticultural show next Saturday, and the flowers I've promised to do for Sally in the church for her and Ashley's wedding – you haven't forgotten that's Saturday week, have you? – I think I've enough to keep me busy. But if you want any help with your investigation just say so, 'cos I'm really interested. The thing that gets me is that if they were young when they died – which seems likely – then they may have family still alive who are missing them. Work it out, Simon. Suppose they were early twenties in 1944 – say twenty-four for sake of argument – then they'd only be approaching fifty now, so their parents may be between seventy and eighty. If they had sisters and brothers they might be anything from forty years old, and might still be hoping for news of them. I suppose Inspector Goodbody has already looked at missing persons lists from that time?'

'Well, he says he looked at all local stuff and he's sent out reports further afield about the discovery, so they've got copies in the Met., and of course to Bristol and Bath. It all takes time; I think that's why he's prepared to let me help him. Anyway, let's turn in now. I've got a busy time ahead.'

The next morning Simon went down to the allotments. Silas and Mike, two weather-beaten old men, were bent over their vegetable plots and grumbling loudly about the small yield of their runner beans due to the excessive wind and rain.

'Excuse me!' Simon called.

Silas straightened up and removed his cap and ran his fingers through his hair.

'Hello, sir. Why, you're the chap from up along, aren't you? The one who found bones in your garden or some such?'

'Yes, that's me,' replied Simon. 'Actually, that's what I want to talk to you about. Can you spare me a few minutes?'

'Course we can,' said Mike. He chuckled. 'We're always glad of a chance to stop, aren't we, Silas? Silas is entering his marrow in the show. What do you think of it, then? Better than his beans, eh! Come to my shed and I'll put the kettle on.'

All three went into Mike's shed. It was well set up with a picnic stove, teapot and mugs and a bottle of milk standing in a bowl of cold water.

'Hard to keep the milk fresh in this muggy weather,' said Mike. 'Let's get the biscuits, Silas.'

'This looks cosy. My name's Simon West, by the way. I'm grateful to you for sparing me the time, especially so near to the show,' said Simon.

'Oh, don't worry about that,' said Silas. 'It can't make any difference now; too late. I don't think a miracle will save these beans but I must say I'm quite pleased with me marrows. Okay, fire away then. How can we help you – if we can?' Silas sat on an upturned box and Simon and Mike used the two stools.

'Well, it's like this,' Simon began. 'I wondered if you were living here during the war years – either or both of you?'

'Lived here all me life, man and boy,' said Silas. 'And me father before me. During the war's the only time I ever left. Two years served me country – Pioneer Corps, then back 'ere – 46 and I never left since. Married Peggy in '48, working up at forestry. We've raised four kids here and raised 'em mighty well. If I say it myself, they're all turned out fine and we've now got three lovely grandchildren.'

'That's marvellous,' replied Simon. 'I'm sure you can help me. You must have heard about there being a room or a structure under our garden. It may have been called an ice house or a well-head chamber—'

'Oh aye, I've heard about that,' interrupted Mike, 'and I haven't even lived here all that time. Moved here after I married in '49, I did, but before that I lived over at Cary and I think I remember my father talking about it. He were a gardener over this way, at the manor, but I'm sure it were your icehouse he used to talk about when I were just a boy. I think actually it belonged to the house next door – you know, where the Doc lives. Before the war both houses were sort of together. No one lived in the one you live in, and the gardens went right along with a stone wall and archways between. Huge place, it was. Old Doc used to have a gardener in sometimes but after the war the arches were filled in an' it came like two separate grounds – half with each house.'

'I remember,' Silas joined in. 'As kids we used to lark about trying to look over the wall at the back. I thought it was just a rumour, we used to tell each other tales about being locked in and left to rot! Never thought it would come true though.'

'My dad said it would have made a good air-raid shelter, had we needed one, but the opening would have had to be widened. He said no one could get down there except a slip of a boy. Funny that, it's coming back to me now, I'd forgotten all about it. Yes, the old ice house… Is that where you found your bones, then? I wasn't really paying attention. Well I'm blowed! Down the old ice house. How many bones you found, then? Whose were they, eh?' Mike was interested now.

'Well, that's what I'm trying to help the police find out,' said

Simon. 'Only it seems from forensics that the bones might have been there since the end of the war. Couple of young chaps, might have been on the run, gone AWOL from the army, or prison escapees…'

'Are you sure they're English? Could have been from over Dimmer,' put in Mike, 'Big prisoner of war camp over there; perhaps they escaped from it. Could've got in and not been able to get out. Oo-er! That's a bit creepy – nasty way to go. But they used to try and escape all the time. Never got far as a rule, 'cos we got to know what they looked like, and the grey clothes, you could always tell them.

'Mind you, they used to let 'em out anyway towards the end of the war. Found 'em useful work to do, you know. Helping on farms, especially at haymaking and harvest, I remember a couple coming to the farm where I used to help out. They seemed friendly enough, but couldn't speak much English. In fact we used to tell 'em a few words. I should think they were glad to get out for an hour or two. Not the officers, of course, they didn't work.

'I bet you what you like it were two of them, probably made a break for it and thought they could shelter until the coast was clear. What do you think? Do you think I'm right? Unless it was prisoners from Shepton. The prison over there used to have deserters – not just in the war, either; it was a military prison right through the Fifties. It could have been chaps escaping from there. I think they got pretty desperate; it used to be a very hard place, so people hereabouts say.

'So I reckon it's one or the other escapees from Shepton or Dimmer. Does that help you?' Mike finished his very long speech and had another swig of tea.

'Goodness, that's given me lots to think about! I'd better get back to the inspector. Thanks very much; I'll let you know what transpires, shall I?' Simon asked them. 'Would you like to be kept up to date? I expect it'll be in the paper in due course.'

'Oh, we'd like to know all right, wouldn't we, Silas?' put in Mike.

'You bet,' replied Silas. 'A bit of excitement – I shall tell my Peggy all about it.'

'Just remember, it's not definite yet. It could be any number of people for any number of reasons. Better not spread it around until we have some proof or evidence or something. I'll let you know what the police say. Thanks for the tea. I'd better get on. Good luck with your marrow. Goodbye.'

Simon left the allotments and took himself into a field where he sat down behind the hedge. He needed to think. He'd received so much information he needed to jot it down while it was fresh in his mind. Details of the gardens first, then the prisoners – from both prisons, the POW camp and Shepton Mallet – and what about the fact that POWs were allowed out to work? He'd forgotten all about that, but now the memories came back. He'd been up in Yorkshire in 1944 and remembered some POW who started a riding school for the local children. Many of them got on so well with farmers that they stayed on after the war as farm-hands. He wasn't sure now whether all his information helped him or hindered him. It certainly offered possibilities for the origin of the bodies, but it also gave him more choices and more investigating to do.

He felt very satisfied with his morning's work; he was very fortunate to have found Silas and Mike as the first two people he'd asked. What should be his next move?

Yes, he must ask Greg's father about the artefacts. If the writing on them was German, he would be able to stop enquiring at Shepton prison and give all his attention to the POWs.

Chapter Eleven

Paulo parked the yellow open-topped Mercedes in front of the apartment block in the Via Maggio. He had come straight from his offices in the via dell' Orivolo which led to the Piazza del Duomo. It was early morning but he hadn't slept much the night before. His mind, for some reason or another, had dwelt on his early life and the father he had never known. He had to talk to his mother as a matter of urgency to ease the frustrating unanswered questions that lingered in his mind.

The apartment was in one of those old established blocks that lined the streets around the Piazza di Frescobaldi and the embankment that fronted the Arno near the Ponte Vecchio. He approached the imposing street door to the block which led into one of those typically Italian courtyards paved in slate tiles and embellished with marble fittings around exotic plant containers.

He climbed the marbled stairs with the easy stride of an athlete. Over six feet tall, with a dark complexion and black hair, he made a handsome figure. He was dressed in an English-styled suit of fine worsted and wore expensive black leather Gucci shoes. He had on a soft white shirt with a conservative tie in a soft blue wool. He looked what in fact he was – a successful business executive. At the age of twenty-six he was the junior partner of Celino, Celino and Lucca, a highly successful law firm.

He rang the brass bell in the centre of the imposing black door. Footsteps approach and the door opened. His mother stood there.

'Ciao, caro mio!' she said, greeting him with an affectionate hug and kiss. Her hair was greying attractively and she had that sort of figure that refused to show the years.

'Perche di primo mattino? Avanti!, avanti!, caro.' Her pleasure in seeing him was undisguised. 'Caffe, caro?'

He entered the spacious entrance foyer. The furnishings were modern and expensive with an obvious feminine touch. 'Yes please, Mother.'

He spoke in English, though he was bilingual and easily slipped into either language.

As Maria busied herself making the coffee she glanced at her son. There hadn't been any further children. Mario's war injuries may have had some bearing on that, but there hadn't seemed any desperation for more offspring, ever since that visit to the doctor in the late months of 1943 that had confirmed she was five months pregnant.

Paul had been missing for two months. His unit had confirmed that he had been shot down over England but that he had managed to bail out and had been made a prisoner of war. At first she had mixed feelings about the baby. She possessed part of Paul, but her future had been uncertain.

The Allied armies had occupied Florence and she had managed to get work as an interpreter for U.N.R.R.A.A. (United Nations Relief and Rehabilitation Agency), the Allied relief organisation that had been established for the civilian population. The German Army had still occupied Bologna and denied the Allied armies access to the Po valley and the northern plains of Italy. The Apennines had proved an effective barrier against further advances during the severe winter months. Most roads had been made impassable with heavy snowfalls and drifting snow.

She had found the Americans and English relaxed and approachable. The Americans had been great fraternisers, particularly with the opposite sex. The English were friendly but more reserved.

The war in Europe had ended in May 1945. There had been no news from Paul since the last letter she had received from some remote address in Southern England in a county called Somerset. Further enquiries through the Red Cross failed to confirm his whereabouts: just 'missing, possibly dead'.

Paulo had been a great comfort and showed a remarkable resemblance to his father, keeping his mother's dark hair and complexion. His eyes, however, were that clear Nordic blue.

With a sharp intellect and a disciplined attitude to his studies, Paulo's academic progress had been assured.

Maria had never quite come to terms with the loss of Paul but time had been a great healer. She had returned to the Academy on the teaching faculty. It was while there she had met Mario, a discharged major from the military contingent that had fought alongside the German Armies against the Russians. He had been wounded in the legs and walked with a slight limp. He had fallen in love with Maria while also working at the Academy. At first she had treated him as a friend but a mutual loneliness had drawn them closer together. Paulo had been no problem, and in fact, Mario had become very fond of the boy.

She broke from her reverie and carried the coffee from the kitchen to the comfortable living room. She sensed that Paulo was troubled in his mind about something.

'*Che cosa c'e, caro?*' What is worrying you?'

'*Mamma, Vorrei! molto molto di palare riguardo del mio padre – il mio padre naturale.*'

Maria had known for a long time that one day she would have to tell her son more about his natural father. She had explained the nature of his birth when he had become old enough and sufficiently mature to be less affected emotionally, but realised at the time that there would have to be much more. Now the time had come and it was important for him to identify more with this father he had never known.

She gazed into those deep blue eyes and realised the confusion that this gap in his life was causing. Despite his Latin looks she could see much of Paul in this son of hers. Here was the sensitivity and compassion of his father's nature, which had been betrayed by the political indoctrination of the militarism by the National Socialism of Hitler's Germany. She recalled the freedom his father had found when he soared into the skies and found a beauty in the heavens denied to him when tied to the regimentation and discipline of the military machine. Oh! if only Paul could have seen this son of theirs!

Maria hesitated, trying to assess what to tell him. Should she leave anything unsaid?

She need not have worried. The story just flowed naturally and she realised a feeling of great relief as the barriers fell.

'*Allora*, said Paulo, '*forse sono le nonni in Germania*. My grandparents might still be alive and living in Germany.' He felt his excitement growing. 'Their name is Langstein and they had two sons – Karl and my father, Paul.' He desperately wanted to find out more about these people – his father's parents.

Were they alive? Did they know more about his father's disappearance? What was his father like as a young man? and so on. So many questions to ask!

He hurried back to his luxuriously appointed office overlooking the Piazza Duomo. Where could he start? How about the most obvious place – the International Telephone Directory for Berlin. Langstein! Not what one would call a common name. His secretary, Nella, found the International Directory in her well-appointed reference files. Yes, there were two pages of Langsteins. Look for K. There were ten names listed under K.

Too many for a long-distance enquiry. 'A long shot too long' – to quote the American idiom. Try the Commercial International Directory under 'Private Investigators' – *Privat Untersuchungsbeamter*. Yes, there were several. Choose a reputable looking firm rather than an individual operator. There they were: Kielmann, Schmidt and Kruger, looking very impressive in heavy black print.

Listing all his questions in order he picked up the telephone.

The receptionist sounded efficient. Paulo's German was limited. '*Güten Morgen, Fräulein. Bitte, sprechen-sie Englisch?*'

'Good morning, sir, can I help you?'

'May I speak to one of your investigators on a tracing enquiry?' He continued, much relieved. 'I'm speaking from Florence, Italy. My name is Lucca, Paulo Lucca.'

'Yes, Mr Kielmann is available, though Mr Kruger is our English-speaking investigator. He is on the telephone just now. Would you like to have a word with Mr Kielmann?' her voice sounded crisp and intelligent.

'Yes please,' Paulo replied, his eagerness overcoming his patience. There was a short pause.

'Kielmann here, Mr Lucca. You wish to make a tracing enquiry. I think you would be better talking to our Mr Kruger. Would you hold just a moment?' His English was heavily accented, with the typical German guttural sounds.

'Hello Mr Lucca!' That efficient voice of the receptionist came back again. 'Mr Kruger is free now I'm putting you through.'

'Mr Lucca, sorry for all that, my name is Kruger. Can I help you?' His English was perfect, almost old English public school.

Paulo repeated his name and the fact that he was speaking from Florence. He then outlined his requirements, giving Kruger as much information as he could.

'Right, Mr Lucca, I think I have all those details. There is enough here to get on with. The Langsteins would be in their sixties or seventies by now. You say the man had an important military position in the National Socialist government of the thirties and forties. That may make matters easier. Quite a considerable amount of information is available from the post-war screening investigations.' Kruger sounded efficient and reassuring. 'If you could send a retaining fee we will, meantime, get on with our preliminary enquiries. I'll put you back to the receptionist and she can take care of all the administrative details. Goodbye, Mr Lucca.'

'Oh! By the way, Mr. Kruger, before you do that... Should you establish a firm lead I will come to Berlin and talk to you personally. I look forward to hearing from you and thank you once again.'

Paulo waited for those efficient tones of the receptionist with increased curiosity.

It was four weeks later, and Paulo was working in his luxuriously appointed office overlooking the Piazza de Duomo. A high profile property development was demanding much of his time and expertise.

'There is a long-distance phone call for you, Paulo, from Berlin.'

'*Grazie, Nella*,' said Paulo.

'Hello, Lucca here'. Paulo spoke into the telephone receiver.

'Mr Lucca, Kruger here in Berlin.'

'Hello Mr Kruger, and how are you?' Paulo replied in a friendly tone. He felt his stomach muscles tense.

'We've located that couple – they are both alive! What would you like us to do now?'

Paulo considered for a moment. The case he was currently on was very high profile and lucrative. He said, 'Mr, Kruger I cannot leave here for a few days but I will visit your office a week from today. Would you be available then?' He tried to hide his excitement.

'Certainly, Mr Lucca. I will make a note in my diary and expect you in one week's time,' replied Kruger.

'Thank you, Mr Kruger. I look forward to seeing you. Good-bye.'

One week later Paulo stepped into the taxi outside Tempelhof Airport, Berlin. '*Zwanzig Willhelm Strasse, bitte.*'

Berlin was impressive. The extensive building programme after the war had created a monument to German creativity. The massive Brandenburg Gate still stood, a symbolic edifice of Germany's former glory: the 'Arc de Triomphe' of Berlin.

'*Danken,*' said Paulo. He paid the taxi driver and entered the impressive portals of an imposing office building.

The illuminated floor index showed Kielmann, Schmidt and Kruger, *Privat Untersuchungsbeamte* – third floor.

The lift rose silently.

'*Güten Morgen,*' he addressed the attractive blonde receptionist. 'My name is Lucca, Paulo Lucca. I have an appointment with Herr Kruger at ten o'clock.'

She glanced over him with her Teutonic blue eyes. Her thoughts were private but were betrayed by the slight adjustment of her posture. She stood up to reveal her shapely figure clad attractively in a casual but carefully tailored suit.

'Mr Lucca, you are expected. Please follow me.'

She led the way down a short, carpeted corridor. She had an barely perceptible swing to her hips. Her shapely legs tapered to a pair of expensive leather-heeled black shoes.

A tantalising hint of expensive perfume teased his senses. He followed her into a comfortably furnished office.

'Mr Lucca to see you, Mr. Kruger' She turned and gave a hint of a smile and hooded her eyelids. Then she was gone.

'Good morning, Mr Lucca. How nice to see you.' Kruger rose from his comfortable chair behind a green leather-covered desk.

The office gave the impression of an expensive and profitable business. Paulo sat down in the proffered chair.

'Mr Kruger, you have some news for me?'

Kruger smiled. A large man, over six feet tall, he had an air of authority. Possibly ex-police or the services.

'As I mentioned over the telephone, we have located the Langsteins, and from our preliminary enquiries they appear to be the people that you are looking for.'

Kruger continued. 'Mr Langstein served in the last war as a high-ranking aide to the Hitler command structure. As far as we know he was cleared of any war crimes. His wife was the daughter of the publisher of the newspaper *Das Volks Politika* which supported the National Socialist government. They had two sons, Karl and Paul, both of whom died during the war. The elder son served in the army, some special commando unit, and the younger son, Paul, was a wing commander in the Luftwaffe, the German Air Force. There were no other children. The Langsteins are now living, modestly but comfortably, in the Viktoria Strasse, one of the many thoroughfares of the fashionable district SW, which lies just beyond the beautiful Tiergarten Park.'

Kruger looked pensively at the file open in front of him on the desk.

'Frau Langstein is frail and showing her years but is still, nevertheless, a very attractive woman. Herr Langstein still has his military bearing. He comes from an old Prussian military family and seems to have worn his years very well.'

Paulo was very impressed with this example of German efficiency. He could feel his excitement rising.

Kruger continued. 'We can, if you wish, arrange an introduction for you. On the other hand, you may wish for a more personal and individual approach, perhaps?'

Paulo had given this some thought on his flight. 'I think I would prefer to make my own introductions, if you don't mind. But allow me to say I'm very impressed by your handling of this enquiry. Very impressed indeed!'

Kruger preened himself, 'We do our best, you know!'

The receptionist smiled at Paulo as he finalised his account.

He realised that he was a stranger to Berlin and would be staying for a few more days. A companion, particularly one so pretty, would be a pleasant ornament to his stay.

Paulo summoned up his courage.

'Do you happen to know a reasonable hotel where I can stay for a few days?' he asked.

'There is the Metropole… it's very nice with a good reputation, and is used quite a lot by visiting businessmen, who also appreciate the entertainment facilities: sauna, swimming pool, music and dancing in the evening,' she volunteered.

'Look – I don't even know your name!'

'Elsa. Elsa Müller.' she offered.

He was finding her increasingly attractive and that almost imperceptible German accent complemented her Nordic good looks.

'Elsa, you don't mind my calling you by your Christian name?'

'Not at all! In fact, I would prefer it,' she answered.

'Look, Elsa, I know this sounds a little presumptuous on my part, but I am at a complete loss here in Berlin. Would you be very offended if I asked you out to dinner this evening?'

Her face remained calm but her eyes betrayed her delight at his suggestion.

'Well, I was going to a concert tonight but I really wasn't looking forward to it… rather too heavy for me. If I can rearrange my times I'd love to meet you. Look, I will write my telephone number down for you. Give me a ring at about seven o'clock and we will take it from there.'

Paulo felt strangely excited. It had been all work for the past few months and he would welcome a little relaxation. Elsa was rather gorgeous – an intelligent stunner!

The dinner was excellent.

A pea and ham soup with pancetta and sour cream.

Caramelised breast of duck with Puy lentils and Mirabeau sauce, followed by tarte au citron, with a vintage Chardonnay. Then coffee, finishing with an excellent brandy.

Elsa looked absolutely amazing. Her long blonde hair hung loosely over her beautifully tanned shoulders, and a simple black strapless dress showed off her shapely figure. She wore very little make-up. Her complexion was wonderfully natural with her slightly shaped fair eyebrows. There was the faintest hint of eye make-up. Her teeth were straight and evenly framed in slightly full lips; she smiled quite often.

Her jewellery was minimal and in good taste. She wore pearl drop earrings and tasteful small pearls around her beautifully shaped neck. She was enjoying herself and basking in Paulo's obvious admiration. That slight almost imperceptible aroma of expensive perfume was tantalisingly provocative.

Their conversation was mostly small talk to begin with, but as the evening wore on and the orchestra played soft background music, they began to tell each other more about themselves.

Elsa was twenty-three years of age and had been born shortly after the war. Her father had been an army officer repatriated from a prisoner of war camp in southern England. He had been captured in Africa while serving with Rommel's Afrika Korps.

His disillusionment had been eased when he met Elsa's mother, who was working as an English interpreter with the screening programme for returning Army and Air Force personnel. Elsa had been born shortly after their marriage, and had a very happy and loving childhood.

Paulo told her of his own background and the reason for coming to Berlin. 'Coincidence,' she said. 'Herr Kielmann, the senior partner, was in the police force in 1943 here in Berlin. He retired in the 1950s.'

Their conversation flowed easily from then on. She was fascinated by his German connections. His looks were obviously Latin, but those blue eyes were definitely Nordic.

'Shall I call a taxi?' he asked after they had wined, dined and danced.

Elsa hesitated a little then seemed to come to a resolution. The evening had been perfect but their relationship was still fragile.

Paulo waited for her reply. He could not understand his feeling of slight apprehension… or was it expectation? Very strange, he thought.

'Yes please, Paulo. It has been a wonderful evening and I have enjoyed myself immensely.' Elsa replied.

'Can I see you again?' Paulo asked trying to hide his eagerness.

'I should like that very much,' she replied enthusiastically.

'I will ring tomorrow evening, after work, then,' said Paulo.

'Yes please,' she replied. 'I'll look forward to hearing from you.'

The next day found Paulo gazing at the large block of apartments in Viktoria Strasse. They were beautifully landscaped. The taxi had skirted the beautiful Tiergarten crossed by the Siegesalle with its marble statues of Hohenzollern rulers. The apartments were near the Viktoria Park in the Kreuzberg district.

The ground floor comprised a large reception area with an elderly porter behind a large imposing desk.

'*Güten Morgen, mein Herr,*' greeted the porter.

Paulo felt his stomach muscles tense. '*Sprechen-sie Englisch?*' he asked.

The porter was elderly and looked as though he had seen his fair share of the world's tragedies '*Ich spräche som Englisch,*' he volunteered. 'Vot can I do vor you?'

Paulo spoke slowly and a stilted. 'Me... I... want... to see Herr Langstein, bitte.' He was embarrassed by this appalling English.

'Ah, *Ja! Herr Langstein. Apartment Zehn!*' The old porter held up ten fingers. 'Zehn!'

Paulo thanked him. '*Vielen dank,*' he said, and went to the lift. Apartment No. 10 was on the first floor. He rang the bell of the imposing door, full of anticipation.

There were footsteps. The door opened. A grey, upright figure stood there. '*Bitte?*'

'*Sie bitte, mein Herr. Sprächen-sie Englisch?*' Paulo asked nervously.

'Yes,' replied the elderly occupant. 'Not as well as I would like to, but enough.' Relief flowed over Paulo. 'May I have a word with you *mein Herr?*'

'You had better come inside and meet my wife. Her English is maybe a little better than mine.'

Paulo entered the Langsteins' spacious apartment. The furnishings were expensive and tasteful. Sitting by an antique writing bureau was an attractive grey-haired woman. Her hair was still thick and pulled back in a classical style. Her face showed lines of suffering – or was it grief? Nevertheless a handsome face.

She rose and stood up straight showing a still shapely figure dressed in an expensive-looking woollen skirt and cardigan in charcoal grey. A gold chain hung around her neck with a locket attached. She held out a long, slim well-manicured hand and looked Paulo up and down appraisingly.

'How do you do, young man,' she said in a modulated voice. She spoke English with a slight accent. The elderly man re-entered the room. '*Liebling*, a young man to see us' he said in affectionate tones. He turned to Paulo 'I'm sorry but I didn't catch your name,' he said carefully.

'Paulo Lucca,' announced Paulo. 'I'm from Italy. Florence.' He wasn't at all sure how to open the conversation. His eyes darted from the old man to the wife.

'Look, may I be frank about my being here?' he blurted out.

'By all means, young man. Reach the point and if we can possibly help we will be only too pleased to do so,' Karl answered.

Paulo launched himself into his explanation, and strangely enough the words flowed easily. He recounted his mother's love affair in 1943 to 1944 with the young Oberst of the German Luftwaffe; the disappearance and presumed death of her lover, Paul Langstein, after his internment as a prisoner of war in England; his mother's subsequent pregnancy followed by his own birth; his desire now to find out more about his natural father's background. The words just tumbled out without much effort.

The Langsteins sat silently, almost mesmerised by his revelations. They gazed at him with a mixture of emotions, sadness and excitement showing on their faces.

If what they were hearing was true, then sitting in front of them was their grandson, whose existence they had never known.

Liesl, his grandmother, was clasping the locket that hung around her neck. She took it off and opened it to reveal two photographs of Paul and Karl in their military uniforms.

She gazed at Paul's image and then at Paulo. The complexions were different. The hair colouring was different. But the eyes were undoubtedly the same. The facial structure was uncannily similar.

She had no doubts whatsoever. Strong emotional convictions came from her own overwhelming inner feelings. Tears filled her still beautiful eyes. Karl himself was fighting to control his mixed emotions. '*Lieber Gott…*' he murmured.

Paulo was filled with a compassion that he could not explain to himself. He had never before experienced such a powerful emotion. A yearning and aching consumed him.

Liesl rose and approached him and gazed longingly into his face.

'*My Liebling*. Oh! my darling boy!' She put her arms around him. He felt her frailty and vulnerability and a sadness and joy filled his whole being. He could not speak for fear of an emotion he would be unable to control.

Karl, her husband, remained stunned, as if a ghost from the past had walked into his life.

All those years ago… Paul and his love affair in Berlin… what was her name… Bunty?' The young *Englisch Fräulein*. The brutal betrayal!

A young life sacrificed for what? A 'cause' not worthy of Germany's great history.

Those atrocious crimes against humanity. No honour! No pride! Just shame! An obscene affront to German dignity…

He looked at this young man, full of youthful vitality and ambition. A face that revealed a sensitivity for all the finer aspirations of humanity.

His whole being was consumed with a guilt and shame, both for himself and the German nation.

'I'll make us some coffee,' said Liesl at last. This seemed to break the spell.

They later all sat and Paulo told about his life in Italy with his mother. Liesl wanted to know everything about his early life and upbringing. He showed them a photograph of his mother and some snapshots taken when he was young.

'We must meet her soon! There is so much to talk about,' Liesl said almost with a plea in her voice.

It was late that afternoon when Paulo left the Langsteins, promising to call again.

He arranged to meet Elsa that evening. They went to a classical concert and listened to some light-hearted Schubert and Rossini. Despite the music, Elsa observed that Paulo was deeply involved with his own thoughts. He had explained his emotional meeting with his grandparents and though she understood the deep feelings that had been released within him, she also knew she could not possibly intrude and left him to his own thoughts.

They returned to his hotel and lingered long over a light meal followed by coffee and brandy. 'I'll get you a taxi,' he said at the end of the evening.

She looked at him and felt his great need for human comfort and reassurance. For him to be alone could be traumatic and almost unbearable.

She placed her hand upon his.

'No taxi tonight, *Liebling*.' A great softness showed in her deep blue eyes.

Their lovemaking had a desperation about it. The need for human contact was overwhelming for both of them. They were falling in love.

'*Güten Morgen. Kielmann, Schmidt und Kruger?*' Elsa felt wonderfully elated, with a deep feeling of contentment.

'*Herr Kielmann, bitte.*' The voice sounded agitated.

'*Moment, bitte,*' replied Elsa.

Kielmann picked up the phone. It was Karl Langstein. They had not communicated for several years, not since the screening trials when Karl had been cleared of any war crimes. His collusion in the enquiries into the English Fräulein's death in 1939 was still a secret held by them both. They both knew that 'accidental death' was a cover-up for murder.

'*Güten Morgen*, Herr Langstein. A long time since we last spoke.'

In fact it had been when Langstein had helped him financially to set up the Agency. Those arrangements had been made entirely by telephone. The matter had been too delicate for them to be seen together.

'Look, Kielmann. There has been a development. It appears that my son Paul had an affair in Italy in 1943 and there is a grandson, Paulo. Definitely no doubt about his identity. There may be a very faint chance that he will probe into his father's early background.

'I thought I would warn you in case his enquiries include the English Fraulein affair. His name is Lucca. Paulo Lucca. He is from Florence, Italy.'

Kielmann still had his old attitude towards safeguarding his own interests.

'Thank you, Herr Langstein, for letting me know. You have nothing to worry about from me. But I will let you know if there should be any further developments.'

'Thank you, Kielmann. That is indeed reassuring. We both know the consequences if the truth was to come out. *Auf Wiedersehen*.' Karl felt somewhat relieved.

'*Auf Wiedersehen*, Herr Langstein.' Kielmann put down the telephone receiver.

He looked pensive. Paulo Lucca rings a bell? Of course! Kruger – that English-speaking enquiry from Italy. He picked up the intercom telephone, 'Elsa! what was the name of that Italian enquiring about the Langsteins? You remember, you put the call through to Kruger because of the English language problem!'

Elsa was a little surprised; Kielmann didn't usually take an interest in cases other than his own. She replied calmly, 'His name was Paulo Lucca, from Florence, Herr Kielmann.'

'*Danken, Elsa*.' Kielmann rang off,

Liesl sat looking at Paulo. Memories, long subdued, came flooding back to her.

'Your father was a fine boy. Very caring and enquiring, life was different for the youth of those days. There was very little choice. National Socialism controlled all the outlets for the young people: college, university, Hitler Youth and the armed forces. If you were young, the opportunities were endless. There was one tragedy in his life. He met a young English girl who was attending the Institute where Paul was studying English. He used to talk to me about her and the English way of life, their customs and their culture. Much different from what he had experienced. He had wanted to go to England, to visit her parents. Her father was a country doctor in southern England, the county of Somerset. Quite near to the prisoner of war camp where your father and his brother, Karl, were held after their capture.

'We did visit there a few years ago after the war when things had settled down and travel was easier. Berlin had been devastated by the bombing and Russian occupation, but normality was gradually restored. We learnt little about Paul and Karl's disappearance. It was assumed that they had attempted to escape and then – nothing. They just disappeared off the face of the earth,' she concluded wistfully.

Paulo could listen all day to these reminiscences about his father's early life. 'What happened to the English girl?' he enquired.

'Oh, that was a terrible tragedy,' Liesl continued. 'Her body was found near the railway sidings. Fallen from a train, the police reported. 'Accidental death.' A very strange affair.' Paul, your father, was devastated at the time. That's why he took up his second passion – flying. Then came the war in '39, and the rest you more or less know about… how he met your mother in Italy. He loved Italy, with its cultural background and ancient historic monuments and works of art.'

She could talk and talk about her lost sons. Karl, her husband, was less communicative, almost guarded in his conversation. Strange, that…

One had the impression he would rather discuss the other son, Karl, who, reading between the lines, had been a more ambitious son, dedicated to the ideals of National Socialism.

Paulo didn't mind; he wanted only to hear about his own father's experiences, and the more they talked the closer he felt to Paul, his father.

Kielmann was worried and edgy. 'Elsa!' he said. 'That young Italian boy who's looking for his father's parents. Does he mention them? I know that you are friendly with him.' He tried to sound casual.

Elsa thought it rather unusual.

Herr Kielmann was never very communicative, and for that matter showed little interest in any of the other cases that the agency handled.

'Oh, he has located them and learnt a great deal about his father's early life, particularly just before the outbreak of the war.

It appears his father had a personal tragedy. An English girl student he was more than a little friendly with was killed in a train accident. The police said that it was an 'Accidental death'. Paulo is trying to find out more about his father's life at that time and the circumstances surrounding the accident might reveal a little more about those early days. I think that he is shifting through the old records or newspaper cuttings that may have survived the post-war chaos. Indeed, he seems happy with what he has found out particularly from old police files,' she continued. You may know something about it. Weren't you in the police force about that time?'

Chapter Twelve

The next day Simon was able to catch up with Greg's father, Steve.

'You know some German, don't you, Steve?' asked Simon. 'I've got these bits of metal, this insignia, or badge – it's very fragile and broken – and these old pieces of leather which look as though they made up a belt or a strap of some kind. On the leather there's some lettering impressed.'

Steve turned the items over gently and picked up the badge.

'Oh, I recognise those straight away,' he said. 'It's a flying officer's badge from the Luftwaffe. Look, I've got a book with it in. It's a bit of a hobby of mine, service badges from any country, but this is definitely German.' He turned the metal over.

'This was probably part of a buckle, it's quite heavy and the engraving is quite deep... No, wait a minute, I think it's part of an identity disc or name bracelet. It's flat on the back and the letters are evenly spaced. Rubbing it over with some tracing paper might show something up – like a brass rubbing.'

They looked intently at the outlines that had come through the tracing.

'If you let the pencil just join up the lines the way they seem to be going you can pick out some letter. Look, this bit is legible now.'

P ^ - L   L .^. I..I -G /` .-N      -53.`2 /

'There's definitely a swastika and what looks like wings, so perhaps it really is from the Luftwaffe,' ventured Simon.

'Oh yes, it definitely is!' replied Steve. 'I've seen several of these... Looks like you've got yourself an officer from the Luftwaffe here. These were with the bones, you say? How long ago do they think they've been down there?'

'Well, they think round about 1944/5, so that would fit in. You see, I was thinking about the prisoner of war camp. You know old Silas who's always down the allotment? He put me on to that tack really. I didn't know anything about the camp at Dimmer but he says there were officers from all three services... previously no Kriegsmarine were held in the camp. Silas perhaps was mistaken. And another interesting thing, he remembers that they were allowed out to work locally; they may have tried to make a break for it. Pity we can't make out the name. I suppose it's the Ministry of Defence we go to next, and see if anyone went missing from the camp towards the end of the war. It looks as if the two would have gone together, so they'd probably be in the records as such.'

'I'll keep looking at these,' said Steve. 'You go and ring the Ministry and I'll keep trying and let you know if I get anything further.'

'Thanks, Steve, it's good of you to spare the time. I've got a bit hooked on this business; it was Lydia saying that she they might have parents still alive that really got me. I'd like to be able to trace any family to put their minds at rest. Then they could have them properly buried.'

Simon got through to the Ministry of Defence. A clerk promised to ring back. She was not surprised by his request, saying that over the years since the war bodies of German pilots and aircrews had turned up on several occasions, but usually they were with parts of old planes or attached to parachute lines. She said, 'If you find anything further let me know, the more info the better, at least, I can look up Dimmer Camp's lists, as they're on microfilm at Kew.'

Steve then appeared at the window. He was waving a piece of paper and Simon eagerly let him in. 'I couldn't definitely make out the letters but I found these numbers and they've come up quite clearly. How've you got on?'

'The Ministry are having a look for me,' Simon replied. 'If we've got some numbers that might help considerably.'

'Looks like 753122 or 753422, or the 3 might be half an 8, but it should help with confirmation. Gosh, Simon, it might not be long before we know who they are after all these years! What a turn-up! Imagine being their parents. It'll be a huge shock but I should think they'd be relieved, there must be nothing worse than not knowing how or where your children died. Let me know as soon as you hear, won't you? I must go, I'm taking Greg to the station. Goodbye.' Steve left by the garden door.

Simon looked at all the information he had got and decided to write down what he knew up to now:

Probably:

German

POWs

One may have been in Luftwaffe (wings on a badge)

No. 753122 or 753422

May have been escaping

Age: 20/30 when died

When: 1944/5

Both male

When Lydia returned, they discussed his list. Lydia was amazed at how much he'd found out in such a short time.

'By the way, Gladys and Hugh have a visitor staying. It's that niece of hers down for the weekend – Monica, she's called, works in London. I said if she is at a loose end we'd be pleased to see her for coffee or a drink. I think she's a lecturer at London University. You know, she's been down before, drives that lovely sports car,' she said wistfully.

'Oh, I know. I've never spoken to her, though. She's about fifty, isn't she? Always looks very smart. Very expensive car. She must have a good job. Yes, it'd be very interesting to meet her. Did you ask Gladys and Hugh as well?' asked Simon.

'No, I didn't see them. It was only a casual remark and she may not come. We'll want to see what happens. That's what we seem to be doing a lot of lately – waiting to see what happens! Well, I expect it'll all come out in the wash as my mother used to say. We just have to be patient.'

Later that afternoon Simon answered the phone.

'Hello, I'm Monica… staying with Gladys and Hugh. I met your wife this morning and she invited me round. I wondered if it would be alright to call about eight o'clock, just for a drink. I'll have already eaten, it's just that Auntie has been telling me about your discovery. It sounds so amazing – and I'd love to meet you anyway of course,' she joked. 'I don't want you to think I only want to hear about your bones, I'd love to meet you properly. I have seen you about when I've been down staying with my aunt and uncle.'

'It'll be really nice to see you, Monica,' said Simon. 'We'll look forward to it.'

Monica had done well since graduating. With her knowledge of German and of Germany's culture she'd remained at university to achieve her Masters and then been offered a lecturer's post in the languages faculty.

She'd never married. Relationships didn't seem to last, and she thought it probably had something to do with her experiences in Germany. The memory of Bunty still haunted her. But she loved her work, and her social life as a senior member of the university was full and very enjoyable. She had many friends, travelled extensively and her home was delightful. She did however often ponder on the lack of a close relationship, and the intimacy she occasionally yearned for. She'd missed out on a family, and it was no one's fault but her own; and now, of course, it was too late.

At times she resented what had happened to her at the end of the war. Quite often what she knew hung over her like a black cloud, and it hadn't got any easier as the years passed. The feeling of unease preoccupied her during quieter moments and she'd never been able to relax totally.

However, that's the way things were. She'd had to make the best of things, and she wasn't going to stir anything up now. It was all too complicated.

Lydia took sometime deciding what to wear for the evening. She knew Monica would look lovely. She didn't want to outshine her, as there wasn't a jealous bone in her body; but she did want to demonstrate that because they lived in a village they were still able to show some sophistication and style. She ended up in a cream silk trouser suit. It hung beautifully and could always be relied upon to help her look elegant. Simon loved her in it, said he could feel all her curvy bits; it really was extremely tactile.

Monica turned up just after eight. As Lydia had expected, she looked quite stunning in a long black skirt and a white sleeveless tunic that seemed to flow over her hips. It must be silk, thought Lydia, pleased that she had taken care with her own choice. Monica accepted a gin and tonic and they sat in the garden.

'How long are you staying with your aunt and uncle?' asked Simon.

'Only until tomorrow night. I've got lectures on Monday and a meeting in the afternoon. I try to keep in touch with them, though. You see, my mother died last year; she was Gladys's sister, and I think she likes to see me because I bring her to mind.' She leant back in the chair and stretched her legs out in front of her and sipped her drink.

'This is really lovely,' she remarked. 'It's so quiet down here, and what a warm evening it is! There are times when I really don't want to go back to London, but I know I always will. I'm not really a country person. I love London. Well, I love most big cities. I went to New York last year, it was so exciting, and I just love Paris. I was over there at Easter this year.'

'Didn't Hugh tell us you'd spent some time in Berlin too?' asked Lydia. 'You have had a thrilling life.'

'Well, that's many years ago now. It was just before the war. I was staying in Berlin with another aunt, on my father's side, when there was a terrible accident. I came straight back to England. Things were getting nasty in Germany at that time.'

Simon, who was a dedicated 'people-watcher', observed Monica's movements. Her fingers were never still and her eyes darted round the garden, never settling.

'Would you like to see where we found our bones?' he blurted out suddenly.

Crash! Monica's glass fell to the stone ground.

'Goodness! I'm so sorry, it slipped through my fingers. Oh dear, it was a beautiful crystal glass too. I'll have to replace it for you. Do you know where it came from?' She was speaking much too quickly, almost babbling, and her face was very pale, emphasising the darkness of her eyes. She looked like a frightened rabbit, Simon recalled later.

'Don't worry, it was only a glass. I'll just sweep the bits away and get you another drink. Of course you mustn't think of replacing the glass. We have plenty and it was only a simple accident. I'm always dropping things myself,' Lydia reassured her. 'Simon shouldn't talk about our bones like that. It's quite ghoulish but it's caused considerable excitement down here, I can tell you. Would you like us to explain it all? Are you all right now?'

'Yes, I'm fine thank you,' Monica replied nervously. 'I don't know what came over me. I think I was thinking of something else entirely.' She braced herself. 'Do tell me all about it.'

Though she smiled, she still looked very pale, Simon thought; but he couldn't resist an opportunity to repeat his tale, and it all poured out while Monica listened intently. When he'd finished he studied her face.

'You know you don't look well Monica, you're ashen! Are you sure you feel alright? It's not something you've eaten, is it?' Monica smiled at him again.

'No, I think it might have been a little too much sun, combined with the drive down here. I feel fine really, and I'd love another drink.'

'I expect you recognised a lot of what I was talking about, having spent time in Berlin, I mean the Luftwaffe and all that. They were about at the beginning of the war, weren't they? I expect you knew German boys when you were studying and some them were probably killed in the war, Oh, how thoughtless of me, I'm so sorry! I'm such an idiot, I could kick myself. Can you forgive me rattling on like that?'

'Well, it did rather take me back. Of course I had quite a lot of German friends, and many were killed in the war, but I was actually thinking of Bunty, my cousin. Did you know she died in Germany? Gladys and Hugh's daughter… that was a terrible time.'

'Yes, actually Gladys told me about it,' said Simon.

'She said they'd never been able to get over it. You know, Hugh still visits the grave several times a week and he still won't talk about her to anyone except Gladys—'

'Oh, he talks to me,' interrupted Monica. Then she bit her lip and seemed to have second thoughts. 'But still, that's nothing to do with your bones,' she said. 'Bunty's body was returned from Berlin and there was a proper funeral with all the family in 1938.

There wouldn't have been German airmen over here at that time, would there?'

'Not likely. Anyway, the pathologist has dated our bones about 1944 or '45... hark at me. *Our* bones! I'm getting carried away. I think the best information we have so far is what Steve noticed. It's a number on what looks like an identity bracelet or disc, and a swastika in some wings of gold wire, which might have been a blazer badge or an epaulette. We should soon be able to identify them with all this gen. I should think the Ministry of Defence will have a name for the number we've got, if they were POWs. Hey, what's up Monica?'

He stared in consternation at Monica as she gradually slid from her chair to the ground, her eyes shut. 'Lydia! Lydia!' She's fainted! I knew she didn't look well. Help me get her up. She doesn't feel hot – in fact, quite the opposite, she's cold. I'll get a rug. Oh good, she's coming round...'

'Monica, you fainted, how do you feel?' said Lydia. 'Here, let me put this rug round you. I think a little brandy,' Simon and Lydia fussed around her as she remembered what had caused her to black out.

'I'm alright! really, I'm okay... I think I'd better get back. I told you I'd had too much sun, I think it may be a touch of heat stroke. I'm not very good in this hot weather, and I was shopping at midday when the sun was really hot,' Monica protested.

'I should sit still for a little while,' said Lydia. 'Just sip your brandy and take your time. The sun can be lethal, although I must say I love it. I much prefer it too hot to too cold. Are you sure you're alright now?'

'Yes, thank you, I'm sorry to be such a nuisance. First time I've visited you and I had to go and faint! You've been so kind, I expect I'll feel fine after a good night's sleep.'

She stood up, slightly wobbly and holding on to the back of the chair. Then she began to move towards the gate. 'Thank you so much, sorry to be such a wet blanket. Perhaps I'll see you before I go back, tomorrow evening.'

'Are you sure you wouldn't like me to come round with you?' asked Simon, anxious to be of help, and thinking Monica still looked rather poorly.

'No, stay there. I'll be okay, it's no distance. I think I'll go straight to bed. Thanks ever so much for asking me round, it's been lovely to meet you. Goodnight.'

'Goodnight, Monica, hope you soon feel better. It's been nice to see you,' said Simon and Lydia together.

'You know,' mused Lydia, 'I'd be surprised if that was all down to a touch of the sun. It was nine hours ago she was shopping. She'd been indoors all afternoon and she's beautifully tanned. It looks to me as if she loves the sun.'

'The strange thing is,' said Simon, 'that it seemed to be triggered off by what I was saying. Think about it, Lyd. When I first talked about the bones she dropped her glass, and then when I said we'd got a number and badges and so on, she fainted. You don't think there could be a connection, do you?'

'Well, if there is I can't possibly think what it could be. But something's wrong. She seems nervous and on edge for someone whose supposed to be confident and self-possessed, I mean she's so successful in her work. A professor of German studies at London University… She wouldn't hold a post like that unless she was very capable and clever.'

Chapter Thirteen

Much of Berlin's archives were salvaged from deep underground storage bunkers.

The city's superstructure had been severely damaged, if not completely demolished, by the day and night bombing raids by the Allied air forces, the Americans by day and the British by night.

The street fighting following the Russian infestation of the city and its suburbs added to the devastation. The German Wehrmacht had been decimated but had resisted to the very end; street after street had been contested with the barbarity born of desperation. The Russians had vented their revenge upon the military and civilians alike.

Prisoners were hanged out of hand by wire nooses from any available beam, lamp post or trees, or just shot where they stood, hands raised in surrender or not.

No woman was safe. Many of the younger women tried to escape by disguising themselves to look old and frail but to no avail. They were treated with the same barbarity after they had been abused. The rape of the city of Berlin was total.

The whirlwind created by the Hitler regime was reaped in full measure upon a once proud city. Hitler, together with Eva Braun, whom he had married on 24 April 1945, took the coward's choice and committed suicide on the early afternoon of the 30th. Josef Goebbels with all his family also committed suicide in the special bunker constructed in the *Kanzlerei* grounds. The bodies of Hitler and Eva Braun were denied to the Russians. His chauffeur doused their bodies with petrol before burning them.

Looting had been thorough, but mostly of consumables. Paper had little immediate value. The deep basements of the *Das Volk* newspaper buildings had given up its records, and with true German thoroughness recently documented and recorded on computer files.

Paulo had no problem gaining access to these old records. Past copies of old issues were readily available. Copies of newspapers from the early 1930s onwards revealed much of the events leading up to the outbreak of war. There was the usual anti-Semitic propaganda. The causes of the *Kristallnacht* and the burning of the Reichstag were well documented. The accused was a communist provocateur.

Hitler's excuse for assuming the Chancellorship was unnecessary. The population would acquiesce to any saviour from either Communism or Judaism.

Paulo scrutinised the copies just prior to the outbreak of the war. There it was – a short passage, almost lost in the political news items.

Young English Fräulein named Elizabeth Fitzhugh found dead on the railtrack in a Berlin suburb. The investigating officer, Chief Inspector Kielmann of the Berlin City police, reported that death was 'accidental' due to a fall from a train and subsequent injuries received by passing rail stock.

Chief Inspector Kielmann... That was a strange coincidence. Could it be the same Kielmann? Thought Paulo.

He must have a word with Elsa.

Liesl sipped her coffee and gazed at Paulo. His news came as no surprise. He intended to fly to England to the camp location in Somerset and if possible see any relations of the girl Bunty who may still be alive. Then he'd make a visit or call to the English Ministry of Defence or central records office to find out any information about his father's disappearance.

His determination showed clearly on his young face and in those clear blue eyes. This was more than a curious search. It had become a vital crusade to fill the vacuum in his emotional wholeness.

'You must follow your own instincts, *Liebling*, for your own sake. Anything you discover would also help to heal my own pain of loss. Not to know where he rests creates an ache that is always with me every waking day of my life. Remember, the camp was located near a small town called Castle Cary.'

His grandfather said very little. There was, however, a strange faraway look in his eyes. It was a troubled look, not necessarily of sadness but perhaps regret for some far-off incident.

Paulo said goodbye to his grandparents with a firm promise to keep in touch with any fresh news that he may discover.

He had arranged to meet Elsa that evening. He had also telephoned his office in Florence and extended his absence from work for a further period. He also contacted his mother to let her know his progress so far. She had been delighted by his success and voiced her desire to travel to Berlin to meet his father's parents.

Events were beginning to touch and take over all their lives.

Elsa looked spectacular. She had an air of tranquillity about her. She was in love!

'*Cara!*' Paulo wished to introduce the subject of Kielmann. '*Cara*, I discovered this old newspaper report about the death of my father's girlfriend in 1938. She was sixteen years old and was killed accidentally in an incident on the railway. The police officer in charge was a Chief Inspector Kielmann… a strange coincidence, don't you think. Could it be the same Kielmann from your office?'

'Quite possibly,' she answered. 'He was in the Berlin police at that time. He may remember the affair.'

They continued their meal together and lost themselves in each other's company. Elsa was saddened by his imminent departure to England but Paulo had promised to ring her every evening.

'*Güten Morgen, Herr Kielmann.*' Elsa addressed Kielmann when he arrived at the office next morning. 'May I have a word with you?'

'Yes, Elsa?' he replied in his usual slightly abrupt manner.

She had long discovered this was a defensive mannerism of his.

'In 1938 you were in the Berlin police force, weren't you?' she went on. 'Yes,' he replied, his manner now even more guarded and abrupt. 'Why do you ask?'

'My friend – Paulo, the Italian boy – has been looking up old newspaper cuttings trying to discover more about his father's connection with the incident that happened then involving a young English girl student who was killed in a rail accident. The officer in charge was a Chief Inspector Kielmann. He was wondering if it could possibly be you?' Elsa asked.

Kielmann felt a coldness as his stomach muscles contracted. Outwardly he remained calm.

'As a matter of fact, I do vaguely remember an involvement in that case. It was rather a long time ago. Tragic incident... a young girl, pretty too. She fell from a train, if I recall correctly.' The casualness of his voice surprised him.

'Would you mind if Paulo had a word with you some time to discuss the case? It would seem that his father was particularly friendly with the girl,' Elsa continued. 'There would be a small problem, however. Paulo only speaks Italian and English. Would you mind if I acted as an interpreter?'

Kielmann felt nervous but was too experienced in dealing with human situations of this kind to allow this to develop into panic. 'Any time, Elsa,' he answered, perhaps a little too tersely. 'Though I don't think I could shed any further light on the case.'

He went to his office and sat down heavily into his chair. He picked up the telephone. 'Elsa, can I have an outside line please?' he asked.

'Certainly, Herr Kielmann. I'm switching you over now.' She was curious.

'Langstein. This is Kielmann here – we must meet and talk.'

Karl Langstein had almost expected the call. 'I'll meet you at the restaurant in the Tiergarten tomorrow morning at 11 o'clock. Would that suit you?' he suggested.

'Certainly, *mein Herr*. Until tomorrow then.' Kielmann put down the telephone.

Paulo touched down at Heathrow in the Lufthansa 727. The sun was struggling through the cumulus-scattered sky.

He could see how Heathrow had earned the reputation as the busiest airport in the world. With three giant aircraft landing in quick succession, he saw others waiting stacked at various levels awaiting landing instructions.

Every airline was represented in the vast public concourse. The sheer ebb and flow of humanity was almost overwhelming.

Yet everyone seemed familiar with the landing and boarding procedures.

He collected his hire car from the Hertz centre. The car was a top of the range Mercedes. White, automatic and effortless to drive. I must remember to drive on the left-hand side of the road, thought Paulo. Easy to forget if one isn't alert.

The traffic flowed smoothly. The well-spaced road signs directed him along the route. Paulo headed west and turned off the M4 for the A303, then took the road for Castle Cary. The minor roads he found slightly confusing, but a clear AA Road Atlas helped him.

Paulo booked into the Castle Inn, a small hotel come public house. It was very homely, very English. His grandmother had instructed him well. This was the nearest town to the old Dimmer location.

The receptionist was in her late twenties. Her fair hair was tied back at the nape of her neck and she had an attractive, open face. She took in every detail of this handsome newcomer. Perhaps he was a traveller, but no, he had an air of a successful business professional about him.

'You would like a double room with full board, sir?' She warmed to her task. Not many good-looking young men called at the Castle.

'Yes, please, if that is possible. I do like a large room.' His grandmother had warned him about English public house hotels. Not exactly luxuriously appointed, they relied on their 'olde worlde' atmosphere rather than modern facilities. A double room usually had a bath or shower en suite. The receptionist handed him a key with an enormous tab attached.

It was nearly six o'clock. She asked, 'Would you like dinner this evening, sir? We serve dinner from seven o'clock to nine o'clock.' She put on her most inviting manner.

'That would be most welcome,' replied Paulo, fully aware that he was being given the 'red carpet' treatment.

'Can I get a drink in the bar?' he requested.

'Certainly, sir. The landlord is in there now. He may show you his three German shepherd dogs. They have a party piece – all drinking a pint of beer from one glass! Will that be all? By the way, my name is Ruth. We like to be as informal if possible here.'

'Thank you very much, Ruth,' said Paulo, and made his way into the bar.

Here he found oak beams, a large open fireplace, comfortable tables and chairs with stools at the bar.

The landlord greeted him warmly.

'Good evening, sir. What can I get you?' He was a jovial-looking fellow, exuding a sense of well-being. About sixty years old, at a rough guess.

'Could I have a pint of your English beer?' Paulo asked.

'Certainly sir. How about our local bitter? You aren't English so you may find it strange; Americans usually like their beer cold,' he added.

'Oh! I'm not American' said Paulo. 'I'm from Florence in Italy.'

'Ah then wine would be your normal drink,' said the landlord.

'Yes, but I have a curiosity to try an English beer,' replied Paulo.

A large glass of bitter was placed on the bar-top and he sipped at the warm brown liquid. He was pleasantly surprised by the flavour.

'Would you like to see my German shepherds? They have a weakness for beer,' said the innkeeper.

'Yes please,' Paulo replied, remembering the receptionist's remarks.

'Here! King! Leo! Rufus!' shouted the landlord.

Behind the bar there erupted a confusion of tails, long tongues and bright eyes. Three huge German shepherd dogs bounded into the bar area. Meanwhile, the innkeeper had filled another brimming glass of beer. Three huge heads jostled to get their mouths and tongues into the foaming brown liquid. In no time at all the beer had disappeared.

Paulo was impressed. The innkeeper was obviously very proud of his three beer-drinking Alsatians. 'Go! Out you go!' he told them. They all three trooped out with their tails wagging with pleasure. 'My three beauties,' declared the landlord.

'I'm very impressed,' said Paulo. 'Have you been the landlord here for long?' he asked.

'About twenty years or more,' the landlord replied.

'Did you know the Dimmer camp?' Paulo added.

'Oh! Yes, the old prisoner of war camp. It was just deserted and derelict huts when I first came to Castle Cary. It's a municipal dump now – you know domestic rubbish, garden refuse and builder's rubble. Very well organised,' he added. 'It's just up the road from here, about five minutes' drive. I'll write down the directions for you.' He scribbled some instructions on a piece of paper and handed it to Paulo.

'You wouldn't happen to know a doctor called Fitzhugh who lived in this area, would you?' asked Paulo.

'Fitzhugh. Hmm! An unusual name,' said the landlord. 'I'll tell you what – see that old chap sitting over there? He may have heard of him. He's lived hereabouts all his life.' The landlord looked across the bar to a corner seat by the window.

'Hey, Tom!' he called out. 'There's a gent here trying to locate a doctor called Fitzhugh. Ever heard of him?'

'Let me see,' said the old man, wrinkling up his face in concentration. 'Aye! There's a Fitzhugh lives in Braunton. A doctor he was, well I suppose he still is. He's getting on a bit. Probably retired long since. Had a practice in the High Street. Next to the newsagent's,' said the old man.

'Thank you very much that is most useful. Can I buy you a drink?' said Paulo.

'Well, that's very civil of you. I'll have a pint of best bitter. Thank you kindly.' The landlord drew up a pint of bitter and handed it over the bar.

The next day Paulo rose early, had a light breakfast and, following the landlord's directions, arrived at the campsite at Dimmer.

It was a desolate place piled high with the flotsam of human society neatly arranged in orderly sections. He felt a strangeness, a strong sense of closeness. Hard to explain. He wandered about trying to analyse his own feelings.

'Can I help you sir?' asked an elderly employee of the dump staff.

'Not really,' said Paulo. 'You see, my father was an inmate of the prisoner of war camp that was here during the war.'

'Ah, the camp. The huts were still here when I started this job, a long time ago. All very orderly. They told me it was a very relaxed place. None of your high security stuff. The prisoners were allowed out to work. Specialised work, mind you. Most of the Fritzes were officer types,' said the old employee.

Paulo thanked him and left for Braunton, a small town not far from Castle Cary.

The newsagent's shop wasn't difficult to find. In fact it was the only newsagent in the town. He entered the shop after parking his car in the High Street. A middle-aged woman was behind the counter.

'Excuse me,' Paulo addressed her. 'I'm looking for a Doctor Fitzhugh. Can you tell me where he lives?'

'Two doors up the road. Turn right as you leave the shop. It's a large black door, you can't miss it.'

Paulo thanked her and left the shop.

He rang the large brass doorbell of the impressive looking door.

Footsteps sounded on the other side of the door. It opened and an elderly distinguished-looking man stood in the doorway.

'Excuse me,' said Paulo, 'I'm looking for a Doctor Fitzhugh.'

'That's me' said the distinguished old gent. 'What can I do for you?'

'My name is Paulo, Paulo Lucca, and I have recently arrived from Berlin. My father was Paul Langstein, who was a Luftwaffe officer in the last war and a prisoner of war at the camp at Dimmer. I am trying to trace his movements. You see, I never knew him as my father until quite recently.'

'You had better come in,' said Hugh. He led the way into a comfortable lounge furnished with solid, antique-looking furniture.

'Take a seat, young man. Would you like a drink? Tea, coffee or something stronger?

'Nothing, thank you,' said Paulo. He was anxious to pursue his enquiries.

'Now how can I help you?' asked Hugh.

'From records I found in Berlin, it seems a very good friend of my father's, called Bunty Fitzhugh, met with a fatal accident on the railway near to the city.'

Hugh gazed at Paulo. His feelings were mixed. Old wounds were being opened and he was afraid. He said carefully, 'Bunty was my daughter, my only daughter. Her body was returned from Germany. She was buried in our local churchyard. That was in 1938. A long time ago… a lifetime.' His voice was strained.

'Thank you,' replied Paulo. He could see the old doctor had retreated into his own thoughts and felt guilty at his abruptness. It was time to leave.

'I'm staying at the Castle Hotel in Castle Cary for the next few days,' he said. 'If you have no objections I would like to visit your daughter's grave before I return to my grandparents in Berlin.'

'By all means,' said Hugh. 'You cannot mistake the plot. It is under the large yew tree in the graveyard. There are always fresh flowers on the grave.' He seemed to have aged visibly.

'Thank you once again. I'll let myself out.' Paulo could see that the doctor had stepped back into a world of his own, of which he was no part.

After visiting the graveside, Paulo returned to the Castle Hotel and found Ruth at her desk. I wish to make a telephone call to Berlin. May I use the telephone?' Paulo requested.

'Certainly, sir!' she answered, a little huskily. 'Use the telephone in your room and the hotel will add the cost to your account. You'll need an outside line.'

Chapter Fourteen

In Berlin the skies were overcast with dark grey clouds. It was quite cool for the time of year.

Liesl had waited patiently for news from Paulo, but then it was early days yet for him to have explored every avenue of his enquiries. Meanwhile she was concerned about Karl, her husband. There were too many long silences and preoccupations with hidden thoughts.

'Karl! Is there anything worrying you, darling? You seem to have had a problem ever since that telephone call the other day,' she asked anxiously. 'Would you like to talk about it?'

Karl had wrestled with his conscience ever since Kielmann's call. The appearance of Paulo, his son's child, had compounded his troubled thoughts.

'Can I talk frankly about a topic that you may find distressing?' he said.

'*Liebling!* We have been married for a lifetime and we have always shared our joys and sorrows. Now is not the time to isolate ourselves from each other's problems.' She spoke tenderly. Karl hesitated, then seemed to arrive at a dramatic decision.

'That telephone call was from a man called Kielmann. He was a Chief Inspector in the Berlin police force in the 1930s and '40s.' The words seemed unstoppable now.

'You remember that case of the young English Fräulein called Bunty, whom Paul was very fond off in 1938?' He watched her intently, but noting the concern and sympathy on her still lovely face, he realised he was still hopelessly in love with her.

'You know that our two sons were quite different in their loyalties to the Hitler movement. Paul was more liberal minded and questioning, whereas young Karl had been completely committed and dedicated, almost fanatical.' There was no stopping now, he continued.

'Karl had voiced his concern about Paul's relationship with the

English girl and the possible harm that could be caused should the affair become more serious. Perhaps you can remember how we discussed Paul's intention to visit England and meet the girl's parents.'

'Yes, I do remember, *Liebling*, but they were strange times,' Liesl said gently.

'Well, I misjudged the situation and thought it a passing phase and that once the girl returned to England it would be an end to the affair. I was wrong.' There was a sadness about his whole being as he continued. 'It was September 1938. Karl asked me to meet him at the Security Headquarters in Wilhelm Strasse. When I saw him his mood was obviously agitated.' Karl paused. The next few sentences would be the acid test of Liesl's loyalties and compassion.

'Karl said that there had been a serious incident involving the English girl. He had decided to confront her and point out the possible dangers in her liaison with Paul, his brother, not only for Paul but for the whole family. Racial purity and complete loyalty to National Socialism were paramount for any ambitious aspirations within the movement.' The strain of Karl's revelations was beginning to show. There was perspiration on his brow. His skin colour had become grey. He continued.

'The girl refused to cooperate, even deriding his arguments as pure fantasy and amateur dramatics. You remember she was so young, with all the arrogance of a teenager. They had taken her by car to the outskirts of the city near the railway sidings to continue trying to persuade her to see the seriousness of the situation. Finally Karl's patience snapped.

'He had become furious at the girl's stubbornness. His Party dagger had been in his hand and he found himself stabbing this infuriating girl. Stabbing – stabbing – as if some fiend had been unleashed within him! His companions looked on in a cruel detachment. The girl was quite dead. She had probably died after the first thrust of the dagger. They bundled the body out of the car and laid it alongside the track before returning to Berlin. They disposed of their bloodstained uniforms and then returned to their quarters.'

Karl had become exhausted by the sheer nightmare of relating these events that had happened so long ago and which he had kept to himself. He continued.

'After I had heard our son's terrible confession of the happenings to the girl, I had decided that I must cooperate or see the ruination of ours son's ambitions – though on hindsight I realised that probably the authorities would possibly have condoned his sins. I approached Kielmann who was in charge of the case and persuaded him to treat the whole affair as an "accidental death". My own high position in the Party had assured the police officer of suitable rewards for his cooperation. In fact, I financed him in setting up in a detective agency after the war.'

Liesl looked at her husband. He was physically exhausted by his confession, though there was relief as well as anxiety showing in his eyes.

She was finding it difficult to analyse her feelings. Her overwhelming emotion was compassion for this man she loved.

'Karl, oh Karl! How you must have suffered all these years with this terrible guilt. But there is only one course of action you must now take. Go to the police and tell them the whole story. Our sons are both dead and cannot be involved now. Your own part was perhaps being an accessory, but the circumstances surrounding the whole affair belong to another world.

'You must go my darling and let the authorities decide,' she pleaded. 'Remember that I love you, my darling, and will support you whatever happens.'

Karl was overwhelmed. He could not overcome his emotions of relief and gratitude. He wept profusely.

Liesl went to him, her heart full of sadness for this man she loved so dearly.

Back in England, Paulo heard the ringing tones at the other end of the telephone. '*Bitte. Liesl Langstein hier.*'

'Grandmother! Paulo here!'

'*Paulo, Liebling*! Are you well? How are you getting along? Are you comfortable in your hotel? What was the journey like?' So many questions. ' I want to hear all your news, my darling.'

'No problems, Grandmother. I met the father of the English girl, Bunty, and I have visited her grave and the site of the camp. I intend to return to Berlin in a day or so and will then tell you in more detail. Are you both well?' he asked.

'Yes, my darling! We are both well, but I have much to tell you. However, it can wait until you return.'

They chatted for a while about Lisa and small matters. '*Auf Wiedersehen, Liebling*,' she concluded.

'Goodbye, Grandmother. See you soon,' said Paulo and rang off.

Kielmann sat at his table in the Tiergarten in Berlin, sipping his coffee and gazing at the strolling Berliners. He appreciated the young and fashionably dressed young people enjoying their parade in the sun.

Karl Langstein approached his table. He looked a little older but was smiling.

'*Güten Morgen*, Kielmann.'

'*Güten Morgen, Herr* Langstein.'

They greeted each other politely. '*Kaffee?*' Kielmann asked.

'*Ja, bitte. Kaffee Schwarz*,' said Karl.

The waiter placed the coffee in front of him.

'Why the urgency, Kielmann?' asked Karl.

'It's the Italian boy, your grandson. He's getting curious about that incident involving the death of that young English girl in 1938.' Kielmann replied.

'Before we go any further with this conversation I must tell you that I am going to the police with the whole story, and I am prepared to face the consequences.' Karl broke in.

Kielmann's eyes narrowed and focussed intently on Langstein's face.

Karl read his thoughts and said, 'Don't concern yourself. You only did your duty. The coroner's verdict was "Accidental death" and left you with no alternative. Nearly all the records have long since disappeared. I had them destroyed during the war.' Karl continued, 'I'm merely telling you in case you are approached by the police, but I'm sure you are experienced enough to know how to handle such an eventuality.'

Kielmann's self-preservation instincts came to the fore. He knew that time and events since 1938 would dull any enthusiasm for resurrecting the whole incident. Karl spoke.

'I think that we no longer need to meet or converse any further. Should my grandson approach you, tell him the facts as you saw them at the time. There is no need for you to worry any further.'

Kielmann was openly relieved.

'I'll leave you now, Kielmann. We need not meet further. *Auf Wiedersehen.*'

'*Auf Wiedersehen, Herr Langstein.* I wish you well for the future.'

They each went their separate ways.

The Berlin police recorded Karl's account of the 1938 incident. There seemed little that they could act upon. The records had long since disappeared.

The perpetrator of the crime was dead, possibly a war hero. His father had condoned the offence by covering up the crime, thus making himself an accessory after the event; but in view of the political background of that time and the parental motive to protect his son and safeguard his future in the service of his country even if the father had not covered up the crime, the chances were more than likely that a Nazi administration would have favoured and possibly assisted in the suppression of the truth. After all, a war of world conquest was being plotted and almost ready to be unleashed. The death of some obscure English teenager would have had a very low priority rating. The State Prosecutor took note that the colonel had been cleared of any war crimes and further prosecution would be difficult to prove. The incident would, however, remain on record.

Chapter Fifteen

Hugh was sitting in his den, sitting very still with his gaze fixed on the garden he could see through the window. He'd been so amazed to find this young man on his doorstep, calling himself Paulo Lucca, that he hadn't known what to say to him. Looking back, he felt he hadn't been very welcoming. He wished he'd been more at ease and introduced Paulo to Gladys and Monica; but in fact he'd been rather abrupt. This was always his way these days. He regretted his terse manner towards people but he couldn't seem to change it.

Perhaps he should go and see him at his hotel. He'd need to prepare himself, think over what he'd like to talk to him about. Quite a few questions came to mind. He wondered how much Paulo knew of his father's life before the war. He'd obviously been on some sort of crusade recently trying to find out all he could. Bunty had been so fond of him, even though she'd been so young. When she mentioned him in her letters, her love had shone through. Her letters had bubbled over with vitality, excitement and animation. As he thought back to reading them, he remembered her vividly.

He hoped Paulo would go to the churchyard. Bunty would have been so happy to think that Paul's son had come over here and been so earnest in his interest.

Hugh wanted to share his thoughts with someone. Gladys and Monica were out. Monica was here a lot lately. Hugh was surprised but pleased, as Gladys seemed very fond of her. They always had their heads together and went out a lot together, shopping or for walks. Monica was lucky in having long university holidays; perhaps she got lonely. Anyway, she was always welcome here.

He decided instead to visit Simon. It was just before lunch time, and perhaps he'd be offered an aperitif.

Simon opened the door to his knock.

'Hello, Hugh, is everything all right? Come in. Would you like a sherry? I was just going to have one before lunch. I'm glad you called... I've quite a lot to tell you about the progress that's been made on the bones. I think we're getting near to it all being cleared up. Inspector Goodbody thinks the Berlin police have located the family. They're called Langstein, apparently the parents are still alive, living in a suburb of Berlin. They're going to see them today.'

Hugh hastily put his glass down just in time to stop himself from dropping it 'Langstein you say? It can't be! It's too much of a coincidence,' he spluttered.

'What's the matter?' asked Simon, concerned at the agitation on Hugh's face. 'What's a coincidence?'

Hugh sat down and picked up his drink, 'Sit down, Simon. I came round to tell you some news I've had and now you come out with the name of Langstein. I can't believe it.'

He told Simon all about the visit he'd had from Paulo and went on to explain the background to the visit and the fact that Paulo was researching his family. He got into his stride and started to relate all his memories, bottled up since before the war, about Bunty as a child, her tragic death in Berlin, and her connection with the Langstein family. The words came tumbling out; it was so long since he'd had such a sympathetic listener.

Simon was startled to discern a connection between Hugh's daughter and his skeletons. Wasn't this what he'd been looking for? He hadn't been really been serious, just turning the idea over in his mind, and now it had turned into fact. He was frightened to hear his thoughts and fantasies confirmed. It had been in his imagination that Hugh may have had anything to do with the death of the Langstein brothers, a sort of fairy tale idea. He hadn't really thought it through, and now here were his musings being talked about in a factual context. But the most striking fact had not yet been revealed.

Hugh was now talking about his niece, Monica. 'You know, Simon, when Monica came back from Berlin, just in time for Bunty's funeral, she told me something very disturbing. She said she'd heard rumours that Bunty's death had not been an accident and that there had been a cover-up. She told me of a large black car and a feeling of being followed and she also mentioned that she'd spoken to an old railway worker who'd found Bunty's body and said that the injuries didn't look accidental, but that he'd been frightened to say any more. Then there was this girl at the Institute who'd warned her about Paul's brother...

'I pushed all this to the back of my mind. For one thing I didn't want Gladys to hear about it. She was upset enough already. An accident she could just about cope with, a murder investigation would have been unbearable. There was nothing you could do in Germany at that time. It would have been dangerous to try and follow it up and very difficult for me to have travelled out there. Besides, where would Gladys have been if anything had happened to me too? I told myself there was always gossip after the violent death of a young person. I felt sure I'd have heard from the Berlin police if there'd been any truth in her suspicions. Now, of course, I'm forced to consider everything over again.'

Simon was silent. He couldn't believe his ears. Hugh had lived with suspicions that his daughter had been murdered for over thirty years. No wonder he was often moody and abrupt! Something like that must really affect you. The revelations explained a lot of things. He must get on to Inspector Goodbody as soon as possible.

Hugh's visit continued as normally as possible. Simon made all the right noises and kept Hugh's glass filled. They talked of other things, inconsequential things like cricket and the horticultural show, and after a couple of hours Hugh left.

On his way out, he told Simon he thought he'd visit Paulo in his hotel or invite him back for dinner, to meet Gladys and Monica. He'd probably be especially interested in meeting Monica who had known his father at the Berlin Institute in 1938.

'I really need to apologise to him. My manner was a bit out of order, but he took me so much by surprise. Thanks for the drink then, Simon, and for letting me bend your ear. Bye now!' Then he was gone.

Simon exhaled a long deep sigh and went straight to the telephone. He must share this information with the inspector. He couldn't bear all this knowledge on his shoulders. A ghastly thought that came to his mind was that Paulo might be in some kind of danger.

Inspector Goodbody was very interested in the call from Simon. Here he was, looking for a connection between Dr Fitzhugh and the Langstein brothers, and Simon was providing him with that very thing. The one thing he did not know yet was whether the Langstein brothers had ever been on a working party that visited or went near to the doctor's house. He had the names from the MOD records of the colonel in charge of the camp and of a few of the senior guards who were thought to be still alive. They had moved all over the country and some had even gone abroad. But the Ministry had helped him find telephone numbers for the colonel and two majors who'd been on his staff.

When Simon hung up, he got straight on to dialling the numbers given to him. There was no reply from the first two he tried but when he heard someone picking up the receiver on his third attempt he was elated. It was Major Smythe. Goodbody introduced himself and outlined his reasons for ringing. The major was interested and cast his mind back to the time he served as deputy to the colonel at Dimmer Camp after being injured in Sicily the year previously.

'Yes, I can remember the working party programme; it was stopped after two prisoners disappeared while out working in the community. It was a shame, because the prisoners enjoyed meeting the locals and it was very useful to use as an incentive for toeing the line. Actually I was in at the inception. It worked very well until the escape.

'How did you know it was an escape attempt?' asked Goodbody.

'Well, of course, we didn't for sure, it was just assumed. After all, that's what prisoners are supposed to do – try to escape – and these two brothers were officers and keen to get back to the front. At first it seemed obvious. Now of course with hindsight I can see how wrong we were. What was it you wanted to know?'

'Well, if you could tell me, if you can remember, to which houses or farms the Langstein brothers were allocated, and anybody who had them work on their land or may have got to know them.'

'That's a tall order, Inspector. I can't recall where many of them went to, but as it happens with these two it does stick in my minds because our camp doctor used to ask for them to do gardening work. They went to his house in Braunton in several occasions. I remember because the doctor was a bit of a misery – he'd had some sadness before the war; his only daughter had died. We were surprised that the Langsteins always volunteered to go to his house. The doctor said they were interested in trees, as he was, and that they were good workers.'

'Thank you, sir, thank you very much,' said Goodbody, overwhelmed by his good luck. 'If necessary, would you make a statement to that effect?'

'Oh yes. If it becomes necessary, Inspector, you can call on me. Is there anything else I can help you with?'

'This is rather a long shot, sir, but you wouldn't know anything else that happened on the day the brothers disappeared? Anything that would pinpoint the date.'

'No, I think it was an ordinary day except that when the working parties returned without the Langsteins we sent out some search parties, but no information came back. They'd just disappeared of the face of the earth; but then they had several hours' start. Leave me your number, Inspector. I'll try and think hard and let you know if anything else comes to mind. The long-term memory is sometimes better than the short-term nowadays. Rest assured, Inspector. I'll set my mind to it.'

'Thank you, sir. I'll look forward to speaking to you again. Goodbye.'

Armed with this news, the Inspector resolved to talk to Doctor Fitzhugh. There were several unanswered questions. Why did the doctor not link the names Simon gave him with those of the German officers he'd come to know during the war? Why had he not mentioned that his daughter had known a young man called Langstein when she stayed in Germany in 1938? And why had he not been in touch himself with the inspector when he'd had a visit from young Paulo Lucca, the son of one of the Langsteins, instead of just telling Simon? Surely he would realise the significance of the name cropping up so often? At the very least it was a huge coincidence. At most it indicated some involvement of

Doctor Fitzhugh in the disappearance of the two officers in 1944.

He decided to visit Paulo at his hotel before finally bringing the doctor to the station for questioning.

Paulo was happy to welcome the inspector at the hotel and they both went into the bar, where the inspector ordered two beers. Paulo assumed further information about his father had been revealed and was eager to hear it, but he was dismayed to find out that his father had not disappeared whilst trying to escape from a prisoner of war camp, which was after all an honourable means of ending his life. Instead it seemed in all probability that he had been murdered – poisoned – whilst undertaking work for the enemy.

The inspector did not mention his suspicions relating to the Fitzhughs, suspicions he wanted kept secret until he was completely ready to charge someone, until he had a safe case with evidence likely to secure a conviction.

Paulo was happy to tell him what Doctor Fitzhugh had been to see him at the hotel also and that they had been to the church-yard together to see Bunty's grave, as she had been in love with his father before her tragic death. He said his mother had told him about this love affair, which she knew of from his father. She had also told him that he may meet a woman called Monica, who was a cousin of Bunty's who was also at the Institute in Berlin and was a friend of his father too. He had asked the doctor about Monica but he'd told him she was out for the day. He'd promised to ask her to ring him, and Paulo felt his visit to Somerset had been very valuable in building up a picture of his father.

Now, of course, it was all spoilt. The news that both his father and his uncle had been murdered was really horrible. Why had it happened? Did the inspector know why anybody would murder them when they were already prisoners of war? It didn't make sense. Inspector Goodbody was still unable to answer Paulo's impassioned question but he was interested in the news – unwittingly given – that Monica had been in Germany at the time of Bunty's death. Perhaps she could reveal a motive. She would be the person he spoke to next!

Chapter Sixteen

The next day the Inspector called on the Fitzhughs, not to see Hugh, not yet, but hoping to catch Monica at home.

Hugh invited him in and called out for Monica, who arrived in the sitting room within a few seconds.

Goodbody was amazed to see her looking pale and drawn. For a successful academic on a long summer vacation she didn't seem at all relaxed. Anxiety was the emotion he thought showed in her eyes and he wondered what she had to be worried about. What disturbing thoughts did she have to live with?

Hugh left the room and Monica invited Goodbody to sit down. He couldn't think of any small talk so he plunged straight in. 'I understand you were in Berlin when the Fitzhugh's daughter was killed?'

'Yes, I was, Inspector, but I prefer to put such a sad time out of my mind. It's a long time ago now. Why are you asking?'

'You may not know, Miss Campbell, but recently some bones – actually two complete skeletons – were discovered in an underground room in the house next door to here.

'We have since ascertained their identity and find there is a connection between them and the Fitzhughs.' Goodbody watched Monica's face carefully. He wanted to register her expression as she assimilated this information but he could detect no flicker of emotion.

'I know who they are, Inspector. The neighbour next door, Simon West, told me when I was visiting him and Lydia at the weekend, but I'm not sure what you mean about a connection with my aunt and uncle. Can you explain?'

Was she being deliberately obstructive or did she genuinely not remember? Goodbody wondered.

'You must remember, Miss Campbell, that it was a Paul Langstein that your cousin Bunty became very fond of in the summer of 1938. In fact, according to the report from the Berlin police it may have been Paul Langstein whom she was waiting for at the marshalling yards where she was tragically killed. I understand you too often spoke with Paul Langstein and appeared to be quite a friend of his. I can't really believe you cannot remember any of this and that you were not affected when you heard the identity of the skeletons?'

Monica still appeared calm as she said, 'It never entered my head it would be the same boy Inspector. Langstein is not altogether an uncommon name in Germany. I didn't even know he or his brother had been in England.'

She appeared so cool. Goodbody was thinking she'd been rehearsing her responses. Suppose she had discussed the situation with her uncle? Suppose he had drilled her to say her lines? He said, 'It may not be an uncommon name but it would surely be a huge coincidence that the brother's name was the same as the family you knew.'

'I suppose it would, Inspector. Yes, you're quite right, it seems it is likely to be the same. How can I help you?'

'You could tell me any reason you could think of that someone in England may have wanted to kill these boys, even if they were prisoners of war in 1944. I should warn you that I have already spoken to a young man who claims to be the son of Paul Langstein and that he knows of the close relationship between his father and Bunty Fitzhugh, and I should further warn you that a Mr Karl Langstein senior, a retired colonel, has made a statement to the Berlin police admitting to perverting the course of justice in attempting to cover up the involvement of his son Karl Langstein junior in the death of Bunty Fitzhugh, and that he used his influence to encourage an Inspector Kielmann to have that suspicious and violent death reported as an accident. I think – and don't you Miss Campbell? – that I have enough information to arrest your uncle and take him to the police station for questioning about the deaths of these two young men.'

'Oh no, you can't!' Monica burst out, showing more animation than the inspector had seen all the time he'd been there.

'Why can't I, Miss Campbell?'

'Oh, I'm sorry, no reason. I'm sorry.' She now seemed really flustered and a greyish pallor spread over her face, but she volunteered no further information except to say, 'I'll call my uncle, then, shall I?' and left the room.

While the inspector waited for the doctor, Monica did not go to look for him. Instead she ran off to look for her aunt. She wanted to be with her when the news of Hugh's arrest broke; she knew how scared her aunt would be and was worried about her. She ran upstairs to her aunt's room but found it empty. She called out, 'Auntie Gladys, auntie Gladys!' but there was no reply. She ran back downstairs and through to the garden, still calling.

Hugh came out of his study. 'What is the matter my dear?'

Monica was nearly hysterical, 'The Inspector's come to arrest you uncle and I can't find Gladys.'

'To arrest *me*? He can't, I haven't done anything. Don't worry, I'll sort this out. Is he still in the sitting room? I'll go and see him. You go and look for your aunt.'

Hugh hurried to the sitting room.

'Look here, Inspector, what's all this about?'

'I'd like you to accompany me to the police station, Doctor. I believe you can help me with my enquiries into the deaths of Paul and Karl Langstein, whose remains were found in the house next door about two weeks ago.

'I must warn you that you are not obliged to say anything but anything you do say may be taken down and may be used in evidence. Now, you'll come straightaway... I hope there won't be any need for me to restrain you?'

'For heaven's sake, Inspector, of course there won't. But I must just see my wife. This is crazy. I haven't done anything wrong. Can I call my solicitor?'

'Yes sir. I certainly think you're going to need him.'

As the doctor walked over towards the telephone, the Inspector watching closely his every move. Then there was a horrendous scream and then another, followed by Monica's voice shouting, '*Oh no! Oh no!*'

The doctor and the inspector looked at each other and then both began to run to the source of the noise. As they chased up the garden, they could hear a car's engine running and then saw Monica dragging someone from the car. Approaching, they both recognised the events unfolding before them. In their respective posts in life they had both seen suicides being pulled from cars before.

'I'll call an ambulance,' said the inspector, and hurried back to the house. 'See what you can do for her,' he shouted to Hugh.

Hugh ran on. Monica had already got Gladys out of the car and on the ground but she was inert, lifeless. Monica was sobbing. Hugh got down beside her still body and placed his fingers on Gladys's neck.

'There's still a pulse I'll try mouth to mouth,' he said. Monica dragged a rug from the boot of the car. She was shaking quite violently from shock.

'Oh my dear! My dear! Why?'

Monica was calmer now.

'She knew the police were here Uncle. I think she was very frightened.'

Inspector Goodbody was coming up the garden, followed by two ambulance men. After a brief examination, they put Gladys on the stretcher.

'We'll take her to the hospital now, sir. Will you be coming with us?'

'I'll go with her,' put in Monica. 'Don't worry, Uncle, I'll come straight back to you when I've spoken to the doctor there.'

'Thank you, my dear, don't worry about anything. If Gladys comes round, tell her everything will be all right. Make sure you tell her that: everything will be all right.'

'I will, Uncle. I'll take care of her; now you take care of yourself. Have you spoken to your solicitor?' Monica seemed controlled and capable.

'Yes, my dear, he'll meet me at the police station. I think I know what I have to do now. You must concentrate on helping Gladys. I'm ready to come with you, Inspector. You won't need any restraints,' he added with a wry smile.

Hugh was able to spend time alone with his solicitor until the inspector arrived to commence his interrogation. The Inspector had been called to the telephone soon after reaching his office. 'A long distance call for you, sir, from Germany, Berlin… a Mrs Langstein,' said his sergeant. The inspector was curious. The case had many strange angles to it.

It was an hour before he was ready to question Hugh. The call from Mrs Langstein had been an emotional one and had presented him with a dilemma. She had been crying and had pleaded with him to drop any charges he may have been going to bring against Hugh because, as she had recently discovered, her son had murdered his beloved daughter.

'I may sympathise, Mrs Langstein, but I can't change anything. We have evidence of murder and there's no way I can drop charges because you ask me to. That's up to the judge. Talk to a lawyer, Mrs Langstein, that's all I can advise.'

What a state of affairs, he thought to himself. I need a drink before I begin talking to the good doctor. He poured himself a very little whisky and added some water; he was not a heavy drinker but he was finding recent events very harrowing.

When he finally sat down, facing the solicitor and Hugh in the interview room, he felt quite sorry for the older man. Investing all one's hopes and ambitions in a child who is murdered at only sixteen years of age must be a heavy burden indeed.

'Don't worry, Inspector,' said Hugh. 'I'm not going to give you any problems. I don't deny anything. You just go ahead and do what you have to do. I'll sign whatever you want.'

'It doesn't work like that, sir. You still need to make a state-ment, even if you're admitting the offence. May I just remind you that you're still under caution. Now, it might be a good idea to start from when you knew the young men would be arriving at your house to do some work. A weekend, wasn't it? By the way, how many times before had those two men been to your house as part of the working party scheme?'

Hugh tried to force his mind back to wartime. Events gradually came back to him. Yes, he remembered now. He had wondered about the two Langstein brothers. He'd been trying to find out more about them from camp records. After what Monica had told him prior to Bunty's funeral he had always been on the lookout for any young men with that surname. He had thought about revenge but he'd wanted to be 100 per cent sure. He'd wanted to check their Christian names, their ages and the area of Germany they had come from with Monica, but he hadn't wanted to arouse her suspicions. That was why he'd asked for them more than any others to help him in his garden. They, of course, did not know his name; he was just *Herr Doktor* to all the prisoners. His surname was hardly used at all. But when he'd returned to the camp one Monday to see some patients, he'd heard the news that they had escaped. He'd been rather glad to be able to stop thinking about them. Once or twice he'd thought about hiring a private investigator after the war but he didn't really want his memories of Bunty disturbed. She'd been a happy child, and he found that was how he could remember her. What all this business was about he hadn't a clue, but he mustn't let the inspector know that. His job now was to convince the inspector that he did do it. A double murder! He knew himself well enough to know he never would have done it, whatever the provocation. It wasn't in him to kill anybody, let alone two young men.

He was just trying to form the words to commence his statement when there was pandemonium outside; two people with raised voices and scurrying feet. Suddenly the door was flung open.

'Excuse me,' began the inspector, 'you can't...'

It was Monica. She was waving her arms at a constable who was hot on her heels.

'Inspector, you must listen to me. You must!' She was screaming now. 'He didn't do it, you've got it all wrong, he wasn't even there!' her voice faded away and she sounded defeated, but the inspector turned to look at her.

'Sit down, Miss Campbell, and calm yourself. I'll listen to you. We must go into another room first. Come with me.' He was speaking quite gently to her. 'How is your aunt?'

Monica looked at Dr Fitzhugh and said, 'It isn't good news, Uncle. The consultant saw Auntie and he thinks there may be some brain damage. He doesn't hold out much hope for a complete recovery but he said to tell you they're giving her the best care possible. She did look peaceful, lying there asleep. Uncle, I'm going to tell the inspector the truth now. You're not to worry, it can't hurt Aunt Gladys now.' She went out with the inspector.

When they were both sitting in a smaller interview room, Monica across the table from the inspector, he looked benevolently at her.

'Now, ma'am, perhaps you could explain. Take your time, and try to keep calm.'

'I'm sorry, Inspector, I'm not usually so highly strung. My emotions have taken a bit of a hammering of late. I know my uncle didn't have anything at all to do with the deaths of those two young men simply because my aunt did it. I know, Inspector, you don't have to say it: am I just saying this to clear my uncle because my aunt is so ill, close to death? No, I'm not Inspector. I can prove to you my aunt killed those young men because I was there; at least, I was at the end.' She paused.

'My uncle was away that weekend. He was at a conference – "Health issues and POWs". He was miles away. He'd told my aunt he would cancel the chaps coming to do the garden but she'd said to leave it. She was quite happy to tell them what there was to do and to give them a cup of tea. She said she was not at all afraid of these two young men and that he was to go off to his conference and not to worry. So he did.

'I was in London that weekend. I remember it so clearly, the details have never left me. I'd been to a concert, it had been a lovely evening with a young man I was very fond of. When I got home, the phone was ringing. It was Aunt Gladys. She sounded distraught. I got rid of my young man – I can't remember what I said; family crisis or something – and drove straight down to Somerset.

'What she'd said, Inspector, was that she'd poisoned two prisoners of war. They were dead, in the kitchen, but they were too heavy for her to move their bodies. I couldn't believe it. I drove like a madwoman but luckily I got there in one piece. She told me she'd killed the young Germans who had murdered Bunty.

'Well, I hadn't been to their house very often during the war. My parents were alive, and I was usually at home; not like now when I spend most weekends with my aunt and uncle.' She started to get upset again, but it was just the thought that those happy weekends were likely to be all over now.

'I didn't know that Auntie even knew there had been a suspicion of murder. I'd told Uncle what had aroused my suspicions in Berlin, but he'd not wanted her to know and we both thought she hadn't heard and didn't know anything.

'You'll never know what I felt when I saw those two prisoners in her kitchen, completely dead. Of course, she was a doctor's wife, so she knew all about poisons. She'd been a nurse herself before she married Uncle, and a very good one. She told me she used cyanide.

'She said she knew they'd killed Bunty, she had heard my conversation with Hugh, and they weren't going to get away with it. If anything could be worse after that, it came then. As I looked round the kitchen towards the bodies, I recognised one as Paul Langstein, the young student at the Berlin Institute whom Bunty had been so fond of. I felt no purpose would be served by telling her she'd got the wrong man. Anyway, I had no doubt that his elder brother, Karl, had something to do with Bunty's untimely death.

'Auntie said she knew a good place to put the bodies, but she needed my help to get them down there. The house where Simon and Lydia live now was empty. My uncle used it for infectious patients and as a common room for the district nurses, who of course weren't around on a Saturday night. It seems very macabre now but we actually used a wheelbarrow and took them round the back way, one at a time. We dragged them to the icehouse, dug down to uncover the trapdoor and pushed them down one after the other, feet first. We replaced the trapdoor, pushed back the earth, and next morning we transferred a couple of shrubs over the spot. Uncle never noticed anything; he was always busy with his own garden, he hardly ever worked on the one next door, as he'd put in trees there to minimise the labour. By the time he next went round there the shrubs were established and that is how they remained I presume until the severe storm the other week.'

Monica was exhausted. However much the inspector may have wanted to charge the doctor, her story did ring true. He knew he'd be able to check the dates of the conference and probably even whether or not the doctor had attended, but he didn't feel it would be necessary.

They went back to the main interview room. Hugh looked up expectantly and his solicitor got to his feet.

'You know, Inspector, I really have to go, unless you are going to question my client further. I have been here for nearly three hours and I have other appointments.'

'It's all right, sir. Your client is free to go but his niece may like you to stay, just for a short while longer, while I get her statement down. I'm not sure whether there'll be further charges for Miss Campbell, but that will be decided later.'

Dr Fitzhugh looked astonished and worried.

'It's all right, Uncle. I have told the inspector the truth. It can't hurt Aunt Gladys now.'

'But I don't know what happened, Monica! What is "the truth"?' He still looked bewildered.

'Of course, Uncle, you never knew anything about it, did you? Auntie Gladys kept her secret for twenty-five years, but I will explain everything when we're at home together.'

The inspector looked at the doctor and went to shake his hand.

'You know not much good has resulted from this whole affair. Three people dead, suspicion and despair, but there's one fact you may want to hold on to. If you're prepared to meet them halfway, the Langsteins would like to be friends – for Bunty's and Paul's sake, and especially for Paulo's.'

Epilogue

The grey sky cast a backcloth to the sombre gathering around the plot in a peaceful corner of the English churchyard. There was a sadness present that seemed to cloak the whole group within its folds.

Karl Langstein stood dignified and soldierly. His wife, Liesl, stood by his side, still an attractive woman, though the years had taken their toll. There was a great compassion in her eyes. Maria and Paulo gazed intently at the headstone. Their feelings were mixed, and Hugh stood alongside Monica, drawing strength from their mutual closeness. Simon and Lydia gazed at the others, overwhelmed by the sheer drama of the whole chain of events that they had unleashed.

The remains of the Langstein brothers, Paul and Karl, had been returned to Berlin for interment in the family plot.

As if in a Shakespearean tragedy, they had been drawn together; and tragedy would ensure their continued understanding and compassion for one another.

ACT TWO:
HIDDEN TESTAMENT

Chapter Seventeen

The air rumbled to the sound of gunfire. A pall of smoke hung over the Petershagen district of Berlin where the 23rd Motorised Division of the SS Niederland was locked in a desperate defensive action with Marshal Zhukov's 1st Belorussian Army.

The assault on the German capital had been launched on the 16 April 1945 by 2,500,000 Russian personnel, over 6,000 tanks, and 7,500 aircraft under the command of Rokossovsky and Zhukov.

Opposed to them were the German defence forces of 1,000,000 men; over 1,500 tanks; and over 3,000 aircraft, 75 per cent of the total strength of the Luftwaffe, commanded by General Weidling, General Heinrich, Colonel Von Duwing and General Keitel. Hitler had assumed the overall command of the defence of the city... the defence force was further supported by 200 battalions of the *Volkssturm*, mostly sixteen to seventeen-year-old youths trained in the use of the *Panzerfaust* anti-tank weapons. These units were performing miracles in defence against the Russian T24 tanks, whose mobility was severely frustrated in the desperate street fighting. The battle was proving the most fearful of the whole war. A vengeful Russian assault against a fanatical defence. Little quarter was shown by either side.

Hitler faced his commanders across the large conference table in the imposing surroundings of the heavily fortified Reichstag building. His body stoop was more pronounced and the strain was visible in the greyness of his face. Joseph Goebbels and Martin Bormann, the deputy Führer, were also there. The Americans had reached Torgau but they had not advanced further onto the city. It was only a matter of time before the Bolsheviks sealed the gap.

Most of those present were aware of the futility of further resistance.

From reports coming in, however, the Third Panzer Army in

the north and the Fourth Panzer Army in the south together with the Ninth Army and 1st Field Army seemed to be holding their positions. The meeting closed and Bormann and Goebbels accompanied Hitler on an inspection of a group of the *Volkssturm* – teenage troops.

The sheer energy of the Russian attack was, nevertheless, gradually eroding the German defence. On the night of the 25 April the Russians carried out a bombing raid of immense magnitude. 543 aircraft took part and 569 tons of bombs rained on the city.

On 1 May, Sergeants Yegorov and Kantariya of the 756th Russian Regiment under the command of Colonel Zinchenko had raised the Russian flag over the Reichstag, though the building was still occupied by German forces.

On 2 May, five days before the final surrender, Hitler called the remnants of the German High Command to a meeting to the bunker in the grounds of the *Reichskanzlerei*. They included Bormann and Goebbels. A peace overture had been made to the Russians but they would not agree to anything other than unconditional surrender, which would guarantee the lives of the armed forces and allow the officers to keep their small arms. This had been rejected. Hitler's policy of Gotterdämmerung would continue.

He would marry Eva Braun and write a will designating the Führer apparent. The conference was dismissed. Martin Bormann was asked to remain behind. Hitler faced Bormann. They had been close associates for so long. He had relied heavily on Bormann's organising abilities and his steadfast loyalty. He could think of no other person more suited to the task.

Bormann gazed at the Führer, who spoke. 'I have written my will and in it I have named you Führer designate. The Third Reich must not perish after my death.'

Amidst all the chaos, Bormann felt sheer elation.

Hitler continued, 'Eva Braun and I will die here in the bunker and our bodies will be burnt to ashes. The Bolsheviks will not have their satisfaction.'

He added further. 'You must take the will and other docu-ments and try to escape from Berlin.'

Bormann had no illusions of the dangers confronting him. The city was heaving with Russian and German forces. Wearing a paratrooper's smock and trousers and using subways and drainage tunnels, he had reached the University building, or what was left of it, and it was here that his luck ran out. Crouching by the ruins of the entrance, he felt a searing pain streak into his back. He knew he had been hit by a sniper bullet. Dragging himself along and stumbling, he entered the building and made his way down to the basement. A slight movement in the darkness alarmed him. Drawing his Luger, he aimed into the shadows.

'If you're German come out where I can see you, otherwise I will shoot!' he called.

From the darkness emerged a dishevelled figure clutching a cello case. On closer inspection it appeared to be a youth of seventeen or eighteen years. He wore a uniform of same kind.

'Come here!' croaked Bormann. Blood was seeping through his clothing from the bullet wound in his back, and waves of dizziness kept sweeping over him.

'Closer, boy. I'm seriously hurt, so listen carefully. Are you a member of the party?'

'*Ya, mein Herr*, but of course. I was a music student here at the University until I joined the *Volkssturm*.'

'Then take these documents in the case. Guard them with your life. There is an address inside take them there make your way to Torgau, where the Americans are waiting, and try to escape into Germany.' His breathing was becoming laboured and a haze hung in front of his eyes.

'Do you understand? This is a direct order from the Führer's office.'

'Yes, *mein Herr*. I'll do as you say. Is there anything that I can do for you' Bormann's head lolled forward. 'Your name?'

'Boris – Boris Schmidt *mein Herr*.'

Five days later on 5 May the Berlin Garrison surrendered.

The long grey train glided into the Hauptbahnhof Station in Berlin. No ordinary travellers were on board this train. Middle-aged men; hollow-cheeked men, men with vacant, lifeless eyes. Some wore remnants of military wear: a field cap here, a leather belt there, with some sort of insignia on the buckle.

On the station platform a group of journalists with their photographers waited expectantly. The train doors slid open and bewildered grey figures descended onto the platform carrying pathetic bundles and old battered suitcases.

The once proud members of the Wehrmacht were returning from Russia. From coal mines, from farm units; from building projects. From a life burdened with toil. A life sentence to slavery.

The year was 1973: twenty-eight years after the end of a world conflict of cataclysmic proportions.

Max Jurgens looked around him. At fifty-five years of age, he looked older. He was a stranger in his own country.

It was a lifetime ago when he had chauffeured the most notorious, ruthless and absolute leader that Germany had ever spawned, Adolf Hitler.

He'd known exquisitely tailored uniforms. The most expensive hand-made limousines. Gone now forever. Now just a shabby piece of human flotsam.

Yet descending upon these tawdry remnants of Germany's once glorious military past were fresh, eager faces, mostly young, asking questions, taking photographs. Almost ghoulish in their seeking out some pathetic victim. Like something out of Rider Haggard's *King Solomon's Mines*, when the obscene Gagool, the wizened witch doctor of Chaka, the Zulu king, descended among the ranks of the terrified warriors paraded in front of the king, seeking out her victims. Then she would strike at the selected individual with her lion's tail to identify the victim for the execution squad standing poised with their spears ready to stab and cut.

'*Bitte, mein Herr*. May I ask you one or two questions?'

He was young. Innocent. He'd never seen humanity at its most savage, consumed with a ruthless all-consuming bloodlust for its tormentors, and ready to tear the guts from a fellow human being.

Yes! He was very young.

'Have you a cigarette? A real cigarette with tobacco?'

'Sorry, but I don't smoke. But come with me and I'll buy you a coffee and a packet of cigarettes.'

Max could see only creature comfort. It had been so long. The

Railway Restaurant reeked of tempting smells coffee and cigarette smoke. Max found himself breathing in the atmosphere like an addict in a drug-soaked opium den.

'Here, let me take your things,' said the reporter.

'Your things! What things? A battered old cardboard suitcase!' Max grinned almost bitterly.

With a steaming cup of coffee and a large cigarette in his hand, and blue nicotine-laden smoke hovering around his head, Max almost swooned with ecstasy.

The young reporter was keen but saw this was not a moment to hurry. 'May I ask you your name?' He finally opened the interview.

'My name? Ah! Yes. I have a name. Max. Max Jurgen, aged about fifty-five; occupation ex-Bolshevik slave. Once a resident of Berlin and Berchtesgaden. Previous occupation, chauffeur to the supreme head of the German State, Adolf Hitler! And member of the all conquering German Wehrmacht. And now, young man, I should like to go quietly mad!'

The reporter looked bewildered. 'Do you mind if I telephone my editor? I won't be long.'

'Be as long as you like – I'm not going anywhere,' Max replied sardonically.

'Get the exclusive rights to his story,' said the editor. 'Offer him 10,000 marks.'

The reporter was mildly surprised at the sum, but then there was still a fascination with the old swastika regime.

Max was more than pleased with the arrangement. Particularly as he was accommodated in an above-average yet modest hotel. He was clothed in a fashionable style, bathed and perfumed. The whole business was almost unbearable.

The story flowed unabated: the triumphal parades through conquered foreign capitals; the excursions to Berchtesgaden, Hitler's mountain retreat; the hidden life of the Führer and Eva Braun. The exclusive was worth every mark.

'Tell me about the final days,' said the journalist.

'Dramatic; heroic; tragic; frustrating; terrifying! The sheer destruction of life and property. From the air and land. Civilians stood no chance whatsoever. Gotterdämmerung was their fate for betraying Hitler's dreams of the 1,000-year Reich.

'Remorse was never an emotion shown within the Nazi Command. For them the survival of the Third Reich was paramount. Hitler before his suicide had boasted its perpetuation. Openly confiding his plans to me, Max, Martin Bormann would continue as Reichsführer and he had personally ordered Bormann to escape from the beleaguered Berlin. He entrusted most of the party's confidential papers to his care, together with Hitler's last will and testament making Bormann Führer apparent.

'He had then ordered me to douse both Hitler and Eva Braun's bodies in petrol and burn the remains absolutely.

'Eva Braun was shot by Hitler, who then shot himself – it had all been very melodramatic. The rest is history. It meant my own imprisonment and confinement, working on various labour projects in the reconstruction of the war-damaged Soviet Union.

'As far as the world was concerned we had become Germany's lost legions. That was until the easing of the so-called cold war.'

The presses rolled. Magazines, periodicals and supplements carried their own versions.

In a moated fortress deep in the forests of Bavaria the articles were scrutinised with intense interest.

Chapter Eighteen

Willi was a gang foreman for the Berlin Municipal Gas Company. He lived in a modest house on the outskirts of Berlin with his lovely wife, Gretchen, and his two beautiful children.

He made a good living, and in the year 1973 that gave quite a comforting feeling – particularly in the West, where consumer goods were plentiful and available. Content with his lot, Willi neither wanted nor sought upheaval.

The day commenced routinely. He had breakfast with his wife and children. Greta, his daughter, was eight years of age, and with her mother's flaxen hair and Nordic good looks was the apple of his eye. Mark, his son, was six years old, and with his father's looks, was Willi's pride and joy.

Both children went to the local junior school.

Kissing his wife and children goodbye, he climbed into his red Volkswagen Beetle and headed for the Gas Depot.

For the past week or so he had been working in the basement of the Berlin University.

The gang were in their usual jocular mood. Ribald remarks fell on droopy tired looks. Too much night-time energy, and so on and on and on…

The ruined basements had to be cleared before new piping could be installed. Some of the rubble must date back to the old wartime street battles and air raids. The whole of the district had taking quite a hammering, from the Chancellery and spreading out through the Behrenstrasse and Wilhelmstrasse and beyond.

My God! Those old Berliners must have taken a pasting! How could they have fallen for all that Hitler spiel and swastika jazz?

The gang had fixed up some floodlights to work under. The work in such a confined space was both hard and sweaty. A JCB would have taken half the time but the site was too narrow.

It was about three o'clock in the afternoon when Jake called over to him. 'Willi, come over here quick!' He was looking at something in the hole.

'What is it Jake?' asked Willi, anxiously scrambling over the piles of rubble. 'Hey! That's not rubble. It looks more like a human skull!'

No doubt about it. The sightless eye sockets and the maniacal show of teeth.

'Right! Everyone stop work and clear the site... All of you – and don't disturb anything further. Karl – get to the site office and call the police!'

The whole area had been cordoned off and Inspector Kruger gazed at the bones. This was not an unusual incident. Bones and skeletons were continually being disturbed in these old ruins. Mostly they were wartime victims of bombs and shells.

'Better wait for the forensic boys. They usually cleared the sites promptly,' he said. Still he was intrigued. You never know. The bones were old and there were metallic pieces buckles and insignia and a rusted Luger pistol one of those normally carried by officers of the old Wehrmacht.

Later at the pathologist's laboratory he cast his eye over the complete skeleton. It looked even more grotesque.

'Well, Doctor, what have you found out?'

'Inspector, this is a strange and macabre case. A bullet was lodged into the lower spine. He may have died from that wound. Ballistics seem to think that it is from a high velocity rifle, perhaps Russian, used in a sniper's weapon! There is, however, something further and more interesting. In the tooth's cavity there are minute traces of glass. Not much; in fact very thin and in small quantities. If I were to hazard a guess, it seems to be in the form of a capsule, perhaps a cyanide capsule. Now that would indicate a high-ranking official. A very high-ranking official, perhaps of the inner government body. I think, Inspector, you have on your hands the skeleton of a fat cat. A very, very fat Nazi bastard cat!'

'You may want to bring in some wartime archivists. Even War Crimes organisations; perhaps the Simon Wiesenthal organisation,' concluded the doctor.

'Thank you. I think you're right. I need to investigate this at a higher level,' said the inspector.

This was definitely different from the normal bag of bones.

The voice at the end of the telephone line sounded cool, efficient and very feminine. Very charming. 'Yes, the Wiesenthal organisation is extremely interested. Look, Inspector, a cyanide capsule means somebody very big in the old Nazi set-up. There weren't many who had access to them. Off the top of my head the only prominent Nazi of that rank not accounted for is the Deputy Führer, Martin Bormann. We've had various false alarms, even one that suggested that Bormann had been a Russian agent and was living in quiet seclusion in Russia. Nothing confirmed. Your find sounds exciting. I think a full-scale investigation would be well worthwhile.'

He thanked her for her advice and promised to follow it up.

There followed an exhaustive investigation. Dental records. The latest blood tests, using samples taken from Bormann's surviving children. There were experimental tests now taking place whereby cells from any body part can be coded with related descendants.

It seemed beyond all shadow of doubt that the skeleton found by Willi and his work gang was that of Martin Bormann, the Deputy Führer of the Nazi Party.

The discovery and confirmation solved one of the mysteries that had puzzled the Western world since the end of the war in Europe.

The newspapers gave the news full worldwide coverage.

These revelations were of particular interest to a group of well-dressed businessmen gathered round a conference table in a moated fortress, deep in the Bavarian forests. At long last the end was in sight.

The road wound its way through the dripping trees. The thick undergrowth encroaching threateningly towards the narrow strip of tarmac.

The journey from Karlsruhe had been tedious despite the creature comforts and luxury of the stretch limousine.

'Not long now, *mein Herr!*' said the chauffeur.

Just then they rounded a bend in the road and passed a few isolated woodland cottages. There, rearing up like some collection of grotesque grey stone stalagmites, stood the massive mediaeval fortress surrounded by a seemingly primeval forest.

Its origins dated back to the feudal home of some local war-lord. The whole structure was encircled by a wide moat and accessed only by the drawbridge.

The car waited on the approach causeway while being vetted by the burly gate attendant. A short telephone conversation with a wall set ensued, and they were allowed to proceed.

A short passage through the thick walls led to the inner court-yard and the main entrance.

A keen observer would spot the watching eyes from the figures scattered around the parapets. Erich descended from the car and entered the massive and imposing double doors through a smaller wicket door.

Inside was an imposing foyer. A large mirror was placed on one wall. Erich knew that it had two-way views. His reflection gazed back at him. He was well set up physically and more than six feet tall, with a thick head of fair hair and Nordic blue eyes. He made a handsome figure, dressed in a fashionable and expensive casual suit, a soft shirt and blue woollen tie with soft tan suede shoes on his feet.

The lobby led into the main hall. It was panelled in oak and decorated with collections of ancient weaponry: swords, muskets, spears etc., interspersed with coats of armour and heraldic insignia. The whole scene was one of Teutonic grandeur.

The whole of the centre of the hall was occupied by a large heavy oak table with solid throne-like chairs. Facing this was a grand wood-burning fireplace with rampant iron lions on the firedogs.

A manservant appeared. 'The Count will be with you in a moment, *mein Herr*.'

A few minutes later Count von Reinhardt entered from what appeared the study. A tall, greying figure, he was dressed in riding breeches and a black Kashmir polo-necked sweater. He wore riding boots in a soft buckskin and carried a riding crop in his hand.

Count von Reinhardt was a former Lieutenant-Colonel of the SS Panzer Lanz that had fought in Russia and Italy in the '39-'45 war. The fortress had been in the Reinhardt family since the wars of the Teutonic Knights.

'Erich, I'm delighted to see you. Did you have a pleasant journey? I know we are somewhat isolated here but believe me it is a small price to pay for the security it affords.' He smiled. 'The helicopter is due back tomorrow so your return trip will be much quicker.'

'*Mein Herr*,' said Erich, clicking his heels in the old Prussian style, 'I'm here as you requested and ready for any assignment.'

'No hurry, my dear boy. I would like you to stay for a few days. I am having some important guests for the weekend and I want you to meet them. I've arranged for you to have the use of the west tower suite. You will find everything you need there, even down to the toothpaste. Felix will show you the way. We dine at seven o'clock. We will meet again then… *auf Wiedersehen* for the present.'

Felix led the way to the elevator. The whole interior of the castle reeked of German history. Fine tapestries and pictures of medieval battle scenes adorned the oak panelled walls.

'This way, sir!' said Felix, as he opened the large panelled door.

The apartment was completely self-contained. There was a large double bedroom with silk sheets and a lounge area with thick pile carpet. Beautifully upholstered furniture. A large bathroom with a separate shower. A miniature gymnasium… and Ingrid!

She had draped herself on the large divan settee.

She also was wearing riding breeches and a sweater. 'Wearing' was perhaps an inadequate description.

The sweater left little to the imagination, for together with the britches they both covered and moulded to her exquisite figure. Her Saxon hair framed the high cheekbones of her face. Two eyes shone almost emerald green in colour and sparkle. A petite nose tilted over slightly full lips. A smile showed her even white teeth.

'I hope you don't mind my being here. Father asked me to see you settled into your accommodation.'

Erich's thoughts were too intimate to express. This beautiful creature looked almost nymph-like in the Bavarian setting of forest and castle. His voice sounded surprisingly calm.

'Very kind of you, but everything seems to have been taken

care of. I had intended to take a shower and change before dinner,' he added. 'Will you be dining with us?' There was a hint of anxiety in his voice.

'Of course I shall, but tomorrow we have guests arriving, I understand Father wishes to discuss some business arrangements. No doubt you are here also for that meeting?' she added.

'Yes. That is the arrangement as far as I am aware,' he replied.

'Do you ride, *Herr*... what do I call you?' Ingrid was curious.

'Erich will do... and what do I call you?'

'Ingrid. Would that do, or must we be more formal?' She was teasing him.

'That will do nicely.' A slightly flirtatious note was creeping into their conversation. 'Yes, I do ride, but I have no suitable clothes...' he replied.

'Um! I think we can fix you up with some jodhpurs and a suitable top. Leave it to me. I'll have a word with Felix, and he will bring them along for you. So that's settled. Tomorrow morning then after breakfast!'

She left, leaving a slight hint of expensive cologne.

The meal was delicious.

There were just the three of them. Ingrid's mother had died five years previously; a haemorrhage. She never recovered from the coma.

Ingrid looked wonderful in her simple black dress and single pearl earrings with one string of pearls around her shapely neck.

'Our guests will be arriving tomorrow in the helicopter. There will be thirteen altogether. I understand that you are both going riding in the morning. Take care – there are wild boar in the forest,' the Count concluded.

After coffee and liqueurs he said that he had some work to catch up on before the morning. Excusing himself, he left the two of them together.

'Would you like to see a stunning view?' Ingrid asked.

'Love to!' said Erich. They made their way to the castle parapets. There was a full moon and the sky was cloudless. The moonlight cast its diffused light over the treetops, creating a symphony of shadows and intricate designs.

146

Ingrid stood close. Erich felt her body heat and caught that teasing hint of expensive perfume. Neither talked; it seemed unnecessary. The whole scene – battlements, forest and open spaces – was bathed in an incandescent light.

'I love this view,' she murmured. 'It's so fairylike, castles and goblins. All very mysterious.

She shivered a little and he placed his arm around her slim shoulders. She pressed closer. 'Do you…?'

She turned her face towards him. The sentence remained unsaid. Slowly he lowered his face towards hers and there was no resistance. They kissed lightly, though stirrings of deeper passions were not far away.

'We had better say "goodnight" until the morning, Erich.' Then she was gone.

He remained for a while, deep in his own thoughts. This was a complication he had not foreseen. His lifestyle did not afford the luxury of falling in love.

To be in love would slow his movements. A partner would be demanding. She'd want to know his whereabouts. Then there is the danger. Obsession with self-protection would frustrate risk-taking.

He could not afford the luxuries of a love affair. Yet Ingrid was making demands on his latent passions, passions that should be disciplined and under cast-iron control.

He must talk to her.

Breakfast was a frugal affair. Fruit juice, croissants, toast and jam and strong black coffee. Erich's jodhpurs fitted comfortably and a sheepskin top sat easily on his broad shoulders.

The stable block was sumptuously appointed for the five superb horses. Ingrid sat on a beautiful roan mare called Sheba. They complemented each other.

Erich sat on a gorgeous black stallion. A satin sheen covered the horse's coat and his muscles rippled. He was in the peak of condition and had two large roaming black eyes. His name was Jason and he was obviously restless for his morning gallop. Erich liked the English saddle. Jason fretted a little but soon realised who was in charge. They wasted little time and cantered across the causeway and out onto the forest trail.

They pushed the horses at a hard gallop for a mile or so through the leafy forest, then reining to a fast trot so as not to wind them. Both mounts were then content to continue at a slow walk.

Occasionally a wild boar broke from the undergrowth and hurried across their paths, but the beasts were more interested in foraging.

They dismounted and sat on a fallen trunk overlooking a delightful forest glen. There seemed a little shyness between them.

'Erich! Something has happened and it is disturbing my usual tranquil self.' Ingrid was not entirely in control of her voice and was finding it difficult to choose the right words.

Erich was aware of her dilemma. 'Look, Ingrid, I think I know what you are trying to say, but let me speak first. You know very little about me: where I come from, what I do, where I am going, my background.' He paused. 'I think that you feel as I do. We have met and we like one another.' He was now beginning to struggle but carried on. 'Please don't take offence at what I have to say. My lifestyle is precarious and most of the time my life is at serious risk. I carry out assignments ruthlessly without too much compassion. I am a political animal and I cannot afford the luxury of human emotions.'

Ingrid was quiet and pensive for some time.

'Thank you, Erich, for being so honest. You don't mind if we remain friends?' There was a sadness in her voice.

'Ingrid, I am finding this extremely difficult, but yes, please. Your friendship would mean so much to me. Friendship would be safe. I couldn't bear to hurt you. You may realise what a strain I am putting on reason and logic!' He felt confused.

'Yes, Erich. I know what you are trying to say and how difficult it is for you to say it. Do you mind if we start back now?'

They rode back in silence.

As they neared the castle there was a loud clatter as a large helicopter landed in the courtyard. The horses shied a little but soon settled.

'I will see you at dinner,' Ingrid called to him, and then hurried inside. Her eyes were moist, Erich noticed. He shivered. There was restlessness within him.

He showered and helped himself to a whisky from the miniature bar.

The internal phone rang. 'Erich, could you come down to the hall?' It was von Reinhardt. Throwing on a jacket, Erich went downstairs.

Seated around the conference table were thirteen prosperous-looking businessmen. Many looked ex-military.

'Ah, Erich, take a seat.' There was one vacant chair at the table.' I would introduce you, but it is better if we remain anonymous; but rest assured we are all united in the same cause.'

It was then that Erich noticed that each of the thirteen had a medal attached to a black and silver ribbon around their necks. Gold oak leaves surrounding the Iron Cross studded with diamonds. It was the highest award for valour – the Grand Knight of the Order of the Iron Cross.

'Yes, Erich, as you can see you are sitting with the survivors of the Grand Order created by Adolf Hitler. Many reached the highest ranks of the Luftwaffe, the Kriegsmarine, the Wehrmacht, the security forces and the SS. Between them they control over half a million patriots; not your rowdy thugs, but middle class professionals in banking, communications, transport, law, government, even the church. Sufficient to paralyse the country should the call arise.' There was a glint of pride and power in von Reinhardt's eyes as he continued.

'Each Knight has his own coat of arms, which you can see displayed on the walls over their chairs. You could say that we represent the present day Teutonic Knights. Unlike the ancients, however, we don't use the lance and sword, but the latest technology and sophisticated weaponry.

'All of which costs vast amounts of money. So far our funds have been adequate to finance the groundwork,' he continued, warming to his subject.

'Before the fall of Berlin, large sums of money were transferred to worldwide capital ventures; bearer bonds; gold, works of art. The plan was to diversify on a global scale. We also used Swiss bank accounts. Now when I say large amounts, I am talking of billions in present values. The whole plan was master-minded by one man, who recorded and listed the total assets and their locations and code numbers. That man was Martin Bormann, the Deputy Führer, who, as you know, disappeared from Berlin in 1945.' Reinhardt sipped some water from the glass in front of him.

'Since 1945 we have searched the world for some sign that he is still alive... without success. However, recently there have occurred three incidents that may provide us with a breakthrough. A returning prisoner of war from Russia was interviewed by the press, as you all know, and disclosed that he had been Adolf Hitler's chauffeur, and was the last person to see the Führer alive. In fact his task was to burn the bodies of Eva Braun and Hitler after they had both committed suicide. Now, this chauffeur has said that Hitler told him that a will had been made conferring the leadership after his death upon Martin Bormann, and that Bormann had also been given highly confidential state documents to take with him in an escape attempt from beleaguered Berlin.'

The Count continued, 'A skeleton uncovered in the vicinity of the Humboldt Universität has been positively identified as that of Martin Bormann. Since then a most interesting revelation has come from an interview with a famous cellist, who is performing at this time with the Berlin Philharmonic Orchestra in Bath, England. His name is Boris Schmidt, and he claims that he met Bormann when he was a young eighteen-year-old music student in Berlin. He was sheltering in the University from the street fighting and shelling. Bormann had been shot, but he had spoken to this Boris Schmidt... some conclusions,' added von Reinhardt.

'Hitler handed to Martin Bormann State documents, including details of large deposits of money, and the last will and testament handing power over to Bormann.

'Bormann was shot in the vicinity of the Humboldt University and met the student, Boris Schmidt. The documents were handed to the student for safe keeping and possible delivery to a safe address.

'All suspicion points to the cellist, Boris Schmidt, having kept the documents; but he does not know their importance. Assuming that he has them they must be in a secure place.'

Reinhardt paused and gazed around the table. There were many heroic faces amongst the group: von Vaerst, General

Halder, Schmidt, Hoth, Klein and Rudiger. With the others, it sounded like a Roll of Honour.

'I have invited Erich here, who is the leader of our number one Kommando. It's one of many Kommandos held in readiness for direct action. These teams have been trained in the style of the old Brandenburgers under the leadership of Skorzeny, who, by the way, is gravely ill but has given us the benefit of his experience and expertise. I propose that we send his Kommando of six men to England to locate these documents by maintaining a round the clock surveillance of Schmidt. The team will make a tactful search of his premises for any possible leads. The whole exercise to be strictly covert so as not to arouse suspicion. I don't believe the cellist knows what he is sitting on. Are we all agreed?'

The thirteen looked at one another and nodded. Rudiger spoke out.

'Count, it must be emphasised that it is important that no suspicions are provoked. We have worked hard and long to keep our organisation secret. Should anything go wrong, no member of the Kommando must subject themselves to interrogation. The leader will ensure this by eliminating any member captured or liable to be captured. This will, of course, include himself. Is that understood?' Rudiger was an aristocrat, cold and ruthless, a man used to hard discipline and immediate obedience.

'Of course, *mein Herr*. This will be a condition put to every member,' said Erich.

'Well, gentlemen, if we are agreed then our business is concluded and the final details we can leave to Erich and we all wish him *viel gluck!*'

The meeting broke up and the Knights adjourned until dinner.

The meal was a leisurely event. Ingrid looked captivating in a simple cadmium red dress. It was ankle length with a square cut neckline, set off with jet-black jade necklace and eardrops, and black patent leather wedge-heeled shoes. The whole ensemble matched her Saxon hair and fresh, outdoor complexion with a minimum of make-up.

Conversation was confined to trivialities, but emotional tensions were not far from the surface.

'When are you leaving?' she asked.

'Tomorrow at midday,' Erich replied, keeping his voice tone as natural as possible.

There was a sadness between them. 'When shall I hear from you again?' She was trying to keep any hint of desperation from her voice.

'As soon as I return from England.' He hadn't intended to disclose as much about his mission.

The evening wore on until finally Ingrid excused herself from the rest of the party and bade them all goodnight.

The Knights and Erich then discussed the final details of their plan of action.

He returned to his room unable to shake of his feeling of uneasiness. There was something in the air, and a feeling of emptiness inside him that refused to go away.

He poured himself a small whisky, undressed and went into the bedroom. Surely, that was the scent he could detect...

Ingrid was lying on the bed, her beautiful body bathed in the moonlight flowing through the large French windows.

Her sheer beauty took his breath away. His restraints deserted him and a surging passion consumed his body. Words were unnecessary, and their pent-up emotions were released in a violence that consumed them both.

Chapter Nineteen

Simon West called up the stairs to Lydia. 'Is his room ready? I expect he'll be here soon. He'll probably come by train and take a taxi from the station. I don't suppose he's well enough to drive yet. I don't know how long it takes to get over a bypass op, but I should think he'll have to lay off the driving for a while. Strange having someone to stay whom we've never met, but we couldn't really refuse. He's sort of a distant relative your sister's brother-in-law, you say? Not really related to us, then. Still it'll be interesting to meet him, being a musician and a German.'

'You're talking about Boris, I presume? Well, we couldn't not let him stay for a couple of weeks as he's had this operation and has nowhere else to go. It's not much fun in a hotel if you're not feeling 100 per cent. Mark says his sister-in-law is really grateful; she was worried her husband would have to come over here and he doesn't want to leave the farm at the moment,' Lydia replied, coming down the stairs.

'I think he's practically better now anyway. He'll be back in the orchestra in a fortnight; he hopes to join them for the concerts in Bath. Wasn't it a coincidence we saw him in that one in London when we didn't even know who he was? He does play brilliantly. I'm so glad Paulo recommended that we go. He said he'd seen him play several times in Italy. By the way, when is he coming over again? It is nice to see him and Elsa as often as we do; it's great that he keeps in touch with Hugh too,' replied Simon.

'It's great to see Hugh so much better, after all that trouble a couple of years ago. He seems, at last, to have got over Gladys's death. I think he really looks forward to seeing Paulo and Elsa. He and Paulo seem to have a special rapport. It would be perfect if they came over while Boris is still here. We could make up a party to go to his concert. Apparently, he'll be playing two solos in Bath – if he's completely better, of course.'

'Well, we'll do everything we can to make sure he gets really well,' said Simon, going to the window. 'Oh, here's a taxi now, this must be him. I'll get the door.'

Simon and Lydia found Boris to be an excellent guest. He was genuinely pleased to have been invited into their home. He spent several hours each day playing the cello, and not only Simon and Lydia, but their neighbours too enjoyed the lovely tones he was able to coax from the instrument. After the first week Simon drove Boris back to the hospital for a final check-up. Given the 'all clear', Boris rang the orchestra to confirm he'd be well enough to join them all at the Bath concerts, and that he'd be please to play his solos.

The orchestra had been waiting for this confirmation. Now their publicity machine could swing into action. Concerts well attended, along with LPs and tapes, should be the mainstay of the orchestra. Posters were completed and distributed. Space previously reserved in papers and magazines could now be confirmed and interviews set up. 'Is it alright with you if I meet reporters here in your house?' asked Boris of Lydia one morning.

'Of course,' replied Lydia, 'we're enjoying being involved. It's quite exciting for us. Will they be taking photos?'

'Maybe,' said Boris. 'There'll probably be quite a spread in the local papers, they like a bit of human interest. I expect they'll want to know about my operation and what pieces I'm going to play, things like that. Since the Florence concerts I'm getting more used to this sort of treatment. You know, Lydia, I do appreciate you letting me stay here. It's been a lovely time, so peaceful; you've been very kind and my room is really warm and comfortable, and the food has been delicious, I've been really spoilt! Much better than if I'd had to go back to my flat and look after myself, and I don't really like hotels. I see enough of them normally and it's difficult to relax properly. I'm so grateful for your friendship. I hope you'll come to my concerts.'

He handed her a bundle of tickets, and added, 'I have no relations over here and we're given half a dozen tickets, so perhaps you'll bring some friends.'

'How lovely, Boris! Thank you. We're just pleased we've been able to help you out and also that you're now fit and well. Six tickets, that's marvellous! Let's ask Hugh, Simon. I think he'd love it.'

There was more good news when Simon and Lydia called on Hugh after lunch.

'I've just been making up beds.' Hugh was a little short of breath, but in his late seventies he looked relatively fit. He'd had a very bad time in 1938, losing his much loved daughter, then later in 1971, his wife Gladys had a complete breakdown from which she never recovered. Paulo was the son of a close friend of his daughter and when he'd come to England in 1971 for news of his father a close relationship had sprung up between Paulo and Hugh. Paulo had since married a German girl, Elsa, and between them they had brought new happiness and purpose to Hugh's life.

'Paulo and Elsa are arriving this Friday for a week's stay. I'm so looking forward to seeing them again.' His eyes were sparkling. 'I've been getting their room ready.'

'That's marvellous, Hugh. We just came to tell you we've some tickets for Boris's concert. Will you come – and bring Paulo and Elsa? And what about Monica... could she come too? We've six tickets, it would make a lovely evening out. You know, Paulo and Elsa have heard him play before, in Florence. They wrote and recommended him when my brother's sister-in-law asked us if he could stay here. Paulo says he's a brilliant cellist, makes the instrument speak. I'm sure he'd love the chance to hear him again.'

Lydia spoke with great enthusiasm, they'd both liked Paulo and Elsa, and Lydia had made great friends with Monica too. She was Hugh's niece and had been a great support to Gladys when she'd had problems after her daughter's death.

Monica was a senior professor at London University in the German studies department and as such had no problem being able to take weekends off occasionally. Hugh said he would ring.

'Goodness, this will make a really special weekend – all of us together again. Let's all have a meal together before we go to Bath. Oh, it's going to be such fun. Hugh, bring them all round to our house on Saturday. Let's make it lunch, then we'll have plenty of time to drive into Bath for the concert.'

Lydia was already thinking up a menu for a Saturday lunch for six and she was really keen to see Monica again. They got on so well and felt so comfortable in each other's company.

Back in their house, Boris was talking to three reporters who had just arrived. One was from a national paper, one was from *The Concertgoer* and one was from the *Western Gazette*, a local paper that covered Bath and all the Wessex area right down to the South Coast. He enjoyed these sessions, which were still a novelty. Although he'd been a member of the orchestra for many years it was only since his success as a soloist when he'd taken the star part at the Florence concerts three years ago, replacing a guest at the last moment, that he'd been sought after and treated as the famous cellist he'd become. There was no doubt he had a magical touch with the bow and the mellow tones he produced and the accuracy with which he interpreted the music had resulted in him becoming very popular with a considerable following.

'Any extra titbits you can give us, Boris – a bit of human interest?' asked one pressman.

'Don't you think my heart bypass op is human interest?' asked Boris.

'Everyone's having one these days,' joked the Western Gazette reporter. 'Any other claims to fame?'

'Did you grow up in Germany, Boris? Were you in Berlin during the war?' asked the other reporter.

'I wasn't old enough to fight during the war. I was at college in 1945. The only involvement I did have with the Nazi Party and Hitler and so on was when I met Martin Bormann... at least, I think I did; that's whom he said he was. I was only eighteen at the time. It was at the very end of the war.

'The Russians were in Berlin and the Americans and British Armies were holed up just outside the city. There was debris and rubble and bodies all over the place. There were tanks about and everyone was trying to find somewhere to shelter, as there was sniper fire. I was trying to get home from college. I was still in the grounds of the university, crouching against a wall when I heard someone calling.

' "Hey! Hey, you! If you're German come and identify yourself or I'll shoot." The voice sounded desperate, he was choking and very breathy. I didn't think, I just called out, "Yes! I'm

German, don't shoot!" This man crawled forward towards me. He was literally dragging himself along. He was in a paratrooper's smock uniform, but he appeared to be almost gone. I went over to him, rolled up my jacket and put it under his head. He had a gun in his hand and he said, "I'm Martin Bormann, the Deputy Führer. I have been named to take over as the Führer if anything happens to Adolf Hitler." He was gasping for breath. I said I'd try and get some help but he pointed the gun at me and told me to leave him alone. He then said, "Just remember the Third Reich will continue and I Martin Bormann, will lead it." Then he collapsed. I looked about for some help, but some Russian soldiers were approaching and I went down into the basement of the College. When I came out about five minutes later the Russians had disappeared and so had the body. I didn't know if he was dead or alive, but I heard later on that he'd been missing since the day of Hitler's death.'

Boris was reluctant to tell the complete truth and hastily decided not to mention the documents he'd been handed at the time. He felt it politic not to say too much to pressmen. They don't always interpret with total candour.

He continued, 'I thought it was exciting at the time, perhaps it wasn't really Martin Bormann. No one has ever asked me about it and now I've almost forgotten the incident, but it might give you something to mention in your columns.'

A reporter quickly spoke up. 'I don't think you realise how interested people will be. There's been quite a lot of talk about Martin Bormann recently because they've discovered the remains of what looks like a high-ranking German officer with evidence of a bullet wound, only a few weeks ago,' said the reporter. 'Anyway, that aside, you're looking forward to playing on Saturday?' he continued. 'Are you completely well now?'

'Oh, yes!' said Boris. 'I'm attending rehearsals with the orchestra now and I'm really looking forward to the Bath concerts. I'm so grateful to my friends here, Simon and Lydia West. They have helped me so much to get better, but I've relied on their hospitality long enough now. I shall return to my flat in Bath after the concert on Saturday and everything will get back to normal. I feel a new man since my bypass.' Boris smiled at the newsmen.

'One last word, I hope you'll give us lots of good publicity.

The orchestra relies on income from concerts. And I hope the critics are favourable. Well, if that's all, gentlemen, I hope I'll see you on Saturday.'

The interview was over and the pressmen left. Boris didn't realise they were more interested in his revelations of 1945 than with the future concerts. But he wouldn't be left in the dark for long. All the following week the news of him meeting with Martin Bormann remained on the front pages, and although they mentioned the concerts Boris was disappointed that the orchestra don't achieve similar coverage.

He attended all the rehearsals that week and felt satisfied that he'd give a good performance on Saturday. With his friends in the audience he hoped the whole concert would be a great success. He was also looking forward to meeting Paulo and his wife from Italy. Apparently, they'd already heard him play in Florence. Discussing that beautiful city would give them something in common and he was curious about meeting Hugh and his niece, as it seemed they'd had some connection with Berlin many years ago, and he'd be able to converse in German with Monica, who was such an expert on not only the language but the history and culture of Germany too.

Simon and Lydia told Boris the arrangements they'd made for the concert during supper that evening.

'Oh! It'll be so good to see Paulo and Elsa again. And I'm sure Monica will just love it. You haven't met her yet, have you, Boris? She's such a nice person.' Lydia turned to Boris.

'Are you sure you're feeling really well now, Boris? Well enough to do this concert and to move back to your flat and everything? You know you can always stay here a bit longer as long as you like.'

Boris laughed. 'I'm fine now, even the doctors say I can return to work as long as I don't do anything really stupid, and I must get back to the flat. When I'm working I need to be in the city, really, and to attend rehearsals without having to travel too far. I'm so grateful to you for letting me stay here, though, it just gave me the extra time I needed to get back to normal.'

'How did your press interview go?' asked Simon. 'I hope they're going to print lots of good things about you, and the orchestra. How many turned up?'

'Three turned up,' replied Boris. 'One from the national press and one from *Concertgoer*. The other one was from your local paper. It went quite well but they seemed more interested in anecdotes than fact. I suppose that's always the way; "human interest", they call it. It seems to attract the readers more.'

'Oh – what anecdotes? Do tell us,' pleaded Lydia, 'they are usually the more interesting bits good to pass on to friends and use at parties. Do tell us what you told them.'

'Well, the thing that seemed to hold their attention the most was something that happened to me at the end of the war when I was still a student at University studying music. I was so lucky I was too young to take part in the war; a couple more years and I'd have had to fight. Anyway, this was a strange incident. Of course I didn't think anything of it at the time because everything was out of the ordinary but looking back, just recently, I've been thinking it might have some significance.' He told them about the injured man who had called to him way back in 1945 and he added facts that he had not told the pressman.

'He pushed a bundle of papers into my hands. They were enclosed in a waterproofed wallet with an embossed swastika on the cover. When I looked through them, they seemed to be mostly accounts, financial-looking stuff. I don't know who the man was, though he did say that he was Martin Bormann, the Deputy Führer. I assumed he died, because he really looked bad when I saw him, and from the fact he'd disappeared and there were Russian soldiers all over the place. I thought that they had taken him away. I did go and look for the house he'd told me to take everything to but it had been completely destroyed, bombed to the ground. I reasoned that they couldn't have been very important or he wouldn't have given them to me, and no one ever asked about them. Not even at the university did I see anyone or hear about anything being missing. It was such chaos. You wouldn't have believed it if you hadn't been there, everything was chaotic. Of course, I didn't throw them away, I couldn't bring myself to do that. Anyway, they might have historical value, as they do have the name of Adolf Hitler mentioned in several places. I might offer them to a historian or a museum one day.'

'That's very exciting,' commented Simon. 'They'll probably have a considerable value, you know. Some people are really into war papers. They'll collect anything. I'd love to see them. Where do you keep them?'

'They're in the bottom of my trunk back at the flat. I always keep them there, as I move about so often. I don't think they're that valuable except perhaps to a collector of historical papers. However, I've been wondering lately about these neo-Nazi groups that have sprung up since the war... Very nasty; I wouldn't like them to get their hands on them, it's the kind of thing they might be interested in. They have some very unpleasant ways, even menacing, I've heard. That's really why I didn't go into too much detail with those pressmen.' Boris paused and looked at Simon. 'You can have them, if you like, you know, to have a look through. When we go into Bath next tomorrow for the rehearsal when you said you'd drive me up. I'll give them to you and you can have a good look at them; I'd trust your judgement.'

'Okay,' said Simon, 'I'd be able to bring them back when we come up for the concert on Saturday. You're staying in your flat tomorrow night, then?'

'Yes,' Replied Boris. 'Actually, Trevor – the orchestra "gofer" – is going to stay with me and help pack up my stuff. You know we're moving up to Edinburgh on Monday for the Scottish tour? He's a useful young man, does all the odd jobs connected with the musicians and their domestic arrangements. He's also a rather handy percussionist; he's helped out once or twice when the regular chap's been double-booked. He'll save me having to do any lifting etc.'

'I hope you two are ready for coffee now. Would you like a liqueur with it?' asked Lydia. 'Have you got all your plans finalised? You're taking Boris up to Bath tomorrow, aren't you? We've really enjoyed you staying here. I hope the concert tomorrow night won't be the last time we see you.' She went on, 'I say, Simon, maybe we could go over to Berlin to stay with Karl and Liesl some time when Boris is playing over there. Do you often play in Berlin?'

'Yes, I do, it's the home base for the orchestra. Have you friends in Berlin then?'

'Yes,' replied Simon, 'a very nice elderly couple. They're more friends with Hugh. It was really strange how we first met them, but that's another story for another time. I'm for bed now. Then tomorrow Paulo and Elsa arrive, and you're going up to Bath, and Monica will arrive in the evening. It's going to be a really busy day. Goodnight, Boris.'

Chapter Twenty

The estate agent glanced up at the tall stranger. Foreign, by the look of him. Well dressed. Expensive charcoal grey suit. Double-breasted and twin vents at the back of the jacket. Turn-up trousers and dark brown suede shoes, soft striped shirt with a plain red tie. There was one concession to English fashion: a tightly rolled black umbrella with a heavy cane handle. The whole ensemble declared wealth, and plenty of it.

'Good morning, sir! What can I do for you?'

Erich looked at him. About thirty years of age, he guessed. White shirt, striped tie and black trousers. The usual casual business dress that is acceptable these days. Eager, but not too pushy. Successful, judging by the comfortable leather office furniture. There were fitted carpets and the ubiquitous filing cabinets, typewriters and copying equipment. In a corner of the large office an attractive girl was interviewing a prospective client. Erich assumed that attractive and efficient girls were also a ubiquitous part of a well-run office these days.

The estate agency was situated in the High Street of Wittersham, a small provincial town not far from Bath.

Bath itself was an attractive town, virtually a city, built mostly of the warm creamy limestone found in the area of the Cheddar Hills. An ancient Roman Spa centre, famous for its hot springs, it became very fashionable during the Regency in the 1800s, when its magnificent terraces had been built to the designs of Nash. The town exuded culture and expensive living. The famous Pulteney Bridge across the River Avon with its shops, a focal landmark, was very much in the style of the Ponte Vecchio across the river Arno in Florence. It led to Milsom Street and the large concert hall, the Connaught Rooms.

'Good morning,' replied Erich. 'I telephoned yesterday enquiring about a suitable property to rent in the vicinity of Bath. My name is Gruber, Franz Gruber.'

'Ah, yes, Mr Gruber, I remember. You would like to lease a detached property. Large, with at least six bedrooms. Yes, I have, I think, just what you are looking for. A large country estate house situated in its own six acres of rural land. Well modernised; ten bedrooms; most of them en suite; dining area; hall; usual kitchens, etc.; garaging for six cars; formal gardens extending into rough meadowland. The whole estate is enclosed within a six-foot boundary wall. Entrance is by large double wrought iron gates. The whole premises are electronically secured and the main gates are remote-controlled.' The estate agent's face glowed with his own eloquence.

'Thank you, Mr...? What is your name, by the way?' Erich asked.

'Welling, sir! Graham Welling. Here, take a card. It has all the information you require. Telephone number, and home number if you need me, with an answerphone. Here is a brochure of the property. It is situated on the A36 Bristol Road, in a very nice area to the north of Bath.'

Erich glanced at the brochure. It seemed too good to be true.

'You can have a short-term arrangement if you wish. The owners are residing in Australia. They have a business in media communication – you know, television, newspapers etc. And they return to England when their business contacts require or they just wish to break the monotony of living in one place. At present they have just returned to Australia and the house is available for six months. They prefer the idea of someone residing in the property rather than have it empty with just caretaking staff. The six-month lease is for thirty thousand pounds.'

Erich listened. The finer details did not concern him, but he knew he had to play the part. 'It seems ideal for my purposes,' he said. 'I have some friends who wish to absorb the English cultural scene. Concerts, art exhibitions, theatre, festivals and historical locations... When do you want a firm acceptance?'

'Well, these properties are popular, particularly when hotel standards vary so much. I would definitely recommend a fairly quick decision if you think that it suits your requirements,' the agent replied.

'May I use your telephone?' Erich asked.

'Certainly sir. You can use the private office.'

Erich dialled a London number. 'Hello Kurt? Erich here. Have the others arrived?'

'Yes, Erich. They are all here,' said Kurt, his second in command.

'Good,' continued Erich. 'I want them to drive down to this address and to arrive in pairs and separately. Bring all the equipment with you and spread the arrival times over three days. You will find three Land-Rovers hired and waiting collection at Hertz.'

'I understand,' said Kurt. 'We will begin arriving from tomorrow onwards. Goodbye.' He rang off. Long telephone conversations could be dangerous.

Erich returned to the estate agent.

'I'd like the lease to commence as from today, if that is possible?'

'Certainly, sir! That can be arranged. No problem. Will you be conducting the documentation, or your solicitor?' replied the agent.

'No I wish to finalise everything now, today!' Erich replied emphatically.

'Very good, sir! I'll get the lease forms for you to complete. If you could let me have your cheque I see no reason for you not to have the keys today. Are you sure you wouldn't like to view the property beforehand?' The agent was anxious not to delay the transaction but thought he should show some business caution.

'No, thank you. It is just what I need and my colleagues are arriving from London tomorrow,' replied Erich.

It was all progressing efficiently.

Erich parked his hired Mercedes near the town centre. Bath truly reflected its glorious past. There was an air of prosperity and Englishness about its shopping precincts. Milsom Street, with its department stores; Pulteney Bridge with its shops; the absence of the bustle of London and other major cities. Traffic-free shopping spread its calming influence and sense of leisureliness. The Roman Spa marked the city's ancient heritage.

Any escape route would have to be planned with great care, Erich realised. After three days the whole Kommando was accommodated. Erich called for a meeting in the lounge.

'Our first task is to study the locations: the concert hall and the flat where Boris Schmidt resides. Then we must become familiar with our escape routes. Bristol is the nearest large town and port. It also has an airport. It is also the most obvious target for any pursuit. Southampton, further south, also has ferry and airport facilities, but once again it's an obvious target for pursuers. There is Heathrow, of course. Large, with that advantage but once again a natural target. My own choice is the harbour of Poole, in Dorset. There we have the use of a powerful motor launch, which a sympathiser to our cause has made available. He is willing to cooperate. He also resides within the harbour limits. Poole would attract less attention from any pursuers. There would, however, be a problem with the land route. He gazed at the group. All hand-picked men with impeccable backgrounds. Physically and mentally at their peak and highly motivated. He could not be more content.

'To avoid any accidental incident all small arms will stay here at base. The transport we have is the Land-Rovers and my Mercedes. We must keep a round the clock surveillance on Schmidt, and I suggest we work in pairs; Joseph and Otto; Horst and Raoul; Ludwig and Kurt. On Saturday evening, the night of the concert, Kurt and myself will search the cellist's flat.

'We will meet together on Friday for a final briefing. I suggest you all make your own arrangements for eating. There will, however, be coffee and small snacks available here. There will not on any circumstances be any alcohol – not until the end of the mission! Everyone clear about these arrangements?' They all nodded in agreement and the group dispersed.

It was the last Friday in May and the Kommando was assembled once again in the large lounge.

On one wall was displayed a large Ordnance Survey map showing Bath and the south-west of the English coastline. They gathered around, and Erich handed each one of them a similar copy of the Ordnance map.

'I want you to study a route to Poole Harbour. Avoid the A37. Use, if possible, the A359 then the A357, skirting Blandford, and then onto the A350. It leads all the way to Poole quayside and terminates near the old Custom House mooring. We shall sail at dusk unless we are subject to hot pursuit. The launch will be tethered to the quayside and ready to sail with full fuel tanks. Our destination will be Cherbourg, where transport will be parked in the dockside car park. Each car will show a red sticker in the windscreen. The ignition keys will be on the nearside rear wheel. From there we travel to Karlsruhe. From the airfield at Karlsruhe a helicopter will take us to a rendezvous in the Bavarian Forest. Any questions on the routes?' The group nodded in acquiescence.

'Good,' Erich continued. 'Joseph and Otto. What have you found out?'

Joseph spoke. 'Schmidt has a flat at number twelve, Queen Charlotte Street. It's loaned to him by the floor manager of the concert hall. He visits a friend who lives in Braunton, a small town south of Bath. The friend's name is Simon West. The concert is scheduled for Saturday evening, tomorrow. It commences at seven thirty and will last approximately three hours. Raoul confirmed all this.'

'Right, we stand by the original plan,' continued Erich. 'Kurt and I will search Schmidt's flat on Saturday evening during the concert. The rest of you will stand by for back-up should anything unforeseen happen. Any questions?'

Dusk was falling. People were walking purposefully to their varied rendezvous.

The Mercedes was parked in the shadows. Erich and Kurt approached the main entrance to the apartment in Charlotte Street. Subdued lighting lit the main entrance. Using plastic and master keys Kurt opened the door without much difficulty.

The flat was in darkness. However, confident that they would not be disturbed, they switched on the lights after drawing the blinds. They searched each room thoroughly and they met in the lounge. There had been no sign of any documents. Switching off the lights they approached the door to the apartment when the sound of a key inserted into the lock made them freeze. It couldn't be Boris – he would be halfway through the concert by now.

The door opened and a person entered. Kurt, who was behind the door, flung his arms around the intruder.

'What the devil! Who are you? What are you doing here?' The stranger spluttered.

'Please do not struggle, my friend, and no harm will came to you,' said Erich.

The stranger was young, probably about twenty-five years old. He was quite well built and certainly not intimidated.

Kurt had relaxed his hold and the stranger, seizing his opportunity, made a dash for the door. Kurt recovered quickly. He pulled out his pistol, complete with a fitted silencer and fired. The stranger staggered but did not slacken his momentum. Then, as he stumbled, his head struck the corner of the door and there was a sickening thud as his body slid to the floor. He uttered a dull moan then silence. Kurt examined the body. An ugly gash was trickling blood and an awful gurgling sound came from his throat. Then there was stillness except for an involuntary shudder. 'He's dead, Erich.'

'We had better make it look like a burglary, now,' Erich replied. 'We hadn't planned on a body. Turn the place over and get out quick!'

They opened the main door and listened. All was normal. They quit the building. People were walking casually about their business. Some young people were laughing together in the flirtatious manner of mixed company.

The two Germans walked unhurriedly to the Mercedes and drove slowly from the location.

The following day was Sunday and the group assembled in the lounge.

Erich was looking pensive. 'My friends, we have had a slight hiccup. Unfortunately we were disturbed at the apartment and there was a fatal accident. There was no sign of any documents. I propose, therefore, that we kidnap Boris Schmidt and bring him here for questioning. Raoul and Ludwig are shadowing him today. The police been at the apartment but have now left. We will make this a combined operation and join Raoul and Ludwig, and when the opportunity arises we take Schmidt and bring him back here.'

Chapter Twenty-one

Simon and Lydia, Hugh and Monica and Paulo and Elsa were thrilled, not only to meet up again but also to be attending the concert where Boris was to play the cello solos. The previous day Simon had taken Boris to Bath. They had stopped at his flat to leave his case and Simon had met Trevor. He had liked him instantly. He had a very ready smile and friendly eyes. He had made it seem as if it was a pleasure and an honour to pack up Boris's things rather than the chore it must have been to an aspiring young percussionist. Then Simon had taken Boris on to the Connaught Rooms for final rehearsals. Boris said he would take a taxi back as he didn't know how long he would be, so Simon returned home in time for lunch having promised they would all arrive in good time for the concert. It was arranged that after the performance they'd all go back to Boris's flat for a small celebration before returning to Braunton.

Simon was keen for Boris to meet Elsa and Paulo, and also Monica, as she would be able to speak with him in German. It might be easier for him to explain more about what happened at the end of the war to someone who understood his native tongue. Of course, Elsa spoke German too but she was of the younger generation. Simon had an idea Boris would like Monica; they seemed to complement each other, in his mind. Surely he wasn't up to matchmaking! No good ever came from that, he said to himself.

'You seem pleased with yourself,' remarked Lydia, over lunch.

'I'm just so looking forward to the concert. I think Boris is really nice. I'm so glad we invited him to stay after all, aren't you? I know we were a bit unsure at first, but it's turned out so well. He's all fit again, and I met the young man who's helping him pack up at his flat. He seems a really helpful chap. He's going to pack all Boris's clothes and get rid of any food etc. that's left and things like that so the flat can be re-let – not that he'll have to do much. There isn't a lot there, and the cleaner's been in regularly.

He should have it all finished by Monday when they'll all be moving on up to Edinburgh. After lunch I'm going to take a good look at those papers he gave me. What time are the others arriving?'

'Some time during the evening... It depends on the traffic coming out of Heathrow and on the M4. Anyway, I told Hugh not to bother with coming round here tonight unless they want to, because they're bound to be tired and we'll see them tomorrow,' said Lydia. 'It's great now we've became such good friends. I think it's particularly special how Hugh and Paulo are so close. Imagine knowing your father was murdered by your friend's wife, and that your uncle had previously killed your friend's daughter! Besides being of different generations... I think it really amazing how well they get on. It's almost as if Paulo has filled the space left by Bunty; and of course his marrying Elsa has helped. For such a young person she is so mature and under-standing.'

Monica arrived later that evening. They heard the cars pulling up, but as it was gone eleven they did not come round to Simon and Lydia's until the next morning. They went out in the garden for lunch together and all the hellos were said amid much hugging and talking.

Simon meanwhile had a good look at the papers Boris had given him. Naturally they were all written in German, and his hold of the language was rather sketchy. He could make neither head nor tail of anything and he had the feeling the documents were in code. He was going to ask Monica to look at them, probably on Sunday, before she went back to London. She was fluent in German, as well as knowing a lot about the country and having studied its recent history in detail; but he didn't want to spoil the atmosphere of anticipation that was present, with all of them looking forward to the concert. The plan was to arrive at the restaurant at about six o'clock so they'd have time for a leisurely dinner before the event.

They left for Bath at about five, Paulo and Elsa going with Hugh, and Monica in Simon and Lydia's car. They arrived together and had a superb dinner. Excellent food and lots of chat made it special, as they delighted in each other's company.

They discussed the pieces Boris was going to play and the other items in the programme too. The cello solos were probably the most popular pieces of cello music performed in public: the part of the swan from Saint-Saens' 'Carnival of The Animals', instantly recognised and very well known, and the Elgar 'Salut d'Amour' – a short but very beautiful piece. There were other movements from Elgar's 'Serenade for Strings', and also Vivaldi's 'Spring' from his 'Four Seasons'.

'A beautiful selection,' remarked Monica. 'All for strings, but I think that's a good idea, you get in the mood and don't really want it broken by a sudden lot of brass and percussion. I'm really looking forward to it, and to meeting your friend Boris, I've heard so much about him.'

'By the way Monica,' Simon broke in, 'there's another reason I'm glad you're down this weekend. Boris has in his possession some war papers. It is quite an unusual story... perhaps you saw it in the paper?'

Monica shook her head. 'No, I don't think so. Are they all written in German?'

'Yes, they are. I can read a little German and usually have no trouble translating, with the aid of a dictionary, but I can't make head or tail of these; except the name Adolf Hitler crops up quite often, and also mention of a "Banque de Suisse". Anyway, let's not discuss them now. Could you come round in the morning and have a look?' Simon asked.

'Of course. Sounds interesting, especially if there is a genuine connection with Hitler. Some neo-Nazi groups in Germany would give anything to get hold of this sort of thing, if it's genuine.'

'Oh, I think they will be. As far as Boris is concerned, he's a very open and in some ways politically naive sort of person. It had never entered his head that he could gain from them in any way. Besides, he's far too wrapped up in his music to give any thought to Nazis. I think you'll like him when we meet up after the concert. He's invited us back to his flat for a nightcap before we drive home, so you'll be able to judge for yourself before you look at the papers,' said Simon. 'Look, it's getting near time. Let's go over to the concert now.'

Three hours later they all emerged onto the pavement, exhilarated by the beautiful music they had just heard.

'He plays so wonderfully, as if he is stroking the strings and trying to be so gentle with the bow, it was fantastic,' enthused Elsa. 'Let's go round to the other door and wait for him!'

She ran on ahead to where the orchestra would be coming out. They all followed and Boris came out just as they arrived. There were introductions and hugs.

'Oh! It was marvellous, Boris, you were brilliant!' said Lydia. 'Look, this is Monica, our dear friend.' She pushed Monica forward. Boris stepped forward and took Monica's proffered hand.

'I'm so pleased to meet you, Monica. I've heard so much about you from Simon and Lydia; you're obviously a very valued friend. Now, I hope you're all going to come back to my flat for a while. It's not far from here. I think I'm going to walk back. I could really do with the fresh air after all that. Would you like to walk with me, Monica?'

'Well, we'd better bring the cars round,' said Simon. 'Give me the keys, Boris – we'll be there before you. Will Trevor still be there? I'll introduce everyone to him. See you in a few minutes, then.'

Before she realised what was happening, they'd all moved off and Monica was walking alongside Boris. In the light from the old-fashioned street lamps used in that part of the city she could barely see his face. She tried to picture him as he'd been on the stage, but he was talking to her so she gave him her attention. There'd be plenty of time to examine his face when they arrived at his flat.

'I understand from Simon that you know a lot about my country,' Boris was saying. His accent was hardly perceptible, he'd spoken English for so long on tours and on the concert platform that it had become almost as easy as German to him; but Monica answered him in German and he felt it was a compliment.

She told him about her prolonged stay in Berlin just prior to the war and also about some of the many visits she had made since. She also told him of her time at the British Institute in Berlin in 1938, and that her studies had been cut short by the war but she did not mention Bunty, Hugh's daughter, or the tragedy surrounding her. Now was not the time. This was Boris's night; his playing had been a triumph and the rest of the evening should be a celebration.

It was after only seven or eight minutes that they rounded the corner by the block of flats. That something was wrong became immediately apparent. The lights were on in most of the block, the double doors on the ground floor were wide open and Simon and Paulo were pacing about on the pavement, looking up and down the street. They ran towards Boris and Monica. Paulo was the first to speak.

'Oh, Boris! Something terrible has happened. It looks like a break-in at your flat. The door was swinging open when we arrived—'

Boris intervened. 'What about Trevor? Where's Trevor? Is he alright?'

'That's the worst of it.' Simon put his arm on Boris's shoulder. 'I think Trevor is dead. Hugh's with him at the moment and we've sent for an ambulance and the police, but Hugh thinks he's been dead some time, so there's not much hope, I'm afraid. We're just out here looking out for the ambulance. Lydia and Elsa are with Hugh, but I don't think there's anything that can be done for Trevor. It rather looks as though he got in their way whoever they are and they just lashed out.'

Boris's tanned face looked grey. Monica was worried that severe shock would set in. 'We'd better go in and find a chair,' she said to him. 'You've had a bad shock, and after tonight's earlier excitement we don't want any further complications. Come on, Boris, come with me. There's nothing anyone can do to help him. Hugh would have known what to do if anything would have helped. Please come inside, Boris.'

She took his arm and he allowed himself to be led into a ground floor flat where his elderly neighbours were ready to ply him with tea and put a blanket round his shoulders. Although it was a warm night, he was shivering violently.

'Poor, poor, Trevor! he was just helping me out. Oh, dear! What about his parents? They're so proud of him. Who could have done this terrible thing? What did they want? There's nothing in my flat. I don't keep any money here or anything of value. Poor, poor Trevor,' he repeated himself.

He looked about him. On finishing his tea he seemed to visibly pull himself together. 'Are the police here now? I must go up. I'm all right now, Monica, the tea's done the trick. Thank you very much.' He smiled at his neighbours, 'not a very good introduction for us, but thank you.'

He stood up, pulled off the blanket and went towards the door, glancing back to Monica. 'It might be better if you stayed down here, my dear.' Monica looked at him. She felt his pain, and a concern for another human being that she hadn't been aware of since Gladys died. 'I'll come with you, Boris, we'll go up together.' She reached out for his hand. 'Is it on the first floor? Come on, it'll be alright.'

On reaching the flat they saw a scene of hustle and bustle. Scene of Crime officers in their white overalls were examining all surfaces. Photographers were snapping away with flashbulbs popping, and in the middle of the sitting room floor a man kneeling beside a body. He was presumably the pathologist, also in white overalls, next to Trevor. Monica was surprised by the youthfulness of the handsome face and also by the look of surprise on his face. How amazing that the look should endure after death. She said, 'What a waste of a young life, what a total waste!' The longer she looked, the more she felt anger rising inside her. She turned away. A police officer came over.

'Just a few questions, ma'am, if you don't mind. Shall we go in the other room? Nothing we can do here except get in the way, if you don't mind, sir.' He gently ushered Boris and Monica into the dining room, where Elsa and Hugh were already sitting.

Paulo and Simon and Lydia joined them, and the policeman ran them through all the routine questions. Where had they been that evening? How long had they been out? What was Trevor doing at the flat? Could Boris think of any reason why anyone would want to ransack his flat? Did he think he had any enemies? Etc. etc. The policeman recorded all their replies. Then a more senior officer arrived and asked Boris if he would come into the kitchen. He introduced himself as Inspector Wilson of the Somerset Police, and proceeded to ask Boris the same questions all over again.

'Not a very nice ending to your lovely evening, sir. I'm sorry you've had such a shock. I understand the deceased was a friend of yours. We're all very sorry, but we do need to get to the bottom of this. It appears the young man was shot and also sustained a nasty head wound. We take firearms very seriously over here, and I feel there must be a reason why men with guns would come to your flat in particular. There are a lot of people living in this block who would have valuable jewels or a lot of cash on the premises, so we have to ask ourselves, why come up the stairs and into your flat in particular? Now you are a German national, aren't you, sir? We know you're over here with the Berlin Philharmonic, but you're also a Berlin resident, are you not.'

'Yes, I am, Inspector but I have no strong political views and I do not belong to any groups, sects or parties. My music has kept me very busy over the years, especially recently. I'm not a genius, Inspector, and I need to practise very many hours to play in the type of concerts I've lately been invited to play, at very grand venues. It is a continuous effort for me to maintain a high standard of play and vary my programmes and play the composers that the audience demands. I do not have a lot of free time, and then I am mostly travelling, or arriving in new countries, so if I do have spare leisure time I usually sightsee. I didn't think I had an enemy in the world. Do you think it could be mistaken identity?' Boris said desperately.

He would not like to be the reason that Trevor had died, even indirectly. He could think of no reason at all that anyone would want to burgle his flat. Nothing seemed to have been taken, although everything was in a terrible mess. He hadn't had anything there that anyone could want. There were some clothes, a spare cello, lots of sheet music, a few books and general domestic appliances, which weren't even his – they came with the flat – and even the stereo was not a particularly good one. Anyway, neither that nor the TV had been taken. He was at a loss, and so was the inspector.

'Well, I don't think we can do anything else tonight sir. Your friend's body has been taken to the mortuary. I'll phone you tomorrow… you'll not be staying here. I presume? Is there a hotel, or some friends you can stay with?'

'Oh dear, Inspector! We're all supposed to be moving up to Edinburgh on Monday, to our next venue. That's why Trevor was here, helping to get me packed up. I know I could stay with my friends who are here now, but you know I'd really rather be on my own tonight, if that's alright. I'll probably drive down to their house in Braunton tomorrow. I can give you their number but for tonight I just want to stay here on my own. And of course I must talk to Trevor's parents. They have been informed, haven't they?'

'Yes, a local police officer went round. They're going to attend the mortuary in the morning identification, you know. A very sad time for them. We don't think there was any motive for the young man's death. He was in the wrong place at the wrong time, I should think. Okay, then, I'll be in touch with you here or in Braunton. Our men will be clearing out now; they've just about all finished. You can touch things again now, but I expect you'll be too tired to do any cleaning up tonight. Goodnight then, sir, and once again, our deep sympathy. If you get any ideas at all, think of anything that's been a bit different lately, any strangers in the area etc. you'll let me know straight away?'

Boris nodded. 'Yes. Goodnight then, Inspector. I wish I could help you further.'

The flat suddenly seemed very silent. 'As silent as the grave' came to Boris's mind. The police left and then the pathologist and his team, and about half an hour later, after trying to persuade him to go with them, the others all left too. He'd promised Simon he would come down the next day.

He had a few moments alone with Monica, gently persuading her that he needed to be alone, to give some thought to Trevor and his parents and to go over in his mind the events of the evening. She understood and didn't press him, and for that he was grateful. He was beginning to think the feelings he was developing for Monica meant one good thing at least was coming out of this evening. He'd held her gently by the shoulders and kissed her on both cheeks. She had laid her head briefly against his chest and promised she'd see him the next day.

Monica had gone with Hugh, and the others all got into Simon's car. It was a very subdued group who returned to

Braunton in the early hours of the morning. Simon especially had something on his mind. He kept turning it over and over as he drove home. It was just as well that nobody wanted to talk, as he was completely preoccupied with his thoughts.

Chapter Twenty-two

Boris had been distraught by the discovery of his friend and colleague's dead body, but he had remained at the flat. The police had questioned him for some time, but no motive for the murder had come to light. Trevor had obviously disturbed an intruder or intruders, but nothing had been taken. The whole thing seemed pointless.

Boris planned to return to the concert hall that afternoon to pick up some music and scores. Then perhaps he'd visit Simon and stay for a few days.

The concert hall was deserted, save for the caretaker, who let him in through the side door.

As he emerged, a fitful sun was breaking through the clouds. He had parked his car at the rear of the concert hall. There were only a few cars in the car park, just a Land-Rover and a Mercedes. As he opened the car door, he became aware of a movement out of the corner of his eye. Then came darkness and muffled sounds. A coat or bag had been placed over his head and hands bundled him into the back of a car.

'Keep still! Don't move and lie low and you won't be hurt.' The voice was muffled. Then, strangely, a voice said in German, 'Drive carefully. We don't need to break any speed limits.'

The whole incident had taken less than one minute.

He was in a large room and his arms and legs were bound to a chair. A blindfold had been placed over his eyes. Voices murmuring in the background. Once again the language was German. '*Mr Schmidt*,' said the voice in English, 'you are no doubt confused, but let me reassure you that no harm will come to you providing that you answer a few simple questions.'

'Are you the people responsible for my friend's death?' asked Boris.

'An unfortunate accident, I'm afraid, but nevertheless a

warning of how desperate we can become.' The same voice.

'Our question is simple. You have in your possession certain old documents of the wartime era. Will you tell me where they are.' There was a menace in the calm tones.

'My God! thought Boris. So that is what this is all about! Those old documents he was given by Martin Bormann, the Deputy Führer, all those years ago, which he had never really looked at properly... how stupid of me!

'I don't have them! A friend of mine is trying to assess their contents and their possible historical value,' said Boris, slightly bemused.

'I will repeat, Mr Schmidt. Where are those papers now?' The menace was more pronounced.

'I wish no harm to come to my friends,' said Boris.

'Rest assured. No harm will come to anyone provided the papers are recovered.' The same voice.

'They are being held by a Simon West who resides at Twenty-seven High Street, Braunton, in Somerset,' replied Boris. The documents were not worth any further tragedies.

'Mr Schmidt, you will write a note to your friend authorising the surrender of those documents as a condition of your release. Do you understand?' It was a cold, dispassionate voice. There were others in the background 'Yes, of course. Give me pen and paper and take these bonds and blindfold off,' said Boris. He wasn't going to be any hero for a packet of old documents.

'You will not look around when your blindfold is removed. Understood?' The menace again.

'Of course, I understand. Just get on with it.' Boris felt calmer now.

The blindfold was removed and Boris found himself sitting in front of a table on which writing paper and pen were ready. Without looking around, he wrote the letter. The blindfold was replaced and his hands rebound.

Erich looked around at the group. 'We will leave Otto and Horst here with Schmidt. The rest of us will proceed to Braunton. Once the papers are in our hands we will continue to Poole Harbour with our equipment and maps will be loaded into one of the Land-Rovers. We will telephone Otto and Horst, and they will leave Schmidt here and follow and rendezvous with us at Poole. Any trouble and it is everyone for himself. But on no account will anyone allow themselves to be caught. Should capture be imminent, you know what you must do. We will sail at dusk provided that we are not subject to hot pursuit. Use the A359, then the A357 around Blandford. Then onto the A350 to Poole Quay. The boat will be moored near the old Custom House. There will be a red pennant flying from the ship's rear flagpole.'

'Chief Inspector Goodbody here.' He had been with the Special Branch for about two years and enjoyed the variation of the workload. One never knew what was around the comer.

'Chief Inspector, this is Inspector Wilson of Somerset Police. We have an unusual situation here in which I feel Special Branch should be involved. A suspected murder and a kidnapping. Both incidents have a German undertone and all are focussed within the Bath area.'

Goodbody was intrigued. This was his old force. 'I think Inspector I had better travel down and assess the problems on the spot. When would it be convenient?'

'The sooner the better. Tomorrow or today,' said Wilson.

'Alright, I'll be with you after lunch. We can talk and you can fill me in then. Goodbye.'

Inspector Wilson was puzzled. A murder with no apparent motive. A kidnapping of a German musician who shared a flat with the victim. No ransom demand. It was a riddle. Goodbody arrived after lunch.

The murder had occurred on the same night as a musical concert in which the missing musician was the soloist. He was also a German national. A perplexing situation.

'Have you checked arrival of any German nationals?'

'I'm circulating hotels and boarding houses and making an appeal through the local newspapers and regional radio and television.' replied Wilson.

'When was the suspected kidnap victim missed?' asked Goodbody.

'The concert organiser reported him missing, and a close

friend who was expecting him on Sunday for lunch said he hadn't arrived,' said Wilson.

'What is the victim's name?' continued Goodbody.

'Schmidt. Boris Schmidt. Aged fifty-three years. Speaks almost fluent English, with a slight accent.'

Later that afternoon the telephone rang. 'Inspector Wilson here. Can I help you?'

'It's the police radio appeal. I heard it on my car radio. My name is Welling. Graham Welling. I'm an estate agent in the High Street, Wittersham. I had an enquiry just over a week ago from a foreign client, He could have been German. He wanted to lease a large property in the vicinity of Bath for himself and some visiting colleagues.'

'Where was this property sir?' asked Wilson.

'On the A36 Bristol road some three miles from Wittersham. Clarendon Hall. You can't miss it,' replied Welling.

'Thank you, sir. We will certainly follow this up.' Wilson knew this could be important.

He turned to Goodbody and told him the details of the conversation.

'Get somebody along there to look into it,' said Goodbody. He felt they were on to something. 'No, on second thoughts, get your coat, Wilson. We are going over there ourselves.'

The wrought iron gates were wide open, and the car screeched to a halt in front of the main door. Goodbody sent a uniform round to the back entrance. Wilson, himself and the other uniform officer approached the front door. It was wide open. The house was silent. Entering with extreme caution, they searched each room. The uniform officer signalled to Wilson and Goodbody. He was pointing into what looked like the main lounge. There bound, gagged and blindfolded, was the figure of a man. Making sure the room was otherwise empty, they approached the imprisoned man and removed the blindfold and gag.

'Thank God it's you! I thought for a moment that they had returned to kill me so that I wouldn't not testify against them,' Boris gasped.

'I'm Chief Inspector Goodbody of Special Branch and this is Inspector Wilson of Somerset Police. Take your time, and tell us what happened.'

'My name is Schmidt, Boris Schmidt. A German musician. This is so bizarre! First my friend is murdered. Then I am kidnapped by a group of German men, who are searching for some old documents that were given to me by Hitler's Deputy Führer, Martin Bormann, at the end of the last war. It seems so macabre.' Boris was bewildered and confused.

'Did you have these documents with you, here in Bath?' asked Goodbody.

'No, I gave them to my friend, Simon West, to assess their historical value. They made me write a ransom note to give him. He was to give the papers to them and then I would be released. They left, and two of them remained behind until a telephone message came through and then they also left.' The strain was beginning to tell and Boris was beginning to quiver.

'Phone for an ambulance, and leave someone here to guard the premises. Get the forensic boys here ASAP. I want a check, particularly of vehicles that may have been parked outside. Then get that estate agent fellow to come and secure the place.'

Turning to Wilson, Goodbody said, 'Come along. We're going to see this chap Simon West. There's no time to lose. I've got a feeling these Fritzes are going to move quickly now that they have what they came over here for. This is just the tip of a very big iceberg. Get an armed response team to follow.'

The Wests' doorbell rang. 'I'll get it!' Simon called to Lydia.

He opened the large front door. The stranger stood there flanked by two other strangers. 'Mr West? Simon West?' He was in his late twenties, fair-haired and athletic-looking.

'Yes that's me. What can I do for you?' said Simon.

He was curious. Jehovah's Witnesses, perhaps? He was prepared to cut the sales talk short, claiming atheism or Roman Catholicism or maybe Buddhism. He hadn't made up his mind. Then he couldn't believe his own eyes. He was staring down the barrel of a vicious-looking pistol with a silencer attached.

'May I come in?' It was more a command than a request.

Simon was gently but firmly pushed back into the house. The other two fit-looking companions followed the gunman. 'Is there anybody else in the house?' asked the leader of the three.

'What is it, dear?' called Lydia from the kitchen.

The gunmen put his fingers to his lips. 'Tell her to come in here. No tricks!' The gun was thrust into his stomach.

'Would you come in here, dear?' called Simon.

Lydia came in wiping her hands on a towel. 'I'm rather busy with the cooking apples. What is it?' She sounded petulant. Then she froze in her tracks at the sight of the gun and three strangers. 'God! What's going on?' she asked Simon.

'It's all right dear. Just stay calm. I think we are about to find out.' Simon was trying to keep his voice steady and not to show any fear.

'Mr West, would you kindly read this note. It is addressed to you.' The stranger kept his eyes on Simon and Lydia.

Simon read Boris's letter. The situation was becoming even more bizarre.

'How do I know that this is genuine?' He was recovering his composure rapidly.

'Here is a telephone number. If you ring that number, you can speak to your friend,' replied the stranger.

Simon dialled the number and a voice answered. 'Hello?' A slightly guttural voice, thought Simon. 'Otto here...'

'Give me the phone, Mr West,' said the obvious leader of the group 'Hello, Otto. This is Wolf. Would you place the phone to Mr Schmidt's ear, and remove the gag?'

'*Jahwohl*, Wolf. Here it is,' Otto answered.

'Would you speak Mr West?' Erich insisted.

'Hello, Boris. This is Simon. What is going on? I've just been shown a letter, supposedly from you,' said Simon.

'Sorry, Simon, to get you involved in this but I'm not sure what's happening myself. They're obviously in deadly earnest in their demands. Don't take any risks, just do as they ask.' Boris sounded nervous. 'Very well, Boris. I'm not looking for trouble. Take care. Goodbye.' Simon rang off.

He turned to the gunman. 'The documents are in the study upstairs.' Erich nodded to Kurt. 'Go with him!'

Kurt drew his own gun from his pocket and nudged Simon towards the stairs. Simon turned towards Lydia. 'I won't be long. Just stay calm and do as they say.'

After a short time he returned. Simon had a package wrapped in a large oilskin satchel. 'I think this is what you are after,' Simon said. He thought it best to keep his comments short.

Erich took the package. It was larger than he had anticipated. The seal on the outside carried the eagle and swastika emblems. 'Is that the whole of the papers?' He was anxious to be on their way but he had to be sure.

'Yes, there are all the papers Boris gave to me, and as far as I know the complete package given to him in 1945,' said Simon. He was beginning to get irritated by the intimidating attitude of these people. Who did they think they were barging in like this? This was England, not some dictatorship.

'There is just one more condition,' continued Erich. 'We must secure you for a while, or take your wife as a hostage to insure your silence.'

'Now look here! Dash it all! You come in here like some cloak-and-dagger brigade, making demands and threats and now this. It's too much!' Simon was really rattled.

Erich was slightly amused by this typically English outburst. 'Mr West, this is no game or charade. We are deadly serious. The stakes are too high to accommodate your sensitivities. Either you agree or you may force us to extreme measures. I leave that to your imagination. Cooperate or else...' Erich was becoming impatient.

'Alright, we have little choice. Secure us both and leave.' Simon saw the futility of resisting.

'Is there a cellar or a secure room to this house?' asked Erich.

'Yes, there is a room that was originally used as a strongroom for the bank who owned the property some years ago.' Simon saw no point in antagonising these people. He was convinced that they would not hesitate to leave two dead bodies behind them if he refused to cooperate.

They were tied securely and locked in the old strongroom. Gags were placed over their mouths. Someone was bound to come looking for them sooner or later.

'Hello, Otto. Erich here. Leave Schmidt secure and make for our rendezvous. Don't take any chances or raise any suspicions. Avoid all roadblocks if possible. We will meet at Poole Quayside. Disconnect the telephone. *Auf Wiedersehen.*'

The Wests' telephone was pulled from its socket and smashed. The team left unhurriedly and drove from Braunton to join the road south.

Chapter Twenty-three

Monica didn't sleep well. It wasn't so much the tragic events of the latter part of the evening that disturbed her as her thoughts about Boris. She could feel that he cared for her and she was exhilarated as she recalled their walk back from the concert hall, but she was also unsure of how the events of last night would affect things and she longed to see him again and be able to touch him. Really what she needed was reassurance that the elation of the previous evening was not the result of Boris's success and a walk home in the moonlight. It was a long time since she'd had a close relationship; there'd been several affairs, usually of brief duration. Before now she'd felt uneasy in long-term commitment and she was surprising herself with the strength of feeling she was experiencing in her yearning to be close to Boris again.

She breakfasted with Hugh. Elsa and Paulo were still asleep, but they both only felt like coffee, and by mid-morning she was knocking on Simon and Lydia's front door.

'Oh, come in, Monica, do you want some coffee?' asked Lydia, welcoming her warmly. 'How do you feel? It all seems like a dream, doesn't it? But I know it's everyone's worst nightmare – and his poor parents! Of course, I don't know Trevor, but Simon had just met him on Friday and he really liked him. I think Simon is worried about the motive. He thinks it was not a random attack but that it might have something particularly to do with Boris. He's in his study now looking at those papers again. It's not just that nothing was taken, but the intruders were armed. That wasn't really necessary, if they thought they were coming to an empty flat, so Simon thinks they're the kind of people that are armed anyway – more like terrorists than housebreakers.' Lydia paused for breath then continued.

'He's going to ring Chief Inspector Goodbody. Do you remember him from last time? Well, he's attached to Special Branch now since his promotion to Chief Inspector. I haven't seen him for two years but I think Simon's spoken to him once or twice on the phone. Because of his background he is occasionally in touch with Special Branch and MI5 and MI6, and they still use him for the odd job. Anyway, I'm holding up the works, do go in. You will stay for lunch?'

'Well, actually Hugh said would you like to come round to us, as Paulo and Elsa are only here for a short time. And Boris may be joining us. It will only be a cold buffet, is that all right? How do you think Boris is this morning? I tried to ring him but the line seems to be dead, perhaps the police have disconnected it.'

Lydia smiled at Monica's attempt to hide her concern. 'You really like him, don't you? I can see it in your face and I'm sure the feeling's mutual, the way Boris looked at you yesterday. Even though you only met last night I can see he really cares for you.' Lydia was keen that her friend should have a long relationship. In spite of her sophistication and her high-powered lifestyle, Lydia often thought that Monica was lonely. It was true that events when she was young had caused her to withdraw into a shell where personal commitment was concerned; it was as if she didn't trust anyone sufficiently, so she was forced to keep relationships superficial. The friendship between them had taken some time to become as close as it was now, but Lydia admired Monica and was also very impressed by the way she had supported her Aunt Gladys during the terrible events of the war, and then her uncle Hugh when he had needed someone at the time of Gladys's death.

'Yes, we'd love to come round. Are you sure Hugh'll have enough food in? We'll bring some wine. Will you be driving back to London tonight? I'd better bring something non-alcoholic as well...'

'No,' replied Monica, 'I'm staying over until tomorrow. I told them I'd be away Monday as well, as Paulo and Elsa are staying. Boris and the orchestra are moving on to Edinburgh anyway, so I must talk to him. I might take some leave and go up there. Do you think that's silly?' She looked earnestly at Lydia. 'You don't think I'm behaving like a young lovesick fawn?'

'It doesn't matter if you are,' said Lydia emphatically, 'but you're not,' she hastily reassured her friend. 'You may have forgotten what it's like to be in love, but I can assure you, we all behave the same. The urge to keep touching and looking and doing everything together is no different just because we're older. Being in love is being in love, it makes us all a bit crazy!'

Monica, smiled, she could rely on Lydia to put things in perspective. She went over to the study. Simon looked up.

'Hello, I thought I heard you. Are you alright, has everyone slept okay?'

'Paulo and Elsa were still asleep when I left. Hugh wants us all to lunch together. You haven't spoken to Boris have you? I couldn't get through when I tried earlier.' Monica sat down next to Simon to look at what he was studying.

'That's funny, I couldn't get him either; but then he did say he'd have to return to the concert hall before he came on down here, some music to pick up, I think. I want you to have a look at these, please, Monica. Your German is so good. I can't really understand them. I mean I can translate word for word but the phrases don't make sense.'

He pushed the pile of papers over towards her. There was an assortment of sheets of varying sizes and some papers in envelopes. As Monica thumbed through them, she noticed that some looked like bonds, officially printed with embossing and gold leaf. They were issued by the Banque de Suisse. They were for huge amounts and mostly dated from before the war and during the early war years.

'I know the currency was in a funny state but these are for amazing sums of money,' said Monica. 'And there's some deposit box slips too. You say Boris had all this in his possession all these years and never examined them? Well, I suppose you wouldn't if you don't believe there's any significance in them, but I think they could be quite sinister. I've noticed Hitler's signature in several places.'

She was opening a brown envelope with the seal of the Third Reich emblazoned on the back. 'Wow, Look at this! Have you seen this, Simon? Do you know what it is? Simon, it's a *will*. I think it's Hitler's will! Look at the way it's set out. It's written in legal jargon and it's witnessed and I don't think anyone has ever seen it; the seal was unbroken when I just opened it. You see it's on very thin paper, it felt as if there was nothing in the envelope. Good heavens! You know what it means if it's genuine? It may not be worth anything to anyone financially, but the interest to the media and historians will be terrific. Taken with the deposit box slips and these bonds, I can see why you think it could have been terrorists targeting Boris. Those neo-Nazi groups would just love to get their hands on this stuff!

'These others do seem to be in code, otherwise it's just gobbledegook. If Hitler's staff took the trouble to write all these out in code, they must contain very sensitive information, or it must have been sensitive at the time. It may not be so important now, but the Nazi groups who still worship him and want to see his evil regime continued and his dreams fulfilled are a fanatical lot and can be extremely dangerous. If they had an idea these were the items in Boris's flat, they could well be responsible for the break-in and they certainly wouldn't have let Trevor's presence put them off. I think this is very worrying, Simon. I'm sure we must get on to someone in authority, tell them what we know. We need someone a bit higher in rank than Inspector Wilson, someone who can close airports and alert docks and get helicopters up.' She paused and Simon broke in.

'I thought they were significant. I've already rung Goodbody, do you remember him?'

Monica nodded and Simon continued, 'I think I'll ring again and tell him that you agree with me. It'll add a bit of weight. I expect they've already got information on Nazi cells in operation. They usually know a lot more than the general public has any idea about. I'll ring now, and then I think I'll ring Inspector Wilson again to see if he knows where Boris is; he might call in at the police station. Don't worry, I expect he's on his way by now. He always enjoys a good lunch, and judging by the way I saw him looking at you last night he won't want to waste any time getting down here to be with you.'

Monica was covered in confusion but apart from a slight blush reaching her cheeks she tried to remain unperturbed.

'I like him a lot, but of course it's very early days. I just hope he's alright. They can be ruthless, these maniacs, and as they haven't got what they wanted there's no knowing what they might think of doing next. I'll just go and talk to Lydia while you phone. Will you ring Inspector Wilson first and see if he's seen Boris this morning?'

She left the room and went through the house to the garden, feeling panicky with anxiety for Boris. She also felt impatient with him for putting himself in such danger by keeping papers like this and not doing anything about them years ago. This was typical of musicians; they were like artists and actors and other creative people. Their heads were always filled with their own ideas, perfecting their own gifts. They weren't of the real world, and it all passed them by. He'd need someone like her – practical and commonsensical – to keep him out of danger. She took some deep breaths as she reached the warm sunshine outside the back door. She mustn't let her imagination run riot. Simon's probably right, she told herself. Boris is probably in his car right now, driving happily along, looking forward to lunch. She went to join Lydia on the patio.

'I'm just off, Lydia. I'm going to help Uncle Hugh get lunch. Simon's trying to contact Boris for me. You will give me a ring if there's any news won't you? I'm a bit worried that we haven't heard from him. I thought he'd ring to say he was on his way.'

'Try not to worry. I expect he'll be here soon, but if Simon gets anything I'll call you straight away. We'll come round about one o'clock. I'm just going to do some baking. I'm right out, and I do like to have a fruitcake and a few scones in the tin in case anyone calls. See you later then.'

They both moved into the kitchen and Monica went on through and let herself out of the front door.

The information she'd discovered in Boris's papers weighed heavily on her mind. Fancy keeping a load of stuff like that! She was sure he'd put himself in danger. The sooner he arrived the better, please God he comes soon.

Lunch time came and went, with neither sign nor word of Boris. When Simon had spoken to Inspector Wilson he'd been unable to shed any light on Boris's whereabouts except from the reports about an abduction from the concert hall, but had told Simon he was liaising with Special Branch because of the German involvement in last night's murder.

Simon and Lydia returned home after lunch. Monica had become more and more anxious as there had been no news, and her uncle had persuaded her to take an aspirin and have a lie-down.

Later that afternoon she was disturbed by vehicles and people coming and going in the street below. On looking out of her bedroom window she saw police cars and police officers, some of whom were armed, and a couple of dogs with their handlers outside Simon's house. She hurriedly dressed and called to her uncle.

'What's going on, Uncle? What do all these policemen want, and why is an the armed response unit here? Is it anything to do with Boris? Do they know where he is? What's happened to him? Why didn't he turn up for lunch?'

Uncle Hugh put his arm round her shoulders. 'Looks like it's all happening next door. Perhaps we should go and see Simon, as the police are actually banging on his door now. Come on, my dear, we'll see if Lydia needs any help. He called Paula, who was scanning the street. 'Will you and Elsa stay here in case the phone rings? We're still waiting for news of Boris. We'll come straight back if we can get any information from the police or from Simon.'

Hugh and Monica were reluctantly let in by the police officer at the front door when they had explained who they were. They were surprised to bump into Chief Inspector Goodbody in the hall; it had been at least two years since they'd last seen him.

'Hello, you two. Got yourselves involved in another drama?' he said. 'You do seem to get in the centre of some strange goings-on! Try to keep out of the way, will you, for the moment. We're doing all we can.'

Monica felt quite sick, but she smiled at Hugh. 'I'll go and find Lydia, make sure she's okay. She must be very shaken up, Uncle. Why don't you go back to Paulo and Elsa and we'll come round when the police have gone.'

Hugh realised there was nothing he could do at the moment. It was best to keep out of the way. He went back to his own house and relayed events to Paulo and Elsa.

'So all this is to do with last night?' asked Paulo. 'I thought it was more than just a random burglary. Boris is a man of mystery, it appears.'

'I don't think he's done anything wrong,' replied Hugh. 'Got himself inadvertently mixed up with some German war documents. Seems a neo-Nazi group is after them. They're the ones causing all the problems – a ruthless lot. Goodbody said he'd explain further when they've finished next door.'

Chapter Twenty-four

Sergeant Miller was at the desk of Poole police station when the 'All Points' signal came through from the Somerset Police.

The CAD communications room was handling the usual domestic calls. 'Tom! Can you put this call out to all the patrol cars, and tell Harold and Mike to get to the quayside area and patrol the moorings for any suspicious activities. They are to look out for a group of males, white, possibly armed and to be approached with extreme caution. Also keep and eye on the harbour area for any suspicious behaviour. The yachting moorings around Evening Hill and Sandbanks.'

'Okay Serge, will do. Control to Sierra Bravo. Receiving? Control to Sierra Bravo. Receiving?'

Erich sensed the tension amongst the others in the Land-Rover. Kurt was driving the Mercedes with Horst and Ludwig and Raoul were in the other Land-Rover. All them were spaced out between other traffic. Blandford had been bypassed and the A350 was taking them to Poole. Several police vehicles had been seen heading in the opposite direction.

This particular patrol car had been on his tail for some minutes since leaving the Blandford bypass. Erich's speedometer was registering 40 mph: no problem there. He glanced at the map. They were approaching a turn-off that joined the Dorchester road. It was a minor road but it might discourage the patrol car.

Approaching the turning, he noticed the signpost to a place called Wareham. Indicating right, he turned. The patrol car turned too. Keep calm. His automatic was by his feet easily accessible.

Still the patrol car did not make a move. Perhaps it was his nerves getting stretched. A road crossing approaching. Dorchester to the right. More traffic on the road. He felt easier. Several cars had slotted in between himself and the patrol car. A left turn coming up. There's Wareham again. Follow it… More traffic from a large public house. Where were the others?

The mirror showed several cars following. Was that patrol car tucked in the queue? No sirens sounding. It must be his nerves. Another major road ahead. Poole on the signpost. Turn left to join it. More traffic. A roundabout. Different system in this country: 'give way to the right.' Keep straight. Another roundabout. So many in this country! Poole, right. The sea or the inner harbour. Many moorings. Keep straight. No sign of that patrol car. More roundabouts. Quayside right. There it was. Large coastal cargo steamers using the docks, unloading and loading, local clay, and petroleum gas from the Wytch oilfields. Largest onshore fields in Britain. Pleasure craft moored along the quayside. Sail and motor launches. Time 6.30 pm. Nearing dusk…

Old Custom House – where? There it was, double-fronted with an imposing staircase, and there moored alongside the quay was a large motor launch, with massive twin outboard engines. A red flag was draped over the stem, and the other Land-Rover and Mercedes were parked alongside. *Keep calm.* Park casually and go aboard.

Otto, Joseph, Kurt, Horst. They were all waiting in the ship's saloon.

What an amazing stroke of luck to have arrived without a single casualty! Dusk was gathering fast and the streetlights were becoming alive.

'Hello there aboard the launch!' Once again, but more persistent. 'Hello there aboard the launch!'

Erich looked curiously through the porthole. 'Hello aboard the launch?' Again, increasingly insistent. No doubt about. The chequered hat band, a white shirt, epaulettes. The police!

'All stay calm. Let me handle this,' said Erich.

Climbing up to the cockpit, Erich looked towards the quayside. The policeman was regarding the launch inquisitively.

'May I come aboard sir?' Constable Harold Seaton was a young man with an air of keenness about him that suggested 'new recruit'.

'Of course, officer. Come aboard.'

Removing his hat – always a peculiar gesture – the young

policeman clambered aboard.

'What can I do for you, officer?' asked Erich.

'This your boat, sir?' PC Seaton enquired.

'No, a friend of mine has lent it to me and my friends to explore the Jurassic coastline along here. I also understand there are some very interesting caves from the old limestone quarry workings,' said Erich. He seemed very calm.

'May I enter the cabin, sir?' requested the policeman.

'Be my guest, officer,' said Erich.

On descending the short flight of stairs, the presence of the group of young men sitting in the lounge of the boat heightened Harold's awareness. They regarded him with suspicion.

He started to pull his handset from his epaulette. The hard metallic feel of the handgun in his neck froze his movements.

'Now, officer. Give me your handset!' Erich demanded firmly. The young officer did as he was told. The pistol had a silencer attached to the barrel. Not the time for heroics. These people looked dangerous.

'Now listen very carefully,' said Erich. 'I have no intention of having any interference in our plan. You will go on deck and you will call your colleague and ask him to come onboard. I will be right behind you. Any attempt at heroics and you will both die here. There will be no noise and nobody will notice your demise. Your bodies will be bundled into your car and driven to a desolate spot. Do you understand?'

PC Seaton knew that this was no idle threat. It was too risky to put both their lives in danger. 'Yes, I understand,' he muttered. Up on deck, he called to his colleague, Mike Hardy. Come up here, Mike! I want you to see something and give me your opinion.' Mike grumbled and, muttering to himself, clambered aboard. As he descended the stairs into the boat's saloon, a pistol was thrust at his throat. He froze.

'No heroics, officer. A dead hero is cold comfort to those left alive. Sit on that bench, next to your colleague,' commanded Erich. 'Give me your radio handset!'

PC Hardy could see that the situation was hopeless.

Erich issued a series of orders. 'Joseph and Ludwig, cast off the mooring ropes. Horst, start the motors. Kurt, take the wheel.

Keep strictly to the harbour speed limit.' Kurt moved the powerful craft forward. Erich covered the two policemen with his silenced handgun.

'You are probably concerned as to your future?' Erich spoke calmly. 'Can you both swim? It is important!'

'Of course!' said Harold.

'Good. Now sit comfortably for a while.'

The launch passed through the harbour entrance and the floating bridge that crossed to and fro between Sandbanks and Studland Bay.

Darkness was creeping forward and a mist was descending as they neared the Isle of Wight with the Needles lighthouse to the port side. Erich handed the two policemen a life jacket each. Both were equipped with bleepers.' Would you please put those jackets on now?' There was no point in objecting.

'Now I must insist that you both jump overboard. You may remove any footwear or clothing you wish,' ordered Erich.

'You can't mean it!' said Harold. 'We must be at least a mile, if not more, from the shore.'

'I'm deadly serious gentlemen. The alternative will be forcible ejection in mid-Channel, possibly ten miles out from the coast... So what is it to be?' Erich was losing his patience.

With the gun aimed at them at point-blank range, the two policemen clambered on deck. They glanced at each other and jumped overboard. A dull splash and they were gone into the murky darkness.

Earlier, the sergeant had put his head round the door of the CAD room. 'Any contact with Harold and Mike?'

'No Sarge.' I'll try again. *Sierra Bravo. Central receiving? Sierra Bravo. Central receiving?...* Strange! No response, Sarge.'

'Call Alpha Charlie.' said the sergeant. There was concern in his voice.

'Alpha Charlie. Central receiving? Alpha Charlie. Central receiving?' The response came quickly. 'Alpha Charlie receiving.'

'Mike, what is your position?'

The sergeant had taken over the head set. 'Passing Poole Park, Sarge.'

'Extend your patrol to the quayside and along the road past Baiter, Evening Hill and Sandbanks. Keep a sharp look out for Sierra Bravo. Their radio is dead. This is a priority one request.'

The patrol car was empty. No sign of the two policemen. 'Alpha Charlie to Central. Receiving?'

'Central receiving.'

'Sarge, Sierra Charlie is parked on the quayside near the old Customs House but there is no sign of Harold and Mike. Stay there – I'm coming down with the van. Ask around. Somebody may have seen something.'

He didn't like this one little bit.

Chapter Twenty-five

There was no answer from number 27.

'Find a way round the back.' Goodbody was anxious.

'They should be in,' the shopkeeper remarked. He had come out to see what all the noise was about. 'They're always in on a Monday afternoon. They were there this morning and I haven't seen them leave and you can hear the dog barking, and that's unusual.'

Just then the front door opened and a uniformed officer stood there.

'The back was open, sir.'

'Find out where that dog is!' ordered Goodbody.

'He was in the garden, but darted upstairs when I opened the back door,' said the officer.

Hurrying up the stairs, they found the dog outside an imposing-looking door. It was locked.

'Break that lock!' Goodbody told the uniformed officer.

Simon and Lydia both tried to talk at the same time.

'One at a time please,' requested Goodbody, bewildered by the sheer gush of words.

Simon told him the whole sequel of events that had happened to them. 'I'm sure that I heard Poole mentioned,' he added.

'Can I use your telephone, sir?' asked Goodbody.

'Sorry, Chief Inspector, but they smashed the phone connection before they left,' said Simon.

Goodbody got through to Poole police on the car radio.

After the preliminary introductions and establishment of rank, he was put through to Chief Inspector Howard.

'Have there been any incidents – anything unusual over the past twenty-four hours?' asked Goodbody.

'We have had some trouble at the quayside,' replied Howard. 'Two of our officers have disappeared.'

Goodbody felt his adrenalin pumping. 'Seal off the quayside.

I'll be with you in about an hour and then fill you in with all the details. Goodbye.'

'Inspector Wilson, you get back to Bath. Let me know any forensic report, particularly how many vehicles were used. I'm taking the armed response team with me.' He turned to Simon. 'Can you tell me anything about those papers?'

'They were German and connected with the Nazi hierarchy. The name *Adolf Hitler* crops up quite a few times. Hazarding a guess, I'd say they are records of locations. Banque de Suisse is mentioned, could refer to Swiss bank accounts. Most of it seemed to be in some sort of code. Who knows – perhaps the Enigma Code.' Simon sounded enthusiastic.

'Thank you, sir! I'll be off now. Carry on, Inspector, and keep me informed of any developments.'

'I'm Chief Inspector Howard.' He was very young for such a rank. Perhaps one of those university graduates on a fast promotion scheme. 'Two officers are missing and there are reports of a large and powerful launch moving from the quayside early this evening.'

'We must move fast. Assuming that your officers have been abducted, and are being held hostage by a group of desperate and armed German terrorists, that restricts any use of force against them for fear of endangering your officers.' Goodbody's mind was working in top gear. The situation was highly sensitive and dangerous.

'Have we any helicopter and patrol vessels that we can call upon?' he asked the Chief Inspector.

'I have been in touch with the Royal Marines training establishment. The Commanding Officer is a friend of mine. They happen to have two Apache gunships available and the Customs people have a fast interceptor patrol vessel. I believe that has a large machine-gun armament. All of them are standing by,' said the CI.

'Get them in the air and out to sea ASAP. But no interception until given the go-ahead from us. Location is all important just now.' Goodbody's mind was racing.

'Set a course for 130 degrees. Maximum revs, Kurt.' Erich knew that a pursuit would be organised if not already in action. The longer those two police officers remain undiscovered, the better. There would be no firefight. The assumption of hostages on board would frustrate that.

At 40 knots this beauty moved like a powerboat. Darkness was falling rapidly and a sea mist was drifting inland.

'Patrol vessel to base. We have a blip on the radar. Could be the motor launch.'

'Apache to base, we are following a high-speed launch. Light is failing but radar has contact. Could be our target. Over and out.'

'Base to patrol vessel and Apache one. Stay clear until further instructions. International sea limit closing.'

Goodbody was frustrated. He could feel these German gangsters slipping from his grasp. 'Inspector, get in touch with the French Sûreté. Let them know the situation. The destination will be a French port, possibly Cherbourg.' Now for the waiting game!

'Sir!' came an excited voice from the CAD room. 'A fishing craft returning to Poole has picked up two exhausted police officers about half a mile from 'Old Harry's Rock. It's Harold and Mike!'

'Good!' Goodbody was elated. The three-mile territorial water line was almost reached. 'Signal Apache one and patrol boat. Challenge and intercept. Repeat, challenge and intercept.'

Erich could now hear the helicopters and the patrol boat. The dark and mist had reduced visibility to nil. All his own lights were doused and the darkness complete. It was a moonless night. Somewhere ahead there was another sound. A powerful craft was up there in front of him. Maybe a mile or so, but getting audibly louder.

A loudhailer sounded. 'Motor launch, heave to! I repeat, motor launch, heave to or we open fire! You will receive no further warning!'

Erich glanced at Kurt. 'Get the automatics out and steer an evasive course.'

Then came unmistakable rat-tat-tat of machine-gun fire. Then *whoosh!* A very near miss. Rockets from the helicopter. The darkness and evasive movements of the launch hindered the sight of the pursuers.

The thump, thump, of heavy engines was getting closer. Then out of the darkness loomed the Truckline ferry with all its lights ablaze. It was the late Sunday night ferry to Cherbourg.

'Get alongside that ferry, Kurt. Quick time!'

'Patrol boat to base! Patrol boat to base, calling!'

'Base here. Receiving.'

'Have a large ferry close by. Too dangerous to intercept bandits. Over.'

'Base to patrol boat and Apache one. Break action! Repeat, Break! Break! Break!' Goodbody was furious.

Tuning the radiotelephone, Erich contacted the ferry. 'Truckline. Heave to. I repeat, heave to! I have a wounded passenger in need of urgent medical attention. Throw down a boarding ladder and hoist. I repeat, throw down a boarding ladder and hoist!'

The Truckline slowed and a ladder and hoist snaked down.

'Kurt, I'm going to board that ferry with Otto, Horst, Ludwig and Raoul. I'm taking grenades and automatics. I intend to hijack that monster and sail on to France. It will act as a diversion. You keep alongside but keep in touch with the radiotelephone. Understood?'

'*Jawohl!* I wish you luck,' answered Kurt. 'One other thing – the documents are in the cabin, in case anything goes wrong. *Auf Wiedersehen*, my friend.'

They clambered up the ladder. Otto was the first aboard and thrust his machine pistol into the surprised face of the waiting officer. 'No sound, if you please!' he ordered. 'Take us to the bridge.'

The ferry master was taken completely by surprise but he could see the determination on the faces of the hijackers. Guns and grenades brooked no protest.

'Set sail, Captain. Keep to a course for Cherbourg. No tricks and nobody gets hurt.

'One hundred revs,' ordered the Captain, signalling the engine room.

'Hello, engine room here. What is the trouble? Why the stop?' The engineer sounded puzzled.

A pistol was thrust into the captain's stomach. 'No trouble, chief. Just an emergency rescue stop for a launch. Carry on!'

In a few hours, they sighted Cherbourg, about a mile off in the morning mist.

'Captain, you will dock as normal' Said Erich. The radio telephone was buzzing. Erich picked up the receiver.

'Erich. this is Kurt. The launch has been holed. It must have been that rocket. She's floundering. In fact she is barely afloat. The cabin's flooded below the waterline.' Kurt sounded desperate.

'*The wallet and papers!*' Erich sounded alarmed.'

'We have made several dives, but they seem to have disappeared – perhaps lodged somewhere.' Kurt was really sounding desperate now.

'All right I will take a compass reading to get the present position. Open any stopcock so that she sinks quickly. Then abandon ship and come aboard.'

The ladders were still in place. A plan was beginning to form in Erich's mind.

'Captain, you will order your second officer to dock the ferry. You will come with me and ten passengers. Otto, stay on the bridge until we dock. Then smash any radio equipment and join us on the unloading deck. There is a coach on the deck. We will use that. Now, Captain, move!'

The passengers gaped at the armed men. Selecting the ten hostages and leaving Ludwig to guard the rest, Erich escorted the hostages to the parking bay. Fortunately the coach was near the front. The hostages were seated inside the coach and warned to do exactly as they were told. Leaving Horst to guard them, Erich returned to the bridge. He tuned the radiotelephone.

'Hello, Cherbourg port. This is the Truckline ferry. A coach will be the first to leave the ship. It will not be stopped under any circumstances and will be allowed to leave the dock area without any interference. Any attempt to hinder the coach will result in the death of one of the hostages we are carrying. The same will happen at every enforced stop. The bodies will be thrown from the coach. Is that understood?'

'We have your message, ferry.' The voice sounded anxious.

The docking procedures were carried out with their usual

efficiency. Then Otto smashed the radio.

Erich came hurrying from the bridge. 'Otto, soak a piece of rag in oil, set it alight and toss it into an empty vehicle. Then get on the coach. Hurry!'

There was no sign of a heavy police presence. A single gendarme stood at the entrance to the dock.

'Horst, Kurt and Raoul – when we clear the dock gate, jump from the coach and hurry to the car park. Pick up our vehicles and follow the coach at a distance. I will stop at some convenient spot. Park some way behind the coach. I will make the hostages lie down on the floor and draw all the blinds and threaten to shoot anyone I see looking through the windows. We will all then drive off in our own cars. Understood?'

They all nodded in agreement. 'Remember, speed is essential in case the coach has been followed too closely.'

Smoke was now billowing out from the landing deck and panic was spreading. The dockside was strangely quiet. Too easy! There were police cars parked discreetly some distance from the ferry.

They rounded the dock entrance and slowed. Kurt and the others leapt clear and raced for the car park. Erich accelerated and sped away from the dockside.

Nobody was following. He had chosen a suitable lay-by for the changeover and they were now speeding along the route to Germany in their own get away cars. A helicopter buzzed along the highway but had continued on. Obviously their identity was unknown.

'Chief Inspector Goodbody? Inspector DuPont here of the Cherbourg Prefecture. We had an incident at the quayside.

'The early morning Truckline ferry was shanghaied by your German terrorists. We had no choice but to let them land. They had hostages. There was also a fire on board the ferry. A coach and escape cars were involved. The whole affair was highly organised. We tracked them to Karlsruhe, where they used a helicopter to lift them to an isolated castle in the Bavarian forests. We are cooperating with the German Polizei and Interpol. We believe there is something more to this than terrorism.

Goodbody was amazed by what he was hearing. 'Thank you,

Inspector, for keeping me informed. We have a possible murder and abduction charge outstanding. I'll appreciate your continued cooperation so please keep me informed of future developments.'

The helicopter landed in the castle courtyard. Erich and the team piled out and made for the main entrance. Ingrid ran out to greet them. Her eyes were, however, searching for one face in particular – Erich's.

There he was, looking a little strained. 'Erich, you are safe!' She put her arms around his neck and kissed him unashamedly. The others glanced enviously at their leader. She was a looker!

'Father is waiting for you in the hall. He has been fretting ever since you left,' she added.

The Count greeted Erich warmly. 'I'm so pleased to see you all back safely. A drink?'

'A stiff brandy would be most welcome,' replied Erich.

The Count handed him a generous balloon of his best Napoleon, then watched him sip it gratefully. 'Felix will see to the others. Now, how did the operation go?'

'The good news is, of course, that we have all returned safely. The downside is that the papers are resting at the bottom of the Channel. But I have the grid references for their recovery.' Erich saw the count raise his eyebrows.

'We were attacked by a patrol vessel and helicopters. The launch was damaged and we were unaware of the extent of the damage. Because of the attack, we had to hijack a Channel ferry.' Erich went on to explain in greater detail the operation and its conclusion. 'Knowing the location, it means that we can recover the documents at our leisure,' he continued.

'Within reason,' cautioned the Count. 'You were not followed?' he added.

'Not that we were aware of. We kept a wary eye out for possible tails,' replied Erich.

'Enough of business,' said the Count. 'I have arranged a magnificent dinner for this evening. Meanwhile your rooms are still available. So go and have a shower or hot bath and we will meet later on.'

Erich retired to his rooms. He stripped off his clothes and

lowered himself into the steaming hot water, with plenty of nice smelly perfumes. A large brandy and a fat cigar completed his luxury.

The door opened. She stood there, gloriously naked. He indulged himself in gazing at this exquisite creature. Everything was in beautiful proportions. Her pert breasts with protruding dark nipples. The inviting thighs. He adsorbed every tiny little detail.

'Join me,' he invited. 'There is so much room in here. I feel positively lost.' A second invitation was completely unnecessary.

They enjoyed each other to the absolute limits of pleasure, basking in a euphoria neither wanted to end.

Kommandant Schultz, of the German Polizei, had exchanged information with Chief Inspector Goodbody and Inspector Du Pont of the Cherbourg Prefecture. These were not your ordinary terrorists, bandits or saboteurs. They were more sinister. Their interest in old 'Third Reich' papers, referring possibly to dormant political fortunes, indicated neo-Nazi links.

A castle in Bavarian forests... No, these were not common criminals. They were well armed and possibly fanatical in their determination. This operation would require maximum concentration and precision planning, possibly including the use of paramilitary units. Cooperation from Luftwaffe air support and armoured units would help. The Luftwaffe could provide helicopter gunships.

The target was isolated, with one access road. That was easily blocked. The forest trails were numerous. That would require all-terrain vehicles. Horses – he understood that there were horses stabled in the grounds. Better have some mounted police units drafted in. There might be an attempt to escape on horseback.

He spent the whole morning on the telephone. By late afternoon he was satisfied. Helicopters. Road pursuit. Forest trails. Had everything been covered?

The whole operation was to commence at dawn the following day. Armed paramilitary police would approach first. There must be no sign of any back-up forces.

There was a stillness in the air. A slight morning mist was rising over the densely packed trees. The whole scene was one of peace and tranquillity; the home of fairies and elves. Quiet, too quiet. That was the unnaturalness of it all. No birds sang. The dawn chorus was missing.

It was that unnatural silence that had roused him. Ingrid lay peacefully by his side. God, She was beautiful, even in sleep! She stirred but didn't waken.

Erich felt uneasy. There was an air of expectancy. But for what? He drew on a pair of slacks and slipped on a pair of shoes, then went onto the parapet. The scene was peaceful. Nothing stirred. He peered more intently. A slight movement in the trees. Was it a wild boar? No, a wild boar would have gone crashing through the undergrowth. There, there was another movement. Not a natural movement, as of an animal, but a controlled movement. He concentrated on the one spot. Yes! There it was a grey shape. It moved stealthily. It was a uniformed man. There was another and another. His stomach muscles tightened.

He Dashed to Kurt's room. 'Kurt! Kurt! Wake up! Wake up! Something's wrong! Quick, rouse the rest of the men. Get dressed and armed. We will meet in the hall.'

They were all gathered together. Count von Reinhardt, Felix, the castle staff, bodyguards and Ingrid. 'We have a problem,' announced Erich. 'As far as I can gather, the whole castle is surrounded. We have about a dozen fighting men. Machine guns, grenades and other small arms. From what I have seen outside suggests a much superior force.

'We have two choices. One we stay and die. The other we make a dash for it. Our escape route is in the air by the Helicopter. Franz, you're the pilot. What do you think of our chances?' Erich addressed the pilot.

'Well, the helicopter can carry up to twenty people. I could have it ready in twenty minutes. Our only chance is surprise. If we are in the air and moving we could elude pursuit. On the other hand, if they have gunships we could have a rough ride.' Franz put the scenario as he could foresee it. There was anxiety in his voice.

Erich looked at the group. 'This is what I propose. The

domestic staff can leave. This is not their fight. They must be ready to leave as soon as the helicopter is in the air. Count von Reinhardt, you will please destroy all confidential files. The rest of you will go to the garage and get petrol cans and sprinkle everywhere with petrol. When I fire a single shot, you will ignite the petrol and all dash for the helicopter, which will take off in matter of minutes from the sound of the shot. Anybody left behind will have to take care of themselves. *But*, repeat, *but* nobody will allow themselves to be taken prisoner. There are too many drugs today that loosen tongues. Everybody understand what they have to do?'

They all nodded in acquiescence. The Count glanced ruefully around at his castle. But Erich had taken over overall command of the situation and there was no time for sentimentality. Too much was at stake.

'Right, let's move. Take only bare essentials. Go! Go! Go!'

They quickly dispersed, and Erich turned to the girl at his side.

'Ingrid, you will go and set the horses free. Turn them into the forest. They will soon be rounded up. Horst, Ludwig and Otto – up on to the ramparts. Take grenades with you. Hold off any surprise attacks.' Erich glanced at Ingrid. They exchanged looks that needed no explanations.

Polizeikommandant Schultz controlled his forces with his walkie-talkie sets. His units were almost in position. Armoured units and helicopter gunships were hidden but tuned up and ready to go. Something was going on in the castle. And there was the whine of a helicopter engine. God! What was that? A sheet of flame shot out from several windows. A group of people were coming out of the front gates. Mostly middle-aged. Domestics, by the look of them. Then a single pistol shot.

'Inspector.' A voice crackled on his walkie-talkie set.

'Yes? Schultz here.'

'Horses are galloping out of the rear gates.'

Things were happening in rapid succession. The noise of the helicopter engine was now rising into a crescendo. God! It was taking off.

Erich fired his automatic. Figures were dashing from all sides. The helicopter rotors were turning faster and faster. It was like some wild animal straining at its bonds. All accounted for. 'Right, Franz, take it up!'

Some small arms fire was coming from below. Schultz turned to his second in command. 'Call up the gunships. They mustn't escape! Then get some men into the castle to tackle those fires.'

The helicopter started to slip into a fast forward flight. Erich looked back. The buildings were well and truly ablaze. Otto tapped him on the shoulder and pointed. There, three evil-looking gunships were homing in on them.

'Franz, can you handle them?' Erich asked the pilot anxiously.

'Depends how aggressive they get. They can be very nasty. Better wait and see what mood they are in!'

'Gunships to command! Gunship to command!'

'Command receiving.'

'We have bandits nearby. What action recommended?'

'Command to gunships. Indicate bandit to follow and land. Tell me the response.'

'They are closing, Erich,' said Franz. 'I can see the co-pilot. He wants us to follow.'

Erich's mind was racing. They were outgunned. Those vicious-looking rocket pods carried a lethal message. But there was no question of them being arrested. He looked at Ingrid. She seemed so vulnerable. Count von Reinhardt seemed resigned. The rest of the group would fall in with any decision he made.

'Can we out-fly them?' he asked Franz.

'Probably, on a long run, but those rockets would be released before we could establish a safe lead,' replied the pilot.

'Try it,' said Erich. His mind was made up; the stakes were too high.

Tilting the large helicopter, Franz gunned the revs. They were pulling away.

'Gunships to command!'

'Command receiving!'

'Bandit trying to escape. Over.'

'Command to gunships. Fire warning rocket. Over.'

They all saw the missile heading their way. It missed.

'That was deliberate,' said Franz. 'Next time, kaput!'

'Try some evading moves,' suggested Erich.

'You'd better hold on,' replied Franz. He began weaving and altering speed.

'Gunships to command. Bandit still not responding. Taking evasive action.'

Schultz had made up his mind. It was the final solution.

'Command to gunships. *Destroy. Repeat, destroy!*' They saw the next missile. And the next one.

A huge fireball filled the air. Gunship to command. Bandit dead. No survivors.'

'Goodbody! Schultz here. All bandits dead. Lair destroyed…'

Epilogue

Back in Bath, Boris was very relieved to be released by Inspector Wilson's officers. He remembered all to succinctly what had happened to Trevor. There was a short debriefing by the inspector but he wasn't able to add much to what they knew already. Simon had heard them discussing pretty much the same things that Boris had heard. His first questions related to Monica. He was haunted by an idea that he'd done the wrong thing by sending the terrorists down to Braunton. He'd known that to resist may have led to more bloodshed, but had he put Monica and Simon and Lydia in greater danger?

The inspector reassured him, that he'd done the best thing; they'd probably suspected Simon had the papers. It would most likely have been the next place they'd have gone as they'd probably have been watching the house the week before. No, Boris had done the right thing, and everyone in Braunton was safe.

Boris was anxious to see Monica and the police car dropped him by his car, which was still parked outside the Connaught Rooms.

He'd phoned through to Lydia. 'I'm on my way,' he called down the phone.

'Thank goodness you're alright, Boris,' she replied. 'Do drive carefully, and don't take any chances we don't want any further disasters.' She hung up and went to tell Monica and Simon the good news.

On the television newscast that evening they saw details of the Truckline hijack and the cross-Channel chase.

They were all in Hugh's house. Boris was sitting on the sofa, his arm around Monica's shoulders. Her face reflected her relief and happiness.

'I cannot believe so much has happened in two days,' he remarked. 'I feel I've caused so much trouble by just hanging on to those papers all these years, and I feel some responsibility for

Trevor's death. How could I have been so naive? I should have shown them to someone years ago – handed them over to the authorities. I have been a really thoughtless idiot. My head is full of music, and not much else!'

Simon intervened. 'Boris, it might have been better if they'd been handed in straight after the war, but you'll never know what might have happened. There was a lot of corruption and confusion then and they might still have fallen into the wrong hands. You must never think you're to blame for Trevor's death. The only people to blame for that are the terrorists. All the time there are people alive who think they can carry on Hitler's dream, there will be danger. They are evil, because he was evil.'

'I wish I'd never set eyes on them,' said Boris with strength of feeling. 'I wish I hadn't ever been in Berlin that day at the end of the war, but I can't do anything about that now. What I can do is make sure everyone knows as much as possible about them so there is less chance anyone else will be killed in their pursuit. And I'm going to set up some sort of scholarship for young percussionists in Trevor's name. I've already spoken to his parents about it, I can afford it now; not only do I give concerts but I'm going to make some records and I'm setting aside a percentage of that money for this project.'

Monica looked at him with pride and he squeezed her hand and smiled back.

'Well, my friends, tomorrow I'm off to Edinburgh. The show must go on, and we'd like to announce something to you. Monica is taking further leave and is coming with me for the concert in Scotland.'

He beamed round at everyone: Paulo and Elsa, Simon, Lydia, Hugh and Monica. 'When Lydia's sister first wrote and said I'd be welcome in Simon and Lydia's house I was very anxious. I didn't feel too well and I thought I would be a burden and spoil my welcome. Now I have to say I wouldn't have missed it for the world! I've made five very good friends and I've found Monica. Wherever else could I have been so blessed? You are all to receive an open invitation to visit us in Berlin whenever we're at home, and to attend any of my concerts you wish – free, of course. So we hope we'll see a lot of you all in the future. Thank you all so much.'

ACT THREE:
THE CURTAIN FALLS

Chapter Twenty-six

Erich gazed at the approaching missile. Ingrid was clutching his arm. Count von Reinhardt, Otto and Ludwig had placed their heads on their knees. The explosion was blinding and there was a sickening judder. The rocket had struck the forward end of the huge helicopter and the sound of rending metal filled the air.

Erich was dazed and mystified – he was alive! Close by lay Ingrid and her father. Otto and Ludwig were staggering to their feet. A fierce fire interspersed with loud explosions came from nearby. His head gradually cleared and he could see that they had been thrown clear of the rear of the helicopter, which had been torn free from the main body and crashed into the dense foliage of the forest.

He staggered to where Ingrid was lying. There was blood on her face but she was alive. He ran to her father, who lay crumbled in the undergrowth. Otto and Ludwig were disorientated but seemed otherwise unhurt.

Erich quickly assessed the situation and dashed to where the two were standing. 'We must clear from here as quickly as possible! The whole area will be swarming with search parties in no time. Otto, take Ingrid's father and head away from the wreckage. I'll follow with Ingrid and Ludwig. Now hurry – there isn't a moment to be lost!'

The four of them set off away from the shattered helicopter.

Chapter Twenty-seven

Hans Liebermann sat in his grand and luxuriously appointed office. He was fifty-eight years of age but still carried himself in a military manner. Life had treated him well. A general during the war, he had organised the expansion and exploitation of the Romanian oilfields during the war and was now the chairman of the vast PETRO Oil Company, based in its prestigious offices in Dortmund.

The post-war era had been one of the economic miracles of the twentieth century. Germany had been shattered. Its vast industrial capacity had been frustrated and destroyed by the imposition of sanctions and controls by the Allied forces. Now through the Marshall Plan combined with sheer German hard work and enterprise, a new and prosperous West Germany had risen from the ashes of defeat.

However, there was an undercurrent of resentment to the new liberal thinking among the intellectuals.

The nostalgia for the old order was ever present though not openly displayed. The nostalgia had contained itself within underground right-wing sympathisers. National Socialism had not perished in the Berlin bunker. A vast network of sleepers was organised waiting for the summons to activate and resurrect the old order.

Hans was thoughtful. The caller on the telephone had given the coded introduction. Two high-ranking members of the party, who would expect his unquestioning cooperation, would shortly make a visit. He had felt that latent excitement that he had not experienced since those heady days of the old rallies.

Order and action: this was the lifeblood of the Third Reich, and he was ready for the call.

He picked up the telephone. Freda, his secretary, answered. 'Yes, Herr Liebermann?' Her voice had the usual calm efficient tone – a tone that matched her appearance. She always wore a tailored suit that accentuated her attractive figure. Sensible but fashionable leather shoes. Her blonde hair was neatly drawn back to show her beautifully moulded face. Make-up very discreetly applied.

Hans counted his blessings. His thoughts had occasionally wandered off in fantasies, but he left the future to take care of these. Who could say? His wife, Trudy, fulfilled most of his fantasies, and the pitfalls of illicit liaisons were daunting.

'Freda, I am expecting two visitors. Would you bring them straight into my office when they arrive and cancel all my appointments for this morning – and no telephone interruptions while they are here.' He had tried to keep his voice businesslike.

'Certainly, Herr Liebermann. There are two gentlemen entering the outer office now. They may well be your expected visitors.' She rang off.

Chapter Twenty-eight

Freda showed in the two men.

'Your visitors, Herr Liebermann,' she announced, as she withdrew and closed the door behind her.

Hans gazed at the two men. One was in his late sixties, upright and aristocratic in appearance, dressed in an expensively tailored pinstripe suit, soft grey shirt and plain woollen tie. His shoes were expensive handmade brown brogues. A soft felt hat was in his hand. The other visitor was much younger, perhaps late twenties or early thirties. Obviously very athletic. Blonde hair and an expensive and stylish haircut. He wore a casual grey woollen suit with a black crew-necked shirt and soft brown leather slip-on shoes. His face showed fitness and an outdoor lifestyle. Shrewd ice-blue eyes betrayed a calculating ruthlessness. An impressive presentation by the two men.

'Good morning, gentlemen.' Hans was wary but did not wish to show any hostility. 'I received a telephone message earlier, and I have been expecting your visit. Now how can I be of any assistance'?

The older man spoke first. 'Herr Liebermann, my name is Reinhardt. Count von Reinhardt, and this is my assistant, who for the time being we will address as Erich.' His manner was relaxed and his voice cultured. 'You are probably aware of our connections from the coded message you received?'

Hans relaxed. 'Gentlemen, please sit down,' he said, indicating the two large comfortable chairs in front of his desk. 'Can I get you something to eat, or perhaps a drink?' he added.

'Thank you, but no. I wish to get to the point of our visit immediately.' The Count continued. He outlined his position within the organisation and recounted the incidents prior to the police raid on the castle headquarters of the organisation, and their subsequent miraculous escape from the ambush and the unfortunate loss of some of their most efficient and dedicated followers.

Liebermann listen attentively, and when the Count had finished his résumé of the past events, he answered, 'Graff von Reinhardt, how can I be of assistance? My loyalty to the cause is unquestioning. Say what you would like me to do?'

The Count spoke slowly, choosing his words carefully. The vast amounts of money that were at stake could test the loyalty of the most ardent of members.

'What we need is the use of oil exploratory equipment: ships; underwater surveillance monitors; a crew of hand-picked men, possibly members of the organisation; and absolute secrecy. Any leak of our intentions would sabotage the whole endeavour and put our movement back decades.'

Chapter Twenty-nine

The representative of PETRO entered the harbour master's office. The clerk looked up from the reception desk. He was a young man with that look of enthusiasm that shows on the faces of people interested in the work they are doing.

'My company has contacted your establishment about our need to base an oil exploratory vessel in Poole Harbour. Our requirements are simple but we want to be discreet. Mention oil and you'd think we were starting a miniature gold rush! My name, by the way, is Roberts, Michael Roberts. This is my card. You can contact my head office at the address on the card to verify my authority.'

The clerk glanced at the card. 'Could you hang on for a moment? I'll contact the harbour master to confirm what you say.'

'Of course – you carry on. I'll just sit here and read some of your tatty magazines.'

The clerk returned with an older man wearing some sort of naval uniform.

'Hello, Mr Roberts. My name is Mulligan, the harbour master. My Irish connections are lost in the mists of antiquity.'

A genial person thought Michael, with a sense of humour. That should make things go smoothly.

'I've heard from your head office in London and there doesn't seem to be any problem. I understand they want the anchorage for six months initially. They did ask for a discreet anchorage and I have organised that; there's no difficulty at this time of the year. We see the last of the tourists and weekend sailors in September. I've shown them a map of the harbour and your anchorage on the quayside. Anything else you may require just get in touch and I'm sure we can sort it out for you.'

Michael thanked him and left to find the nearest expensive hotel. After all, the company were paying.

Erich gazed at the ship tied up alongside the quay in Bremerhaven. She was larger than he had expected, more like a small version of a luxury cruiser. The upper deck bristled with antennae and discs. The huge gantries showed a powerful lifting force. Ludwig and Otto were with him. Their brief was to mix with the crew, who, although selected for loyalty, could have human weaknesses – too fond of female company, perhaps, and a liking for the seamy life where their tongues may be loosened by the company or liquor. They had their instructions. Any suspected defections were to be eliminated decisively and permanently.

Chapter Thirty

Captain Steiner gazed at the three men who had entered the bridge house. He was a man in his late fifties with an aura of command. His life had been the sea since he had commanded U333 during the war. He'd been a legend in the Kriegsmarine with over 100,000 tons of enemy shipping to his credit. His tour of service had ended in Naples Harbour with his surrender to the Americans. This humiliation had stayed with him ever since and he was a dedicated member of the underground movement.

Erich spoke first. 'Commander, my name is Erich and these are my colleagues.' He gestured towards Ludwig and Otto and introduced them. 'I believe you are aware of our task.'

Steiner regarded each of the three men. These were clearly tough, ruthless men dedicated to their ideals. He had seen such men in the Kriegsmarine: capable of enduring unbelievable hardship, yet always with that hungry look when hunting their prey.

'Gentlemen, welcome aboard. You will have my complete cooperation. If you will follow me I will show you your quarters and take you around the ship.'

Their quarters were compact but comfortable. Each man had his own cabin.

'We have a crew of twenty. Most are experts in their own field,' Steiner continued as they toured the ship.

At the stern, a small helicopter pad served the small two-man Sikorsky. Behind the bridge house was a vast area filled with complicated-looking electronic gear. In front of the bridge, secured to the deck, was the underwater surveillance pod fitted with manoeuvrable arms controlled by the three-man crew. The lifting gear towered above the deck and was capable of raising objects of up to ten tons in weight from the seabed.

'A very fine ship, Captain. You seem to be equipped for any underwater task.' observed Erich. 'Well she is *PETRO 1*, the flagship of the company. A sort of floating demonstration of the company's technology,' replied Steiner, with just a hint of pride in his voice.

'When can we sail?' asked Erich.

'Now you are on board, we can set sail on the high tide tomorrow at noon. The crew are all here and we are fully stocked for a three-month expedition. I understand you will give me my sailing instructions once we have set sail,' replied Steiner.

Chapter Thirty-one

Michael sat on the bar stool in the bar of the Miramar.

The bar waitress was the chatty type, attractive and shapely. Her hair was cut in an elfin style, which suited her boyish looks. Her make-up was simple and unobtrusive. A trim figure with a neckline that flirted with the imagination. Curvaceous hips accentuated by the clinging black one-piece dress. Her long fingers tapered to modestly painted fingernails.

Michael was aware of her attractiveness, and he was feeling lonely. The bar was empty except for a few long-term residential types.

'You're not from these parts?' she asked. Her voice had a soft flirtatious tone.

Sylvia had noticed the lone stranger when he had entered the lounge. A well-dressed city type, she observed to herself. About early thirties. Expensive casual hairstyle for his dark hair. Clean-shaven. Good-looking, with a hint of a tan from expensive holidays or travel abroad for business trips. Around six feet tall with a slim athletic body. Nice lounge suit from an expensive tailor. Loose open-necked shirt and casual slip-on brown leather shoes.

She was feeling a little bored, preferring to be busy and the centre of attraction to her appreciative customers. She had no illusions about their fantasies and she enjoyed a spot of flirtatious banter.

'No, I'm down from London on some business at the harbour,' he responded, not too eagerly, he hoped.

'Your business is with boats, then?' she asked, gazing straight into his attractive hazel eyes.

'Yes, fixing up a berth for an oil exploration ship from Germany.' He thought he'd raise his status a bit.

'German ship?' she said in a manner that indicated more than a casual interest. 'We had some bother here with some German gang some months ago. You may have read about it in the papers, or seen it on the television...'

Michael showed interest, adopting the role of the good listener. His thoughts were more on chatting up this delightful creature than on the content of her conversation.

'No, can't say I remember. Why, what happened?' he replied, wanting to prolong the 'chat'.

'Strange business. My boyfriend was involved. He's a policeman at Poole.'

Pity about the boyfriend, Robert thought. He was slightly irked by the reference to him, and that this attractive creature could be interested in a policeman of all people. Not his idea of a romantic!

'Oh? What happened?' Anything to keep her chatting.

'Well, there was this launch tied up to quayside, and my Harold...'

Michael winced slightly. *Harold* – what an unromantic name.

'...He was patrolling on the lookout for a car carrying some wanted men connected with a kidnapping – somewhere in Bath, I think,' she continued, now in full spate.

'To cut a long story short, Harold approached this boat and went aboard.' She was getting to the climax now and it was showing on her face.

'You'd never believe it but there was this gang of Germans. Right villains they looked.' She was really making the most of it. 'The leader was pointing this vicious gun at my Harold, and told him to call his friend on board. Well, they were both taken prisoner. It gave my Harold a nasty turn, I don't mind telling you,' she added with a twinkle in her eyes and an impish smile on her lips.

'But that's not the finish of the story,' She was off again. 'They then took my Harold and his friend with them out to sea – and guess what happened next?'

Michael hadn't a clue. Harold was now beginning to be really irritating. He hadn't the faintest idea but wished Harold had gone to kingdom come.

'I haven't the foggiest notion,' he heard himself saying.

'They made them both jump overboard to swim about a mile

back to shore. Mind you, they did give them life jackets.'

She was looking wistful now, and this irritated him still further. To think of Harold as a hero was just too much.

'Sounds exciting,' was all he could muster.

'My Harold was furious. He said if he ever met those Germans again, it wouldn't be him going for a swim!'

Michael found it all getting out of hand. This wretched Harold was sabotaging his progress with this attractive but misguided creature.

'And how is Harold now?' he asked, not believing the words were coming from his own mouth; a blatant contradiction of his own true thoughts.

'He's got over it all now. Particularly as he heard that the Germans had all died in a helicopter crash.' She continued. 'We are getting married at Christmas, thank goodness. His night duties are driving me mad.' She added.

'Excuse me, I must serve this couple.' She moved along the bar.

Michael drank his whisky and made his way disconsolately to his room. Somehow the evening hadn't concluded as he had planned.

Ah well, win some, lose some... He must remember never to call any sons he should have in the future *Harold*.

Chapter Thirty-two

PETRO 1 quietly slipped its moorings as the two powerful diesel engines turned the twin screws. The subdued throb conveyed the feeling of the immense power of the 1,000 horsepower engines.

The engine room telegraph rang down to the engine room where the chief engineer, another veteran of Steiner's wartime crew, watched and listened lovingly to the power thrust of his impatient charges. Erich stood next to the commander at the navigation charts spread over the table in the spacious bridge house.

A course was set for the open Channel. There was an air of nostalgic excitement. Steiner was setting out on another mission. Not in the cramped space of U333 but in command of this powerful spacious and state-of-the-art craft.

He felt the invincibility that Admiral Gunther Lutjens must have experienced on the German flagship *Bismarck* when he set out on his fateful mission in May 1941.

'Set a course for latitude fifty degrees North, longitude two degrees West. This will bring us outside the territorial waters north of Cherbourg,' instructed Erich.

'When do you estimate the time of our arrival?' he added.

'At a steady fifteen knots we should arrive in six to eight hours' replied Steiner.

The sea was calm. A low mist hovered over the vast expanse of water, giving an eerie sense of isolation.

Sylvia snuggled up to Harold. It was his night off. Night duty was one week in four, and she savoured this time together.

The flat was hers, but Harold was a frequent visitor and sometimes lingered until morning. She was, however, adamant that there would be no joint tenancy until the wedding bells had rung.

It was a cosy flat and she had furnished it simply and without clutter. The decor was definitely feminine: pinks and pastels. The large settee dominated the lounge, as the equally large bed with wrought iron framework dominated the bedroom. Deep wool carpets covered the floors except for the kitchen, where a concession had been made to the practicalities of cooking and work surfaces. The bathroom was spacious with a large pedestal bath in the centre of the room. The walls were tiled from floor to ceiling. The overall colour scheme pink with a mix of white. Yes, Sylvia was very proud of her niche.

They had been looking at the television. The programmes were more of a background to their togetherness.

'Harold...' She had a way of saying his name that never failed to excite him.

'Yes, Pet,' he replied. She would have liked a 'darling' but this was the nearest to any verbal endearments that Harold allowed himself.

'I had a smart "City" type in the bar the other evening.' She was watching for a reaction.

'Smart chap, and very good-looking. I think he fancied me,' she continued. 'In fact I know he did.' She needed more emphasis to gain Harold's attention.

'Oh, really? You must get that all the time. Maybe you ought to consider finding something else after we are married.' His voice was too matter-of-fact for her.

'I like my job,' she protested, quite aware that he was showing a reaction. Jealousy was there, even if it was camouflaged with indifference.

'Well, this chap was telling me that he'd arranged for a German boat to be moored in the harbour.'

'*German!*' Harold replied with a snort. 'I'll keep an eye on that lot! You can't trust them. Never know what they are up to.' He was definitely biased against anything German. A long unsolicited swim can cloud anyone's liberal thinking.

'Are you going home tonight?' she asked.

'Up to you... I'm not on duty until late tomorrow.'

'Let's go to bed,' she replied. She needed a more active scenario from him. He became more stimulated by the bedroom scene.

They unwound themselves and he gave her a friendly slap on the bottom. 'I thought you'd never ask!' he added.

That's better, she thought. Too much talk isn't good for a girl's ego.

Chapter Thirty-three

PETRO 1 hove to north of Cherbourg.

'Can your sonics sound the seabed with a reasonably accurate assessment of any objects – say, the size of a large motor launch – that may be down there?' Erich asked Steiner.

'They could certainly detect the object, but a more accurate assessment would be made with our remote cameras,' replied Steiner. 'I would suggest an initial sweep of the seabed with sonar over an area that you suggest. Then a remote camera scan of any object detected. Our three-manned diving pod would then make a final confirmation of identity.'

'The object of our mission is to retrieve a waterproof container from within the launch,' Erich continued.

'This may make retrieving the launch a delicate operation. Should the boat disintegrate, the container would be more difficult to trace amongst the debris.'

Erich voiced his concern. Steiner was thoughtful and finally deliberated over the safeguards that could be taken. He said, 'When the launch has been finally located, depending on its size and its being in one whole piece, then canvas straps could lift it using our derricks; then a large net could be passed under the craft so that it is cradled completely. A slow lift would then bring it to the surface. '

Steiner was confident such a manoeuvre was possible. His curiosity was, however, aroused about the importance attached to the case and its contents. Instilled discipline subdued this curiosity. Orders were orders and must be carried out without question.

'Good, Captain, I like your plan.' Erich felt a great sense of relief.

Chief Superintendent Goodbody sat at his desk in New Scotland Yard. It was a modest office for such a high-ranking officer but a long way from his humble beginnings in Somerset. His hair was a little greyer since those days in Bath and he had put on a little weight with all the deskwork.

Promotions had come quickly over the years.

He gazed thoughtfully at the memo on his desk. The message was short and headed, 'Ministry of Trade and Industry'.

Please contact Sir John Blake, Minister of Trade and Industry, at your earliest convenience. A telephone number was given.

Goodbody picked up the telephone and dialled the number. A smooth male voice answered, 'Minister of Trade's office. Can I help you?'

'This is Chief Superintendent Goodbody of the Metropolitan Police, and I have received a memo to contact the Minister.'

'Ah yes, Chief Superintendent,' came the smooth reply. 'The Minister would like to discuss an incident that has arisen. Can I make an appointment that will be convenient for you?' The unruffled voice gave nothing away.

'I can call anytime after lunch. If that suits,' replied Goodbody, intrigued.

'Shall we say three o clock?' The smoothy replied.

'That will be fine. Three o'clock then.' Goodbody confirmed. 'Thank you Chief Superintendent. Goodbye.'

Sir John Blake greeted him warmly.

'Please sit down, Goodbody.' The minister indicated a large comfortable chair. In fact the whole spacious office was comfortably furnished.

'I'm sorry to drag you here, but the matter is a little delicate,' said Sir John. 'We have granted an exploratory licence to the German oil company, PETRO. The area is off the French coast in what is international waters north of Cherbourg, but the ship wishes to be based at Poole in Dorset.'

Goodbody was curious. He had some dealings with the Poole police during the kidnapping incident.

Sir John continued, 'There may be nothing suspicious but the Sûreté were heavily involved with an international incident some time ago. A cross-Channel ferry was hijacked by a group of German terrorists. The whole incident climaxed in Bavaria, where the German Polizei and Interpol, together with units of the German military, destroyed the terrorist cell and all its members.'

Goodbody was not entirely without knowledge of the affair. 'Thank you, Minister, for filling me in. I was involved in this case, as you are undoubtedly aware.'

'I know, Goodbody, and that is the reason for my asking you to call here,' replied the Minister.

'There was something more malevolent in that clandestine organisation. There is a vast network of "sleeper" cells in Germany dedicated to a resurgence of the political right wing of the old Third Reich. The presence of this German oil exploratory ship may of course be quite genuine.' Sir John was choosing his words carefully 'The French are, however, very sensitive to the German connection. Interpol is also keeping a watching brief and the German authorities are on a constant alert.'

Goodbody took in the wider implications of what he had always treated merely as a local criminal operation.

'What course should we take, Minister?' he inquired.

'I think our task is to keep an eye on any developments on our side, particularly the use of Poole as a base for their operation. Any hint of a deviation from the norm must be investigated. That's where you will come in. Be alert to the situation and liaise with the French and German police on any developments,' concluded Sir John.

'Very well, Minister. Thank you for the briefing. I'll contact our European colleagues straight away. Were there any other matters to discuss?' asked Goodbody, sensing the meeting was at an end.

'No, Goodbody. Thank you for coming, and keep in touch.'

They shook hands and Goodbody left. His adrenalin was on a low pump.

He nodded cursorily to Sir John's smooth PA, and departed.

The weather was beginning to break up. The cumulus-darkened sky indicated that a storm was brewing. The dark forbidding sea was restless.

PETRO 1 had covered a five-mile box-search with its sonar. Nothing of significance had shown on the screen, and Steiner was acutely aware of the approaching storm.

He turned to Erich. 'We may have to abandon any further search for today.'

Erich sensed his restlessness. 'Give it a further hour, and if there is no positive response steer a course for Poole Harbour and we will wait for a further clear spell.'

He felt frustrated.

Steiner grunted his assent.

Harold called in at the harbour master's office.

The enthusiastic clerk was tidying his desk ready for the end of his shift. 'Hello, officer,' he said cheerily.

He quickly scanned his memory banks for any personal cause for this visit by the law. 'What can I do for you?'

'Oh, just a routine visit,' said Harold. He'd seen that guilty look on many faces in his career. Everyone has some hidden conscience for past law infringements that had gone undetected; usually car violations.

'You expecting any new berths in the near future?' Keep everything low key, he told himself. For the time being this would be a personal vendetta.

'There is a clay container due in from Spain tomorrow,' the clerk replied.

Much of the fine Portland clay was now shipped to Spain for fine art pottery. The heyday for Poole had been in the 1800s. The quayside would have been crammed with three-masters loaded with timber from Newfoundland. Heavy coarser clay for building was exported to all parts.

The famous limestone and marble of the Purbeck Hills was shipped to London and used for grandiose buildings such as St Paul's Cathedral, the Victoria Embankment beside the Thames, the Houses of Parliament, and various bridges spanning the river.

Most of this trade had disappeared except for specialised structures requiring architectural grandeur. Today it was light commercial trade and tourism. Wytch Farm, the largest onshore oilfield in Europe, created some trading, as did small boat-building for the luxury market.

Though one of the largest natural harbours in the world, Poole had a very shallow draft, an average of two or three feet in most places. The channel for larger craft had to be constantly dredged.

The whole of the harbour was scattered with islands of various sizes. The largest was Brownsea, the birthplace of the Scout movement, and where Henry the Eighth had sited a cannon to repel Spanish marauders, and later, any Napoleonic inquisitiveness. The earliest raiders were of course the Vikings, who laid waste to the hinterland. Before them, the Romans also used the harbour extensively to reach the inner settlement of Wareham and beyond. Trading flourished then with galleons coming and going from all parts of the Roman Empire, importing wine and oil and exporting clay and lead brought down from the Mendip hills.

'Oh, there may be a visit from a German oil exploration ship. It has berthing facilities for six months. The harbour pilots are on standby for its arrival early tomorrow morning.'

The clerk was being very helpful. It must be a relief to him that the call wasn't more personal, thought Harold. He made a mental note to visit the quayside the following day. 'Thank you for being so helpful,' he said. 'By the way, has your car had an MOT recently? Only I noticed that your licence is nearly due.'

He left with a wry smile on his face. Once a copper always a copper. He couldn't break the mould now.

The enthusiastic clerk was puzzled. What car? He didn't have a car...

Chapter Thirty-four

The shoreline of Dorset lay across the horizon. Dawn was breaking and the coastline was still a smudge rising from a white crested sea. The storm had followed *PETRO 1* for most of the journey across the Channel. The heavy cumulus sky was, however, showing breaks. Steiner ordered his lookouts to scan for a sight of the pilot boat.

Street lights were still twinkling from the vast holiday resorts of Bournemouth and Poole. 'Pilot boat ahead!' came the call over the ship's intercom.

Dead slow. Steiner rang the engine room telegraph.

There, coming out of the shadows, was the blue and orange pilot boat, a navigation light at its masthead.

The radio crackled.

'Ahoy, *PETRO 1!* Pilot here. I'll come alongside your boarding steps, if you will hold your speed and course steady, please,'

'Thank you, pilot. Board when convenient. My speed and course will remain steady.' Steiner spoke into the hand microphone.

They passed the famous 'Old Harry' landmark to the west and picked up the deep-water channel with green and red marker buoys.

The pilot had taken over control of the bridge.

The narrow entrance to the harbour was dead ahead. The old chain bridge remained stationary on the western bank to give Steiner free passage.

The pilot was alert but relaxed. Using the two-screw drive helped the tricky ninety-degree turn after the entrance. Alternate forward and reverse gave steering an extra edge in this tricky manoeuvre. Brownsea Island straddled the entry channel.

'Dead slow!' called the pilot.

PETRO 1 eased herself along the deep-water channel.

'We shall be mooring on the western quayside, Captain. I understand you wanted to avoid the busy eastern mooring?'

The dockside was beginning to come alive. Several early morning tourists and locals watched this magnificent boat being docked. The black and yellow flag was causing some curiosity, not least among the occupants of a police patrol car parked in the shadow of Anthony Caro's metal sculpture.

Erich briefed Otto and Ludwig to keep a low profile. They had been members of the original group involved in the ambush of the two policemen.

Steiner addressed the crew in the dining area.

'We will be anchored here for a few days while we wait for a favourable weather report. In the meantime you may go ashore but you must return each evening by 11.30 p.m. Avoid fraternising, particularly with women.'

There was a low murmur of good-humoured protest.

'I will post a roster for a five-member watch. They will ensure that there will be no uninvited visitors. Is that all clear?'

They all mumbled their assent.

'In case of an emergency I will give three blasts on the ship's horn. Wherever you are return to the ship immediately. Remember to pull up your pants beforehand. Enjoy yourselves.'

The crew gathered in groups and chatted for a while before moving off to various rendezvous.

Goodbody picked up the telephone. 'Jane, can you get me Kommandant Schultz of the German Polizei and then Inspector Du Pont of Cherbourg Prefecture. The numbers are in the book.' He replaced the telephone and gazed at the file in front of him. The file was headed 'TOP SECRET – LIMITED ACCESS'.

Jane, Goodbody's secretary, had some knowledge of the file and its contents and sensed the urgency in Goodbody's voice. Dressed casually but neatly, she brought a little glamour in an otherwise austere office.

'Is that the office of Kommandant Shultz?'

'*Ja, ja!* Who is calling?' The German voice quickly slipped into English. Jane made a resolution to take up her language studies again.

'Chief Superintendent Goodbody of New Scotland Yard would like to speak to the Kommandant if possible?'

'Hold on one moment.' She pressed the intercom button.

'Kommandant Schultz is coming on the line, sir.'

'Thanks Jane' said Goodbody.

'Hello Kommandant Schultz here.'

'One moment, sir. I'm putting you through. You're through now.' Jane put her receiver down.

Goodbody, after the usual salutations, broached the subject of Sir John's concern. They spoke for a good half an hour.

'Thank you, Herr Goodbody, we are in a state of constant alert to this situation. I'll put some of my best men on this particular case and let you know if anything suspicious turns up. We will keep you informed of any developments. Goodbye and thank you again.'

The same reaction came from the Inspector of Cherbourg Prefecture. A state of 'Red Alert' was now in place.

'Jane, can you have a car on standby to take me to Poole in Dorset?' Goodbody spoke into the intercom.

'There is a police officer at the gangway, Captain, and he would like a word with you,' the crewman told Steiner as he entered the bridge house. Erich and the commander had been studying the sea charts around the approaches to Cherbourg.

They both went to the overhang window that overlooked the gangway.

'Damn!' exploded Erich.

Steiner looked puzzled.

'It is that policeman we had to deal with on the other mission,' said Erich.

'I'll deal with him,' said Steiner. 'You make yourself scarce, and take Otto and Ludwig with you.'

Chapter Thirty-five

Goodbody relaxed in the back of the spacious chauffeured black Humber.

The Yard did provide comfortable transport for its executives. One of the few good perks that went with the job.

He always found this form of transport preferable to any other.

Sitting back, thinking, sightseeing, musing: the ultimate in relaxation and not a secretary in sight.

The traffic flowed, albeit slowly sometimes, but it flowed. None of those frustrating hold-ups. It was early afternoon. Whitehall had its usual throng of sightseers – mostly foreign tourists – who never tired of the sheer pageantry of London.

Whitehall Palace, outside which Charles the First was beheaded by the Cromwell parliament in 1649. Opposite were the brightly uniformed sentries of St James's Palace, standing rigid, while the throng of photographers took pictures of Harry, Tom and Dick with an occasional Mabel standing alongside them, to be shown lovingly to the folks back home.

Trafalgar Square, with its fat urban pigeons, getting fatter with the peanuts from more doting tourists. Nelson gazing down from the top his column.

The Mall: the stage setting for those magnificent parades and processions that the British do so well. Nash's imposing terrace to the right and St James's Park on the left. What a setting for military bands, horses, carriages and colourful marching men! Enough to soften the hearts of the most ardent critics of the monarchy.

Queen Victoria's figure gazing solemnly from her setting in front of Buckingham Palace. The palace, with its grand façade; quiet and dignified.

More tourists, and the never-ending procession of the ubiquitous black London cabs in which seasoned users always referred to the driver as 'George'.

Past the magnificent Wellington Memorial, which stands opposite No. One, London – Apsley House – the historic London home of the Duke of Wellington, victor of the Battle of Waterloo in 1815, the final Napoleonic battle.

Hyde Park on the right. Rotten Row where Society once displayed itself so beautifully on horseback. Knightsbridge, where fashion was de rigueur for the gorgeously attired lady shoppers. Harrods, the 'jewel in the crown' of the retail world, where exotic goods are displayed for the rich of the city.

On and on over the Hammersmith flyover along the Great West Road, past Gillette's Art Deco facade.

The hubbub of the great metropolis was slipping away and giving way to the green swathe of Richmond Park, easing into that great artery to the west, the A30 trunk road.

Soon the Humber was leaving behind the vast urban spread of London that devoured everything with bricks and mortar and mile upon mile of tarmac. The soft colours of the Green Belt gave way to the undulating landscape of Hampshire.

The countryside changed subtly as they approached Dorset. They were now on the A31 traversing the New Forest, that ancient hunting ground planted by William the Conqueror as his own game reserve, and where Will Rufus met his mysterious death from a huntsman's arrow. Now it was a free-range preserve for wild ponies and dedicated walkers.

The undulating landscape flowed down to the urban spread of Bournemouth, now the new home of many of the light industries and administrative centres removed from London, and yet still a magnet for vast numbers of tourists and holidaymakers. A centre of communications with its main-line rail link to Waterloo and air links to far distant places. Comparatively modern in its development, it was just over one hundred years since it had been a scrubland wilderness.

Bournemouth quickly gave way to the county of Dorset, with its coastline fragmented by bays and coves. Evidence of its past quarrying industry, which still thrives, but more discreetly on the vast limestone mass of the Purbeck Hills. Sprawling at the foot of these heights is the expanse of Poole Harbour, with its historic town of Poole, whose origins are cloaked in trade with ancient empires and the woodland expanses of the New World.

Chapter Thirty-six

Chief Inspector Howard was still in charge of the Poole police forces. He was one of the breed of fast-track promotion officers recruited from the universities.

He greeted Goodbody warmly. The Yard had forewarned him of his arrival. He was puzzled. The message had given no hint for the purpose of the Chief Superintendent's visit.

Goodbody wasted no time in his briefing and the sensitivity of his mission. The presence of the German oil exploration ship and the use of Poole as its base for the next six months had become a matter of international concern.

Howard had been involved in the previous incident involving German terrorist activity and was alert to any further threats.

'This must be kept highly confidential,' Goodbody informed Howard. 'The whole enquiry is based on supposition, but we cannot take any chances. There are the much bigger issues at stake.'

Harold kept his eyes alert during his escorted tour of the ship. Karl, his escort, gave very little away and kept to factual information on the complex equipment. There was, however, a distinct absence of any other members of the crew. He had heard muffled voices deep in the recesses of the engine room, and two mechanics were working on the two-seater Sikorsky. They wore special leather headgear and were absorbed with the helicopter's engine and rotor blades. The area was restricted, however, to aircrew members only.

He thanked Karl and left the ship. The two helicopter mechanics were observing him from inside the cockpit.

Later that evening, he told Sylvia about his visit to the PETRO 1.

'You know, I had a funny feeling they were all behaving warily, almost as if they had something to hide. It was a bit scary, I don't mind telling you, Pet.'

There's that 'Pet' again, thought Sylvia. She would definitely have to work on that one. 'It's just your prejudices making you think that way,' she told him. 'Keep an open mind and concentrate on me and you'll feel much better. So will I.'

He could feel the warmth of her body and caught the hint of that perfume, and soon the German ship slipped into history.

Steiner turned to Erich. 'The weather is becoming more settled, and there is a "high" over southern England that looks like staying with us for some time.'

'Right,' said Erich, 'we sail tomorrow and continue with the box-search.'

'I will inform the crew tonight and we can sail on the midday high tide.' Steiner sounded relieved.

'I'll stay for a few days and keep a watching brief,' said Goodbody to Howard. 'Do you know of a reasonably comfortable hotel? Not necessarily five star.'

'I have heard that the Miramar provides a good service. It's not the Hilton but then they don't charge Hilton prices, which always looks better on the expenses sheet. The Royal Bath is, of course, the premier hotel. Five star and very exclusive,' replied Howard.

'No, the Miramar sounds fine. You can contact me there. Could you ring through and book rooms for me and my chauffeur? I'll hang about in case there aren't any vacancies,' said Goodbody.

Five minutes later, Howard confirmed the booking. It was late when they arrived at the hotel.

'Good evening, sir. Your rooms are all ready,' said the receptionist as she handed over them the keys to their rooms. 'If you wait here I'll get the night porter to help you,' she added.

Joe had worked as night porter at the Miramar since the war when he and his wife, Mary, had moved down to Bournemouth from London to escape the extensive bombing raids on the East End, particularly around the dock area.

Small in stature, his cockney upbringing was reflected in his mannerisms and distinctly London accent. He also had that rolling gait usually associated with sailors, or which could have been acquired through pushing a barrow around the street markets of London. Both notions, however, would be far from the truth, for Joe had started work as a young press photographer in the days of the magnesium strip that flared to give additional light for the cameras. He had been present at the Sydney Street siege where units of a Guards regiment were returning the fire of the cornered anarchists. A young Winston Churchill, then the Home Secretary, was observing the siege. Unfortunately, Joe had a mishap with his magnesium strip and lost an eye, but one would be hard-pressed to identify which was his glass eye.

He and his wife, Mary, who was crippled with arthritis, now ran a bed and breakfast business.

'Joe,' said the friendly receptionist, 'can you show these guests to their rooms? I hope that you will both be comfortable, sir,' she added, turning to Goodbody.

'Right,' said Joe in his croaky accent. 'Follow me, Gents.' They had only hand luggage. He led the way. 'If you want a sandwich or anything during the night just ring down to the reception and I'll bring it up to your rooms.'

It was late afternoon.

The sea was calm and the sky was a light hazy blue streaked with wispy white cirrus cloud.

It was their second day on site, and the sonar had searched the seabed for a further two five-mile boxes, without, however, much success. The sun was beginning to sink down towards the horizon, when there was a commotion around the screens. Walter, the sonar supervisor, called to Steiner and Erich.

'We are getting strong signals on the screen!' he announced. Excitement was rising amongst the onlookers.

'What do you think, Walter?' asked Steiner.

'Well, there is definitely something down there. It could be any number of things – old wartime wreckage, a boat perhaps. Who knows? We need to take a closer look with the cameras.'

Steiner was thoughtful. 'We will heave to, and get a better look in the morning.'

Goodbody had slept very well. He telephoned Howard and heard that *PETRO 1* had left port on the high tide. He also contacted Jane to see if there had been any further developments from the Continent.

'No sir. There is, however, some post that I can send down to you by dispatch rider, if you wish.'

'No, thank you, Jane,' said Goodbody. 'It can all wait until I return.'

'By the way, sir,' Jane continued, 'the Home Secretary has been in touch, so I gave him your telephone number.'

'Good, Jane. You know where to find me for anything urgent. I will either be here at the hotel or at Poole police station. Goodbye, and thank you again.' He rang off.

Sylvia arrived for work and began organising the bar area, checking for shortages and generally getting ready for the lunch time session.

She met Joe as he was going off duty.

'Good morning, Joe. Had a good night?' She liked Joe. A rough old diamond in some ways, but a real bit of old London. Quite a rarity. He had lost his only son in an air crash up in Scotland. He'd been photographing isolated farms during the heavy snowstorms in the winter of 1947 for a documentary film. A pilot error, the enquiry had said. Something to do with merging horizons. Shame, really; he'd gone all through the war with a Guards tank regiment, unscathed.

'You'd better watch your step, young lady,' Joe said with a twinkle in his one good eye.

'Oh, why?' she said in mock innocence.

'There's a bigwig down from New Scotland Yard staying in number 64,' Joe said.

'Nothing but the best for me,' she teased.

'Don't say I didn't warn you, my girl,' Joe called as he went through the swing doors on his way home.

'Bye, Joe!' She called to the retreating figure. She just loved that old man.

The remote camera scanned the object in the murky waters. Definitely an old wartime bomber. Looked like a Dornier. It was

241

covered in debris and underwater growth. The wings were, however, still prominent and the fuselage showed the black cross of the German Luftwaffe.

It was a bitter disappointment.

Steiner gave the order to continue the search. He was conditioned to long searches. Those long tedious missions in the grey expanses of the Atlantic were something to which U-boat crews became accustomed.

The sonar was relaunched.

Sylvia recognised Goodbody. He had that presence that policemen have, observing everything with a studied casualness.

'Good morning, sir,' She said cheerily. The bar was open for the lunch session and Goodbody was feeling the need for a little light conversation.

'A small bitter, please,' he ordered.

'You're new here, aren't you?' It was Sylvia's opening remark to most of her new clients and it always worked.

'Yes. I'm down here making inquiries into some official business.' Goodbody never gave too much away but she was an attractive girl and her ingenuous approach was somewhat disarming.

'You're a police officer, aren't you?' she continued.

'Does it show that much?' He wasn't too surprised; after all it was partly her business to sum people up.

My boyfriend is in the police,' continued Sylvia. 'He's stationed at Poole.' Goodbody showed a mild interest.

'He was a sort of hero. Got himself kidnapped by some German terrorists, but then he managed to escape.'

Sylvia was motoring now on her favourite subject, Harold, and romancing a little at the same time.

'He can't stand those Germans now! He was telling me about a German ship tied up in Poole, which he had given the once-over. Couldn't stop himself, he said, but I told him he was paranoid.'

Goodbody's interest was raised. 'What is your boyfriend's name?' he asked casually.

'Oh – Harold. Harold Seaton. Here, I hope I haven't got him into any trouble?' she sounded a little apprehensive. I do tend to talk too much. But then he is my Harold and we are getting married soon.' Sylvia wasn't too concerned about her loose tongue. After all Harold did deserve some praise.

'No, of course not,' Goodbody reassured her. His interest was now definitely roused.

'Seaton, this is Chief Superintendent Goodbody from New Scotland Yard.'

Chief Inspector Howard opened the interview. He said 'I understand you visited the German oil exploration ship in the harbour the other day.'

Harold felt distinctly nervous. He hadn't told anyone officially about the visit.

'Yes, sir. I thought I would just give it the once-over. A sort of goodwill gesture – "entente cordiale" and all that, you might say.' That sounded a genuine excuse, Harold reasoned.

'Notice anything unusual?' the Chief Inspector continued.

'No, sir. Everything seemed in order. More like a spaceship with all those electronics!' Harold replied. 'Though I thought it strange that there were so few crewmen on board, and I had to have an escort for my tour of the ship. I had a distinct feeling that I was being watched. A bit spooky, really.'

Chapter Thirty-seven

They were into the fourth day of searching when a shout from Walter brought Steiner and Erich to the sonar screens.

There it was, a definite object sixty feet beneath on the seabed.

'Stop engines!' ordered Steiner through the engine room telegraph. 'Lower the camera.'

At first the screen showed the murky green of the sea afloat with marine life. Then, slowly and imperceptibly at first, a dark shadow showed as the white outline of a large motor launch. It was not yet covered with sea growth.

'This would be worth a closer look in the underwater pod,' Steiner told Erich.

The pod was eased out from its mountings on the deck and then lowered by the powerful derrick onto the sea's surface. It was an evil-looking craft, more like an alien spaceship.

The three-man crew closed the airtight hatch and the voice came through the intercom. 'All aboard, Captain. We have gone through all the safety checks and everything functioning perfectly. Time to go.'

'Cast off the lifting gear,' ordered Steiner to the deck crew.

The pod was slowly swallowed up beneath the green waters like some eerie deep-sea creature.

The visual scanner was transmitting to the television screens in the control room. Soon the murky translucent daylight gave way to the brilliant artificial light of the powerful searchlights fitted to the front of the pod.

For a short time there was only the floating and swimming sea life. Then the seabed came into view; sand and rock formations. Then the outline was unmistakable: the white streamlined hull of the launch. The searchlight picked out the name, *Seabird*. That was it. They had located their launch.

Steiner turned to Erich. 'She's too deep for a diver. It will mean a lift.'

He picked up the intercom and spoke to the pod.

'Hans, stand by, I'm lowering the canvas straps. If you can loop one forward and one aft of the launch, we will lift her off the seabed. Then the net will be sent down to cradle the whole launch. Understood?'

'Understood, Captain. We are standing by,' came back the voice of Hans, the pod commander.

The whole operation was carried out slowly and with great care. The powerful derrick showing little strain from the weight of the launch.

After two long hours the white hull of the launch broke the sea's surface. 'Hold it at sea level,' ordered Steiner.

PETRO 1 could not accommodate such a large vessel. Steiner turned to Erich. 'If I lower you onto the deck of the launch, you can search the interior once it has drained of sea water.'

'Right,' replied Erich. 'I'll get down to the derrick and get a lifting line onto the launch.'

The interior of the launch was a scene of complete chaos. Everything was sodden and the debris lay where it had settled.

Erich wasted no time. He searched the rear cabin without success. Then went to the forward control room. It was here that he located the large waterproof case. His adrenalin was pumping now.

After tying the case to another line, he waved to the deck of *PETRO 1*. He and the case were then gently lifted onto the main deck.

Erich, clutching the waterproof case, stepped onto the deck. There was a smile of triumph on his face.

The case was looking a little battered but was otherwise intact. 'What is the range of your Sikorsky, Captain?'

'A direct flight without refuelling would cover about 300 km,' replied Steiner.

'I would need to reach Frankfurt, which is about 800 kilometres from here,' said Erich.

'You would need to refuel for that distance. You could take spare fuel and refuel on the way. We have plenty in reserve,' Steiner advised him.

Chapter Thirty-eight

Sir John Blake gazed at the paper on his desk.

It was a report that he had requested from the giant oil company, Shell; a complex document regarding oil exploration of the Channel and the North Sea.

Shell, it would appear, had explored extensively in these waters. The finding on the North Sea had shown the possibility of vast reserves. The oil prospects off the Dorset coast also showed the presence of large reserves.

Further searches of the continental shelf had failed to locate any reserves off the French coastline.

Most of this knowledge was available to the major oil companies and *PETRO* would be included.

He picked up the telephone.

'I'm sorry, Sir John, but Chief Superintendent Goodbody is in Dorset. Would you like his telephone number, or can I give him a message?' said Jane.

'Would you ask him to contact me as early as possible?' requested Sir John.

'Certainly sir.' Jane rang off.

She dialled the Poole police.

'Goodbody here.' He was with the chief inspector. 'Hello, Jane. What is the problem?'

She explained the content of Sir John's telephone conversation. 'Thank you, Jane. I will give him a ring.'

'Sir John? Goodbody here… you rang my secretary.'

Sir John gave Goodbody the gist of the reply from the Shell Petroleum Company.

'Thank you, Sir John, that does give rise for some concern. One questions the motives for the search. I think we need to have a closer look at what is going on out there in the Channel.'

Sir John agreed and asked to be kept informed. Goodbody turned to Howard.

'We have a problem here. I need a closer look at what is going on out there in the Channel. Any suggestions?'

'Well there are the Royal Marines based here in Poole, the Special Boat Service. We could ask for their help,' suggested Howard.

'Do you know the officer in charge, or any officer that we can liaise with?' asked Goodbody.

'Yes, Colonel Harris has a good record in cooperating with the police. I can set up a meeting if you wish?'

'Would you do that? I feel that we need his opinion on this matter,' replied Goodbody.

The Green Beret marine looked at Goodbody's identity card. He saluted smartly and waved the Humber through the barrier.

This was the home of some of the British Army's finest troops. There was a remarkable absence of the usual marching and drilling. There was, however, an atmosphere of deadly efficiency.

Small craft dotted the water's edge. A large tank landing craft was anchored a little way offshore. A group of black wetsuited marines were embarking for parachute practice in Studland Bay. They would be taken to the RAF airfield to board the big lumbering Hercules transport plane, the workhorse of the armed services.

The meeting with Colonel Harris was very fruitful. Goodbody insisted that any surveillance must be discreet so as not raise any false alarms.

The colonel added that the marines had access to the 'Nimrod' high altitude flights which were equipped with the latest high-tech cameras that could pinpoint with visual accuracy any activity at sea level.

'When can we expect some feedback, Colonel?' asked Goodbody.

'I can get things moving and under way within a few days and a result to you in, say, four days.'

Meanwhile, Erich felt his excitement increasing with the success of the mission. The launch had been salvaged and the case recovered. There were momentous implications for the right-wing movement. Speed was of the essence in getting the case back to Count von Reinhardt, who was waiting with Ingrid in his large villa on the outskirts of Frankfurt.

'Steiner,' he said, directing his gaze towards the captain, 'when can I leave for Frankfurt?'

'The helicopter is fully serviced and ready for flight,' replied Steiner. 'We can place extra fuel drums on board and provide a mobile hand-pump to refuel. I would suggest that you fly low to avoid any radar scanners and choose an isolated spot for refuelling.'

'Thanks, Steiner. The Movement owes you a great debt and no doubt you will be rewarded when we have achieved our final goal. *Auf Wiedersehen.*'

'Goodbody – Colonel Harris here. Could you pop over to the base? I have some very interesting photographs you will wish to see.'

'Right, Colonel, I will be over in about an hour's time.' This sounded exciting.

Goodbody gazed at the pictures in amazement. One could pick out the details of the ship with extreme accuracy. Several figures were shown. A launch was secured at sea level alongside the ship's derrick. A strange-looking capsule was also alongside the ship.

'What do you make of it Goodbody?' asked the colonel.

'I don't think that it has any connection with oil exploration,' said Goodbody. 'And I have a shrewd idea what is going on. That launch has been lifted from the seabed. Not for salvage, but for something that was on it.' He was beginning to fill in a few gaps. 'You see, Colonel, some time ago we had an incident in which a group of neo-Nazi Germans were involved. A launch was used in their escape. That launch was damaged by one of the pursuit helicopters from this base. They eluded pursuit because of thick mist and the presence of a cross-Channel ferry – which, by the way, they hijacked. I strongly suspect that what you see in these photographs is the salvaged launch. But why? Something in that launch must be of extreme value to them.'

'Can't we board them?' suggested the colonel.

'No. They would only say they had located the launch during their searches. The Nimrod – is it still available?' enquired Goodbody.

'Oh yes. There is a constant surveillance over our airspace. Part of our defence strategy. I'm sure the RAF would be only too pleased to be involved.'

'If you can organise that and let me have a constant report of any activity, it would be invaluable. Perhaps you could send any findings to me marked "My eyes only" to the police station, addressed to Chief Inspector Howard?'

Chapter Thirty-nine

Erich made his farewells to Ludwig and Otto, and then clambered aboard the Sikorsky. The pilot had already been briefed on the route and the precautions to take.

The engine whined and the rotors slowly revolved. It was a robust craft, the end product of Italian and British technology. The rotors increased their speed and the engine whine gave way to a purposeful roar. The deck crew cast off the hawsers that secured the plane to the deck. A wave to Steiner and his crew and the helicopter rose into the air and veered off on its course to the European mainland.

High up in the near stratosphere the patrolling Nimrod's cameras were whirring. Goodbody had alerted Interpol, the French Sûreté and Kommandant Schultz of the German polizei and voiced his concern about the presence of *PETRO 1* so near to the French coast.

The telephone rang in Howard's office.

'Hello, Chief Inspector. Colonel Harris here... is Goodbody available?'

'Hold on Colonel, he is sitting next to me. I'll hand you over. Just a minute.'

'Goodbody here, Colonel.'

'Chief Superintendent, you may wish to know that air surveillance has just reported that a helicopter has taken off from *PETRO 1.*'

'Thank you, Colonel. Does your air surveillance extend over the French mainland?'

'I would have to clear that with the Ministry of Defence and the French authorities. I can't foresee any strong objections. After all, this is an international incident,' replied the colonel.

'Good. If they give you the green light. I would like to know the destination of that helicopter. Failing that we will have to rely on our continental friends to do the tracking. I will get on to them immediately. Thank you for keeping me informed. I will get back to you as soon as I can. Goodbye Colonel.'

Kommandant Schultz, the Sûreté and Interpol were all alerted and were now equally anxious to locate the Sikorsky's route and destination.

The German Luftwaffe launched one of its F111s to patrol the south-eastern German borders. The French had two Mirage jets patrolling their coastline.

Erich was completely unaware of the furore of activity that he had stirred up.

Count von Reinhardt had been contacted by Erich informing him of their success. He had used the agreed code: 'The oyster is open and the pearl intact.'

Ingrid was overcome with relief. The disaster of the air crash had left her extremely sensitive and nervous for Erich's safety.

Refuelling had been carried out without a hitch, first in France, and then a quiet meadow deep in the German countryside had lent itself perfectly for the operation.

Still flying at a low altitude, they avoided any large conurbation. Their destiny was now the grounds of Count von Reinhardt's spacious villa.

Chapter Forty

Herr Gunter was extremely wealthy. In fact he had no idea how many millions of German Deutschmarks, American dollars, British pounds and other powerful currencies he possessed. His control of German and Swiss banks and financial consortiums in South America and South Africa meant that his fortune was continuously growing and diversifying.

He also held vast amounts in gold deposits and art treasures in trust for clients who wished their wealth to remain discreet and known to themselves only.

His financial empire was controlled from a vast building in the centre of Frankfurt. His office occupied the whole of the twelfth floor. Here, an army of clerks, secretaries, accountants and lawyers toiled for his own personal gain.

Money had to a large extent cushioned and isolated him from the mainstream of life but he had few illusions on the transience of human behaviour.

The person sitting in one of the many comfortable armchairs in his sumptuous office disturbed him: an aristocrat with a military background. *Graf von Reinhardt*, the visiting card showed. One of the old school, possibly with Prussian ancestry.

'Well, Graf von Reinhardt. What can I do for you?' he asked. There was a cautious note in his voice.

The Count took his time and chose his words carefully.

'Herr Gunter, what I have to say must not under any circumstances go beyond these walls. Should there be a leak the consequences to both of us would be catastrophic.'

Gunter was well used to threats and had a well-oiled organisation quite capable of dealing with them. Yet there was an air of menace about this man in front of him that went far beyond personal danger.

'I understand, Count. Please continue.'

'You may or you may not be aware that there is in existence a vast underground organisation of right-wing sympathisers.' The Count spoke cautiously. There was much at stake.

'These sympathisers are not your mindless thugs of yesteryear but intelligent blue and white-collar workers. At their core is an elite group of former leaders of the old Third Reich: Army, Navy and Luftwaffe commanders of the highest ranks. All of them are dedicated to avenge the defeat of Germany and restore this country to its former glory.'

Gunter was listening but showed little emotion. The Count continued.

'To achieve the realisation of such a mission, vast sums of money are necessary. I'm not here cap in hand but to unlock such treasures that rightfully belonged to the National Socialist Party, you understand.'

Gunter's emotions were being tested by all this talk of the old Germany. He wasn't without idealism, despite his great wealth. Often in his financial dealings the intrigue and lack of morality motivated by undiluted greed had appalled him. The sleaze and patronage he often found sickening, and often recalled with nostalgia the days past when loyalty and discipline were dedicated to a greater cause other than personal gain.

The Count was continuing.

'We have in our possession certain documents that survived the tragedy of the bunker. These documents include the last will and testament of Adolf Hitler, under which Martin Bormann inherited the leadership and the title "Führer of the Third Reich". There are also itemised lists of places, banks, and industries in which there were vast amounts of shares and bonds that have accumulated interest over all these years. These shares give ownership to large mining enterprises. Many works of art are stored in secure vaults in trust to banks, etc.'

Gunter sipped some iced water and offered some to the Count, who declined gratefully. The Count went on.

'To access this wealth we need inside help to handle our legitimate claim and to make it available when and where it is needed. This is where you may be able to assist, Herr Gunter.' Now the plutocrat could see the purpose of the Count's visit.

'You will have time to consider what I have told you,' continued the von Reinhardt.

'In one week's time, I shall contact you again for your comments. Needless to say, any leak of what I have told you will result in the elimination of you and your family and eventually your whole financial empire. We are playing for extremely high stakes and cannot allow any deviations. Dedication to the cause is matched by our determination to react with utter ruthlessness to any threat to its final fulfilment.'

Chapter Forty-one

Ingrid was overjoyed to have Erich back. The estate had extensive grounds. They rode regularly and swam in the heated swimming pool amongst immaculate lawns, designer plants and patios with inviting loungers and colourful sunshades. The sheer joy of each other's company consumed them both. Their lazy evenings of wining and dining followed by nights of intimate closeness deepened the bond between them.

The Count had been busy making contacts with the organisation. There had been several meetings at the villa to discuss future policies in the light of the possible access to unlimited funds.

A training base for military activists was a top priority. A location remote from prying eyes was needed. A suggestion was made that the Arctic could lend itself to their purposes under the guise of Arctic exploration. Desert regions could also be used. Sympathetic dictatorships such as those of Iraq and Argentina could be approached. Finally it was concluded that not just one base but several locations would lend themselves to an overall plan to train a force of some thirty thousand highly trained and disciplined men after the style of the old SS units. These would provide the nucleus for a much larger force that could challenge the existing establishment. Such a force would take an oath of allegiance to the new party.

There was, however, a shortage of recruits. Frustrated 'Old Guards' would quickly enrol and a vast reservoir of expertise would be harnessed as a training cadre. Young Germans would respond to this inherent national militarism that had lain dormant for too long. Such an organisation would require rigid discipline to remain underground.

Herr Gunter cooperated to the full, and vast amounts of money were soon made available.

The German Polizei were on full alert. The helicopter had eluded them, but Schultz had deployed every man he could spare to scour the underworld for any unusual activity or rumours.

Joseph had worked at the garage for over a month. He was a good mechanic and an astute undercover policeman.

He had made a number of friends, and Friday nights were for relaxation. *Der Braun Bar* biergarten was the rendezvous for young unattached workers and a sprinkling of young blue-collar couples. Overflowing beer mugs, raucous laughter and outbreaks of spontaneous singing were de riguer.

Joseph and his companion Hans, joined a group of friends. The atmosphere was one of merriment and laughter. Beer had a way of banishing the workplace and giving Bacchus his rightful status.

Joseph was aware that Hans was more sober than usual. Even the buxom fräulein sitting on his lap was having a tough time. The sight of her ample breasts had never failed before, and she had more than enough to send any male rampant with lust.

Later, Hans became increasingly confidential. His tongue was loosened by his overgenerous beer consumption.

'Joseph,' he began, 'we are close friends, aren't we?'

'Of course, Hans. We work together and we share the same apartment and sometimes the same women. What more can a man expect from a friend?' replied Joseph.

'I have a problem', Hans continued. 'You see, I have been approached by certain people. People who are a little political.' He hesitated for a moment. After all, he had been sworn to the utmost secrecy. He seemed to make up his mind and went on.

'It appears that these people are looking for skilled workers – technicians and those sorts of people.'

He was feeling considerable relief in confiding with Joseph.

'They are recruiting politically for a right-wing movement. It would mean leaving here and going to a training camp. Wearing a uniform and training in weapons. The works.'

'Are you going to join them?' Joseph asked.

'Well, I must say that I do agree with their politics. We need some control and discipline in the political arena. This immigration problem is getting out of control.'

'So what is the next step?' asked Joseph casually.

'I'm to let them know in a week's time. If I agree, I'm to report to an address in Frankfurt. I don't suppose you would be interested?'

'I might,' said Joseph. 'I could do with a bit of action in my life. Tell me more.'

Joseph's contact in the Polizei was Kapitan Prowski. He made contact and reported the conversation he had had with Hans and requested advice on the matter.

Kommandant Schultz read the memo. To act now would achieve little. Some small fry perhaps. He picked up the telephone.

'Kapitan Prowski? Kommandant Schultz here. Your memo: this could be a break for us. Tell your man to go ahead and get involved with this recruitment campaign. We do need someone on the inside and this could be the answer, but tell your man to exercise extreme caution. The situation could be fraught with danger. Keep me informed of any progress. Goodbye.'

Goodbody picked up the telephone.

'Schultz here, Chief Superintendent. We failed to track the helicopter but we do know the course it took. Somewhere in the Frankfurt area. It shouldn't be too difficult to narrow down its destination. In the meantime, there has been some low-key activity here and some useful information may be forthcoming from this source. At present I would suggest that you take no further action from your end. We need to penetrate this organisation. So far we have only seen the tip of the iceberg. Keep a watching brief on the oil exploration project but don't precipitate anything that may arouse suspicion. The last thing we need is for them to go completely underground and perhaps suspend their activities. Keep in touch. *Auf Wiedersehen.*'

Chapter Forty-two

The group had been travelling for two days up the River Salando.

The boat had a shallow draught and was powered by a sturdy three-litre diesel. It made good way against the strong current that carried the brown murky waters from the Andes to the Atlantic coast of South America.

There were twelve in the group. Mostly young artisan types with a sprinkling of white-collar workers.

In charge were two fatigue-clad older men who had a definite military bearing and a commanding manner, ex-services at a guess.

They had said little since they had left Montevideo after disembarking from the SS *Karuana*, a small cruise liner that had left Bremerhaven a week previously.

The passage had been uneventful. Most of the time had been taken up by daily briefings on the group's purpose and future.

A campsite had been established high in the slopes of the Andes. There they were to undergo a period of intensive military training in weaponry, tactics and technical know-how.

The camp accommodated 200 recruits in basic but comfortable conditions. Contact with the outside world would be minimal, if any.

Joseph sat next to Hans as they watched the thick jungle slip by. In the distance rose the massif of the Andes.

Jungle noises rose to a crescendo as they proceeded upriver. The alien thumping noise of the diesel sent alarm signals throughout the indigenous bird and animal population. The boat negotiated a bend in the river and revealed a purpose-built landing site with a scattering of prefabricated buildings.

Standing on a landing pad squatted a large double-rotor Chinook. Its landing ramp was down and stores and small vehicles were being loaded.

The group were conducted to the aircraft and escorted aboard.

A two-hour flight over more dense jungle ended at an extensive compound of buildings set in a large clearing.

Their civilian façade was dropped and uniforms donned.

Steiner docked *PETRO 1* alongside Poole quay. Otto and Ludwig and the rest of the crew, except for the security watch, disembarked to sample the shore life.

Harold sat in his panda car. He had been on watch as soon as he had heard that *PETRO 1* was returning to Poole.

The crew would have to pass the panda. It was then that he had recognised them. Yes, there were definitely two in the group who had kidnapped him.

He spoke into to his handset.

'Put me through to the Chief Inspector,' he said to the duty sergeant.

'Howard here' He heard the voice announce.

'PC Seaton here sir,' Harold said. 'I've been checking on the German oil ship and there are definitely two of the gang that kidnapped me amongst the crew.' He was in a high state of excitement. 'Shall I bring them in, sir?'

'Hang on, Constable,' came the reply.

Howard turned to Goodbody and repeated the gist of the call.

'Tell him not to take any action whatsoever and to continue his patrol,' replied Goodbody.

Harold was puzzled, but then orders were orders. Something was strange about the whole business, he thought.

Goodbody himself was excited. Here was a definite lead and connection to the previous incident.

He telephoned Schultz.

'Interesting development, Chief Superintendent. *Ja*, we seem to have a definite connection with the terrorists. Excellent! Keep an eye on things and let me know what develops.'

Sylvia glanced at the two strangers. They were smart but casually dressed. One was in a suede and the other in a black leather jacket. Athletic looks and movement. Perhaps they were off-duty marines from the Special Boat Service unit based in Poole.

They approached the bar and gave her an approving all-over

inspection. She warmed to them. It always gave her a reassurance when given this masculine look-over. She bent over the bar a little further.

'What would you like, gentlemen?' she cooed knowingly.

'We would like to try some of your English beer, if you please.'

Well that was a surprise! Their English seemed fluent, but its pronunciation definitely foreign.

'Two pints of our best bitter, then, should give you a good example.' She was intrigued. 'You're not from these parts, are you?'

'*Nein, mein Fräulein*, we are from Germany and we are working in Poole.'

Ludwig was cautious not to say too much about their activities. But then, she was a stunner and that dress left little to the imagination... Female company had been a scarce commodity over the past few weeks.

They took their beers and retreated to the lounge.

Harold sat back on the comfortable settee. His thoughts were obviously elsewhere. 'Harold, what are you thinking about?' Sylvia asked. Her voice was showing her resentment at being ignored.

'Well, it's a strange thing that happened yesterday. We were keeping an eye on that German oil ship in Poole. The crew were disembarking – and you'll never guess who I saw?'

'Of course I won't! So tell me.' More irritation showing. Anything to get his mind back on her.

'Two of the crew were members of that gang that kidnapped Mike Hardy and myself. But when I phoned the Super he told me not to take any further action and to continue my patrol. Most strange, that.'

'Well as a matter of fact two young Germans were in the bar last night.' Sylvia warmed a little to this conversation.

The men were seated around the large oak table set in the ballroom of the villa with its spacious walls hung with modern impressionist and post-impressionist art: Cézanne, Monet and

Chagall, interspersed with the occasional Ingres and Titian.

The furnishings here were more modern than their previous venue in the Bavarian castle. The thirteen members of the Grand Order of the Iron Cross, each had their individual cross, emblazoned with diamonds and gold oak leaves, suspended about their necks on a silk black and silver ribbon.

Von Reinhardt sat at the top of the rectangular table. Before each member was a crystal glass decanter of water and crystal drinking glasses, with an ink blotter, notebook and an ornate inkstand.

'Gentlemen, my apologies for our humble setting. Since the destruction of our previous venue this will be our temporary base. You all know Erich, our executive member.' The Count turned towards Erich, who sat at the far end of the table.

Erich felt their eyes scrutinising him. They all knew of the helicopter crash. His injuries were, however, not visible.

The Count continued with a brief résumé of the events following the crash. He detailed the setting up of a military training programme and the availability of vast financial reserves.

'We now have three objectives,' he continued. 'One: the overthrow of the present government. Two: the present government to be replaced by a right-wing order. And three: the unification of Germany and an effective opposition to any further communist expansion.

'I feel we shall have many sympathetic supporters in the West and we will get tacit support from these sources.'

The council listened attentively and murmured their approval.

Helmut Fuchs sat at his desk. His office was modestly furnished with solid German furnishings that lent an imposing backcloth to his office as leader of the Social Democratic Party, the SPD, and Chancellor of the Bundestag, the German Federal Parliament. It was a post he had held for the past two years. A majority of 298 seats out of the 656 gave him a healthy lead over the Opposition, the Christian Democratic Union, the CDU.

As overall commander of the Bundeswehr, the German armed forces and the internal security forces, he was sensitive to the threats posed by the Russian-controlled East German state, symbolised by the presence of the Berlin Wall. He drew comfort, however, in the presence of a highly trained elite military backed by a powerful air defence that could be expanded rapidly from the reserve units of trained militia. Most importantly, there was also the membership of NATO, the North Atlantic Treaty Organisation. Nevertheless, constant vigilance was essential.

Fuchs's companion, Kommandant Schultz, head of internal security including the Polizei, was no stranger.

'You say, Kommandant, that there exists a right-wing underground organisation that has penetrated nearly every institution in the Federal Government and the professional classes?'

'Yes, Herr Fuchs, that is the conclusion I have reached from information gathered by my own undercover sources,' replied Schultz.

'What do you propose, Kommandant? What action can we take?' Fuchs was anxious.

'My first recommendation is to initiate a low-key state of alert to avoid arousing any suspicions of our awareness. If we can root out the leadership, the rank and file membership may wither away harmlessly.'

Schultz paused. The next suggestions were delicate and not strictly within his terms of reference. He was, however, a seasoned fighter when it came to state security and his duties had often spilled over into the political arena.

'Secondly, there is a political agenda here. The grievances held by these people are concern at the increased influx of ethnic groups seeking political asylum and an increased awareness of the rise in crime and the need for strong measures to root out those who control the criminal syndicates. A nil tolerance policy towards drug traffickers, for instance.'

Schultz paused to assess the Chancellor's reaction. Then he continued.

'Now, these suggestions are naturally political, and need further consultations given with your colleagues. Maximum publicity given to these grievances and the governments proposals on how to tackle the problem may go some way to allay the discontent that builds breeding grounds for recruitment into these subversive groups. I'm fully aware of your dilemma, Herr

Chancellor, and merely put forward these suggestions for consideration. A strong line against communist expansion would also be popular.'

Schultz wondered if he had pushed Fuchs too far.

'Thank you, Kommandant. You have given me much to think about. I will consult with my colleagues and of course keep you informed. Thank you once again... Have you ever thought of taking up politics?' He was smiling now.

Schultz gave an imperceptible sigh of relief.

Six weeks had passed since their arrival at the training camp. Joseph had never felt fitter. There had been many comings and goings. New recruits coming and fully trained graduates going. Training had been scrupulously thorough. Not only with the latest small arms and machine pistols but with explosives, detonators and subduing gases.

Joseph had been aware of an increase in activity among the leaders of the cadre. Something was causing a flurry of activity. The Chinook had brought in many visitors who had carried out inspections of the camp and its recruits, particularly the training programmes. He must get a message back to Germany.

Ingrid sensed the tension building up in Erich. Too many nights lacking in fulfilment; days spent alone while he attended various meetings and travelled to parts of Germany and Europe.

Erich had listened to the Count's ambitious planning and had recruited another strong commando unit of thirty handpicked men.

Chapter Forty-three

Kommandant Schultz read the coded telex. Activity, gathering of leaders. It all indicated movement towards a climax. But where and when, and where was the German base of operations? He picked up the telephone.

'Get me Chief Superintendent Goodbody,' he requested his secretary. 'Goodbody speaking.' The link was quick.

'Ah! Chief Superintendent. Schultz here. We have a problem. Something is brewing and it is going to be big. I need a lead to the German base of these people.'

Goodbody could feel the tension in Schultz's voice. 'How can I help, Kommandant?'

Schultz continued. 'You had one of your men eyeball one of the terrorists and I told you to keep a low profile for the time being. I've changed my views. Can you put a tail on this man and the boat and let me know immediately of any activity? I think that this may be the link I have been looking for. On no account arouse their suspicions.'

'Right, Kommandant. Leave it with me. I'll be in touch. Goodbye.'

Harold found himself facing Goodbody and Howard.

'Seaton – how would you like to go undercover?' Howard put the question.

Goodbody scrutinised his man. A typical PC plod. He would have wished for someone with a little more spark. But then, this man knew the suspect. Perhaps an accomplice from the Met would help?

'Seaton,' continued Howard, 'the man you recognised from the German oil ship. We need a twenty-four hour surveillance put on him. It must be done with the utmost discretion and secrecy. You must keep this to yourself and tell nobody – and I do mean nobody, even your most intimate friends and colleagues, and in particular girlfriends! Do you understand?'

Harold felt his ego expanding. Plain clothes! Secrecy! Discretion! 'You can rely on me, sir, completely,' he declared.

Howard continued. 'I'm bringing a man down from the Met, and you are to work closely together. His name is Inspector Rawlinson. He will, of course, be your senior and in charge of the surveillance. Now, have you any questions to ask me?

Harold felt a little deflated. This was not to be his show completely. However, without him the whole operation would never get off the ground.

'Very good sir. No questions. When do I start?'

'Immediately,' said Howard. 'Inspector Rawlinson will be with us this afternoon and I've arranged for you to meet him in this office at three o'clock. Any more questions?'

Howard finalised the interview.

'Back here in plain clothes at three o'clock sharp. Off you go, Seaton.'

Bob Rawlinson was twenty-eight years old and one of the new fast-track promotion police candidates recruited direct from the universities. He had graduated from London University with a good degree in Law and Sociology.

Policing was, however, in the family. His father had retired as Chief Constable for Plymouth and his grandfather had been involved in the Dartmoor prison riots.

The number of times he heard the old man recall the subduing of the rioters. 'Take your batons to the bastards!' the old man's commanding officer had instructed, 'and don't stop until the buggers are down on the ground. Then if they move give them some more. It's either you or them, so make sure it's not you!'

Ah! How many times had he heard that epic story? How times have changed, thought Bob. Perhaps for the better. Time would tell.

Six feet four inches in height and athletically built, he still played in the Met rugby team. He had dark hair and sallow skin. A hint of his hidden intellect showed in his studious looks. He had, however, inherited a certain gentleness from his mother.

He knew his mission was important and highly confidential.

He glanced at *The Times* headlines. The European summit of Heads of State was scheduled for November and would be held in Bonn, West Germany.

That will be a headache for someone in the German security forces, he said to himself.

Chapter Forty-four

Bonn is situated on the left bank of the Rhine; it has a cathedral dating from the thirteenth century and a university instituted in 1918 by the King of Prussia, making it an intellectual centre.

During the Second World War it suffered much destruction. The palace of the Archbishops of Bonn was seriously gutted by fire, although other historic buildings, including the eighteenth-century town hall, the museum of Academy of Arts, and the provincial and municipal museums, and Beethoven's house, converted to a museum since 1889, all escaped damage. The Romans called it *Castra Bonnensia*. It was one of the most important of their camps. At the end of the eighteenth-century it was occupied by France; then it passed into the possession of Prussia after the Congress of Vienna in 1815, following the defeat of Napoleons armies at Waterloo.

It was in this setting that West Germany had established its seat of government in the newly built government buildings. Its population of just over 100,000 had nearly doubled since the end of the war.

It was here that the summit for the heads of the European states would be held.

The usual noisy demonstrations would be expected from the dissident political groups, boosted by the fringe troublemakers that such gatherings attracted.

The local police reinforced by the state police and units of the militia would anticipate all of this. Mounted units, for crowd control, would be on standby, and the ubiquitous water cannons would be at the ready.

Erich surveyed the buildings. The pavements were glistening with the sheen created by the steady drizzle of rain that enveloped the city.

People hurried about their business huddled under umbrellas and wrapped in their stylish waterproofs.

National flags drooped forlornly in front of the government buildings.

A police presence was evident, but it was low-key. People entering the buildings showed some sort of pass, otherwise they were quietly questioned on their business interests within the buildings.

Erich moved casually. The camera draped about his neck and his pac-a-mac rainwear identified him with the usual attendant tourists. He used his camera extensively, on the buildings their exits and entrances, on the approach roads and the surrounding buildings.

Steiner held the coded telex in his hand and directed his gaze towards Ludwig and Otto. 'Erich wants you both back in Germany. You are to travel by air from Heathrow to Köln airport for Bonn, and book in the Hotel Stern, where he will contact you within a few days. You are to book a flight and leave within the next day or so.'

Harold sat opposite Chief Inspector Howard and Chief Superintendent Goodbody. Inspector Rawlinson sat next to him.

He felt quite intimidated and impressed by so much 'brass'.

His first impression of Rawlinson was his youthfulness. The inspector wasn't much older than himself. Quiet, unassuming, but no fool. They would make a good team.

Bob Rawlinson had slight reservations on his assessment of PC Seaton.

Their briefing was short and thorough. Rawlinson would book into the Miramar, where he would be in close proximity to Goodbody. They would not know one another as far as the rest of the guests were concerned.

Both officers would have the use of an unmarked police car equipped with a radio contact direct to Chief Inspector Howard's office.

The Germans were to be kept under surveillance twenty-four hours a day.

They were known to frequent the Miramar when ashore, and PC Seaton was to identify them to Inspector Rawlinson at the first opportunity. They were aboard *PETRO 1*, and Goodbody suggested that they take their surveillance from there. Seaton would undertake this immediately while Rawlinson booked in at the hotel.

'Any questions? No! Then off you go, and keep in touch with this office – and good luck.' Chief Inspector Howard terminated the interview.

Sylvia was troubled. Harold had not shown up for two days. This was most unusual. She knew that his resistance, whatever the circumstances, could be counted in hours. He must have a very good reason to last this long.

The telephone rang. She answered in her husky telephone voice, 'Harold? Where have you been?'

He sounded tense. Could that be abstinence, or work? she mused.

'You are at the hotel but I'm not to what? What sort of a game is this? And don't call me *Pet!*' Her hackles were rising rapidly.

'I see! It's official – confidential – and you can't explain yet… Not even to me?' Sylvia couldn't handle rejection. It just was not one of her strongest points. 'Listen, if you turn up with some blonde on your arm, policewoman or no policewoman, you can have serious doubts as to my availability in the future!'

She rang off.

Must be important, she mused. He's never pulled this one on me before!

Otto turned to Ludwig.

'Our flight isn't until tomorrow. We can have a break at that hotel this evening and get an eyeful of that sexy bar hostess. What do you say?'

'Why not?' replied Ludwig. 'It sounds as if we are going to be busy from here on.'

Chapter Forty-five

Joseph sensed the air of expectancy within the camp. All training sessions had been cancelled and the recruits were told to pack their personal belongings. Squads of work units were busy dismantling the buildings that had been used for training and lectures.

The orders had been posted.

'All training personnel were to be on standby ready for transportation back to Germany.'

Ludwig and Otto left the ship as dusk was falling; Harold spotted them from his unmarked car. He picked up the radio handset.

'PCS. Receiving?

Inspector Howard's voice came through almost immediately. 'Go ahead, PCS.'

'Suspects leaving dockside and boarding waiting taxi. I'm following. Over.'

'Follow, but keep a safe distance between you and the taxi. I will contact IR at the hotel and alert him to the situation. Over.'

Bob Rawlinson was in his room unpacking a few belongings. He was travelling very light. The telephone rang.

'Rawlinson?'

The chief inspector relayed Harold's message.

'Stay alert, and be on standby for possible visitors.' He rang off.

The bar lounge was quiet. A few early visitors and guests. Rawlinson approached the bar, where he was greeted by the attractive bar hostess.

She had a figure that went in and out at all the right places. A friendly smile from a generous mouth. She gave him an abashed look-over from her wide inquisitive blue eyes. 'What can I get for you, sir?'

The way she said it could easily cause a body stir. Rawlinson was, however, on his guard and alert. Nevertheless, to direct any suspicion from watching eyes, he showed an interest. 'Do you have a draught bitter?'

'Of course, sir,' she said demurely. 'We have our local Dorset brew, Storrington's of Blandford.'

'May I have a pint in a stemmed glass?' He preferred this to the usual glass with a handle. She placed the glass on the counter.

'Put it on my account, please,' he asked. 'Room Eighty-four,' he added.

'Certainly sir, no trouble. You're not from these parts, are you?' Sylvia was getting into her stride. She liked the look of him.

No I'm visiting family friends who moved down here from London. We like to keep in touch.'

London. She might have guessed. The clothes casually stylish. She liked his dark and interesting looks.

'Excuse me while I serve these two gentlemen.'

Ludwig and Otto had just sauntered into the bar lounge. 'Good evening, sirs. You must like it here?'

'*Ja, mein Liebling*. We just couldn't keep away,' said Otto. English girls, he had found, responded to foreign phrases. To them it always seemed to have romantic connotations. 'Two glasses of your excellent English beer *bitte!*' He gave her a flashing smile.

Bob Rawlinson showed a friendly but casual interest in this flirtatious banter. His mind, however, was fully alert. Germans – and two of them. This was too much of a coincidence. Sylvia was thriving on this mating game. The bar was always a protective barrier and she could exploit a flirtatious encounter to the full.

'Your business finished in Poole, then?' she asked Otto.

'We shall miss our visits here and our chats,' he replied. Then he felt Ludwig's warning tap on his leg.

Sylvia was called away to another customer.

Rawlinson called 'Goodnight' to her and went outside to the car park.

He spotted Harold parked in the shadows. He hesitated alongside the car and took out a cigarette.

As he lowered his head to light up he heard Harold's whispered voice. 'Two of them. They have just entered the hotel. Did you spot them?'

'Yes, they came to the bar and spouted a bit of German for the benefit of that attractive bar hostess.'

He moved away towards his own car. He needed to contact Chief Inspector Howard urgently. Harold couldn't understand the slight pangs of jealousy rising within him.

His radio buzzed.

'Seaton! Chief Inspector Howard here. I understand you are still in contact. There may be a move tomorrow. Inspector Rawlinson overheard a remark in the hotel that hinted at a possible move away from the ship. Be extra vigilant. We don't want to lose our friends. You may need your passport if they travel abroad, and carry sufficient cash. Don't worry, you can reclaim all expenses that you incur. Keep in touch.' He was gone.

Joseph landed at Bremerhaven with ten other newly trained recruits. All were dressed in casual clothes. Their instructions were explicit: to disperse and rendezvous at an address in Frankfurt. Secrecy was essential. Each man was given an envelope containing 500 marks.

The Grand Council was gathered around the table with the Count at the head. Erich sat at the opposite end.

'As you are all aware, the summit for the heads of state is arranged for 11 November at Bonn.

'Erich has reconnoitred the venue and drafted a course of action. You each have this draft in front of you. All copies will be shredded after this meeting so commit the details to memory as no notes will be taken for you to take from this room. Is this understood?'

They all nodded their approval. General Rudiger addressed the assembly.

'Are we to understand that the summit is to be hijacked and the state representatives held as hostages?'

'That is precisely what will happen, General. Each one of you must be ready to take command of various departments.

'Similar actions will take place in the major towns, where the heads of the police and local authorities will be detained. In fact, gentlemen, we are to implement a 'coup d'etat'. The biggest in

Europe since the overthrow of Napoleon the Third and the establishment of the French Republic!'

'An ambitious plan, Count von Reinhardt,' added von Vaerst. I presume that we have the resources?'

'We can muster 3,000 fully trained and equipped commandos. These will be allocated to various centres of communication. All television and radio stations will be seized, together with the control of all telephone and telegraph channels. Major road, rail and air routes will be seized.

'It is hoped that the use of force will be minimal. However, resistance will be crushed ruthlessly. The stakes are too high to be jeopardised by any heroics.

'A further 30,000 volunteers will be recruited once the situation has been stabilised. The armed forces may react violently. We have, however, infiltrated our members into their ranks to cause maximum havoc by sabotage and defections.

The silence lay heavy over the council. The sheer audacity of the action left many stunned. The objectives were breathtaking, but the establishment of a right-wing order amply justified the audacity of the plan. This they all realised.

'Erich has been coordinating the practical measures,' the Count continued. 'And I suggest we register our approval and endorse any action to be undertaken. A show of hands will be sufficient to show a vote of confidence in the operation.'

All hands were raised. There were no dissenters.

Chapter Forty-six

Schultz was worried. They had heard from their man Joseph.
The recall of the trained recruits and the closure of the camp in South America would mean only one thing: that something big was being planned.

The summit of the heads of states was scheduled for November, and that was a month away. He didn't want any embarrassing incidents while they were in Germany. His forces would be stretched enough with the ragtag demonstrators that such meetings seem to attract.

Bob Rawlinson and Harold Seaton stood in the main reception concourse of Heathrow Airport. Neither acknowledged the other. They had agreed that they would travel separately. Other passengers stood around gazing at the flight schedules that flashed on the display boards. Some were slumped on the banks of seats. Frustration, boredom, excitement and anxiety – all of these human emotions were visible on the faces of the travellers. The whole concourse held a microcosm of human passions, all gathered under one roof. Such is the nature of the mass movement of humanity.

Police patrolled amongst the milling throng, a sharp reminder of the social violence that had crept into modern society. However, for the most part, people ignored this evidence; they were too preoccupied with their own uncertainties.

Ludwig and Otto collected their boarding tickets and made their way towards the Lufthansa terminal, unaware that two sets of eyes were following their every move. A quick phone call to Goodbody had smoothed any difficulty in getting flight reservations for the two police officers.'

All four, watched and watchers, mingled with the passengers for Bonn.

Goodbody spoke to Schultz.

'Our two suspects are boarding flight Alpha 201 for Bonn and will depart at 1100 hours, British time. My men have them under constant surveillance but they will, however, need your help in Germany. The language may present some difficulty.'

Schultz was well aware that non-German-speaking travellers would attract attention. 'Don't worry, Goodbody, I will have my men meet flight Alpha 201. They will act as if meeting old friends. If your men could carry a newspaper, preferably English. They will be approached separately and they can discreetly identify the two German suspects, and we can take over from there.'

Goodbody acknowledged Schultz's plan and rang off. He then picked up his telephone.

Bob Rawlinson's radiotelephone buzzed and he withdrew to a sheltered corner. After the call he bought two copies of *The Times*.

The lounge of the Kaiserhof Hotel was modestly furnished with comfortable deep leather chairs.

Joseph and Hans booked into separate rooms. The other members of the group had either arrived or were still travelling. They should all be at the hotel within the next two or three days.

Greta and Jake were well suited to undercover surveillance police work. Both in their mid-twenties, they were presentable in appearance yet capable of merging with groups without drawing attention to themselves. Greta, fair-haired and blue-eyed, would have appealed to the old National Socialist ideal of Aryan womanhood. She had an athletic figure hidden beneath her sober clothes that were fashioned in a slightly masculine style with a jacket and flared trousers. Jake, on the other hand, could pass as an academic. Thick black-rimmed glasses, dark hair. Not muscular, but wiry. Both of them were enthusiastic police officers. And both preferred undercover work. Together they looked an average couple. Separately, they would pass as career chasers.

They picked out the two English policemen standing near to the newspaper kiosk. English newspapers were tucked beneath their arms.

'Tom darling!' she called to Bob Rawlinson. 'Long time no see! How's Barbara? I've so many questions to ask.'

He greeted her with a kiss and a hug, entering into the spirit of the occasion. It was quite enjoyable, he mused. While they were close, he whispered, 'Your men are standing by the telephone kiosks.'

She glanced casually in that direction and spotted Ludwig and Otto. They stood out from the crowd like two shining beacons. Suntanned and looking extremely fit. Otto even sported one of those funny English pudding hats.

'Darling, it is so nice to see you again,' Greta continued. 'I have a car in the car park, but first let us have a cup of coffee and talk in the restaurant.'

They took a seat outside the café where the reception area could be observed.

Hello, Edward,' said Jake, holding out his hand in greeting.

Harold shook his hand and smiled in return. He felt a little awkward but quickly got into the spirit of the occasion.

'Let's have a cup of coffee, old boy, and chinwag about old times,' he responded.

As they strolled towards the café, Harold froze. He had glanced to where Ludwig and Otto had been standing and saw that they had been joined by a third person whose back had been towards him. Now he'd turned full profile. There was no doubts in Harold's mind it was the leader of the hi-jack gang. He quickly turned his back on the group and hurriedly put Jake in the picture.

Jake knew that on no account must Harold be recognised. Their whole cover would be blown. He jostled Harold behind the newspaper kiosk.

'You and your colleague must leave and return to England! Greta and I will take over from here. Now hurry – disappear!'

Bob Rawlinson had been watching the mini-drama and realised they had a big problem. He left Greta and hurriedly followed Harold from the reception concourse.

Goodbody listened to their report and realised what a narrow squeak they had experienced. He had not heard from the German Polizei, so presumed all was still going according to plan.

Meanwhile, Greta and Jake drove slowly passed the massive wrought iron gates with high wails extending from both sides surmounted by vicious iron spikes. Security cameras scanned the gate area. The roof of a large villa could be seen beyond the cultivated gardens and lawns.

They had followed the three Germans at a discreet distance from Frankfurt Airport, where their car had been waiting following their telephone call ahead. The route had been taken them beyond the suburbs of the city and out into the surrounding countryside. 'Villa Jasmine' was secluded on a minor road off from junction ten of the Autobahn to Mainz and Wiesbaden, some fifty kilometres west of Frankfurt.

Jake spoke into the radiotelephone.

'Goodbody! Schultz here. Your lead has been an outstanding success. The bandits journeyed to Frankfurt and then on to a Villa Jasmine. It looks very much as if we are making contact with the hierarchy of the organisation.'

Goodbody acknowledged the Kommandant's information and rang off.

Chapter Forty-seven

The three heavy military personnel carriers entered the villa's gates and were driven to prepared sites, hidden from prying eyes.

Von Reinhardt and Erich inspected the vehicles, which had been purchased from the Eastern Bloc. Each was capable of transporting twenty fully armed men. They were lightly armoured and ideal for their purpose. Ludwig and Otto joined them.

'You will each be in charge of one of these beauties,' said Erich, 'and have twenty fully trained men under your command. We will now adjourn to the villa and join the rest of the Council where your briefing will begin.'

Erich turned to Ludwig. 'By the way, how was your journey from England?'

Ludwig recapped the uneventful journey. They had been alert for any surveillance but had not spotted anything or anyone suspicious.

The whole of the Grand Council were seated in the main hall, where Erich had erected a film projector and screen showing a large map of the city of Bonn.

The Bundeshaus lay alongside the River Rhine on the southern bank. The approach road, the Konrad Adenauer-Allee, was shown extending almost the full length of the rambling building whose entrances and exits had been marked.

The Count opened the proceedings with a message of greetings and an introduction to Ludwig and Otto. He then indicated to Erich to commence his briefing.

Erich preambled his plan by emphasising that success would depend on a combination of daring and surprise. The Rhine provided an easy route for infiltration, and several powerful launches were to be used, each carrying twenty to thirty fully armed and trained commandos. All members of the units would wear military camouflage uniforms and helmets and would pose initially as military police, wearing red tabs on the epaulettes. This would make identification easier. Maintaining their pose as military police, they would occupy all strategic entrances and exits within the Bundeshaus. They will also occupy the main conference hall and subdue any resistance and hold the delegates hostage. The hostages would then be informed of the aims of the coup.

Meantime a commando detachment would occupy and overcome the Headquarters in Karl Marx Strasse. Other units would set up roadblocks on all approaches to the city centre. Television and radio centres would also be targeted.

Erich continued, 'Once we have established control of the situation the foreign delegates will be allowed to leave. Our political grievances are purely with the Federal Government. Needless to say, all heads of federal states will be detained.

'A state of emergency will be pronounced and a National Socialist Government declared. The remainder of our 30,000 trained militia will then be mobilised followed by the call for a declaration of intent by a further 100,000 underground members by the wearing of white armbands.'

Erich finished his summary and allowed time for his words to be considered by the Grand Council and his commanders.

'A bold plan,' the count declared to the assembly. ' I think we are all agreed on its execution – but are there any questions?'

'Just one point,' said General Holst. 'Politically, there will have to be a governing caucus. Have we made provision for such a body?'

Chapter Forty-eight

Sylvia glanced at Harold, who was sprawled out on her comfortable settee. He had changed in some subtle manner since that hush-hush job in Germany. She couldn't quite put her finger on anything particular. It was more his manner than his behaviour.

Superior! That's what it was; he had somehow become superior. When he visited the bar where she was working, he seemed to be looking for recognition, regarding other guests as potential criminals who should be wary of his presence. You would think that he had been watching too many 007 films...

She had decided that undercover work was definitely a no-no for her Harold. The sooner wedding bells were ringing the better for their relationship. She could better sort out this problem at close quarters.

Luckily, 'Pet' seemed conspicuous by its absence among his terms of endearment. A definite bonus.

Schultz was puzzled. His inside contact was now back in Germany and staying in a hotel in Frankfurt.

The Villa Jasmine, and now this. Why Frankfurt? Too much of a coincidence for him to accept. His police instincts were alerted. He picked up the telephone.

'Get me the Commissioner of the Frankfurt Police,' he told his secretary. 'Heinrich Sawatzki speaking.' The voice sounded crisp and efficient. After the formal introductions, Schultz explained his concern for the activities taking place in the Frankfurt district.

'Commissioner Sawatzki, I would like you to put a surveillance team on the Villa Jasmine and the Hotel Kaiserhof. I need a handpicked team and on no account are they to raise any suspicions. Air surveillance would also be useful, and can you please treat this as very top priority, Commissioner? And let me know the instance there are any developments. If you can also have someone infiltrate into the hotel so much the better. I leave the local arrangements to you. Thank you and goodbye.' He rang off.

'Good of you to see me at such short notice, Herr Chancellor. I know that you have a busy schedule ahead of you with all the arrangements and organisation for the summit meeting.' Schultz opened the interview he had hurriedly arranged with the Federal Chancellor.

'There have been developments on the subversion problem. Increased activity has been recorded and we have, I think, located the core of the organisation.

Now, my security forces are going to be stretched to their limits during the European summit. Can I, therefore, impress upon you and your colleagues the need for increased alertness towards your personal security? This will also apply to the visiting delegates.'

The Chancellor listened attentively to Schultz' warnings.

'Thank you, Herr Schultz,' he replied. 'Rest assured I will alert the delegates and take extra care over my own personal security. Thank you once again for keeping me informed. My secretary will show you out.'

The meeting ended.

Chapter Forty-nine

The delegates were assembling in the large conference hall of the Bundeshaus. Temporary six-foot metal barriers enclosed a large area in front of the building. Police vans were drawn up along the front facade. More armed police were posted strategically at all exits and entrances.

The bulk of the riot police confronted the gathering crowd of demonstrators. These demonstrators were carrying a curious assortment of banners declaring their support for a multiplicity of grievances. *Down with bureaucracy, Down with wealth, Down with poverty,* the 'downs' competed with the 'freedoms'. *Freedom of speech, Freedom of political prisoners* etc., etc. The permutations were endless. For the most part the crowd was good-natured. However, hovering on the fringes were the militants, the troublemakers, and the opportunists for violence and disorder. Heads shaven, clad in aggressive clothing and wearing intimidating headgear, they were the norm for most political gatherings. They seemed to emerge from all parts of the misguided intellectual and middle-class woodwork, with an admixture of disenchanted working-class dropouts, prepared to enter into any confrontation with law and order, full of 'rights' but with little evidence of responsibility. To these, the enemy was the police and any agents of law enforcement. The police themselves were taking no chances, with shields, body armour, shin pads, heads clad in riot helmets and batons drawn. Mounted police and water cannon were held in reserve.

The three armoured personnel carriers approached from the Franz-Josef-Allee where the crowds were more scattered and the police presence lighter. The police checkpoint was manned by armed riot squads.

Erich, in the uniform of an oberstleutnant, was in the first carrier. The police inspector approached cautiously.

'I haven't been informed of any military support,' he told Erich.

'There have been reports of armed infiltrators in the demon-strators. A detachment of military police was considered necessary to counter any use of firearms,' replied Erich. The inspector could see that this was indeed a strong detachment of armed military police and it did make sense.

Just then a series of minor explosions came from the direction of the crowd. Someone had thrown several loud fireworks at the police nearby. This seemed to dispel any doubts that the inspector may have had.

'Open the barrier!' he called to his men. 'Let this convoy through and then close the barrier immediately.'

The carriers continued to the front of the Bundeshaus. Sixty fully armed commandos disembarked and hurried to the main entrance hall, their weapons cocked and safety catches released. Meantime three military transporters had drawn up in front of the Headquarters in Karl-Marx Strasse. Further transporters were disembarking military personnel at strategic positions on the main thoroughfares leading into the city centre and setting up barriers and defensive strongpoints. Three powerful launches had sped up the Rhine and docked by the Palais Schaumburg. Commandos were also taking up defensive positions on the northern side of the Bundeshaus.

Everything was happening so quickly. The security forces were bewildered and hesitant, many assuming that these manoeuvres were all part of the overall security measures. Firing could be heard from inside the Bundeshaus. Erich had led his group to the main conference hall. There had so far been little, if any, opposition. They entered the main assembly hall; armed security guards were present. The sight of uniformed militia carrying arms at the ready and acting aggressively called for a challenge, but before the guards could raise their weapons, the intruders had fired several volleys and their bodies lay sprawled grotesquely where they had fallen.

Erich faced the delegates with his machine pistol at the ready. 'Stay where you are, gentlemen, and no one will be hurt,' he ordered.

The gunfire and the casualties stunned the delegates. They sat apprehensively in their seats.

More gunfire could be heard within the building and outside on the forecourt.

Joseph and Hans gathered in the hotel lounge. There were some forty plus trained recruits assembled. An instructor from the South American camp addressed them.

'There are coaches outside which will take you to your rendezvous. There you will be issued with uniforms and weapons and given instructions.'

He approached the receptionist and handed over an envelope that obviously contained a large amount of cash.

'*Auf Wiedersehen, und Danken,*' he said, and then departed outside the hotel to muster the recruits into the waiting coaches.

Jan Puhle had been in the police force for over five years and he always found surveillance work intriguing. Never the same situation twice running. He was working alone on this mission. Perhaps the inspector had reasoned that he would be less noticeable.

The many comings and goings to and from the hotel had all been recorded and reported. But today was different. Several coaches had drawn up outside the hotel and a large number of young men were boarding. They looked fit and tanned and could easily pass as a football team, or teams. Jan was using a maintenance van and wore a white coat. The radio crackled. The station officer took his message and handed it to the inspector.

'Good – tell him to stay in touch. I think I'll raise the helicopter on this one.'

Schultz was trying not to believe his own ears. The commander of the Bundeshaus security was in no doubts whatsoever. A well-organised mercenary force had been successfully launched at the summit meeting. There had been casualties, and all the delegates were now hostages. The building and surrounded were firmly in the hands of the mercenaries.

A further message came through. The foreign delegates had all been released but the federal leaders were still being held.

'Why oh why had he not foreseen such a coup? The target was obvious but the sheer audacity of such a manoeuvre he hadn't even considered. The mercenaries now held all the trump cards. Any action now would endanger the delegates' lives, including that of the Chancellor.

Something was missing in this jigsaw and he wasn't seeing it.

A further message confirmed that all radio and television stations were firmly in the hands of the intruders.

The telephone rang. It was Heinrich Sawatzki, Frankfurt's Commissioner of Police. 'Herr Schultz, there has been some activity here. Three coach-loads of young men have been seen entering the Villa Jasmine, and an air surveillance shows a great deal of activity within the grounds, with uniformed men manning defensive posts all around the house and a convoy of vehicles lined up along the drives. It looks as though they are ready to travel.'

Ah! The missing piece in the jigsaw, thought Schultz. Little, if any, news was filtering out of the city of Bonn. 'Commissioner Sawatzki, listen carefully. I want you to muster all your armed response units and contact your local military commander and surround the villa and do not let *anybody*, repeat *anybody*, leave. If there are telephone lines and radio masts at the villa I want them cut and the mast destroyed and, if possible, a jamming device set up for any mobile telephone communications coming from or to the villa. In fact, I want Villa Jasmine completely isolated from the outside world. This is of the utmost importance. Do you understand?

'Yes, Herr Schultz, I understand perfectly,' replied Sawatzki.

'Good,' continued Schultz. 'Implement this action immediately! We have a dangerous political situation on our hands. If necessary use the military and their attack helicopters.' Schultz rang off and sat back. A cobra without its head is no cobra at all, he mused. It's all a question of waiting...

Erich was congratulating himself on the complete success of their mission.

The crowds had dispersed at the first sounds of gunfire. Demonstrating is one thing, but getting oneself killed is a bit much.

All key strategic points had been seized and defence posts established. It had all gone like clockwork.

He called Ludwig over.

'Get in touch with the villa and report all is secure. It's time for the politicians to take over.'

Sawatzki had taken personal command of the villa operation. The major of the local Fallschirm unit, which was stationed permanently on the outskirts of Frankfurt, had joined the police units with two companies of his parachutists. A force of some 400 men now surrounded the villa. His request for two Apache gunships had been granted and were now airborne and the pilots in radio contact.

'Major, can you seen the radio mast? It must be connected to a powerful radio transmitter and we want it knocked out and the whole unit destroyed – kaput, finished utterly – and I want it done now.

The major took over the radio handset. 'Ground to gunship. Are you receiving?'

'Loud and clear. Gunship one here. What is the target?'

'Major Braun here. Large radio mast and station beneath it situated in the north wing of the villa. Obliterate, repeat obliterate!'

'Got you loud and clear, Major. We will have visual in two minutes.'

They scanned the sky. The two menacingly shaped gunships roared overhead. 'Gunships to ground control. We now have visual of the radio masts. Attacking, attacking now, over and out!'

The deadly swish of four rockets was followed by four thunderous bangs. Smoke, dust and rubble hurled into the air. The northern wing of the villa disappeared in a series of brilliant flashes.

Some small arms fire came ineffectively from the ground.

'Gunships to ground control. Target obliterated. Will land nearby for further assistance if required. Over and out.'

The Count and the Grand Council were all dressed in military fatigues and gathered in the hall. Debris from the northern tower had showered around the whole villa.

This had not been foreseen or expected. Somehow there had to be a leak. One of the commanders dashed into the hall.

'The villa is completely surrounded by the police and regular army units!' The Count turned to the gathered Council.

'We have several choices, it would seem. A dash in the convoy and bulldoze our way through the opposition; escape by a few using the helicopter still moored to the helipad; surrender; or a fight to the finish.

In Bonn, Ludwig returned hurriedly to Erich. 'We have lost radio and telephone contact with the villa. Something must have gone wrong.'

The telephone rang on the reception desk. Erich picked up the receiver. 'Hello? Who's speaking?' he asked.

'My name is Schultz, chief of federal security. To whom am I speaking?'

'I am the commander of the occupying force of the Bundeshaus,' replied Erich. 'Our aim is to achieve a successful coup d'état and install a popular right-wing party which will bring to the people the government they wish, namely a strong, patriotic regime, a barrier to any further communist expansion. We want the unification of Germany and the establishment of Germany as a world power once again.'

'Commendable aims, Commander, but bad timing and the wrong methods. The days of the putsch are over and consigned to history. I have to inform you that the Villa Jasmine is at this moment completely surrounded, with its communications systems destroyed or non-existent. Perhaps you would care to think about your situation. I will make contact again in two hours from now. If you choose to continue your action I can assure you it can only end in a bloodbath.'

Chapter Fifty

The newsflash on the television screen was short and startling. The European summit in Bonn had been the scene of a coup d'état by right-wing militants. Foreign delegates had been released unharmed, but the Federal German heads of state, including the Chancellor of Western Germany, had been detained. They were now all held as hostages until the terms of the insurgents had been met. Several West German city councils had also been attacked and their offices occupied.

On the phone, Schultz sounded calm, though his anxiety was not far from the surface of his emotions. 'We have the situation contained, Goodbody and thanks to your lead we seem to have isolated the militants from their political backers. We have what I believe is termed a "A Mexican stand-off". The next few hours will decide how the final chapter will unfold. I will keep you informed, but the news media now have the story and will, I'm sure, keep up a running commentary.' He rang off.

Erich summoned his commanders together and gave them the news. Their military operation had been an outstanding success. The fiasco of the Frankfurt operation had robbed them of a completely successful finale. Any harm to the hostages would provoke a 'bloodbath', and without an assured victory their back-up support might then fade away.

The loudhailer could be heard in the villa.

'This is the Commissioner of Police to the occupants of the Villa Jasmine. You are completely surrounded. You will open the main gates, lay down your arms and surrender. If you fail to do this you will receive a sustained attack by air and ground forces and will certainly suffer many casualties. You have one hour to comply with these demands. A white flag or similar sign will show your compliance together with the opening of the main gates for our access. There will be no negotiations on these terms. I will give you one hour from now.'

The Count and the Council had heard most of the demands, and others had confirmed their contents.

They were all ex-commanders who had endured severe conflicts during World War II, and there was no lack of courage and determination amongst them; but they were also strategic realists. There was a time for determined action and a time for the assessment of the strength of the opposing forces arraigned against them. Gratuitous heroics played no part in the success or failure of an enterprise.

General von Vaerst spoke. He had been an outstanding Panzer Corps Commander on the Russian Front. His empty sleeve gave testimony to his involvement in those ferocious battles.

'Count van Reinhardt, we are beleaguered by superior forces. The enemy is not vengeful, unlike those Russians who bayed for German blood during the war. The situation is desperate and our forces are cut off without effective leadership. Alive, we have a future. Dead, our cause dies with us. I would suggest compromise and life.'

General Klein, a veteran of both the North African and the Italian campaigns, spoke. 'Count, the North African and Italian campaigns were battles of successful strategic withdrawals: Rommel in North Africa and Kesselring in Italy. Monte Cassino was held against all odds by the Herman Goering Parachute Corps, despite the utter destruction by the American air bombardment of the monastery, but the escape routes were open for the strategic withdrawal of our forces to the prepared Gustav Line. The whole of the Italian campaign was conducted on the policy of strategic withdrawal, and Italy was the last theatre of war to surrender. I am inclined to agree with von Vaerst. We are not dealing with a fanatical dictator at our backs. Compromise and live to fight another day would be my advice.'

General Holder spoke.

'Count, we have neither the vicious SS nor the Gestapo or any other fanatical spectres of vengefulness to impose on us a Rommel-type exit. Our aims are for order and a strong Germany are genuine. We seek no personal gain and our sympathisers are many. We can achieve our goals politically, but we must be alive to provide that political stimulus. I am also for compromise.'

Schmidt and Rudiger also nodded in assent.

'If we die our cause dies with us,' confirmed Rudiger.

The Count was swayed by the arguments put forward. He said firmly, 'Gentlemen, it would seem that our cause must not die in the rubble of this beautiful setting.'

Joseph, standing at the rear of the hall, sensed the pathos of the situation. Defeated but not subdued, these veteran military leaders had chosen a tactical withdrawal rather than a fanatical defence for the sake of what they considered a greater Germany...

Chapter Fifty-one

Commissioner Sawatzki walked through the open gates with its white sheet draped over the crowning spikes. Uniformed men stood on either side of the drives, their weapons grounded before them. These were no scowling enemy but fresh-faced young men. The Count and the generals were in the hall. Sawatzki spoke.

'Count von Reinhardt, I will need your assistance in resolving the situation in Bonn.'

'Schultz here.' The message was from Frankfurt.

'This is commissioner Sawatzki, Kommandant. The insurgents have surrendered and their leader, Count von Reinhardt, is willing to cooperate to save further bloodshed.'

Schultz felt a great surge of relief.

'Good man, Commissioner. Do you think the military could get an aircraft or helicopter to bring the Count to Bonn?'

'I cannot see any problem, Kommandant. I'll organise that immediately; in fact there is a civilian helicopter here in the villa grounds. I could probably get one of the gunship pilots to transport the Count in this helicopter to Bonn.'

'Excellent, Commissioner. Have him land on the Sportpark Wasserland where I will meet them by car. Again, congratulations, Commissioner. I'll not forget your cooperation.'

Erich was overwhelmed by the turn of events. The military plan had worked to perfection. All objectives achieved, and loss of life minimal. Morale was high. There had been maximum security and meticulous care in the planning. Could there have been a leak that had betrayed the Frankfurt operation? How could he maximise his military success without any political back-up?

Otto came running in from the main entrance.

'Erich, come quickly – a convoy of police cars flying a white flag of truce is approaching!'

They dashed to the entrance to the Bundeshaus and saw, standing around a large black limousine, a number of high-ranking police officers. A police car equipped with loudspeakers stood alongside the limousine and there, unbelievably, was Count von Reinhardt emerging from the limousine! He was led to the car with the loudspeakers. An important-looking uniformed officer held the handset for the speakers.

'*Achtung! Achtung!* The Bundeshaus. I have Count von Reinhardt here alongside me and I am handing the microphone over to him.'

The Count spoke into the handset.

'Erich, this is Count von Reinhardt, and I am here quite voluntarily. Villa Jasmine was overwhelmed and an infiltrator may have betrayed us. The Grand Council considered all the options, and death, no matter how noble, would not have furthered our cause. To avoid further bloodshed we advised a cessation of military action. Life means hope, and I am giving you the facts. The ultimate decision must be yours. I understand Kommandant Schultz has a telephone link to the Bundeshaus, and we can talk some more later. You have nothing to blame yourself for. Your operation has been a brilliant success. By the way, Ingrid is safe.'

The Count then handed the speaker over to Schultz.

'You have heard the Count's advice, and I hope you will heed his words. Either an unconditional surrender of your forces and the laying down of their arms, or my men will use the utmost force to free the hostages. You have two hours to consider what action to take. Meantime my men will remain fully alert and await my orders.'

Schultz closed his message and returned to the limousine with the Count.

Erich gazed around at the hostages. Most were talking in small groups. One group in particular was gathered around the Chancellor Helmut Fuchs, having what appeared to be an earnest discussion.

Erich approached this group.

'Herr Chancellor, you are unaware that there has been a dramatic change in events. Our political leaders have surrendered to a situation that became untenable and would certainly have ended in a great loss of lives. For our part, however, we have complete control of the situation here. There is, therefore, a dilemma. To surrender and release our hostages would incur various terms of imprisonment, and some of my men may wish to continue the conflict rather than be incarcerated in a German prison cell. It would help if I could offer an inducement for my men to surrender.'

The Chancellor was thoughtful.

'Would you permit us to hold an assembly without the presence of your guards?' Erich consulted his commanders.

'Very well, *Herr* Fuchs, we will withdraw so that you can have your debate.'

Herr Fuchs was a realist. The whole situation could quickly turn very ugly. Desperate men can perform desperate deeds. These militants had been driven by their frustration with his governments' policies. No matter how misguided, they were Germans wishing for a greater Germany. The fact that the world had moved on from those old insular power politics with an inclination towards racism in all its archaic guises could not come within consideration.

'Gentlemen,' said Fuchs, addressing the Assembly, 'we have to resolve this situation without father bloodshed and at the same time not be seen to surrender to intimidation. These, therefore, are my recommendations.

'The militants must surrender and lay down their arms. They will be detained as political prisoners and agree to a period of indoctrination and political education. I would suggest the use of a suitable secure university campus rather than prison. Finally, the acceptance by these prisoners of a "Citizen's Charter", which would mean their immediate release on parole.

'Non-acceptance of these conditions would result in a political trial and a prison sentence of not less than five years.'

The delegates considered the terms, and many thought them politically idealistic if not downright naive. At the same time there was the realisation that some hope must be offered to the insurgents to avoid a desperate shoot-out in which many of themselves would, no doubt, become casualties.

Erich was informed of the result of their deliberations and

agreed to surrender at 0900 hours the following morning. After all, some of his men were merely young adventurers rather than diehard fanatics, and it did give them some form of option instead of a prison sentence.

Meanwhile, Chancellor Fuchs would convey the terms of the surrender to the security forces.

With these arrangements confirmed, Erich summoned Otto and Ludwig together. They had heard the conditions of the surrender and neither of them was happy with the outcome.

'I have decided these conditions are not for me,' Erich declared.

'Therefore I intend to make a break for it tonight after dusk. The motor launches are still moored at the Palais Schaumberg and I intend to use them for my escape. I'm offering you the choice of joining me or staying for the surrender.' Neither required any further urging.

'Good!' Erich was pleased with their response. 'Choose a dozen picked men who you think feel the same way and get them assembled in the reception area at 2000 hours. They should carry small arms and machine pistols with faces and hands blackened.

Chapter Fifty-two

Dusk had fallen and the additional floodlighting, erected by the security forces, was bathing the buildings in brilliant light.

Erich looked at his men. Young, keen and eager for action. Their camouflage suits and black woollen hats, together with their blackened faces and hands, would make them merge with the shadows and hidden from the patrolling security guards.

The Bundeshaus had been constructed alongside the River Rhine and the 'Ufer', a beach and promenade extending to the north to the Palais Schaumburg, a distance of about one hundred metres. The walkway was hidden in the shadows. Crouching low and in absolute silence, Erich led his men cautiously towards the moored launches. He froze and raised his hand for the others to do the same.

Voices could be heard coming from ahead. The sound was conversational, usual for men when bored with inactivity, domestic chat or girlfriend topics. There was a glow from a burning cigarette.

Erich signalled for Ludwig to follow and the others to remain behind.

Edging forward cautiously, they spotted two silhouettes of armed security police, unsuspecting and off their guard, and with their backs towards the two stalkers. They were within earshot.

'Don't do anything foolish! There are two machine pistols aimed at each of your heads. Any false moves and you are both dead.'

The two guards stood quite still; they were not looking to make heroic gestures.

'Put your weapons down and raise your hands above your heads.'

Erich and Ludwig approached with their weapons at the ready and removed the guards' machine pistols.

'How many guards are there on the launches?' Erich asked.

'We are the only guards posted to guard the launches,' said one of the men, who was obviously a ranker.

'Good. You will come with us!' commanded Erich.

The three launches were moored alongside one another.

'Ludwig, you will take one launch, with four men and one prisoner, and Otto, you will take another together with four men and the other prisoner. I will take the third launch. We may not be able to keep in touch, so the plan is to slip away under cover of darkness and proceed slowly so as not to raise any alarm until we reach the city limits. Then, if not detected, we will continue south. You may make Frankfurt, but if we are detected then it is every man for himself. All agreed?'

They nodded their assessment.

'Our ultimate rendezvous will be the Villa Jasmine, but this may take time – a month, two months, maybe longer. Free the prisoners after 0900 hours tomorrow morning. Good luck.'

They boarded the launches.

Schultz, accompanied by Count von Reinhardt, appeared at the main entrance to the Bundeshaus at exactly 0900 hours, escorted by a strong police escort.

An ominous silence hung over the reception area.

Herr Fuchs stepped from the entrance to the assembly hall, followed by the other delegates.

'*Güten Morgen*, Herr Schultz. The militants are inside. They have laid down their weapons but their leader has gone. He left at dusk yesterday evening.'

Just then, a senior officer of the security forces hurried into the reception hall. 'Kommandant, the launches have gone, so too have the security guards!'

Schultz turned to the Count. 'Did you know about this, von Reinhardt?'

'Of course not! This whole thing has been organised on their own initiative.' The Count was just as surprised as the Kommandant.

'Alert the police helicopters and carry out a search of the Rhine to the north and the south,' Schultz directed his senior commanders.

Chapter Fifty-three

Victor Holst was one of life's opportunists. He had come a long way from his early days as a small-time wheeler-dealer, and he now dealt in any commodity, legal or otherwise, that gave him a good return on his investment. For the most part these commodities were of the lethal variety: weapons of destruction. Anything from a pistol to an aircraft, all carrying huge profit margins. Viktor was extremely wealthy, a millionaire several times over. Morality played no part in his business enterprises, and the highest bidder was sole arbiter of who he had dealings with.

The owner of several palatial properties, with apartments in New York, London and an extensive villa on the French Riviera. His business offices were situated in most of the world's capitals.

He had now acquired a medieval castle on the banks of the Rhine due south of the spectacular landscape of the Lorelei Gorge. Money had provided Viktor with most of life's luxuries, including his beautiful young wife. Most of his friends were business acquaintances, whose activities fluctuated around the borders of legality. It was a hard and mercenary world with little room for compassion; a dog eat dog world. The idea of being a feudal lord had appealed to him, and the thought of inhabiting a castle appealed even more to his primordial marauding inclinations.

'*Liebchen…*' The word sounded unnatural coming from him. 'How many have you invited to this weekend get-together?'

'There will be at least thirty, maybe more; after all, it is a house-warming.' She had a way of pouting which he always found attractive; in fact, he always responded to her sultriness.

'They should be arriving sometime this afternoon – I sent instructions on how to get here. Come off the A3 at Wiesbaden and stay on the road to Assmanshausen, and then we are sign-posted from there. Don't fret, my love, everything is organised and taken care of. The caterers are here already, all the bedrooms are prepared. We have enough of them – I lose count after thirty – and all have a bathroom en suite. After all, you spent a fortune on this place, so sit back and enjoy it.'

She was also very businesslike, Viktor reflected. A true case of beauty and brains. Money could just about buy everything, he mused.

Some of his business associates had been invited, so a little business could be mixed with pleasure.

Erich had checked the launch and found two jerry cans of reserve fuel stored below. He was assessing their chances of successfully eluding any pursuit. He had come to a decision and sounded the klaxon. The other two launches drew alongside, and he called Ludwig and Otto aboard.

'A change of plan,' he told them. 'Put all your spare fuel cans aboard this launch. Then one of you stay aboard your own launch and open the water-cocks, then return aboard. To make good our escape we will need civilian clothes, transport money and open communication channels. We are now travelling downstream and at daybreak the Rhine will become busy with tourist and ferry traffic. By then, we need to be long gone.'

They had watched the two launches sink beneath the deep murky river waters and were now passing through the Lorelei Gorge. It was then that Erich spotted the castle. It was a blaze of light and the sound of music drifted over the waters. People were silhouetted on the terraces. The evening was warm for the time of year. A landing stage was situated below the parapets.

Erich's mind clicked into action.

'Head the launch to that landing pier. Put it under the sheltered part.'

Steps led up to the castle. Weapons at the ready, they climbed with stealth. Viktor and his associates were gathered in the lounge and his guests mingled and danced in the main hall. It was a sumptuous setting with the oak panelling and the broad staircase rising majestically to the upper floors. The walls were adorned with medieval armour. All that was missing were the period costumes; doublets and hose and low cut bodices topped with fantastic hairstyles.

Viktor was aware that the band had stopped playing and could hear commotion. The guests were staring towards the huge sliding windows. Other guests were entering from the terraces, faces pale with alarm.

'*Mein Gott!* What is going on?' he called as he entered the hall. It was then that he saw the armed men, faces blackened and weapons at the ready. A raid, a robbery, a kidnapping – all these things were flashing through his mind as he dashed for the staircase. The police...he needed the telephone in the study upstairs. He had reached the third step when the viscous sweep of bullets thudded into his body and he fell grotesquely across the stair, his sightless eyes gazing up to the chandeliers, a look of utter surprise on his lifeless face.

There was a stunned silence and then an hysterical scream and his wife collapsed like a puppet into a senseless heap.

Some of the male guests made to move, but a second volley over their heads stopped them in their tracks.

Erich issued a string of orders.

'Otto, the kitchens. Ludwig, the upstairs, and don't forget the bathrooms. Anyone attempting to use a telephone, cut them down!'

He ordered the guests to sit down. 'No heroics, please, and you live.'

To his men he said, 'Choose someone near your size and escort them to their rooms and borrow some civilian clothes, preferably casual wear. We also need cash, so find the safe. It's probably in the study. Empty it. There are over a dozen cars outside and we shall need the ignition keys.'

He located the telephone.

'Ingrid, this is Erich. We are safe but need your help. Are there any vehicles in the villa grounds?'

He had taken her by complete surprise but she quickly recovered.

'Yes, *mein Leibchen*, there are two coaches that brought your men from Frankfurt, my father's Mercedes, and an assortment of smaller vehicles.' She spoke calmly.

'Are you alone?' he asked.

'Just some domestics and me. The rest have been taken to police headquarters for questioning and detention.'

'Good! Now listen carefully. Can you bring the smaller coach to the A66 past the turn-off for Wiesbaden, but continue on the east bank of the Rhine to Rudesheim, and we will rendezvous with you along this road. Keep your eyes alert. I will be waiting with about a dozen men. Can you also bring my passport, which it is my valise. Do you think you can manage that, *Leibchen?* It is vitally important!'

'Don't worry, I will leave immediately,' she replied, and rang off.

His men had managed to find an assortment of civilian clothes. 'Keep your faces blackened,' he told them.

He addressed the guests.

'You will remain in this room for the next two hours. Two of my men will be outside and they have orders to shoot anyone attempting to leave.'

He directed Otto to cut all the telephone wires and then gathered his men in the parking area. 'Take those three large Mercedes and immobilise the rest. Pity about the Rolls Royce, but it might be spotted. Throw all the spare ignition keys into the river. Now let us get out of here.'

'Who is staying?' asked Ludwig.

'Nobody stays!' said Erich. 'These people are too traumatised to make any move for the next two hours or more.'

They roared out of the castle grounds and headed for Rudesheim.

Schultz was puzzled. There had been no sightings of the launches, the helicopters were equipped with infrared night sights. It was as if they had been spirited away into thin air. He picked up the telephone.

'Commissar Sawatzki, what is the situation at the villa?

'The occupants have been removed to police headquarters for detention, and Count von Reinhardt's daughter and the domestics are staying at the villa,' Sawatzki replied.

Schultz was pensive. 'I suggest that you arrange a surveillance of the villa in the morning,' he said.

'Of course, Herr Kommandant. I'll instruct my security people immediately. Will that be all Kommandant?'

'Yes, Commissioner, I will keep in touch and inform you of any further developments. We have a breakaway group that may be heading your way.' He rang off.

Erich had driven the three Mercedes into the deep waters of the river. The roads were deserted except for a few late night revellers returning home. It would be four hours to daybreak.

Ingrid had been driving for over an hour and left the A66 beyond the Mainz bridge and was on the Rudesheim road. She had slowed to a crawl when a figure stepped out of the shadows and stood in the road. It was Erich.

They greeted each other affectionately.

'Ingrid, *mein Leibchen!* Take these men back to the villa before daybreak if you can, and farm them out on the estate as gardeners, handymen, cooks, whatever... and they have been with you the whole time, you understand. Drop Ludwig, Otto and myself off near Frankfurt Railway Station.'

She gave him his passport and 10,000 marks she had taken from the villa's safe. 'When will I see you again?' she pleaded.

'I will contact you within a few days. In the meantime I must lay low. Keep calm. Now we must hurry!'

Chapter Fifty-four

It had been a week of hectic activity. Her father was still detained, so also were the generals. The Frankfurt Police had made further enquiries of any further new arrivals at the villa but had been satisfied with Ingrid's responses. She knew that they were keeping surveillance on the villa.

The news of a daring robbery had broken, but the police were still baffled. A postcard had arrived from Florence in Italy.

> Cara Ingrid
> > Sta bene
> > Ciao, E

The curtain falls. The tale is told.
Adieu.

Printed in the United Kingdom
by Lightning Source UK Ltd.
118670UK00001B/10